Breakaway GOALS

BETH BOLDEN

AUTHOR NOTE

BREAKAWAY GOALS TAKES PLACE in the wider Beth Bolden universe: a universe that is more inclusive and welcoming than our own.

In Beth-world, the first professional athlete to come out of the closet was Colin O'Connor (*The Rainbow Clause*), and after this happened, approximately ten years ago, there have been numerous players, coaches, and even owners who are living their best queer lives freely.

Earl Gray Publishing LLC

www.bethbolden.com

beth@bethbolden.com

Publisher's Note: This is a work of fiction. Names, characters, places, and incidents are a product of the author's imagination. Locales and public names are sometimes used for atmospheric purposes. Any resemblance to actual people, living or dead, or to businesses, companies, events, institutions, or locales is completely coincidental.

Book Layout © 2023 Beth Bolden

Book Cover © 2025 Ozark Witch Cover Design

Photo © Cadwallader Photography, LLC

Model: Aaron Wolber

The people in the images are models and should not be connected to the characters in the book. Any resemblance is incidental.

Ordering Information:

Quantity sales. Special discounts are available on quantity purchases by corporations, associations, and others. For details, contact Beth Bolden at the address above.

Breakaway Goals/ Beth Bolden. -- 1st ed.

CHAPTER 1

"Morgan, you haven't played on a national team for eight years. What about this team, *this* tournament made you want to come back?"

Morgan drummed his fingers on his knee. It wasn't that he expected the questions to suddenly *not* suck, but he'd expected the interviewer to at least work up to the crappy ones. The ones that hinted without actually saying it that he didn't give a shit about playing for his country.

The interviewer gazed at him expectantly, a sweetly neutral expression on her face. He wondered if she'd been born like that. Just popped out of her mother with the ability to school her face into something bland and non-threatening as she poked him right where it hurt.

His son, Finn, would tell him that if he didn't want anyone to complain about him not playing for the US team, he should play for the goddamn US team.

"Well, uh, that's a great question." *Lie.* "How could I miss this tournament? Four countries sending their best players? A tune-up for the Olympics?" *That's three fucking questions and not a single answer in there, Reynolds.*

She nodded, clearly encouraging him to actually answer the fucking question.

"It's just such a great opportunity." *And such a shitty fucking answer.*

He was sweating, could feel it under his arms, in the damp patch at the small of his back, underneath his Team USA polo. *Ridiculous.* Morgan had been doing this for a long fucking time, fielding questions starting back in his early teens, when he'd first entered the USA hockey national team development program. Then he'd been drafted first overall, and the media interrogations only became more intense from there. And yet, he was totally fucking this up, anyway.

He saw a flash of annoyance cross her features before it smoothed away, like it didn't exist.

"And you?" She'd clearly decided that was the best she was going to get out of Morgan, because she turned to the man next to him.

He should've known that the NHL media team wouldn't be able to resist putting them together for interviews. Morgan had been hearing his name next to Hayes Montgomery's for years now, usually uttered with breathless anticipation. The chosen one and the next one.

It wasn't Hayes' fault that he made Morgan feel old.

But he did.

"Oh, well . . ." Hayes stumbled over his words a little, and Morgan didn't have to look over to see the guy's face was full of hero worship. It made Morgan want to crawl out of his skin. *I'm not so fucking great, bud, I promise.* "How could I pass up a chance to wear the stars and stripes on my jersey and play next to

Morgan Reynolds?" It turned out Morgan didn't have to look at him, because Hayes' voice was brimming with adoration. The kind that made Morgan want to shake him.

It was weird, 'cause normally Morgan *liked* it when people stroked his ego.

He was a damn good hockey player. Had the stats and the awards and the Cups to back it all up.

But Hayes made him feel like he was halfway out the door, not because he wanted to be, but because everyone else was pushing him there, ready to move on. *Yeah, Morgan, you were damn good, but look at this kid, he's going to be even better.*

"I heard a rumor," the interviewer said lightly, "that you're going to be playing on the same line during the tournament. What's that going to look like?"

Hayes looked over at him, like he was giving Morgan the first crack at answering the question. But it was another one he didn't want to touch with a ten-foot pole.

"Good hockey, that's what it's gonna look like," Morgan said, a little brusquely. What else would it fucking look like? They hadn't even gotten on the goddamn ice yet.

"Even though you normally play center, you're okay shifting to Morgan's wing?" She directed this one entirely at Hayes.

"Oh yeah, for sure. It's not my natural position, but I'm excited to feed him the puck. Morgan's a legend," Hayes said. That note of reverence was back and even more pronounced now.

Morgan wanted to roll his eyes. Hayes was making him sound a hundred and five, not thirty-five, and he *hated* it.

The interviewer asked a handful of additional questions which Hayes actually attempted to answer and Morgan gave brief one-word retorts to.

Then, finally, *thankfully*, the interview ended.

The interviewer stood and, after shaking both their hands, ducked out of the conference room they'd rigged up to deal with multiple interviews at once. The camera operator exited too, leaving them alone.

There were only two days of practice—not much time at all to try to find some chemistry and gel on the ice—so they'd been trying to get through the media bits as fast as possible. Frankly, Morgan thought they could've skipped them altogether, but they weren't asking him his opinion for a reason.

"Hey," Hayes said softly, unsure.

Morgan turned to him. They'd met before, he was sure of it, but when Hayes had been younger, he'd left even less of an impression on Morgan. Unassuming, he'd always believed. But when he looked at Hayes now, that wasn't the word he'd pick.

Sure, his voice had been unsure, almost questioning, but when Morgan met his eyes, he was surprised at how direct they were. A clear green, almost fierce, and staring right at Morgan.

Like he was daring Morgan to see him.

Huh. That was interesting.

The hair prickled on the back of Morgan's neck.

"What's up?" Morgan asked, realizing that he'd just been *staring*. Staring and not saying anything, like a complete idiot.

"I just . . ." Hayes shrugged. "You wanna grab some coffee or something? We've got a few hours until we have to be on the ice for practice . . ."

Morgan did not want to share a coffee with Hayes Montgomery. If he did, it was going to become a whole fucking thing, the chosen one and the next one hanging out, and that was a whole level of obligation he didn't want to deal with.

But also . . .Hayes *was* going to be playing on Morgan's wing. Maybe they could keep the conversation solely on hockey and on the plan Morgan had heard about during the dinner he'd had with the coaching staff last night.

"We could do that," Morgan said.

Tyler Thompson was going to be the head coach, and he'd brought in an old friend, Gavin Blackburn, who'd coached mostly at the collegiate level but was now with the Seattle Sea Monsters, to assist him.

Both Thompson and Blackburn seemed to believe the team would have plenty of fire power; they were more concerned about how all the different puzzle pieces would come together.

Hayes' face broke into a big smile, lighting his eyes up even more, and that prickle on the back of Morgan's neck itched again. "Yeah? That would be so freaking great. I'm—"

Morgan had to cut this off before the guy drove him crazy. "Yeah, only great if you stop looking at me like you're going to fall to your knees and worship me."

It was kind of an asshole thing to say—maybe a better man than Morgan would've just accepted the uncomfortable squeeze at the base of his stomach every time Hayes gazed up at him like he was hockey Jesus—but even the slightly asshole flavor didn't explain the way Hayes went so pale. Morgan reached out and grabbed his arm to steady him.

"Who told you?" he asked under his breath, going from looking happy and excited to anxious only a second later.

"Who told me what?" Morgan didn't want to be concerned, but it was hard to look into those green eyes, full of apprehension, and not worry.

Maybe he'd only be Hayes' captain for ten days, but he was still technically Hayes' captain, and the instinct was too ingrained for Morgan to resist.

"Who told you?" Hayes asked again, this time his voice dropping to a harsh whisper.

"Told me what?" If Hayes was going to repeat the question, then so was he.

"About—" Hayes broke off and waved at himself. "That I like, you know . . . *men.*"

Morgan jolted. He hadn't even thought about how his words could be interpreted. Finn, who was queer too, would be seriously judging him right now, and while he couldn't say he *always* deserved that look in his son's eyes, he'd have deserved it this time.

"Shit, man, nobody did. I didn't know. I was just . . ." A wave of shame crashed over him as he rubbed his neck. "I was just talking shit."

"Oh. *Oh.*" Hayes' eyes were very wide now.

"Yeah."

"Well, uh . . ."

"It's alright, you know? I won't tell anyone. I'm an ass, but I'm a circumspect ass, at least. My son, Finn—"

"I know Finn, or *of* him, rather," Hayes said, nodding.

"So you know, I'm not gonna be shitty about it." Morgan winced. "Other than what I stupidly said just now."

"It wasn't that stupid. *I* was being dumb and paranoid," Hayes said, looking like he was five seconds away from apologizing to *Morgan.* That was crazy, because he'd been gunning for the opposite, to remind Hayes that Morgan wasn't that great. That he didn't really need to gaze at him like he was Wayne Gretzky and Bobby Hull wrapped up in one single player.

"Really—it's fine." Morgan didn't love that he'd put his foot into it, because he never loved when he did that. It was bad enough that most of the other NHL players he knew totally fit the dumb hockey stereotype. Always more brawn than brain.

"Alright." Hayes seemed to relax then. "Do you uh . . .still . . ."

Morgan rolled his eyes. Didn't even bother to try to hold it back this time. After all, that's what he'd been *trying* to tell Hayes before he'd stepped in it. "Yes," he said. "We'll go to coffee. But *only* if you stop looking at me like you're five seconds away from apologizing. *Again.*"

Hayes wet his lips. "Alright. Sorry—God, *sorry.*" He flushed red this time, which was way better than the sheet white he'd been before.

Cute, even, the pink flush staining the apples of his cheeks.

"No worries. Let's go." Morgan patted him on the shoulder. He did it instinctually, the long habit of affectionate touching ingrained after so many years of teammates, but also because Finn had told him once how important a casual touch could be after a guy came out.

Means you're not afraid of us, he'd said, and Morgan had lost nights of sleep after that, worrying about his son. Worrying if Morgan would end up in jail because if Finn's teammates ever did the shitty thing and avoided touching him on purpose? Morgan couldn't be responsible for the consequences.

"Alright." Hayes grinned at him, a dimple emerging in his cheek.

Morgan pushed the door open, Hayes following him. There were various personnel scattered in the hallway, the interviewer leaning against the wall, talking to her boss, someone high up in the commissioner's office. They'd just dodged her, on the way to the coffee shop that Hayes said was just across the street, but then they ran—nearly literally—into a problem. Because there was, *ugh*, Jacob fucking Braun.

His nemesis.

Morgan never knew what bothered him more—that Braun always saw right into his brain and knew exactly where he was going to shoot the fucking puck and somehow *always* blocked it, or that he gave way less of a shit about Morgan than Morgan gave about him.

"Oh, there's Braun," Hayes said brightly. Did he not *know*? Morgan thought everyone knew about him and Braun.

The last game they'd played against each other, he'd pushed his way into the crease, and one of Braun's teammates had pulled him out by the back of his jersey, and the next second, Morgan had been swinging his fists.

Morgan hadn't been able to punch Braun, but his teammate had been a decent enough stand-in.

"Yeah," Morgan said, shoving his hands into the pockets of his trackpants.

Last night Thompson had asked if he and Braun on the same team was going to be a problem, and he'd said no, because he wasn't stupid enough to think Braun wasn't really fucking good. He gave their team the best chance of winning, and he wasn't back on Team USA, after eight years of pretending he was above national tournaments, to *lose*.

A second later, Hayes made an aborted noise. "Oh God, I'm sorry. You two—"

That, of course, was the moment they came face-to-face.

"Reynolds," Jacob said, tilting his head. "I'd say it's good to see you but—"

"Just do your fucking job on the ice," Morgan said between clenched teeth.

The corner of Jacob's mouth turned up in an insufferable smirk. "Aye, aye, Captain," he said.

Morgan made a face and then, thank God, they were moving on, heading down the escalator to the ground floor of the hotel, away from the conference level.

"Shit, I'm sorry, that was . . ." Hayes didn't finish his sentence. Because he'd realized he'd apologized again, or because he didn't know how to? Morgan wasn't sure.

"It's fine, I'm fine, it's just a thing." Morgan didn't usually feel compelled to offer an explanation for why he disliked Braun so much.

How he'd set up semi-permanent residence in his brain, constantly taunting him with the goals he'd never score and the records he'd never set.

Hayes shrugged, and they headed out the front door and towards the coffee shop.

They were settled at a table, Hayes drinking some long-winded multi-hyphenated drink that made it clear, from the way he rattled it off, that his order was not as simple or straightforward as Morgan's "large black coffee," before Hayes brought it up again.

"So what is it about you two?" Hayes asked, his nail picking at the edge of the paper sleeve on his cup.

"I just don't like him. He's smug."

Hayes shot him a knowing look. "Really? That's why you don't like him?"

"I think I liked you better when you were afraid of me," Morgan muttered.

"But you like me!" Hayes said brightly.

"Of course that was what you took from that sentence." Morgan hesitated. "And I'm *not* smug." But he could be. Maybe it was more deserved than Braun's smugness, but it was annoying that Hayes, who'd seemed barely able to utter a whole fucking sentence in Morgan's presence before now, had decided to call him on it.

"Are you kidding me? You're Morgan Reynolds." Hayes said it all hushed and reverent.

"We're not back to this again, are we?" Morgan asked with a groan punctuating his question.

"No, I mean, it's not like that, it's just . . .you've got the shit to back you up, if you want to be smug. But then so does Braun, frankly."

"Don't say that," Morgan muttered. He didn't want Hayes to think Braun was good, even if that was objectively true.

"I mean, he saved an absolutely *sick* shot I took last year in the playoffs, so yeah, he's good. He's one of the reasons I'm here."

Morgan took a long drink of his black coffee. "Come on. Don't pretend. You leaped at the chance."

"I . . ." Hayes made a frustrated noise. "Okay. Fine. Yes."

"We're all a little starstruck." Morgan wasn't, but then he'd been doing this too long to worry about other people. Other than Braun, that was.

"Not you," Hayes scoffed.

"Okay, not me," Morgan conceded.

Hayes went back to picking at the sleeve on his coffee cup. "I just want you to know . . .I've never bought into the whole *next one*, thing. That's not what I consider this, even if other people do."

Morgan told himself that he liked this kid—could he still call him a kid when he was in his mid-twenties? *Probably*—even when he was being really fucking stupid.

"Are you serious with this?"

"Uh yes? Yes. Yes, definitely." Hayes punctuated this with a sharp nod of his head, like he'd just finally decided.

"Your lack of ego's not gonna do you any favors. You're really fucking good, kid."

Hayes looked happy, then at the end bristled, unexpectedly. "I'm not a kid. I'm twenty-five."

"Okay. You're really fucking good, grown ass man."

"You're not funny," Hayes said, but he was choking back a laugh.

"No, of course not," Morgan deadpanned.

"I just meant . . . I'm not here to push that bullshit narrative." Hayes wouldn't look at him, those piercing green eyes glued to the wood tabletop. "That's not why I'm here. I just want to play hockey."

Morgan decided that this was the best time to change the subject. If Hayes didn't want to look at his own skills frankly and realize just how unbelievable they were, that was his problem. "I guess the most important question is *can* you play wing?"

Hayes looked surprised. "Yeah. Of course."

"It's not that straightforward."

"Sure it is. It's fine, I've got this." At least Hayes *sounded* confident. "At practice, you'll see."

"Here's what I was thinking," Morgan said, going on to describe what he envisioned for their offense, generally, and for their line specifically.

Hayes cocked his head, and Morgan wasn't surprised when he asked one good question after another, poking and prodding at the plan, because even though he downplayed his abilities, Morgan had seen enough through the years, against each other and more, to know how good Hayes was. It even got to the point where Morgan got up, grabbed some paper and a pen from the counter, and drew it up so they could dissect it further.

"Canada's always good, and so's Sweden," Morgan said, leaning back after he'd finished his coffee. "And we can't count Finland out, even if they're shorthanded because of injuries. This isn't going to be a gimme."

"I never thought it would be," Hayes said earnestly.

"No, you probably didn't," Morgan said, barking out a laugh and patting him on the shoulder. "Come on. Team lunch, then we've got practice this afternoon."

"I swear to God, I thought I was going to have a heart attack about ninety-five percent of the morning," Hayes said as he stepped out of the elevator onto his floor.

His best friend, Zach, on the other end of the call, scoffed.

"He's just a guy," Zach said.

"He's not *just* a guy. I can't believe you'd say that." But Hayes could believe that Zach would. He wasn't ever intimidated by anyone on the ice. No matter who their team, the Los Angeles Mavericks, faced, Zach was always level-headed.

During the more surreal parts of the morning—the interviews, the unexpected and humiliating coming out, and then their coffee shop hangout—Hayes had wished he could be more like Zach.

Of course, Zach hadn't spent his whole life being compared to Morgan.

"Okay, he's not just a guy. He's a hockey player."

Hayes rolled his eyes. "I wish you were here. You'd keep me from exploding out of my skin or saying *I'm sorry* one more time and annoying Morgan so much he never talks to me again."

"I'm sure you haven't been that bad," Zach said.

He'd have to be a lot dumber to miss how Zach sort of avoided the subject he'd broached. How Zach was not here. How he hadn't been picked to play in this tournament.

And really, even though Zach was good, *solid*, Hayes hadn't been all that surprised. It was insanely tough to whittle down the US players to just one team's worth. Canada had a similar problem. It was slightly easier for Sweden and Finland—they had a smaller group to pick from. But lots of good players—including Zach—had been left off the four rosters.

Next time, Hayes had promised Zach, when the list had come out. Zach was two years younger than him, only twenty-three, and had lots of time to improve and make national teams. Even in the four years since he'd been drafted by the Mavs, he'd come a long way, working his way onto the top six, now solidly anchoring the second line.

"I was pretty awkward," Hayes admitted as he slid his keycard into the lock, pushing the door open. "You'd have been so fucking embarrassed for me."

"Probably," Zach said. "But hey, you told me you wanted to ask him to go to coffee, and you actually *did* it. And he actually said yes."

"You make it sound like a date," Hayes grumbled. It had been very much *not* a date. They'd talked about hockey basically the whole time. Besides, Morgan was one of those guys you just *knew* was straight, no question about it whatsoever.

"I mean, you said you were gonna do it and you did it. Give yourself a pat on the back for that one. Now Morgan Reynolds drinking coffee in front of you is gonna be a permanent part of your jerkoff routine."

Hayes squawked. "I'm not *that* bad."

"You totally fucking are."

"Well, it got real awkward after I asked him, because he said sure, but only if I stopped falling to my knees around him—"

"Oh, shit," Zach interrupted.

Hayes flopped down onto his partially made bed. He had ten minutes before he had to be back downstairs for team lunch. "Yeah, *yeah*. Of course, that wasn't what he was meaning, but I, like a complete fucking idiot, thought that was exactly what he meant, and I freaked."

"Please tell me you didn't come out to Morgan Reynolds today."

Hayes knew Zach wasn't saying it like that because Morgan wouldn't be understanding—more than once he and Zach had discussed how great he was about his son, Finn—but because with every person he told, the chances of it staying under wraps got smaller.

Hayes wasn't against coming out of the closet. He wouldn't be the first professional athlete to do that. Not by a long shot. But he wasn't ready. He still wanted to imprint his legacy in the NHL, before he became known as the "gay one" instead of the "next one."

"It was practically an accident," Hayes said.

"You just wanted to see if he was going to fall to *his* knees and thank God 'cause he's been wanting to get up on you *forever*," Zach teased.

It was impossible not to smile. "Like that would ever happen."

"Exactly," Zach said.

"It didn't, by the way. He was cool about it, though. Especially considering how embarrassing the whole thing was."

Zach hummed. "You do anything else humiliating that I missed?"

"Totally spaced that Morgan and Jacob Braun hate each other?"

"God, you're really batting a thousand over there. Maybe I *should've* stowed away in your luggage. You need someone to keep you from tripping over your own goddamn skates at this point."

Hayes sighed. "It was not my greatest moment. In a whole series of them, honestly."

"You're gonna be fine." Zach didn't sound like he really believed that was true, but at least he was saying it.

"I hope so." Hayes took a deep breath. "They're definitely putting us on a line together."

"God, you and Morgan Reynolds. You're gonna be on his wing. Try not to die of happiness or from a permanent hard-on." Hayes didn't need to see his best friend to see how hard he was smirking.

"Zachy—"

"Maybe something else to use when your coffee date jerkoff material gets old," Zach teased.

"Contrary to popular believe, I do *not* jerk off to hockey highlights."

"Maybe not to anyone else's. But Morgan's? Hell yes you do."

Hayes really regretted that one time when he and Zach had gotten drunk, two or three years back, and Hayes had confessed how Morgan Reynolds did it for him in all kinds of ways. The hockey way, for sure, but the *wished he was not as straight as he seemed* way, too.

Morgan was just *hot*. On the ice, of course, with his soft hands and quick feet and unreal puck handling, sliding between defenders like they barely existed, muscling guys around like he was born to do it, and *off* it, too. His eyes were more blue than green and sometimes even a deeply attractive hazel in certain lights, and his light brownish-red hair curled just right over his forehead when he went too long without cutting it. Hayes had spent way too many nights imagining Morgan rubbing the caramel-colored scruff edging his perfect jawline all over Hayes' body.

It was never going to happen, of course, but it was still a fantasy he couldn't seem to help.

"I'm kind of pathetic, aren't I?"

Zach scoffed. "No way. You're Hayes Montgomery. You're gonna be top line for Team USA and you're gonna be playing on Morgan Reynolds' wing. Kind of the last thing from pathetic."

"Okay, chill out," Hayes said, laughing. "My ego's gonna grow out of control."

"Not likely," Zach said flatly.

"Morgan gave me shit about that too. Being too modest."

"Did you shit yourself?"

"When he said I was really fucking good? Yeah. But I'd already embarrassed myself enough . . ."

"Yeah, you really did."

Hayes laughed. He'd felt weird and apprehensive about this whole tournament. He didn't often blend well with other hockey guys, other than Zach and a handful on the Mavs—who weren't going to be here. "Don't hold back."

"You're damn good. You're already a star, and you're gonna be a superstar," Zach said solemnly. "Now remember that when you go out there this afternoon with Reynolds, okay?"

Hayes said he would, tucked his phone in his pocket. Checked and then fixed his hair in the mirror, flicking the dark brown strands around—not that he thought it made any difference, because it wasn't like he was going to be picking up here—and went down to lunch.

Calvin and Noah were there—they'd played together at the USA development program—and it was easy to sit with them and let their bullshit and snark flow over him.

Morgan was at a table with the coaching staff and the other goalie on the roster, Bram Jones.

Jacob Braun was on the other side of the room, laughing with some of the older guys.

Then they headed to practice, taking a bus to the arena.

It wasn't the first time he'd played for Team USA; Hayes had won medals at the U18s and at World Juniors. The Mavs had gone deep enough into the playoffs the last few years that he hadn't had a chance to play at senior Worlds.

Still, it didn't get old to tug his jersey on, feel the fabric settle over his gear.

He went through his normal warmup routine on the ice, not hurrying, just eyeing the different groups forming around the ice—the goalies on one end, the defensive core on the other, the forwards fanning out around the middle of the rink.

Hayes was just finishing up his stretches when Morgan skated up to him. "We're gonna run some plays," he said. "Danny's gonna play left wing."

Matt Daniels—better known to everyone as Danny—had played with Hayes in the development program. He was a powerhouse center, had won the Cup last year, and had a rep for being aggressive on the ice and outrageous off it.

"Sure," Hayes said. His style was a little more finesse than that, but if Morgan thought he and Danny could gel together, he wasn't going to argue.

Except, they didn't gel together at all.

"When I'm fucking calling for the puck, you gotta pass it to me, Monty," Danny complained after he'd taken another bad shot.

Like his stomach wasn't already crawling with shame for letting Morgan down. For taking such a shitty angle in front of him. He was better than this, he *knew* he was, but Danny was pushing him, not speed wise, but too close, not letting him have the space to work he was used to, and it was throwing him off.

"Give him a break," Morgan threw out offhandedly.

Danny made a scoffing noise. "You never give anyone a fucking break, Mo."

"Maybe *you* fucked it up," Morgan retorted. "Let's try it again."

They did. Over and over again, until Hayes was dripping sweat, the exhaustion on his face mirrored on Danny's.

"Better," Morgan finally said. He turned to Danny. "You gotta skate as fast as Monty does, or you're never gonna find me."

"Good luck with that," Hayes muttered under his breath, but it must've been loud enough that Danny heard, because he made a face.

"Not my fault that the next one is so fucking fast," Danny said, wiping the perspiration off his forehead.

Hayes wanted to tell him not to call him that, that he *hated* being called that, but he'd learned the hard way that if he hated something to *never* let anyone know, because he'd never get away from it. Hockey players were generally a good-natured group but they were also relentless.

"Don't call him that," Morgan snapped.

"Hey, it's not *me* that made it up," Danny said.

"It's bullshit. There's no *chosen one*. No *next one*. We're all just doing our fucking best." Morgan shot Danny a hard look. "Or we *should* be doing our fucking best."

"Hey that's cold, man," Danny said, apparently unbothered by Morgan's lecture. Hayes wished he could be that relaxed about it, but he wasn't.

It was probably the way Morgan had been featuring in his fantasies since he was old enough to start jerking off.

Hayes didn't know how he felt about Morgan speaking up for him. If it made him want to worship Morgan even fucking harder, or make him shy away from it, embarrassed at needing to be protected.

"Is it cold if it's true?" Morgan asked as he picked up his water bottle, squirting some into his mouth.

"Ouch," Hayes said.

Danny elbowed him in the side. "If I gotta skate faster, you gotta push harder into the corners. Be aggressive, Monty."

"I can be aggressive."

Danny's eyebrows skated up under his visor. "When?"

"Kids," Morgan broke in. "Let's run it again."

CHAPTER 2

It was a risk putting Danny and Monty on his wings, but Morgan had specifically convinced Thompson to do it because he thought it could create a kind of alchemy that might work out there.

Morgan really hated it when a plan didn't come together.

He hated it even more when a plan just plain fucking *sucked*.

"You want to switch things up?" Thompson leaned in midway through the first, eleven minutes down, nine to go, and asked Morgan when he'd gotten back to the bench after his last shift.

But the thing he hated the most was admitting that he'd been wrong.

"No," Morgan said. "We'll find it."

He didn't need to turn his head to see the flash of incredulity on Thompson's face.

"We'll get there," Danny said, patting Morgan on the knee.

"Yeah, if you find another gear," Hayes huffed on his other side.

"It's not my fault you're the fucking energizer bunny out there," Danny bitched. Good-natured at this point, still, but probably because they were still up 1-0 against Sweden, Calvin Miller getting a great rebound from one of Noah's shots.

Braun was steadfast on the other side of the ice, blocking shot after shot effortlessly in a way that would totally chap Morgan's ass if they weren't wearing the same fucking jersey.

"It's early still," Blackburn soothed, leaning in.

But Morgan had a feeling he needed to do something, and the remaining two shifts he spent on the ice told him exactly what that was.

On their way into the locker room for the first intermission, he grabbed Hayes' arm.

"Hey," he said, pulling him gently to the side of the hallway next to the locker room entrance.

"What?" Hayes looked momentarily apprehensive before he smothered it, his face smoothing out.

And that was the whole problem. Hayes was playing afraid out there.

Afraid of making a mistake. Afraid of checking. Afraid of skating the way he normally did. Afraid of taking charge of the puck the way he might, if he was in Morgan's position.

Maybe he'd been wrong, and Hayes *couldn't* play wing.

Danny had made his share of fuckups, sure, but he was working hard, especially to keep up with Hayes.

Of course, Morgan wasn't sure if that was because he was genuinely trying to find a new gear, or if Hayes hadn't been pushing the way he normally might.

Morgan wasn't sure how to say it. Normally he might just say it, bluntly, with no attempt at tactfulness.

But Hayes seemed like a good kid. A good hockey player.

Then there was all the staff lingering in the hall, and if Morgan chastised Hayes here, someone would leak to the media that the chosen one thought the next one was playing like shit.

"You okay?" Morgan settled on.

"Yeah. Yeah. Of course. I know we're—"

"Yeah," Morgan agreed. Not sure if he wanted to hear Hayes' assessment of the garbage fire they'd been in the first period.

"Danny's . . .well, I'm adjusting."

"He's adjusting too," Morgan reminded him. "Adjust faster."

Hayes nodded, eyes huge in his face.

Morgan didn't think he'd ever seen eyes that color before, sharp as emeralds. He looked away. "Come on," he said gruffly and led Hayes into the locker room.

During their third shift of the second period, Morgan began to realize he'd made a serious tactical error.

Hayes wasn't any better. Danny wasn't either.

Their line was sluggish, awkward, and getting dominated by the Swedes, barely getting one shot off. Not what anyone would've expected from the offensive powerhouse that this starting line was supposed to be.

The second line scored again, and at least there was that—they *were* winning. But Morgan had never settled for "good enough" and he felt anxious and restless, sitting on the bench, watching the other guys celebrate.

Hockey was a team sport, for sure, but Morgan liked—*needed*—to be in the thick of the action.

Next to him, Danny let out a frustrated noise.

Morgan thought about saying something to calm him down—he was the captain, after all, and that was kind of his job. But maybe if Danny got worked up, Hayes would match his energy.

He turned towards his other side. Instead, Hayes' face was blank. Wiped clean of emotion.

"You got this," Morgan said to him, nudging him with his gloved hand.

"You better," Danny said, leaning right over Morgan.

Morgan liked to think that he preferred Danny's brash, almost complete disregard for who Morgan was over Hayes' hero worship, but at least Hayes wasn't annoying.

Hayes rolled his eyes.

"Yeah, you'll find your feet," Morgan said encouragingly.

"Gustafson just picked the puck right off my fucking tape," Hayes muttered.

Morgan didn't mention that the last time the Bandits had played the Mavericks, Morgan had attempted a very similar play, and Hayes had just blocked him out effortlessly, like Morgan hadn't even fucking *been* there.

Only a great defensive play after the takeaway by Danny and then an unbelievable save by Braun had kept the Swedes from cutting their lead in half.

"He's sharp," Danny agreed. "But you're sharper."

Hayes *was*.

Morgan had watched enough hockey over the years and then there was the two times a year the Bandits played the Mavs for him to know that Hayes was better than this.

"Lock in," Morgan said, a little more harshly than he had before.

It didn't help.

And by the end of the second period, Sweden *had* cut their lead and were pushing.

They needed another goal, and there was absolutely no fucking reason it couldn't be Morgan or Danny or Hayes, except that they looked like beer leaguers out there.

This time he couldn't be nice. Not if they wanted to win this game. Not if they wanted to win any more fucking games.

Instead of lingering in the hall or taking him into the locker room, Morgan dragged Hayes down the main hallway and then around the corner, deeper and then deeper still into the arena, until it was just them.

"What the hell is wrong with you?" he demanded and then hated himself a little when Hayes shrank back even more.

He was fucking this up.

"Nothing," Hayes muttered under his breath. He was looking down at the ground. Wouldn't even meet Morgan's eyes. And suddenly, Morgan hated that even more than the shitty ass way their line had been playing. Wanted Hayes to look up and meet his eyes. Wanted that bright green on him, seeing him. Challenging him. Being brilliant, the way Morgan knew he could be.

"That's bullshit. You hurt?"

Hayes shook his head.

"Then what the fuck, dude?"

Finally, Hayes lifted his eyes up. "You're just . . .I'm just . . .I'll get it together, I promise. Don't take me off your line."

Morgan was beginning to understand what this was. He knew what pressure could do to a person. Make you crumple like a damp piece of paper or crush you until you became as hard as a diamond.

He'd have assumed Hayes was more the latter than the former, but there was no question there'd been a whole lot of media bullshit around this tournament. About Hayes and Morgan playing together for the first time. Even if you thought you had your shit handled, it could still sneak up. Being locked in one day didn't mean that you were locked in forever.

"Listen," Morgan said, "you gotta forget about all that bullshit. About how you watched me as a kid. Thought I was the greatest thing you'd ever seen—"

"Presumptuous," Hayes interrupted, and Morgan saw a little of his fire flame back to life.

"Hey, I'm not the one who's playing afraid of fucking up, of making a mistake in front of my childhood hero," Morgan retorted.

"Did you even have childhood heroes?" Hayes sounded annoyed now. Which was better than afraid, at least.

"You gotta be more like Danny. Don't be afraid to tell me to fuck off, okay? I'm just . . ." Morgan put a hand on Hayes' chest and paused, suddenly and horribly aware of how close they were standing. They had all their gear on, sure, but it felt intimate.

Morgan told himself he was just trying to bridge the gap between them. For *hockey*.

Not because there was a frisson of something like awareness skittering through him, suddenly wild and untamed.

Hayes was a very good-looking guy, even dripping sweat and wearing all his smelly gear. It was the eyes, but it was more than that too. The sharp jawline. The wet strand of hair falling across his forehead. The plump pink lips.

Hayes bit that bottom lip and the sight sent a jolt through Morgan. "You're just what?"

Morgan couldn't remember the last time he'd felt this flustered—suddenly or otherwise. "Uh." He tore his eyes away from the indent in Hayes' bottom lip. "I'm just a man, Monty."

Hayes looked like he'd just been hit with a puck to the head. "What?"

You're doing this for hockey. You do everything for hockey. That had been true for so many years Morgan barely even remembered when he'd had other priorities. Could he even *have* other priorities?

Morgan was still touching Hayes' chest. Hockey players were super touchy, always, but this felt like a step further. He curled his fingers into Hayes' jersey. Right above the eagle's wings that were spread across his chest. "I'm just a man. I'm not special. I'm not anything—"

"Untrue," Hayes said.

Morgan shook his head. "You gotta forget about . . .I don't know . . .any of the times that you jerked off to my hockey highlights, okay?"

He'd been seventy-five percent joking, but the way his words hit Hayes, making him flush bright red, told him that he'd hit the nail on the head.

Oh, God.

"I didn't . . .I wouldn't . . ." Hayes stammered. He smacked Morgan on the arm and pulled back. He looked annoyed, now. Like he hadn't liked being called out on it. Annoyed was better than timid, any day of the week. Morgan was a self-professed asshole; he could work with *annoyed*.

"You sure fucking did, and I can't even blame you. They're some damn good highlights." He shot Hayes his best cockiest smile. Ignoring the flames licking up inside him at the idea that Hayes thought he was hot.

It was hardly the first time that had ever happened. He was rich and famous and successful and hardly ugly on the eyes, either. But this was *Hayes*, who was all those things too and was still looking at him like there was something worthy deep down inside Morgan, something he'd lost sight of a long time ago.

"They were okay," Hayes said, and the corner of his mouth quirked up in a grin. "You're really an asshole, you know?"

Morgan knew. "I'm gonna remind you of that fact when Danny's being a dick. In fact, maybe we should move Danny to center, you can make some plays for him."

Hayes made a face. "Don't."

"Then fucking play better," Morgan said.

Hayes didn't know whether he was burning with anger or embarrassment.

Or something else, entirely.

He still didn't know what the fuck had happened during the second intermission. Morgan had dragged him off to this abandoned section of the arena, where it was only the two of them. At first Hayes had been sure that Morgan was trying to let him down easy, give him some privacy when he kicked him off his line.

But instead he'd been earnest and then cocky, something burning between them that Hayes still couldn't explain.

He only knew his breath had come short, his mouth had dried out entirely, his tongue feeling too big in his mouth.

Then Morgan had touched him and teased him and held him accountable.

It shouldn't have been hot.

He should still be feeling humiliated that Morgan had correctly guessed that he'd starred in way too many of Hayes' wet dreams, and there was definitely a bit of that.

But there was more, too.

"Morgan," Coach Thompson barked, and he and Morgan and Danny went over the boards for their next shift.

He'd known he was fucking this up. But he couldn't get the thought out of his head that this was *Morgan Reynolds* and he was supposed to pass him the puck, make him a play that was equal to his skill and would only buff his glory to an additional shine.

The thought hadn't seemed so overwhelming when he'd been warming up, but the moment the puck dropped, he'd lost the thread, the pressure climbing up him, all the way up to his throat, until he felt like he was drowning.

"Come on," Morgan yelled, skating hard towards their end of the ice, and Hayes pushed away the embarrassment, the worries, *everything*, focusing hard instead on the annoyance. How dare Morgan Reynolds act like he was nothing? Maybe he was Morgan Reynolds, but *he* was Hayes Montgomery.

He'd won the Calder and the Rocket twice, and the Mavs had gone to game seven in the conference finals last year. Maybe he hadn't won a Cup yet, but everyone talked about how it was only a matter of time. *You know it's only a matter of time.*

He followed and then skated past him, taking the puck when Danny passed it to him, and he went hard around the back of the net, coming out the other side, surveying the way the players were arranged around the zone.

Morgan had a defender glued to him and so did Danny, but Morgan was Morgan, and if anyone could get open, it was going to be him.

Hayes dug his blades in and turned abruptly, hoping that Morgan would mirror him, and sure enough he moved with him, just enough that he shook his guy free. *Make a play. That's what you're here for.* And he did, shooting the puck between the defender's legs. It hit Morgan's tape and he barely held it for a second, before he shot it, going top shelf. The puck hit the net above the goalie's left shoulder.

"Sick play!" Danny yelled as they crashed together in celebration, Morgan joining them, his elated smile tinged with something knowing when he knocked his helmet against Hayes'.

"Great pass," Morgan said.

It had been a great pass and an even better play.

And he knew he'd only been able to pull it off because he'd gotten out of his own head. Played up to the skill he knew he possessed instead of focusing too hard on the pressure, on the player that everyone else expected him to be.

The additional goal had been exactly what the team need-ed because the Swedes slipped one more in, right at the end of the game, after they'd pulled their goalie.

But a win was a win, and as Morgan said, none of these teams were going to go down easy.

"That pass was absolutely filthy," Danny said after, when they were stripping down to their base layers, sweat congeal-ing on Hayes' skin.

"Thanks," Hayes said, nodding as he leaned down and began to unlace his skates.

"Good team win," Coach Thompson said, striding into the locker room, clapping his hands. "That last goal—that's what I want to see. Good passes, good plays."

Hayes flushed, tucking his head down. He'd gotten the main assist sure, and he'd made the play happen, but Morgan had been the one to take the shot. He'd barely even had a split second to consider the multiple factors before he'd just done it.

But then that was what made Morgan so good. He didn't need to hesitate. He just *knew*.

"Come on," Danny said, wrapping his arm around Hayes, apparently not caring how gross he was. "I think you deserve a drink for that."

Hayes shucked his arm off—not smiling, but not frown-ing either. "I didn't even score the goal."

"Yeah, but Mo wouldn't have even got a chance at it if you hadn't made that play."

"Maybe. Maybe not." He wasn't going to argue Morgan's brilliance with Danny.

Danny grinned. "I'm not debating this unless it's over a beer. Come on. Shower. Get dressed. Team's going out."

Hayes was going to do those things anyway, but when he finished, Morgan appeared by his stall.

"You coming?" Morgan asked, raising an eyebrow.

Part of Hayes wanted to go back to his room, crawl into bed, order room service, and watch some particularly trashy reality TV, but he knew he should go out and be social with his teammates.

Hayes hesitated just long enough that Morgan leaned in.

"Come on," Morgan said a little impatiently. "Don't go all bashful shrinking violet on me. That guy wouldn't have made that play or gotten me the puck the way he did."

"You asked me to do it," Hayes muttered.

"I asked you to remember what you're fucking capable of." Morgan met his eyes with a challenging look. "And you did."

That much was true.

"Yeah," Hayes agreed. Kind of hoping—and not hoping—that Morgan might give him another pep talk. Might call himself "just a man" again, like Hayes had ever needed that reminder—but if Morgan wanted to give it to him, wanted to *show* him, he wasn't going to argue.

"Celebrate with us then," Morgan said. "I owe you a drink for that pass."

"Hey, you took the shot," Hayes said.

He'd asked Hayes to be a playmaker, and he'd done it.

"Sure," Morgan said, smiling now. "Maybe you owe *me* a drink, then."

Hayes thought this was ridiculous. They both made a hell of a lot of money. What did it matter?

But half an hour later, he found himself in a bar, buried in the back of a big booth, pressed next to Danny on one side and Noah and Calvin on his right, Bram lounging with his hip pressed against the exposed side of the table. Everyone was shooting the shit, discussing the game they'd just played and what the next game—against Finland—might bring.

Morgan rolled up to the table, four bottles of beer dangling from one hand.

Hayes' pulse accelerated at the thought of those big competent hands.

It wasn't like his hands were really any bigger than Calvin's or Bram's, or even, God forbid, Danny's, but somehow it was only Morgan's that made his heart stutter and fall right at his feet.

It was that childhood hero worship, for sure, but it was more too. The way Morgan met his eyes and nodded slightly, just a dip of his chin, and the look in his eyes. Like he could see right through Hayes.

There weren't many first overall draft picks, tasked as the savior to a whole franchise, who carried that burden and the burden of all of hockey's expectations.

Part of Hayes wanted to ask him how he'd done it. The other part of him didn't want to talk at all. Only wanted to tuck his head into the sinful curve between Morgan's chin and his neck and suck a mark there until everyone knew that Morgan didn't belong to anyone else but Hayes.

It was really stupid.

Hayes knew it and felt it anyway.

"Here," Morgan said, sliding one of the beers right at Hayes. "You deserve this."

"What about me?" Danny squawked. "I set him up with the puck."

Morgan slid a look towards Danny. "Like you could've ever made that play. Not at that speed."

Danny made an annoyed noise, but he was still grinning.

Hayes wondered if that was the secret: not being good at everything and getting used to acknowledging it.

But Hayes—and Morgan—had always been considered full skill players, without any obvious holes, and so when one cropped up, everyone micro-focused on it, until Hayes wanted to scream.

"He kept up," Hayes said, on one hand hoping to reward Danny for being so fucking honest about his own short-comings, and on the other hand kind of envious that he could admit it so easy, as easy as breathing.

"Barely," Morgan muttered.

"You're such an asshole," Bram said, but he was laughing. So was Danny. Calvin and Noah, too.

Danny elbowed Hayes. "God, you're so starstruck. It's cute."

"Is it?" Morgan wondered before Hayes could deny it.

Hayes took a long drink of his beer. Kind of hoping that everyone might forget that he was sitting right here.

It wasn't *cute*. It was embarrassing as hell.

"He's got it under control, right, Monty?" Danny teased, elbowing him again.

"Maybe you're the asshole, Danny," Hayes said in his most unimpressed voice. He couldn't let Danny sense the blood in the water; he was a pest on *and* off the ice.

Morgan smiled and Danny *cackled.*

"Baby's got claws," Danny said.

His eyes met Morgan's again.

"'Course he does," Morgan said. "You think being a first overall's a breeze, Daniels?"

Danny looked surprised for the first time.

"That's what I thought," Morgan retorted.

"There room for one more?" Hayes was surprised to see Jacob Braun approach their table. They'd taken over several of the booths. He could've stayed separated from Morgan pretty easily.

Hayes wasn't the only one, either. There was a wide range of reactions—from shock to apprehension—on all their faces as Jacob shifted from one foot to the other.

Morgan glanced over at Jacob, looking annoyed but not murderous.

Bram's voice was full of straight-up worry when he nudged Jacob. "You sure, man?"

"We're all teammates here," Jacob said, and Morgan made a face.

And yeah, Hayes liked Jacob—at least when they were wearing the same stars and stripes, not really when he denied him goal after goal—but he could see a little where Morgan was coming from. There was a smug kind of superiority in Jacob's voice. Like he *liked* being the better man.

"Yeah, we are," Morgan said after a long, fraught pause. He slid one of his beers over in front of Jacob. "Great game. Have a beer."

Jacob's fingers curled around the bottle. "Thanks."

"See?" Morgan said, turning back to the table, grinning, his own brand of smugness radiating out of him. "Danny *is* the asshole."

"Said like there can only be one," Calvin muttered.

"Maybe I think all of you are assholes," Noah agreed.

"Monty isn't. He's too sweet," Bram said, reaching over and pinching his cheek.

Hayes laughed.

"Oh, he's plenty bitchy when he wants to be," Morgan said, and their eyes met again.

Something jolted deep inside Hayes. There was no real reason for Morgan to keep looking at him like this, but he kept doing it. Over and over. A whole tableful of hockey players, and Morgan knew all of them. Had played with and against them for years, but he seemed to only have eyes for Hayes.

He'd even looked away from Jacob, like once he'd made his peace offering, the guy didn't even matter.

"I'm telling you, it's nice to have those magic hands directed at the other goal instead of at me," Jacob said, gesturing towards Hayes.

"No kidding," Bram said. "That fucking pass?"

"I thought the goal was way better than the pass," Hayes said quietly.

Morgan chuckled. "You would."

"Monty's got no ego, it's kind of ridiculous," Danny teased, ruffling Hayes' hair, still damp from his post-game shower. Hayes resisted the urge to fix it, because what did it matter how shitty it looked? These were teammates, not potential hookups.

"That's cute, too," Calvin said, but his tone was affectionate.

Hayes wasn't particularly happy with the adjective they kept settling on, but what did it matter? He wasn't trying to be sexy for these guys. He never wanted any of them to want him—or for him to want them in return. He'd smartly kept his sex life far, far away from hockey.

"I still wanna know how you knew Mo was there," Noah said.

Hayes shrugged. "I knew I had to go to someone else. They were about to converge on me and I couldn't keep the puck. I could pass it to Danny or send it to Mo. And I thought if I made a move—Mo's been around a long time. I had to assume he'd figure out what I was doing."

"Aw," Danny said, wrapping a big arm around Hayes' shoulders. "I'd have figured it out, Monty."

"Ten seconds too late," Hayes pointed out sweetly.

Danny just laughed. He *could* be an asshole, no question about it, but considering his rep, Hayes was surprised at how little ego he really had.

"Yeah, probably," he agreed.

The whole table didn't stick together very long. Calvin and Noah went to the bar to get something stronger than beer. Danny left to talk to Walter, one of the defensive guys at the other table. Even Bram and Jacob found a quiet corner to chat in, leaving just Morgan and Hayes in the booth.

Hayes shifted awkwardly on the bench seat as Morgan finished his beer and then pushed the bottle aside.

"I meant it, you know," Morgan said, turning to him.

Hayes wanted him to mean *all* of it—the compliments to his game, the entreaties, the looks, and that strange, unexpected heat that had bloomed between them in that empty hallway.

But he had a feeling he knew what Morgan meant.

"It was a good pass, but a sick goal," Hayes argued. "You didn't even *think* before you shot it."

"If I'd waited, they'd have been on me and blocked the angle," Morgan said matter-of-factly. "Sometimes hockey is about thinking, but sometimes you gotta just take the shot."

Morgan's gaze was knowing and warm on Hayes' face. "Like you did," he continued. "You made the play. Didn't overthink it. Or worry about making it happen. Or what might happen if you didn't."

"Yeah." That was true. He'd shed all that bullshit like a snake shed its skin. Left it behind and refused to let himself pick it up again.

"You don't usually worry about that shit," Morgan stated, didn't ask, as he slumped farther into the booth, arm lifting to the top of the cushion. There was still a good few feet between them. But even though they weren't touching, Hayes swore he could feel the heat from Morgan's touch.

"How do you know that?" Hayes asked, only to be contrary. Yeah, Morgan might be kind of an asshole, but what was most annoying about him was that smug certainty he wore like a cloak.

Morgan shot him a look. "Because you don't. You know what you're capable of and you do it, regularly. When we play each other. When I watch other games. But you froze today."

Ugh, Hayes didn't want Morgan to bring up the jerking off theory again.

It had been humiliating enough the first time.

"It's not you," Hayes claimed.

Morgan's eyebrow rose. "No?"

"It's not," Hayes stressed.

"So you didn't have a poster of me above your bed."

He'd had *two*, actually, but he wasn't telling Morgan about the contents of his childhood bedroom.

"Of course not," Hayes blustered.

Morgan slid a few inches closer. Hayes swore he felt the brush of Morgan's fingertips on the fluffy ends of his hair. "You're lying. You said it in an interview, once."

Hayes' pulse picked up. "And you remembered that?"

"The chosen one is supposed to keep an eye on all-comers," Morgan said wryly, making a face.

"You hate it as much as I do," Hayes said, suddenly realizing how true that was.

"'Course I do. The moment you're on top, there's always someone who's younger and better and hungrier than you coming to knock you down."

Hayes was all too familiar with that phenomenon. He'd been hearing about some kid headed to the US developmental program, the oldest of three hockey-playing brothers, who everyone thought was going to be the next generational player.

Hayes had wanted to scream that *his* generation was only in their early to mid-twenties and he'd barely gotten a chance to do anything, yet. He hadn't lifted the Cup yet, but he could already taste the silver when he licked his bottom lip.

So he got it.

It wasn't fair, but then so much of this just wasn't fucking fair.

"It sucks," Hayes agreed.

"I even want to hate you, a little bit," Morgan admitted. There was a flash of shame in his eyes before he looked away. "But Danny's right. You're cute."

"I'm not sure that's any better than being an asshole," Hayes muttered. He didn't want Morgan Reynolds to think he was *cute*. He also didn't want him to think he was hot, because what the fuck could even happen if he did?

Also, he reminded himself, *Morgan Reynolds doesn't think men are hot. Cute's allowed. Cute's straight enough.*

"Don't change, okay? Don't let this . . ." Morgan huffed out a breath. "All this fucking bullshit pressure and media narratives and always looking over your shoulder change you, okay?"

Hayes didn't want to know what he meant, but he did, a little too well. There'd been a picture circulating that he'd tried not to see but had been nearly impossible to avoid: four figures superimposed next to each other. Gretzky, Morgan, him, and the oldest Barnes brother, who was still so young he had yet to lose his baby face.

"I'll try," he said.

Morgan nodded. "Good. Or the next time we play each other I'm gonna kick your ass."

"Like you could," Hayes scoffed. But Morgan probably could, even at thirty-five. He'd looked sharp out there in the game today, skating as well as guys years younger than him.

"Come on, superstar," Morgan teased, nudging him with a shoulder when he yawned into his beer. "It's getting late. We should probably get some sleep. I'm gonna round up everyone else."

They slid out of the booth, but Danny gave them a side eye when they wandered over to their group, mingled over by the bar.

"Time to call it a night," Morgan announced, and that was definitely his Captain voice, and Hayes definitely didn't find it hot. At all.

"You two eager to go to bed?" Danny asked slyly.

As far as Hayes knew, Danny didn't know for sure about him—not many people did, though he supposed he could count Morgan among the enlightened—so this was just regular run-of-the-mill heckling.

That he could handle.

"Some of us like our beauty sleep," Hayes said, pasting a faux-innocent look on his face as Morgan laughed and Danny's jaw dropped.

He didn't stay outraged for long, because that wasn't Danny's kind of thing. He met outrage with something even more outrageous.

"See? *Cute*," Danny teased, squeezing him. "No wonder you like him, Cap."

"Never said I did," Morgan grumbled, but he met Hayes' eyes and Hayes realized he didn't have to say it because he *did*. Maybe not like Hayes had always secretly, ludicrously hoped might be true—but this was enough. Of course it was enough.

Because if Morgan liked him like that, then Hayes would have to figure out how to break his lifelong, ironclad promise to himself that he'd never fall in love with another hockey player.

"Didn't have to, Mo," Danny joked. "Alright. I'll get everyone together."

It took ten minutes for Danny to convince the team to close out their tabs and head outside into the cool air.

The bar was only a few blocks from the hotel, and Hayes hoped the chill might clear his head, help him look away from where Morgan was chatting with Bram and Calvin.

It didn't quite work, so he slipped to the back of the group, glad not for the first time that he could be unobtrusive.

He glanced at his phone. Zach had texted him. **You gonna ever come down from that assist?**

Hayes smiled. **No**, was all he said, because Zach would get it. Zach *always* got it.

Before Zach could text him back, they were at the hotel, streaming as a big group into the lobby. Some of the team got distracted by the fact that the lobby bar was still open.

But Hayes was done for the night and slipped off towards the bay of elevators, pressing the up button.

"These idiots forget we've got a practice tomorrow."

Hayes looked over, surprised to see Morgan standing there, wry smile on his face.

"I didn't forget," Hayes said.

They exchanged knowing looks, already anticipating how hungover and cranky three quarters of the team was going to be tomorrow morning.

The elevator dinged open, and Hayes almost wanted to say, *let's hold it, in case any of these idiots come to their senses,* but that would mean admitting—even to himself—that he didn't want to share a private space with Morgan.

Morgan rested against the back of the elevator. Hayes glanced back at him. "Same floor?" he asked, after pressing seven.

Morgan shook his head. "I'm on eight."

"Alright. Okay." Hayes hit eight. Tried to even out his breathing and *not* look.

He even stupidly thought Morgan might appreciate that, but Morgan clearly didn't, because he caught his attention, again. "You want to grab breakfast together?"

Hayes' breath caught. He kept trying to put some space between them, but Morgan kept closing it.

Kept pushing right into it.

"Uh. Yeah. Sure."

The floors ticked by. Hayes' breath felt caught in his throat, his gaze tangled with Morgan's. His hazel eyes were steady, but intent.

"Good," he said. "I'll meet you downstairs at eight."

Hayes nodded.

Morgan chuckled a little under his breath, like he knew what Hayes was trying to do. But he couldn't. He *couldn't.*

"That really was a great pass, you know?" Morgan said absently.

Hayes' throat went dry. "Thanks."

He didn't want to make conversation. He wanted to stay silent until the elevator reached his floor. Until he could get to his room and scream into his pillow like the thirteen-year-old he wasn't anymore.

"You're something else," Morgan said.

"Not what you were saying earlier."

Morgan shrugged. "You needed a reminder. That's all."

That hadn't been all, and Hayes knew Morgan wasn't stupid enough to think that was true.

"I—"

"It's all good. Really." Morgan reached out and put a reassuring hand on his shoulder, squeezed. Awareness prickled across Hayes' skin. *This is what he'd do to anyone. To Noah. To Calvin. Even to Danny.* But then Morgan's touch lingered a second too long, only disappearing when the elevator finally came to a stop on Hayes' floor.

Hayes wanted to yell that he'd wanted it before, but now he was wishing he could stay. But there was no reason to stay. This was his floor.

"I…uh…I'll see you tomorrow morning, then," Hayes said, meeting that frank gaze one more time before he tore his eyes away and walked off the elevator.

Before he did something he would—and wouldn't—regret.

CHAPTER 3

His son's voice was bright and easy in his ear. The brightness was normal, but Morgan couldn't say that the ease of it was routine.

And whose fault is that?

Morgan shoved the voice away and focused on Finn.

He was sixteen and thought he knew everything.

"Braun was so good last night," Finn said, and the teasing lilt in his tone meant he knew exactly how annoyed that would make Morgan.

But teasing was good. Teasing was better than the alternative, which was sullen frustration—or worse, silence.

"I hope you're taking notes," Morgan said, focusing on the one positive of Braun's performance, besides the obvious one, which was that it had helped them win the game. "He's got skills."

"And you hate him for them," Finn said slyly.

"I'm sure you're going to end up playing against some guys who wish you weren't so good in the net," Morgan reminded him.

Knew it was a mistake as soon as the words were out of his mouth, because Finn went dead quiet for a long second.

It was a difficult line to walk with Finn—impossible, actually—between praising his developing goalie skills and heaping too much pressure on him to have a successful future.

As a Reynolds it was hard to avoid; the pressure came with the last name.

But Morgan knew he could be a total fucking idiot too, and lay it on too thick. He *meant* well, but sometimes it felt like all he could talk about with Finn was hockey. It wasn't his fault that hockey was loaded for his son, but he ended up taking the brunt of it, sometimes with his foot in his mouth to boot.

Not surprisingly, Finn changed the subject. "So, how's it playing with Monty? You guys looked a little off to start the game, but then the third period? Jesus, it was like it all clicked."

Morgan told himself to be normal. To say something fucking normal but then, "I . . .uh . . .yeah," came out instead.

Finn, not an idiot, focused in on his dad's obvious discomfort.

"It's not good?"

"It's fine."

"You're lying."

He was. Probably even to himself.

Morgan steeled his resolve. He'd called Finn, not just to check in on him, but also for . . .well, maybe some advice that only Finn could give.

"I've got a friend," he said, and Finn probably assumed he was changing the subject. But he wasn't.

"You have a friend?" Finn faux-gasped.

"Shut up," Morgan grumbled. "You know I do. People like me."

"No. People are afraid of you," Finn said succinctly.

Some deep, painful part of Morgan wanted to ask if Finn was one of them, but he wasn't sure he could hear the answer. Besides, this wasn't supposed to be about the sometimes fraught relationship he had with his son.

"So I have this friend," Morgan started again, "and he's . . .uh . . .well, he always thought he was straight."

"A common problem," Finn joked.

Morgan rolled his eyes. "He thought he was straight, but then he met someone—"

"A guy?" Finn interrupted.

"*Yes*," Morgan said, trying not to let his frustration and annoyance seep into his tone. This whole charade was stupid. Maybe Finn would even see right through it and pin him down. *Who made you think you weren't straight, Dad?*

But Finn only made an impatient noise. "Okay, so your friend thought he was straight and then he met a guy and he's attracted. What's the deal?"

What's the deal? Like this wasn't a life-changing, life-altering occurrence. Like Morgan wasn't going out of his mind wondering how to shift things back to how they'd been. He felt divided, between *before*, when Hayes Montgomery had just been another hockey player, a *good* hockey player, that far too many people compared to him, but *still* just another hockey player, and *after*, like he'd been chemically altered by the five minutes they'd spent in that empty hallway.

He couldn't see Hayes the same way anymore. He'd lain awake far too late last night, going over everything again and again in his mind. The interviews. Them grabbing coffee. Practice. The game. Their first intermission conversation, when he'd tried to be gentle. The second intermission conversation, where he'd been honest, and that honesty had lit Hayes up and subsequently set Morgan on fire, too. Then the bar. Sitting too close in the booth, his fingers only millimeters from Hayes' neck, from the spiky ends of his dark brown hair. He'd wanted to *touch*, even though he knew he couldn't.

That he *shouldn't*.

The elevator ride, where Hayes had tried to put distance between them, and Morgan should have let him, but he didn't, because he just didn't *want* to.

If Morgan had leaned in and kissed him goodnight, would that hero worship in his gorgeous green eyes grow hazier and hotter?

Then this morning, when he'd been soft and cuddly in his oversized hoody, his hair mussed from sleep, eyes filled with a sleepy affection as they'd sat across from each other and eaten their eggs in silence.

It was that ease, combined with the warmth blooming at the base of his stomach, that had driven Morgan to call Finn before they had to head to practice.

"Earth to Morgan." Finn's voice broke through his thoughts. "I asked, *what's the deal?*"

Oh. Right.

"Well, he's never . . .he's *not*," Morgan said. Not that it mattered. He was open-minded, far more than a lot of the other hockey players he knew. He'd started out vaguely accepting, and then the older Finn grew and the more Morgan understood about the challenges he faced, just by being who he was, the more stringent he'd gotten about his beliefs.

Two years ago, a player on the Bandits had uttered a shitty homophobic slur and Morgan had gotten him traded to another team. A *crappy* team.

He knew he was accepting, but it turned out that accepting queerness in other people was easier than accepting queerness in himself.

"That doesn't mean anything," Finn said blithely. Clearly he had bought Morgan's story about a "friend," hook, line and sinker.

Morgan didn't know if he was relieved by his son's obtuseness or regretful.

"What do you mean?"

"I *mean*," Finn said, chuckling, "that sexuality is on a spectrum. Your friend probably leans towards women, but he found the one guy that really cranks his motor."

Did Hayes crank Morgan's motor?

Morgan wanted to say no, but the answer was way too obvious, flashing neon lights in his head. He could lie to himself, but he'd always made it a habit never to do that. *Yes.*

Morgan wanted to laugh and to cry. "What should he do about it?"

"Is the other guy open to it?"

"Uh yeah. He uh . . .yeah he's queer."

"Well, just because he's queer doesn't mean he's interested," Finn lectured.

"From what I've seen, he'd be receptive," Morgan said. Hero worship wasn't attraction, not exactly, but Morgan didn't think he was the only one who'd felt the heat between them in the empty hallway yesterday.

"Wait," Finn said.

Here it comes. Morgan braced for the inevitable lecture that he'd obscured his own questions with a very stupid *I have a friend* story. *Hey,* he could imagine saying to Finn, *you bought it at first.*

"Wait," Finn repeated again, "you said, *from what you've seen.* It's someone there? At the tournament? Your friend and this other guy? They're both hockey players?"

"Uh," Morgan said, not expecting that question and finding himself unable to field an answer that didn't immediately give it away.

"Don't answer that," Finn said, laughing. "It's fucking obvious it is. Well, I'd tell your friend that this isn't a bad time to explore some possibilities, if everyone's open to it."

"Seriously?" Morgan didn't know what he'd expected from a sixteen-year-old, but maybe it should have been this blithe approach.

At sixteen, with all the time in the world ahead of him, Finn probably thought it *was* a good idea to explore possibilities.

"It's only what, nine more days? Kind of a good bookend. Makes it just a hookup and a good, string-less way to see if he likes it. You know?"

It occurred to Morgan that maybe if he'd dispensed with the stupid *I have a friend* story, Finn might have given him very different advice. He probably assumed that Morgan's "friend" was closer to his age than Morgan's. Did guys Morgan's age still "hook up"?

"Uh, yeah. I can . . .um . . .see that."

"You don't sound like you do," Finn teased.

"Is that normal?"

"*Yeah*," Finn scoffed. "Just make sure your friend communicates and it'll be fine."

Still, Morgan hung up five minutes later not sure, despite Finn's certain attitude and persuasive advice, that he was going to go for it.

Hayes was another player. It was inherently messy, just because of who they both were. Might make things awkward later.

Maybe he should just let the idea of doing something about it go.

But Morgan knew that wasn't going to be in the cards. Whether he acted on his attraction or not, it was still going to exist, hard and real, pressed right up against his breastbone. Every time he saw Hayes. Every time their eyes met. Every time he made Hayes laugh. The way he understood exactly how Morgan felt, because he was in the exact same position.

Morgan had only met a few people in his life who really truly understood what it was to be him. Of course Hayes was going to, he should have realized that sooner, but it was one thing to *know* that fact, and it was another to begin to know *him*.

So really, the only question wasn't if the attraction was going to exist. It was only if Morgan was going to act on it.

"Better," Morgan called out, taking a tight line behind the net, gaining speed with the puck as Danny and Hayes fanned out in the zone.

Hayes slid behind a defenseman, caught Morgan's puck, and then hit the net by shooting a clean top shelf shot, right over Bram's right shoulder.

"Goddamn," Danny yelled. "That's fucking sick, boys."

Morgan rolled his eyes, but it had been good.

They'd just been working out the play, nobody playing full-out, but it had gone better than he'd anticipated.

He didn't think he'd be giving Hayes any lectures about letting the pressure or the moment or his linemates get to his head. Not today. And not tomorrow, when they played Finland.

"Better," Morgan said, giving Hayes a nod as they skated over to the edge of the rink.

"Yeah?" Hayes still had that look in his eye, like if Morgan gave him a compliment, he'd die a happy man. But Morgan couldn't do anything about that. Even if he could, he wasn't sure he would. Something about Hayes' awe soothed the worry inside. The worry that wondered every day if today was time he'd begin to feel every one of his thirty-five years and it would finally show on the ice.

"Not perfect," Morgan added. "But better."

Hayes smiled, and if Morgan had hoped or dreamed or anticipated that he'd been wrong about the way that made him feel, he'd be wrong.

He almost said something really stupid like, "you've got a nice smile."

But he wasn't stupid. Or he was trying really hard not to be stupid, no matter what Finn had suggested he do.

"Thanks," Hayes said.

Danny skated over, slinging arms over both of their shoulders. "You two are all buddy-buddy over here," he teased.

Morgan forced his body not to tense. Danny didn't know. He couldn't possibly know. *Morgan* barely knew.

Next to him, Hayes looked over it. Clearly more used to brushing off teammates' jokes than Morgan. "You're obnoxious."

"Aw, Monty. No love," he cooed.

"Not for you, you dick," Hayes retorted.

"We should get some reporters over here. They'd lose their shit, seeing you all cozy and chatting."

"We talk," Morgan said, trying not to sound defensive. "We did *hours* of interviews together the day after we got here."

"Yeah, and everyone fucking creams themselves every time you do."

Hayes was frowning now. Morgan fought the urge to slide his glove off and reach over, smoothing out that crease between his brows. He shouldn't let Danny's stupid shit get to him.

"It's not . . .it's not *fun*, Danny," Hayes said slowly.

"For everyone to think you're really fucking good at hockey? Yeah, a real hardship," Danny said.

"Monty's not wrong," Morgan said, and Hayes shot him a grateful look.

Danny made a face. "Ugh, now you're actually making me *feel* like a dick."

"That must suck for you," Hayes said matter-of-factly but he was smiling again.

Morgan felt a weight lift, just seeing that smile.

"Come on," Morgan said, "let's run it again."

Hayes pushed off with him, skating towards the middle of the rink. Morgan pointed his stick at Hayes, wiggling it teasingly.

"Want you to try to impress me again," he said, lowering his voice so only Hayes could hear it. Aware, as his blood pounded in his ears, that he was definitely flirting. Maybe he was shit at it, but he was still making the attempt.

But Hayes only grinned, like he didn't get it. "Oh, yeah? How's that any different than Danny's bullshit?"

Morgan leaned in a bit closer. Close enough to pick out the hazel specks in Hayes' eyes, watch as his breath came a little shorter.

"It's different 'cause you're not impressing the fucking media. Just me."

Then shorter still, as Morgan closed more distance between them, until their visors were nearly hitting. The closeness wasn't *that* unusual, but it was way more standard during a goal celebration. Just like this, during practice, when the skate time was winding down and most guys were just fucking around, it wasn't exactly normal.

But Morgan didn't care.

"I don't think you're very easy to impress." Hayes wet his lips, pink tongue flicking out.

"Good thing you're so fucking amazing at hockey, then." Morgan curled his gloved hand over Hayes' shoulder. There were so many layers between his skin and Hayes', but all the padding felt like nothing. Like he was already touching him.

"Don't flatter me," Hayes said, the corner of his mouth turning up.

"It's not flattery if you've got it." Morgan squeezed his shoulder. "So let's see it, baby."

Hayes' jaw dropped open. And yeah, that had been very stupid. Flirty, yes, and stupid, yes. Even stupider that he hadn't even thought about it before the word was out of his mouth.

He'd said it because it felt natural and right. Teasing and affectionate.

Hayes looked like he wanted to say a whole lot, but then snapped his mouth shut again.

Morgan wasn't ready to explain why he'd said it so he reached out with his stick and grabbed a nearby puck, taking off, and just hoping—praying, really—that Hayes would follow without questioning him.

One second. Then two. And then there he was, a shadow behind him.

Morgan wasn't quite up to full speed, but when Hayes pulled even with him, he was barely breathing hard. Hayes shoved his stick in, trying to steal the puck as they headed towards the empty goal.

"Come on, baby, take it if you can," Morgan said under his breath, hoping that Hayes could still hear him.

Hayes' movements grew more determined, and a second later, the puck was bouncing off Morgan's skate blade and it was on Hayes' tape.

He took off, twirling in a tight circle, still fast as anything, proving with every move he made just how fucking incredible he was. Morgan took off after him, not quite as sharp at changing direction at that speed, and then Hayes changed again and again, using his edges in that way that it felt like only he could, until Morgan finally had to give up, sliding over in front of the goal, hoping to play some more general defense.

He wasn't a goalie, by any stretch, but he'd won the Selke twice. He could still hold his own, even against the league's new hotshots.

And Hayes, no matter how much he tried to deny it, was one of them.

Was *the* hotshot, frankly.

"You gonna play goalie, *baby*?" Hayes retorted, grinning so brightly it took Morgan's breath away.

"Against you? Hell no."

He let Hayes get lulled into a momentary complacency as he passed the puck back and forth to himself, and then he took off, intending to steal it back.

But before he could, Hayes shot the puck off and to Morgan's surprise, there was Danny, smug smile on his face as he and Hayes tag-teamed him all the way to the crease.

Danny flicked the puck behind him, and it took a full second for Morgan to realize he'd been passing it back to Hayes, who took the shot, practically skating around Morgan and sinking the puck right into the net.

Danny screeched behind him, but Hayes was only staring at Morgan, and brilliance looked fucking amazing on him.

Flushed cheeks, bright eyes, the knowing edge to his smile as Hayes reached out and tapped Morgan's thigh with his stick.

"Good showing," he teased.

"You cheated." Though that goal had been ninety-five percent Hayes and five percent Danny.

"Thought we were supposed to be practicing our plays, Cap," Hayes said, all innocence, but Morgan knew better at this point. Maybe he hadn't said *baby* again, but Morgan could feel it, as good as a brush on his cheek, the back of his neck, a brief touch, Hayes' hand warm and firm, on the small of his back.

"I . . .uh. Yeah. We're good."

Coach was on the other end of the rink, signaling the end of practice—it had never been meant to be a long, grueling one, with a game the day before and another game tomorrow.

In the locker room, after he'd gotten showered and changed, Danny crowded into his space before they headed towards the bus. "What the fuck was up with that?" he asked lowly.

Morgan's heart started to beat a little faster. On the other side of the room, Hayes' back was to him, all slim muscles as he pulled on a T-shirt.

He hadn't let himself look before now, and he told himself he *still* wasn't looking, but that was a lie. He'd *just* looked.

"What the fuck was up with what?" Morgan retorted evenly.

Danny shot him an unimpressed look. "You know what I'm talking about. You and Monty, flirting."

"We were practicing. I gotta know what he's capable of."

"Yeah, but me and you aren't playing sexy keep-away," Danny pointed out.

That was true. Before Hayes, Morgan never would've been tempted to play sexy keep-away. The thought never would've even occurred to him.

"I already know what you're capable of," Morgan said dismissively.

Danny made a face. But Morgan knew his feelings weren't hurt; he was just annoyed that Morgan wasn't telling him what was going on. Nobody was a bigger gossip than Matt Daniels.

Morgan had hoped that shook him, but he wasn't surprised when on the bus, Danny dropped down in the seat next to him. They'd been the first ones on the bus, so Danny could've picked any seat he wanted.

"You're really not gonna tell me what's up?" Danny asked incredulously.

Morgan rolled his eyes. "There's nothing to tell."

"Lie. The tension between the two of you could power a small city."

Morgan froze, but of course Danny kept talking.

"And I already suspected about Monty, but *you* surprised me. Of course you'd go for another first overall pick. Is it like some special club—"

"Matthew," Morgan hissed under his breath, lips numb. He grabbed Danny's arm and squeezed it, hard. "You don't—"

"I *know*. You don't out people without their permission. I'm not stupid."

Morgan wanted to tell him not to *act* stupid then, but of course Danny kept going, because when had he ever shut up in his whole fucking life? Never, that was when.

"I don't know for sure about Monty, of course, but the guy's never even looked at a girl. Even when they shove themselves at him. And I figured you already knew, 'cause of the whole first overall thing and then because of the way you kept looking at him. Last night. And today."

"I wasn't looking at him any kind of way," Morgan lied.

Danny shot him an unimpressed look. "So you're in denial then."

He was freaking out. That wasn't denial. Not even close.

"No," Morgan huffed out, trying to keep his temper and his wits.

"So *is* it a super special first overall thing, then? Get picked first, then the chosen one agrees to fuck you? I guess I missed out. Only went sixth. Too bad."

Morgan smacked his palm over Danny's mouth. "God, do you ever shut up?"

Danny grinned under his hand. That was all the answer he needed.

"No, it's not. It's not . . .maybe it's a little like that, only 'cause I know how he is, how he feels. But yeah, maybe it was a little . . .flirty today."

"A little flirty?" Danny answered, sound muffled through his hand.

"It was . . .we were mostly just giving each other shit."

"I know what that's like. *I* give you two shit. You two were on some other level. And you know what, that's okay. It's not a big deal."

If Morgan could've predicted how Finn would react—even though he'd been using his very stupid *I have a friend* story—he might not have been surprised at his son's advice. But he did *not* expect that Danny would echo it.

"What?" Danny retorted. "It *isn't* a big deal. Considering your situation, I didn't think you'd end up being shitty about it."

"I'm not being shitty, it's complicated. Hayes is a teammate. I'm his *captain*," Morgan hissed. Other players were beginning to walk onto the bus. In a second, someone could maybe overhear this conversation, and that would make it all so much worse.

"Yeah for what, another week? If I swung that way, I wouldn't let a little messiness stop me from hooking up with Monty. He's hot."

God damnit. Morgan wanted to close his eyes, wish this nightmare over, and sink right through the seat and off this bus.

"What? He is."

"How do you know you don't swing that way, then?" Morgan asked more for time to comprehend his own sudden sexual revelations than because he really wanted to know about Danny.

"I mean, I'm fundamentally not *against* dick, if you get my drift, and we all had our share of brojobs in the program, but a guy's never really done it for me like *that*, you know?"

"Maybe you just haven't met the right guy yet," Morgan said, and then wished the moment the words were out of his mouth that he hadn't let them slip.

Danny's eyes lit up. "Oh my God, that's it, isn't it? Monty's the guy who made you want dick."

"If I hear even a *hint* of this from someone else, I will kill you. Slowly. Painfully."

"Well, duh," Danny said, like this was a no-brainer. Like he didn't personally power the NHL gossip train.

"I'm just saying."

"I'd never out either of you, swear to God," Danny said, smacking a hand over his heart. "You want me to take a blood vow?"

"No. *No.*" If he asked Danny, he probably would, and that would make everything even messier—literally—than it had been before. And the mess was already overwhelming him. "Just . . .uh . . .score a goal for me tomorrow, alright?"

Danny grinned. "Aye, aye, Captain."

"Or a sick assist. That would work too."

"I got you, Mo. We're gonna come through."

"We're?"

Danny elbowed him. "Me and Monty. We got your back. I mean, Monty more than me, 'cause even though you're still hot, you're kinda old—"

Morgan buried his head in his hands. "Please, for the love of God, stop talking."

CHAPTER 4

Hayes felt like he hadn't been able to take a deep breath since yesterday.

Since the game. Since the elevator.

Then today, Morgan had done all the other normal Morgan things while also cranking it up another notch. Flirting. Teasing. Egging him on. Calling him *baby*, twice.

If Hayes pressed his palms to his cheeks, he knew he'd feel his heartbeat, careening out of control.

"You okay?" Danny leaned over right into his space.

Morgan was sitting across the table, and for a second after he'd snagged that seat at dinner, Hayes had almost been disappointed. *But I want to sit next to you. Feel your shoulder press into mine.*

But instead Danny had taken that spot. Annoyingly.

At Danny's question, Morgan looked up from his plate, where he was cutting his chicken.

"I'm fine," Hayes said. But was he? He was slowly going out of his mind, alternating between total panic and total exhilaration. Maybe he was reading the signs wrong, or maybe Morgan hadn't *meant* to send any signs, but he didn't think so.

The *baby* had sealed it.

"You don't seem fine," Danny said. His gaze narrowed and that teasing, knowing expression that *never* boded well when it was on Danny's face, emerged. "You seem kinda . . .hot."

"Oh. Uh. No."

It was early February in Toronto. Hot was something he wasn't. Unless Danny was talking about the raging inferno inside him whenever he thought of Morgan calling him *baby*, and the possibility that he might do it again. Softer this time, and more earnest, pressing him next to his hotel room door . . .

"You *look* hot," Danny leered.

"Stop it," Hayes said, smacking him on the arm. "Nobody wants to know about your secret crush on me."

He'd learned, a long time ago, how much easier it was to go on the offensive sometimes. To push back on guys who tried to make him uncomfortable.

Not that he really thought Danny was doing it on purpose.

"We really don't," Morgan said through clenched teeth.

If Hayes hadn't been present for his own accidental coming out, he'd have assumed Morgan's discomfort was about the possibility a guy might have a secret crush on another guy, but he knew Morgan better than to believe that was true.

So what was he pissed about? About Danny hitting on him, in the most straight-bro way ever? That was ridiculous.

"How about *your* secret crushes, Mo?"

Morgan rolled his eyes. "You are the most outrageous person I know."

"And you say that like it's a bad thing."

Hayes laughed at the disgruntled face Morgan made.

"Are we gonna go out tonight?" Danny asked, changing the subject.

"We have a game tomorrow," Hayes pointed out. "Against Finland."

"Yeah, Danny. You *do* remember you're here to play, not to party, right?"

Danny ran a hand through his wild blond curls. "Yeah, I did get that memo, Captain and Captain's shadow."

"I'm not—" Hayes protested, suddenly flustered and unable to hide it.

"No, you're just a very good boy. No wonder Morgan likes you so much." Danny flashed Hayes a toothy grin.

"I *like* that he doesn't want to go out and get drunk the night before a game," Morgan said.

Hayes knew Morgan's praise shouldn't hit him as hard as it did. But it was impossible not to feel the thrill of it.

"Too bad," Danny said.

"You're not still—"

But Morgan didn't get even half his admonishing question out before Danny just shook his head. "No. No. I hear Cal's getting up a Mario Kart tournament. You two in?"

Hayes didn't want to play video games. He still wanted to curl up in his bed with the trashiest TV he could find. Try to go to sleep early, be extra ready for the game tomorrow. The Finns weren't going to go down easy. They never did.

But Morgan nodded and then turned to Hayes. "You in?"

How was Hayes supposed to say no when *Morgan* asked him? Not especially nicely, but with that extra affectionate glow that Hayes might or might not be wishfully making up in his hazel eyes?

Which was how he ended up pressed up against Noah with Danny on his other side, lying on the floor next to one of Calvin's beds, as Morgan kicked Bram's ass in Mario Kart.

Jacob wandered in at one point—the tournament had grown big enough they'd ended up split between two rooms—but hadn't stayed, which was better for everyone, because Hayes hadn't missed how Morgan's back tensed even as he tried to clear the sour expression off his face.

When Bram finally lost, chucking his controller onto the bed in frustration, Morgan was laughing, as relaxed as Hayes had seen him since the tournament had started.

"How did you get so damned good at this?" Bram whined.

"You guys forget I've got a sixteen-year-old son?"

"How *is* Finn?" someone asked.

"Good. Good. I've been trying to get him into the juniors draft, but he keeps saying he wants to do the program and then a few years of college." Morgan made a frustrated noise and ran a hand through his hair. "You know how they are, always wanting to pave their own path."

"If he wants to be smart, let him be smart," Danny teased. "He's gonna be smarter than you, at any rate."

"Not that hard for him to get there," Morgan said, smiling even as he ducked his head.

A few minutes later the party broke up, and Hayes found himself on the way back to his room with Morgan.

Hayes pointed out, trying not to stammer with nerves, wondering what was happening—if *anything* would happen, that the elevator to Morgan's floor was the opposite direction.

"Shush, now you're gonna make me feel even worse," Morgan joked, knocking their shoulders together. "I wanted to tell you something."

Hayes' breath caught in his throat. Tried not to gaze up at Morgan with that same hero-struck expression he knew he wore around him so much of the fucking time. Wasn't quite sure he pulled it off.

"What is it?"

Morgan chuckled. "Just something I talked about with Danny today. You know he . . ." He paused awkwardly. "I thought you should know that he's uh . . .guessed about you."

"Oh. *Oh.*" This was not even in the realm of what Hayes had expected him to say.

They stopped in front of Hayes' door. Hayes shoved his hands into the pockets of his sweatpants, feeling for his key. Dug the edges of the plastic card into his palm and tried to calm his breathing.

This wasn't Morgan saying anything specifically. This was only Morgan trying to be a good teammate. A good *captain.* Keeping him informed and all that jazz.

"I didn't confirm anything," Morgan said seriously. "I just thought you should be aware."

"Okay. Um. I don't mind. I kind of assumed he'd guessed. With the whole secret crush thing. And there was a lot of talk in the program." He'd been kind of an open secret there. A lot of guys were, including Zach, even though he'd ended up going to college instead of staying in.

"Right. Well." Morgan lingered, even though it was clear he didn't really have a reason to.

Hayes wanted to invite him in, but he didn't know what they'd even do—besides the obvious, and he wasn't even sure if Morgan wanted that. He looked more awkward than turned on right now, if he was being honest.

"I really don't mind, but I appreciate you telling me," Hayes said, reaching out and squeezing Morgan's forearm, and didn't let go even though he knew he should. "Danny's more circumspect than he seems, at the outset."

"I hope so," Morgan said under his breath.

"He's probably suspected about me for years, and it's not like he's outed me in that time," Hayes reassured.

"I just . . .I worried." Morgan *looked* worried. Conflicted, even, a crease between his brows that Hayes wanted to lean in and smooth out with his fingertips.

"You don't need to worry about me. I'm a big boy. I can take care of myself."

Morgan's gaze flicked up and down, and Hayes went cold and then very hot. He hadn't really *meant* to flirt this time. Not late at night, because even in the fluorescent light of the quiet hotel hallway, the air between them felt intimate. Private.

"Believe me, I know," Morgan said softly.

If Hayes wasn't knee-deep in some kind of fantasy-fulfill-ment right now, he might think Morgan swayed an inch or two closer. At the very least, he should stop touching Morgan. It had gone on way longer than it already should've, but instead, he curled his fingers around his forearm.

There was a thick layer of sweatshirt between his skin and Morgan's, but just like in that empty hallway during the second intermission against Sweden, it felt like nothing.

Like Hayes could already feel him.

Like Morgan wanted to be felt.

He certainly hadn't tugged himself away, either, even though there was no reason to stay.

There was a part of Hayes that wanted to cut through all the haze and ask bluntly, *what are we doing? What are* you *doing?* But if he did that might spook Morgan, and God knew, if Hayes never got anything else but this, he was going to hold on to this scrap forever.

"I was unfair to you," Morgan said, still very quiet. "When we met."

They'd run into each other casually, incidentally, so many times. It was impossible not to. But yes, this tournament was the first time they'd exchanged more than just basic pleasantries. Morgan must be talking about the first day they'd been here.

"It's awkward, everyone talking about how I'm the new you," Hayes soothed.

It was awkward, too, being the person doing the replacing.

"Not just that." Morgan huffed out a breath. He was so close Hayes could feel it against his cheek. "You made me feel old."

"You must've hated that." It was actually a fucking miracle Morgan had given him even a passing consideration if that was really true.

"I didn't love it."

"What do I make you think now?" Hayes knew he shouldn't push. But he gazed up at Morgan and hoped his eyes said what he really meant. *Tell me something else. Something better.*

Morgan swayed closer. Or maybe that was Hayes. They were rapidly running up against the point of no return. Hayes knew it. Morgan had to know it too. They couldn't be this close in a hotel hallway for this long without eventually getting interrupted.

Hayes opened his mouth, to ask again, to maybe suggest something even crazier, which was that they should continue this inside the privacy of his room, but before he could, a door way down the hall slammed shut. Morgan sprang back, eyes wild. Like he'd just gotten caught, even though they hadn't actually done a goddamn thing.

"I should go," Morgan said and looked like he regretted the words the moment they came out of his mouth. "It's late. The game. Tomorrow. Finland."

Hayes' tongue felt thick and swollen in his mouth, his brain even more sluggish. "Yeah." For a semi-insane split second, he considered again inviting Morgan into his room. But he didn't. "Alright."

Morgan turned and, without a word, headed back down the hallway towards the elevator.

Hayes waited one second, then two until he was almost out of sight down the long hallway before he pulled the keycard out of his pocket, opening his door.

Then proceeded to flop down on the bed and scream loudly into his pillow.

Why hadn't he just *said* it? Morgan hadn't seemed freaked out by their closeness, only by the possibility they might be discovered, which frankly, was more likely than not, considering where they'd been.

Hayes rolled over. Wondered if he should call Zach. It was late. And what would Zach even say? *Geez, dude, you totally just whiffed. And with Morgan freaking Reynolds. You've only adored him forever.*

Because Morgan had been right. There'd been two posters. One above his bed, the other across from it.

He might have more chances, but Hayes wasn't sure that was true. This tournament wasn't that long and then it would be over and their only reasons to see each other would be when the Mavs played the Bandits, twice a year.

Maybe he wouldn't get another chance. Maybe that had been it, and he'd fucking blown it.

Hayes groaned. Leaned over to grab his phone from the charger, but before he could dial Zach, there was a muffled knock on his door.

Shit, it was probably Danny, too keyed up to sleep still. Hayes slid out of bed and padded to the door, pulling it open.

It was not Danny.

It was Morgan. He looked even wilder around the eyes. "Can I . . ."

Hayes felt shocked into silence, and only pulled the door open farther, stepping back to let Morgan in.

The door shut behind him with a decisive click, leaving them in silence.

"I . . ." Morgan huffed out a breath. "You asked me what about now? And I never answered you."

"Yeah?" Hayes gazed up at him. They were alone now, crowded into the little space by the door. He'd only turned on one light, the one by the bed, so it was dim, Morgan's face shadowed.

If the hallway had felt intimate, this was so much more.

"Now you make me feel like . . .like *this*." Morgan leaned in and, reaching down, cupped Hayes' cheek before very carefully pressing their lips together.

Hayes had known it was coming from the moment he'd opened the door and Morgan was standing there. But he hadn't realized the kiss would feel like a thousand fireworks exploding under his skin.

Or that Morgan would make this unbearably hot questioning groan in the back of his throat and kiss him deeper. Like one taste of Hayes wasn't enough and he wanted more, so much more.

The way Morgan's calloused fingertips stroked his cheek was both tender and erotic.

Hayes didn't ever want to stop, no matter how insane this was, ignoring the laundry list of why this was a terrible idea, but then did something even more insane and pulled back.

He *had* to know, had to understand exactly what Morgan meant. If he somehow meant something that wasn't this, that wasn't Hayes pulling Morgan to his bed and pinning him to the mattress, he needed to know *now*, before he fell even deeper into this Morgan-sized hole.

"Like what?"

Morgan stared at him like he *was* insane, wanting it spelled out, when they'd just been kissing and they could keep kissing. Part—the dick part, mostly, but not entirely—of Hayes agreed with him.

"Are you serious right now?" Morgan sounded a little exasperated and a lot fond.

Hayes stuck to his ground, even though he nearly just leaned in and kissed him again. "Yes. I don't want you to like . . . I don't know . . . panic about this."

"Do I look like I'm panicking?" Morgan's tone wasn't accusatory but almost gentle.

No. He did not. It seemed like Morgan Reynolds wasn't just an overachiever when it came to hockey, but to sexual awakenings too, because he seemed steady about it.

"No?" It was only then that Hayes thought that maybe the NHL gossip train had let him down and despite his belief to the contrary, he *wasn't* Morgan's first guy. "But maybe, I'm not . . .maybe you've done this before?"

"Never wanted to kiss a guy before you." Morgan's lips quirked up into a surprisingly soft smile. "Guess Danny wasn't totally wrong about a secret crush."

Not a hard-on. Not just wanting to hook up. But a *secret crush*.

How was Hayes supposed to do anything but kiss Morgan after that?

As Hayes pushed him back against the wall, Morgan going easily, their lips meeting again, everything short-circuited into an endless cycle of *yes-more-yes-more* as their mouths moved together.

Morgan felt even more solid than he did on the ice, muscles tensing and then relaxing as Hayes pressed him into the wall. But even though he wanted to lose his head, he kept his hips back. Despite that Morgan seemed unnaturally chill about the whole *kissing a guy* thing, he wasn't going to be the one to shove his increasingly hard dick against Morgan's.

And why would he even need to when just the kissing was so damn good?

Morgan made that same aborted groan again, tongue in Hayes' mouth now, and them making out—Morgan's hand back on his cheek and Hayes' fingers pressed into his broad shoulders—was in the top five hottest moments of his whole life.

Pulling away, Morgan stared at him, like he was a defense he needed to solve. Hayes' breath was coming in short pants and he nearly chased Morgan's mouth with his own.

They didn't need to stop. They could keep going just like this.

But that was Morgan's other hand reaching out and taking his. Leading him deeper into the room.

He had two queens—one clearly occupied, from the way the pillows and comforter were mussed from his aborted screaming session—and the other pristine.

Morgan couldn't have had more than one brief look, because his gaze was glued to Hayes the whole time, but he guided them to the bed Hayes had already been using.

Sat on the edge and pulled Hayes in between his spread legs. Kissed him again.

It was a really good move. Smooth and sexy and earnest. All of Hayes' insides jellified, and he didn't feel any shame about it, because Morgan had to feel his dick, pressed against his thigh, and hadn't flinched away from it yet.

Once the realization crossed Hayes' syrupy-slow brain, he found it increasingly difficult to stop himself from just humping Morgan's thick, muscular thigh.

But he hadn't confirmed yet that they were actually getting off. Morgan hadn't made any moves to do anything but kiss him, even if he was kissing him as thoroughly as Hayes had been kissed in *years*.

His hands were firm, wrapped around Hayes' waist, and he hadn't moved them an inch. They hadn't drifted down, even to a PG-13-rated area, even though Hayes had been told multiple times that he had one of the best asses in hockey.

If all this was the world's hottest make-out session—like surface of the sun, concrete in the middle of a Jersey summer kind of hot—then Hayes wasn't going to complain about it.

Morgan made that tiny groan in the back of his throat again, like Hayes was unwinding him, one hot press of their mouths at a time, everything spit slick and intense, and then his lips slipped away, down his neck.

Before this moment, Hayes wouldn't have said his neck was particularly sensitive, but he couldn't help the long, liquid moan that left him when Morgan found the one spot that lit him up inside.

"God," Morgan murmured roughly, "you're so fucking hot."

Hayes lost the fight with himself and pressed his cock more firmly against Morgan's thigh even as Morgan sank his teeth into that spot. There'd probably be a mark there in the morning. Any other time, with any other guy, Hayes would be all up in his head about that, but right now he couldn't find it in himself to give a shit.

Not when it felt so goddamn good. Or maybe it was because Morgan's hands had finally drifted lower and he was squeezing Hayes' ass now, going straight from PG to X-rated.

Hayes dug his fingers into Morgan's hair, dragging him back to his mouth, the kiss turning hot and filthy.

But even though Hayes was increasingly feeling like he was on a hair trigger, like he might just spontaneously come in his pants from how goddamn sexy Morgan was when he was growling under his breath, ten fingertips digging into his ass, tongue halfway down Hayes' throat, a minute ticked by and then another where he didn't escalate.

Hayes wasn't precious; he'd been idling, waiting for the go-ahead, but if he didn't do *something,* coming in his pants wasn't just a possibility, it was an inevitability. And if he only got one shot at Morgan Reynolds, he wanted to at least *touch* his dick and maybe if he was really lucky, Morgan would recip-rocate.

But clearly if he wasn't the one pushing them forward, it wasn't going to happen. Hayes couldn't even be that surprised by it. Sure, Morgan was most definitely not having a gay freak-out, but he was also new to this.

Hayes was not.

He slid a hand down from Morgan's shoulders to his chest, to his abs, tucking it under his sweatshirt for a moment, feeling rather than hearing Morgan's hiss as he touched bare skin.

Morgan leaned back a fraction, moving one hand from his ass to the bed, resting back against it. Hayes considered chasing his lips but decided maybe for this it was best if they weren't actively eating each other's faces off.

Then Hayes went lower, not touching anything, but definitely getting within the vicinity, watching as Morgan bit his bottom lip, hard. He knew if he went another inch over and another down, he'd find Morgan's cock, throbbing and hard in his sweatpants. It would be so easy to ghost his palm over it and then slip his hand in. Touch him for real.

It was stupid to want Morgan to *ask* him to do it. Wasn't this more than he'd already hoped for, in any possible universe?

"What . . ." Morgan swallowed hard. "Are you . . ."

"Do you want me to?"

Morgan laughed, almost desperately. "Um, *yeah*. Definitely."

There was nothing stopping Hayes now. He felt a tiny frisson of nerves—once he did this, there'd be no going back from it—but pushed them away as he skimmed his fingers lower, finding exactly what he'd hoped.

Morgan's cock was thick and hard, pressing against the fabric, twitching as Hayes traced its outline.

"Please," Morgan groaned.

Hayes shouldn't let the sound go to his head, but it was impossible. "You want more?"

Morgan tipped his head back. Bit his lip again. It was like he'd bitten Hayes, and he was shocked by it and craving it, all the same.

Heat surged through Hayes, erasing the last of his doubts.

He was here and Morgan was here and he wanted him to touch him. It would be stupid to not do everything he wanted—or to at least start on the very long list.

Still, it was obvious Morgan wasn't expecting it when Hayes sank to his knees in front of the bed, not only from the shocked arousal that crossed over his face but the little gasp he tried to muffle.

"Yeah?" Hayes asked, pausing as his fingers gripped the waistband of Morgan's sweats but went no farther.

For a moment that felt elastic and endless, Morgan didn't say anything. Just stared at Hayes. Then finally, he nodded and pulled his own sweatshirt off. The look in his hazel eyes was intense, focused. Telling Hayes to make the play.

Hayes wasted no time.

He'd gone long enough without doing this.

Tugging down Morgan's pants and his underwear, he leaned in, getting his first good look at Morgan Reynolds' dick.

It was so unfair that his cock was as gorgeous as the rest of him, but right now, Hayes wasn't going to pretend he wasn't more than a little flattered that the closer he came, licking his lips, the tighter Morgan's thighs tensed.

"You're such a fucking tease," Morgan groaned, not sounding like he hated it at all.

"Just admiring the view," Hayes murmured. He let himself for another breath and then he slipped it into his mouth, the taste of Morgan's precome coating his tongue as he wrapped it around the head, sucking hard.

Morgan let out a wordless groan, and when Hayes glanced up, he was digging his fists into the comforter.

"You can put your hands in my hair," Hayes said, letting up for a second. "Just . . .uh . . .don't pull too hard."

The flush on Morgan's face deepened, winding its way down his bare chest.

"Shit, that's hot," he said, and he reached out with one hand. But as Hayes took Morgan's cock back into his mouth, he didn't use it to dig into his scalp or pull his hair, hard or otherwise. Instead, his touch was sweet, almost reverent, tracing the lines of Hayes' face, feeling the bulge of himself against Hayes' cheek.

When he finally settled in Hayes' hair, he was still gentle, caressing his scalp.

And that only encouraged Hayes to take Morgan deeper, to let the tip of his cock ghost at the back of his throat.

Morgan moaned louder. He was almost babbling now, an endless litany of *baby* and *please* and *good*, that was the encouragement Hayes needed to double his efforts.

Too soon, Morgan's hand finally tightened in his hair, a warning for Hayes right before Morgan was gasping and he was coming down his throat.

"Holy shit," Morgan exhaled as Hayes licked him clean and let him slip from his mouth.

He was breathing hard, not just from sucking cock, but his own arousal, now that he was able to focus on the fact that he was more turned on than he'd probably ever been in his whole life.

Just the fact that he'd sucked Morgan's cock was going to be a top three sexual experience. Nevermind anything else that happened.

Morgan's hand drifted down to his shoulder and he gripped it, encouraging him to lift himself up.

Hayes was not expecting Morgan to want to kiss him after that—straight guys, or guys who'd *thought* they were straight, were understandably usually weird about come and anywhere come had just been—but to his shock, Morgan immediately kissed him hard and deep and eager.

And it was his hands, not Hayes', that were suddenly at his waist, shucking his sweatpants off.

"Shit, you *are* so fucking hot," Morgan murmured, pulling back a fraction. "Just look at you, baby."

He short-circuited the rest of Hayes' brain by licking up his palm and then reaching down, no hesitation whatsoever, and wrapping his hand around his cock.

Hayes jolted at the first touch, the pleasure rocketing through him.

"Is this good—you gotta tell me if it's good," Morgan pleaded, a surprisingly earnest look in his eyes. "You made me feel so good, I wanna give it to you, too."

Hayes had never let himself really think about what Morgan Reynolds would be like in bed, but he supposed he'd assumed it would be similar to how he was on the ice: confident and brash. Sure of himself, even if he wasn't sure of himself at all.

"Fuck yeah, it feels good," Hayes told him.

There was an addicting vulnerability in Morgan's face right now, and if Hayes was honest, that was the hottest thing about this whole experience.

Sure, Morgan's hand felt good, especially after how long the windup had been, and how much sucking cock in general and sucking Morgan's cock specifically had turned Hayes on. But that was the thing that was unwinding him, finally. The need in Morgan's eyes.

"God, yeah," Hayes said and kissed him, crowding into him enough that he could feel their bodies touching in half a dozen places, not just Morgan's hand on his dick.

It was probably the most basic handjob he'd ever gotten, but it didn't matter.

A minute later, with Morgan's mouth eager and hungry against his own, he came his brains out.

"Shit," Hayes sighed happily. He wanted to lean in, his knees wobbly post-orgasm, and rest his head on Morgan's shoulder, but he wasn't sure what the deal was. Was the touching over the moment they'd both come?

Had Morgan gotten what he'd wanted from him and cuddling wasn't part of it?

That seemed likely, as Hayes had never pegged Morgan as a cuddler.

Of course he'd never imagined that Morgan might give him an orgasm either, so maybe they were just in uncharted territory.

"I . . . uh . . . we should clean up," Morgan said, and he didn't look uneasy, not even remotely, but there was an understandable awkwardness.

There always was.

"Yeah," Hayes said, nodding, and deciding to hell with it, pushed his pants and boxers off the rest of the way and headed towards the bathroom.

He grabbed a wet washcloth and was back a second later.

Most of his orgasm had ended up on Morgan's hand but there were a few drops of come on his chest and his thighs.

It was definitely not a hardship to clean those up. To linger at how fucking gorgeous Morgan was, now that Hayes was letting himself look. Sure, he could've done it in the locker room, but he'd never let himself before. Not with Morgan, not with any other guy.

Morgan watched as Hayes cleaned him, not saying a single word.

Hayes sort of got it; what even was there to say? It was wild this had happened at all, and there was an inherent messiness in here that Morgan wouldn't like. Hayes wasn't even sure he liked it. He'd never hooked up with another hockey player before. He'd gone out of his way *never* to hook up with another hockey player.

And now he'd not only done it, but he'd done it with one of the most high profile guys in the sport. The guy whose footsteps everyone expected him to follow in. The one who he was playing with for the next eight days.

No big deal.

It was okay if Morgan was freaking out about this, because *Hayes* was kind of freaking out about this, and he'd known he was gay for a really long time.

"Are you—" Hayes cut himself off. Suddenly unsure he'd started that the right way. "You're okay, yeah?"

Morgan nodded. "Uh. Yeah. I'm good." A small smile emerged. "Really good. This was good."

"You got any other adjectives, or are you sticking with 'good' for the time being?" Hayes teased.

Morgan flushed red. "No. Good is . . .um . . .good." He made a self-deprecating noise. "You kind of sucked my brain out with my dick."

"Noted," Hayes said, unable to help his own smile now as he pulled his briefs and sweats back on.

Morgan stood and re-assembled his clothing as Hayes flopped down on the edge of the other bed.

"Finland tomorrow," Hayes said, deciding that the best course of action was to move onto a different subject, and hockey was always safe.

"Yeah." But once he was dressed, Morgan still seemed like he was lingering, eyes glued to where Hayes sat on the other bed. Hesitating like he wanted to go over to him.

Maybe he didn't want to just fuck and run? Hayes gave him some credit for that. Post-nut clarity was a real thing, and he wouldn't blame Morgan for freaking out.

"We feel pretty ready," Hayes said, sticking to hockey because that was safer than suggesting Morgan come over here and kiss him again.

Morgan shot him an incredulous look. "We *barely* escaped against Sweden."

"One goal or three, doesn't matter, just that we won," Hayes reminded him.

Morgan began to pace in between the two beds, and Hayes regretted bringing up Finland, because a second ago Morgan had been relaxed, and now he wasn't.

"Yeah, we can't get away with those mistakes every time. We gotta be on our best game," Morgan said.

"We will be," Hayes reassured.

"But—"

But Hayes had had just about enough of this. "Come here," he interrupted.

Morgan's eyes met Hayes'. "What?"

Hayes sighed. "Come here," he repeated, gesturing this time.

He didn't come immediately. Which tracked, honestly. Had anyone ever told Morgan Reynolds what to do in years? Had anyone *ever* told Morgan Reynolds what to do?

But he did eventually slink over, blinking away a mixture of astonishment and confusion as he approached where Hayes sat on the edge of the bed.

"What?"

Hayes curled a hand around his shoulder and tugged him down a few inches until their mouths were nearly slotting together.

"Stop worrying," Hayes murmured against Morgan's lips.

He'd never have been this aggressive normally. He'd have believed that the hookup ended with their orgasms and wouldn't have assumed Morgan wanted to chat or debrief—or even to cuddle—but then he'd lingered even though he had no reason to stay.

Except if he wanted to.

"I'm not—"

"Yeah, you are," Hayes interrupted again. This time he gave Morgan a soft peck. Not sexual, just comforting. Unsurprisingly Morgan didn't fight him and finally softened underneath his touch.

"You get it," Morgan mumbled. "I'm . . .I'm me. And if I don't . . ."

Morgan didn't finish his sentence but he didn't have to, because yeah, Hayes *did* get it. Probably better than almost anyone else.

"Yeah," Hayes agreed, "and if that happens, we'll cross that bridge. But there's no point in angsting over something that hasn't happened yet. Worrying isn't going to change anything. It's only going to make you miserable, and I don't like you when you're miserable."

Morgan barked out a soft laugh. "No?"

"No, you make everyone else miserable too."

Morgan didn't argue. Just stood there for a minute in silence, letting Hayes slip his fingers underneath his sweatshirt, humming as he stroked the skin between his neck and his shoulder.

Finally, he straightened. Hayes wanted to snatch him back, but he looked calmer now, and it *was* late. There was no reason for him to stay any longer.

"Thanks," Morgan said, his voice rough around the edges.

"Any time," Hayes said with a smile.

Morgan, already half-turning to head towards the door, turned back. "You mean that?"

Hayes let his smile widen. Say everything he didn't necessarily know how to say with words—or maybe he *did* know, but he knew Morgan wasn't going to be able to hear them. "Yeah, I do. Wouldn't have said it otherwise."

CHAPTER 5

Morgan didn't think he'd ever been so worried that when the puck dropped in a game, he wouldn't be able to lock in the same way he always did.

After all, Hayes was *right there*, just across the ice in warmups and right there on the bench, an inescapable presence at his right shoulder.

But to his surprise, it felt like their connection made him play *better*. Elevated his game and seemed to do the same with Hayes.

"Sick shift," Danny said, leaning in from his left.

It would be easy to say Danny was the singular reason he was forcibly prevented from obsessing about Hayes. About his eyes and his jawline and the way his sweaty hair swooped over his forehead. The way the skin above his cheekbones flushed just faintly pink when he'd met Morgan's eyes over the breakfast buffet this morning, like he hadn't sunk to his knees and sucked Morgan's cock less than twelve hours earlier.

It wouldn't be easy to forget about Hayes—not after last night, anyway—but Danny was annoying enough he'd probably make it possible.

But to Morgan's surprise, he *was* able to decently compartmentalize, separating the soft, scorching hot half-naked Hayes from hockey Hayes.

"Thanks," Morgan said, keeping his eyes on the ice where the second line was taking the puck past their blue line towards the Finns' goal.

He and Danny and Hayes hadn't scored, but they'd made a good effort, two decent shots on goal, but what brought him the most optimism was the way they'd played together. Like the line was finally beginning to come together.

"Yeah, it was good. Decent rebound attempt," Hayes agreed, leaning in. His leg was pressing against Morgan's. It was the first time out of thousands where it made his breath catch, but he was still able to mostly push the feeling away.

Danny grimaced. "I was an inch away from getting the puck in the net."

"You'll get it next time," Morgan said, patting him on the knee.

Hayes nudged him, shooting him a little grin. "You gonna give me any encouraging bullshit, Cap?"

Morgan rolled his eyes. "Not bullshit," he claimed, "and you don't need it. You had a great angle, that was just a pretty decent block by Saros."

"Yeah, that bastard," Hayes whined good-naturedly.

"Hey—" Danny only got part of the sentence out before the whole bench was erupting, Noah sinking a deep shot between the post and Saros' left pad.

"Sick!" Danny screeched in his ear as the players shot to their feet, crowd raucous at the first goal of the game. They might be in Toronto, but no doubt they were excited to see scoring so early in the period.

Morgan sank one of his own less than a period later, and Danny finished it off with a great rebound—this one Saros *didn't* block—and they won handily three to zero.

Morgan almost, *almost*, felt bad that he didn't have any reason to drag Hayes out to that empty hallway and chastise him.

He announced to the room, already celebrating as he walked in, "Great game, guys. Let's keep it going. Canada in two days. That's gonna be the championship preview."

At 2 – 0 in the tournament so far, that was increasingly looking likely to be the case. Not that anyone was probably surprised. Sweden and Finland could play spoiler, but they were only dark horses. The favorites were, without question, the US and Canada, and after the US had taken care of business and avoided losing to a team they should have beaten, there was no question they'd be in it.

Morgan made his rounds, even stopping by the goalie end of the locker room, giving Braun a brief pat on the head. He'd shut out the Finns, which was hardly a given. They had some real firepower on that team, and he'd kept them out of the net.

That deserved, at the very least, some kind of acknowledgment, even if Morgan personally hated his guts

"Good game," Morgan muttered.

Acknowledgment didn't mean he had to be *friendly* about it.

Jacob glanced up, a knowing glint in those dark brown eyes. "Thanks, Reynolds."

"Keep it up," Morgan said.

"Or what?"

Morgan grimaced. "Or I'm gonna light you up when we're done with this."

Jacob just laughed. "Oh yeah, like you normally do?"

Ugh. He really hated that guy. The one goalie in the NHL that always seemed to have his number. Admittedly, Braun had a *lot* of other players' numbers, too, considering how good he was. But Morgan wasn't just anyone; if he was the best like everyone claimed he was, then he should be able to score on the best.

But points always seemed to elude him where Braun was concerned.

"Yeah, yeah," Morgan muttered and stepped away before he said something very un-captainly.

He had his gear half off when Danny leaned in, the music and the general celebratory atmosphere making it so barely anyone could hear him except for Morgan. "Did I sense something between you and Monty?"

Ugh. What happened to Danny being a self-centered dick who wouldn't notice subtext or subtlety if it hit him over the head? Maybe Danny was finally growing up, but Morgan thought he kind of liked him better as a clueless idiot. Especially when he was giving Morgan shit. *Especially* when he was giving Morgan shit about Hayes.

"I don't know what you're talking about," Morgan said, not looking up from the laces on his skates.

"Sure you do," Danny said knowingly. "There was tension before, but this is a new kind of tension. You finally do something about it, Mo?"

"Maybe *he* did something about it," Morgan said under his breath. Told himself he wasn't confirming anything.

"Yeah right," Danny scoffed. "Monty? He wouldn't dare unless you gave him a green fucking light."

"Maybe I did."

"Lots of *maybes* here, Cap," Danny teased.

"Why does it even matter?"

Danny had the nerve to look hurt. Real hurt or faux-hurt? It was impossible to say. Morgan hated it either way. "Aw, I'm hurt. Here I am, caring about you two because of the intrinsic goodness of my heart. Why shouldn't I hope that my two lineys get their dicks wet?"

"I'm just shocked you know the word *intrinsic*," Morgan said, chuckling despite his annoyance.

"I've got a word of the day calendar in my bathroom. It's a nice routine, you know? Take a shit. Learn a word."

There was nothing Morgan could say to that so he said nothing. Nothing was definitely safer.

But then Hayes wandered over, down to his base layers, sweaty hair curling over his forehead, and the overwhelming *want* that Morgan had kept tamped down all day and throughout the game surged back.

Don't look, don't look, don't look.

But Hayes was looking at him and speaking now, so he couldn't do anything but helplessly raise his eyes. "Hey, a bunch of us are going out and grabbing some food," he said. Including Danny with a sideways glance. "You wanna join?"

What Morgan wanted was to follow Hayes back to the hotel, crowd him in the elevator, and then drag him to his room and see if he'd have the guts to put his mouth on Hayes' pretty cock.

But that was definitely not a plan he could disclose in the locker room or with Danny hanging on to every word they were saying to each other.

He wanted to say no, because he didn't want it to be him, three quarters of the team and Hayes. He wanted it to be just him and Hayes. But *some* Hayes was better than no Hayes at all. And maybe he could take advantage of the low light of some Toronto bar and flirt with him a little. Convince him that their hookup should continue.

"Sure," Morgan said. "Count us in."

Hayes smiled brightly, like Morgan had just made his whole fucking night. "Great."

"Oh, Cap," Danny said in a commiserating tone after Hayes walked away, "you are so fucked."

Morgan elbowed him on the way to the showers. "Shut up," he told Danny who only grinned, like the two of them were the best entertainment he could imagine.

This whole thing was awkward enough without Danny being there, offering his nonsense commentary.

He wasn't fucked. He had this under control.

But then he caught sight of Hayes laughing with Cal, and he nearly tripped right over someone's skate guard.

Totally under control.

Okay, maybe Morgan was a little bit fucked.

He couldn't remember a time when he'd *ever* been interested in someone—for sex or for anything else—and couldn't tear his eyes away from them. Morgan didn't think he *ever* had, frankly. Even his ex-wife, whom he'd been in love with and had Finn with, hadn't captivated him like this.

But what was he doing now, in this Toronto bar?

Sitting in a dark booth and glowering as Hayes talked up the whole fucking joint, charming teammates and random Canadians alike.

He was wearing this long-sleeved dark green henley and it clung to all his slim muscles and brought out the color of his eyes. Then the jeans that fit him like a glove, calling attention to how delicious his ass and thighs were. Reminding Morgan that he'd *never* really given a shit about a guy's ass and thighs before but now couldn't get over this particular set.

It was unfair. Life was unfair.

Morgan debated standing up and going over to the bar, where Hayes was seemingly holding court, and charming him right back.

He could do it.

Probably nobody would bat an eye—except Danny, of course, and Morgan was beginning to think he didn't really count.

"You're sitting over here and frowning. Monty ditch you already?"

Speak of the fucking devil.

Morgan shot Danny a half-hearted glare. "No."

"Sure seems like it from where I'm standing," Danny said, shifting his gaze from Morgan to where Hayes was leaning against the bar, yet another random Canadian guy flirting with him like the world was ending tomorrow.

Random guy put a hand on Hayes' forearm and squeezed, all friendly chatter, and Morgan wanted to remove his whole arm from its socket.

It was not normal. Morgan was at least aware of that. But that only made it weirder. He never got jealous. Envy was not an emotion he was used to feeling.

But that had to be what this sensation was, like worms crawling around in his stomach.

"Come on," Danny coaxed. "Come over to the bar with me. I promise if you were there, Monty wouldn't be flirting with randoms. He'd be flirting with you."

"You don't know that," Morgan said. But he wanted it to be true, so badly it made him squirm.

"Yeah, I kinda do," Danny said impatiently.

How had he gone from the state of finding Hayes annoying and like a prickly pointed reminder of his fading opportunities to Hayes being the most appealing person he could remember meeting?

You actually got to know him. You talked to him. You figured out that you and him? You're the same underneath.

That seemed to be the biggest issue. Before this tournament, Hayes had been a generic outline, another guy taken first overall, who everyone had universally decided was going to be great, as great as Morgan, or maybe even greater.

Up until this point, Morgan had resisted actually having a real conversation with the guy. What good would that serve, he'd always imagined, if he'd thought about it at all. But now he couldn't unwind the clock.

Couldn't pretend that he and Hayes hadn't made a connection.

Morgan finished his beer. He could go over to the bar. Get another one.

"Don't be stupid about this," Danny lectured.

Morgan shot him a look. It did not escape him how painful it was that Matthew Daniels was lecturing him on stupidity.

"You'd know," Morgan said, grinding his molars together.

"If I was him, I'd think the sex was bad, if you're over here and not even *trying* to stop that guy from touching me," Danny said.

And yep, then there was the sexual tension.

He'd hoped, maybe a little stupidly, that the sex would have dispensed with that. It often did, in Morgan's experience, but then he also had never hooked up with someone and then wanted to *stay* after, either. He hadn't done it last night, but he'd *thought* about it, and that was the scariest part of all.

If Hayes had asked, he'd probably have said yes, and then where would he have ended up?

Maybe the end result of all this was Hayes holding his dick like a leash, but how was that any different than what Morgan was doing now, staring daggers at a guy who kept daring to touch Hayes' arm?

"Fine, fine, I'm going," Morgan said, sliding out of the booth and getting to his feet.

He didn't miss how Hayes' gaze flicked over to him as he sauntered over to the bar. He took his time ordering another beer, making more polite small talk with the bartender than he might normally tolerate.

Only when it was over and he had a fresh bottle in his hand did he make his way over to Hayes.

"Hey," he said, interrupting some story the guy was telling. Something about a Leafs game. Morgan barely held in his eye roll.

Hayes glanced over. "Hey, this is—"

The guy made a trilled embarrassed noise. "Morgan Reynolds. Of course."

"Yep," Morgan said. He did not shake his hand. He was still contemplating yanking the whole arm from its socket. The guy was shrimpy, he probably had weak tendons.

"You finally decide to stop being antisocial?" Hayes asked, eyes crinkling with amusement.

Morgan wanted to shake him and demand answers. *How did you get so fucking attractive? I'm dying here.*

"Yep," Morgan repeated.

The smile lines around Hayes' eyes and mouth deepened. He tilted his head up towards Morgan's face. Morgan was reminded, viscerally and suddenly, of kissing him.

Morgan licked his lips. He hadn't wanted to come out at all, and now he had to extract both of them from this bar and this stupid idiot in front of them who had the nerve to imagine for even five seconds that Hayes was good enough for him.

"You're just . . ." The guy was still making embarrassing noises. "Just so damn good at hockey."

And yeah, it had gotten worse, because his interested gaze had moved from Hayes to Morgan.

"I know," Morgan said.

"Yeah, he knows," Hayes said, grinning now.

"That goal in the first game, against Sweden—"

"Now that," Morgan drawled out, because he was done with this shit and more than ready to end it, "was *all* Hayes."

Hayes' cheeks pinked up. "No, it wasn't. I told you . . ."

"Yeah, you did, and you were wrong. That pass? You made that play happen."

Hayes flushed even darker but looked pleased. Not as pleased as hopefully Morgan could make him in about half an hour, but it was a good start.

Even better was the fact that Hayes was looking at *him* now.

"Maybe," Morgan continued, unwilling to stop now, "I'll get lucky enough to send you one of those during this tournament."

"Not against Canada," the guy said.

"Dude, that's pretty much who we're playing for the rest of the tournament," Hayes said, his eyes flicking to the stranger's briefly, like he didn't want to stop looking at Morgan and any time he was forced to, it was an annoyance.

"I mean, Sweden's won all their games except—"

"It's going to be the US and Canada," Morgan said, nearly growling. "It's practically a done deal."

"Well," random guy said, drawing himself up, like he suddenly realized he'd overstayed his welcome, "that's probably true. Good luck, then."

Hayes murmured his thanks under his breath but Morgan didn't even bother. He wasn't sad this guy was finally leaving and wasn't going to pretend otherwise.

"You could've been nicer," Hayes said, but he didn't seem all that surprised that Morgan hadn't been.

"You mean I could've flirted with him, too?" Morgan hadn't meant the words to leave his mouth, because there was no question they exposed him—his jealousy, his soft, vulnerable underbelly, his *feelings*.

Hayes flushed again. "I wasn't. *He* was flirting with me."

"Smart man," Morgan said.

"I wondered if . . ." Hayes trailed off.

Finn had told him specifically that if he wanted a tournament-long fling, he should say so. He hadn't been explicit last night, but maybe he should be.

"Any time I can have you, I'm going to take it," Morgan admitted in a low voice. *I'd take it and probably beg you for more.*

"Oh." Hayes looked surprised and then thrilled. "Why didn't you just say? I kinda assumed or rather I didn't *want* to assume. . ."

"Because I'm stupid."

Hayes laughed and then nudged him with his elbow. "Not stupid. Well, a *little* stupid."

"Stupid to not walk over here half an hour ago and tell you that I wanted to go back to the hotel."

"Ah, but then you wouldn't be all cute and jealous," Hayes teased. "And it would've been a damn shame to miss that."

Morgan thought of how just a few days ago, Hayes had still seemed half-afraid of him, definitely worried about saying or doing the wrong thing. And now he was gently puncturing his ego one softly pointed joke at a time. If you'd asked Morgan a week ago if he'd like that, if it would *turn him on*, he'd have said no, that was crazy.

But he'd have been wrong. So wrong.

Because Finn had gotten it the first time; Hayes really cranked his motor. Everything about him from his hockey to his sly sense of humor to the way he filled out those jeans.

How had they started out with Hayes worshipping him and then ended up here? Morgan didn't know, but he'd clearly lost the lead somewhere.

"Do you want to?" Morgan asked gruffly.

Hayes' gaze heated up. "Yeah," he said.

"Come on, let's go," Morgan said.

"Do we need to . . .I don't know . . .say goodbye?" Hayes looked around the bar where the team was spread out at multiple tables and a handful even strung along the other side of the bar.

Morgan caught Danny's eye and nodded once.

"No," Morgan said. "Danny's got this." He pressed his palm to the small of Hayes' back, turning him towards the exit.

"Danny? You mean Matthew Daniels? *He* has this?" Hayes laughed awkwardly. "Are you serious?"

"Braun's here too, somewhere. As shitty as he is, he's not going to let anyone do anything stupid."

They grabbed their coats from the booth and headed towards the front door, Hayes pushing it open.

"God, it's cold," Hayes complained as soon as they were outside, on the way to the hotel. It was only a few blocks away, but it was still way fucking cold, and it made sense, considering how they were bundled up, to knock their shoulders together and then for Morgan to wrap his arm around him.

Nobody was going to know it was them, not with the snow swirling around the dark, and all the layers they were wearing.

"Better?" Morgan asked under his breath as they paused under an awning, the snow starting to come down harder.

Hayes' smile was brilliant as he glanced over at Morgan. "Maybe we should've taken an Uber."

"Afraid of a little snow, Monty?" Morgan asked, nudging him.

Hayes tipped his head back. "No. Just not used to it, I guess."

"Not much snow in Los Angeles." Morgan had a split second where he really thought about it; how frequently it snowed in upstate New York, where he lived. And how far away Los Angeles really was.

Morgan shoved the thought away. He didn't like it and there wasn't any reason to dwell on it, besides. They were together now, and who even knew how he'd feel in a week?

He was pretty sure the last time he'd slept with the same person for a week it was his ex-wife and it had been ten years ago.

"Actually, it's kind of nice," Hayes said and glanced over at Morgan. His eyes were shining, and it was really, unbelievably hard not to lean in and kiss him now.

He didn't. But it was a near thing.

Instead, Morgan squeezed his far shoulder and dipped his head down, closer to where Hayes' beanie just grazed the top of his ear. He even had an attractive ear, all soft small whorls. For a second, Morgan imagined putting his mouth there, *too.*

"Come on," he said, clearing his throat. "Let's go."

"Impatient much?" Hayes teased as they walked back out into the snow.

Morgan wanted to deny it, but it was kind of hard to when it was so obvious. He wanted to get Hayes alone. Wanted to stop having to hold back.

"Aren't you?"

"I wasn't the one who spent half the night sulking in the booth," Hayes said, nudging him. Honestly, he sounded delighted and between that and the use of the word *sulking,* that usually would be enough to piss Morgan off.

Grown men did not sulk.

He did not sulk.

Nevermind that he had definitely been sulking.

"I—" Morgan started laughing. "God, you are such a brat."

"But you like it," Hayes said, grinning at him as they passed under a streetlight.

He wanted to deny *that* too, but how could he?

"Yeah," Morgan said in a low voice. *I like you.*

Finally they reached the hotel. As they walked into the lobby Hayes pulled off his beanie, shaking the snow out of it. Morgan's fingers twitched, wanting to touch his hair, to smooth down the ruffled strands, but instead he shoved his hands in his pockets as they made their way to the elevator.

When the doors opened, Hayes shot him a look, raising his eyebrow as his fingers hovered over the buttons.

Morgan tilted his head. "More guys on your floor," he said, and Hayes nodded, pressing eight.

Morgan didn't say that gave him a whole extra floor to slide closer to Hayes. To reach up and do exactly what he hadn't been able to in the lobby, which was cautiously reach over and stroke the back of Hayes' hair, smoothing the damp tufts down.

Hayes looked over at him, grinning. "You fix it?"

"Yeah."

"Just gonna mess it up again," Hayes teased.

"Is that wishful thinking or a specific request?"

Hayes tilted his head, clearly considering the question. "Can't it be both?"

The elevator hit the eighth floor and the doors opened.

Hayes trailed Morgan down the hall. His room was almost all the way at one end, which was another reason Morgan had suggested it.

He dreamed about making Hayes loud. About listening to him moan. About being the source of those sounds.

He pulled his room key out of his pocket and opened the door, Hayes slipping in behind him.

When it shut behind them, finally giving them privacy for the first time in what felt like all fucking day, Morgan hesitated.

Hayes didn't say anything. Didn't push. Just leaned back against the wall, expression unconcerned but eyes speaking volumes just from the way that sharp green skimmed over Morgan's body.

He clearly wanted it, but he wasn't going to force Morgan.

Morgan took a deep breath. He knew they actually needed to talk about this, even though the last thing he wanted to do was use his words. "Yesterday was good."

The corner of Hayes' mouth tilted up. "Yeah. I think we both enjoyed ourselves."

"I want to keep doing this—while we're here."

Hayes' eyebrows lifted. He'd surprised him. Well, good. It was Hayes' turn. He'd been surprising and shocking and blowing up his brain since Morgan had arrived in Toronto.

"How do you feel about that?" Morgan told himself he shouldn't keep pushing. That he should be cool. Casual. But he didn't feel particularly cool *or* casual about this, and he wasn't sure he could keep hiding that fact. Danny had even picked up on it and Danny was not the most observant person in the universe.

"How do *I* feel about it?" Hayes chuckled. "I'm good with it. Surprised. But good with it."

Morgan opened his mouth to argue about why it was stupid for Hayes to be surprised. That he should *get* why he was so attractive and special and *fuck*—but he could try to use his goddamn brain to convince Hayes how awesome he was, or he could just kiss him.

Kissing him won out.

Hayes kissed him back, opening his mouth under Morgan's, making these little aborted groans in the back of his throat that cranked Morgan up even more. He pressed Hayes against the wall, wanting to feel him. Wanting Hayes to feel him in return.

Unable to help the noise coming out of his own mouth when Hayes ground his cock against his thigh.

"Bed," Morgan said breathlessly, grabbing Hayes' hand and practically dragging him towards the main part of the room.

He'd been wishful thinking this morning, because he rarely made his bed, and yet he'd done it today. Been hoping, even though he hadn't been sure if he should, that Hayes might be coming back to his room later.

Hayes gazed up at him, green eyes hot on Morgan's face.

Yesterday, he'd let Hayes make all the moves. He hadn't been . . .not *nervous*, not exactly. More like worried he'd do or say something that was wrong. That Hayes didn't like, even though Hayes had seemed to really enjoy everything they'd done yesterday.

But even then, Hayes had been the one to push them to the next level, to go from kissing to more, and after that incredible blowjob, Morgan—while definitely enjoying the feel of having his mind blown—had only gotten to give Hayes' cock a few strokes of his hand. Barely different than anything he might do to himself, if he was alone.

Morgan was determined to do better this time. Maybe he hadn't done this before but that didn't mean he couldn't at least make an effort.

"You're so hot," Morgan murmured, leaning in and kissing Hayes again.

The kissing had been so good yesterday—Morgan couldn't remember the last time he'd just made out for the hell of it, and he wanted more of it.

More of Hayes' incredible plush mouth, moving against his own, the pleased sounds he made in the back of his mouth, the way his body seemed to melt into Morgan's, like they'd been designed for each other.

So he took what he wanted, doing more of the driving today. Stripping Hayes' jacket off and then his own and then that stupid henley that had haunted most of his evening, absorbing the gasp Hayes made when Morgan's mouth moved lower.

Unlike Morgan, Hayes wasn't bulky, his muscles slim and lithe, but there was no question that he was a guy. The swell of his pecs were still flat-ish, capped by tiny nipples. Nipples Morgan wasn't sure were as sensitive as a woman's. But if he didn't check, he'd never know, and to his own surprise, he really wanted to know. He wanted to know everything about Hayes, every little spot that made him writhe and moan, so he leaned in, licking across the tip.

Hayes tensed and then groaned, clearly into it, so Morgan did it again. It was everything he was used to, but so different too, and he *liked* that.

He worked them until Hayes dug his fingers into Morgan's hair and gently began to push him lower. Morgan's mouth moved lower, his tongue dampening the hair of Hayes' happy trail, enjoying the way the muscles of his abs contracted under him.

How had he never realized how hot this was? His cock was twitching in his boxers, and if he hadn't started humping Hayes' leg yet, it was probably only a matter of time.

He glanced up and let out a moan at how gorgeous Hayes was. Back arched. Chest flushed. Nipples shiny and hard. Teeth sunk into his lower lip.

"Shit, baby, you look so good like this," Morgan murmured into his skin, fingers trembling as they worked Hayes' jeans down over his thighs then down to his ankles.

His cock was a hard line in his black briefs, and as Morgan pressed a palm into it, his own dick jerked at the wet spot he discovered on the fabric.

Ducking his head, he tongued at it, loving the way Hayes' fingers tightened in his hair and the pleased noises he made.

But then Hayes actually said words that made sense. "You don't—" He paused. "I don't expect—"

Now that was absolute bullshit. Morgan not only wanted to, Hayes *should* expect that kind of reciprocal action. He deserved it. He was beautiful and kind and funny and so good at hockey it was hard for even Morgan to be jealous of his skills.

"Nope," Morgan interrupted that absolute horseshit of a statement. "I do want to and you absolutely should expect it."

Hayes let out a humorless chuckle above him. "I just didn't want you to feel pressured."

"Baby," Morgan ground out, as he tugged down Hayes' briefs, "I appreciate your concern about my gay awakening but I promise, I'm into this. I'm *way* into this."

Hayes laughed again, but this time it sounded easier. Actually amused. "Okay."

"I *am* probably gonna be shit at this though," Morgan murmured. He wrapped his hand around Hayes' cock. It was red and wet at the tip, Hayes barely able to keep his hips still as Morgan gave it one stroke and then another.

"Don't care."

Morgan looked up again because it was hard not to, especially when Hayes was so goddamn stunning like this.

Hayes grinned. "Just don't bite it off, and we're gonna be good."

Just for that, Morgan had to wrap his other hand around one of Hayes' glorious thighs and pull it open even more. Just enough that he could lean in and nibble at the muscle there. Sink his teeth in just enough he—and only he—could see the imprint of them in Hayes' skin.

"Shit," Hayes panted. "*Shit.*"

Morgan didn't tell him he had more where that came from. Figured that actions spoke louder than words and finally got his mouth where it belonged, which was on Hayes' cock.

It was smooth and slick against his tongue. So easy to slide it in farther, to want more of it. To want *all* of it, even though he knew there was no way he could take it. Not yet, anyway.

Hayes gasped, high and tight in the back of his throat, as Morgan tried to find a rhythm he could keep up. It made him sweat under his arms and his hands shake.

He'd never imagined being on his knees for anyone, but now he knew that was because he was meant to do it for one person and one person only: Hayes Montgomery.

Morgan tried to remember every glorious trick Hayes had employed yesterday when he'd done this, but his mind had been wiped slippery clean and he couldn't focus on anything.

Not with Hayes' taste and his cock thick in his mouth, the heat of his arousal burning everything else out.

"Yeah, yeah," Hayes moaned. "God, you're good at this. Of course you're good at this."

Morgan didn't know if he was telling the truth—probably, because even a bad blowjob was a decent blowjob—but he decided it didn't matter. He was going to make Hayes come, was going to make him shake and lose it in a haze of pleasure so thick he thought about this moment every time he touched his cock after this.

Morgan sucked harder, dipping his head down, taking as much into his mouth as he could, choking a little as the head hit the back of his throat.

"Fuck," Hayes cried out, and then, "I'm gonna—"

Morgan stroked his thigh and groaned too as Hayes' cock kicked and then began to shoot its load down his throat.

He'd never imagined, not in a million fucking years, finding *that* hot. He'd always imagined women tolerated swallowing. But *Jesus,* that was a turn-on, too.

Licking Hayes clean, he finally let him slip from his mouth, and only then did he realize just how desperate and hard *he* was. Hayes' bare thigh had never looked better to him than in that moment. Thick and muscular, the pale skin covered with a thin dusting of dark hair.

If he just . . .pulled his jeans down and . . .humped it, would that be okay?

Use your words, that voice inside Morgan chided him.

But before he could, Hayes gave a happy sigh and said, "That was . . .well, it was fucking incredible."

"Yeah?" Morgan could hear the roughness in his voice as he wobbled to his feet, his knees jello from how fucking turned on he was right now.

"Get up here," Hayes ordered and Morgan went, shucking his jeans and briefs before he crawled up Hayes' body and kissed him hard and insistent.

Forget Hayes' thigh. He was just going to rub off on Hayes' stomach, the wetness of his precome slicking the way, Hayes' abs tensing underneath him.

He just needed a little more, pleasure sliding through him in a wave, and then Hayes kissed him deep, tongue tangling with his, and dug his hands into his bare ass, and that was all it took. Brain whiting out, making embarrassing noises, the whole nine yards.

When his orgasm finally petered out, he collapsed right into the mess, Hayes laughing underneath him.

"You came all over me," he said, sounding delighted by this. But he couldn't be as delighted by this as Morgan was.

Satisfaction was following quicky and inevitably after pleasure.

He didn't want to roll over, but he didn't want to crush Hayes either. So he finally did—regretting it only until he could see the remains of his orgasm, smeared all over Hayes' stomach.

"You liked it," Morgan teased.

The way Hayes' eyes lit up at this made it clear that he *did*. "Yeah, and so did you," Hayes retorted fondly, smacking Morgan lightly on the arm. "It's okay, 'cause it was hot."

"Understatement of the century," Morgan admitted.

Last night he'd felt like he should leave pretty much the moment he'd come. Though from the way Hayes had smiled softly when he'd lingered, even briefly, Morgan wondered if he should ask Hayes if he wanted him to stay.

Maybe that wasn't hookup etiquette. It certainly wasn't hookup etiquette for Morgan. But he was comfortable, shoulder to shoulder with Hayes, and when he looked at him, eyes sleepy and content, Morgan thought it wouldn't be an imposition to fall asleep just like this.

But before he could decide if he was going to say something—and what he *would* say if he did—Hayes lifted himself up out of bed.

Morgan could hear the faucet running. Knew Hayes was cleaning up.

He returned with a wad of tissues and a rueful smile on his face. But to Morgan's surprise, he didn't hand them over. Instead he climbed half over him and wiped up the smears of come himself.

"I . . .uh . . .guess I should go?" Hayes said, but it wasn't a statement. It was definitely a question.

"What's our schedule for tomorrow?" Morgan asked, sitting up.

He shouldn't make it dependent on the schedule. Who cared what time the alarm was going to go off if he could stay with Hayes tonight? But even if he rarely did this—and not ever with a guy—even *he* knew it was pretty unhinged to say that literally the fourth day they'd been hanging out and only the second time they'd had sex.

But Hayes leaned down and plucked his phone out of the mess of their clothes on the floor anyway. "Um, yeah, practice in the afternoon. Some media in the morning."

Morgan did not groan with annoyance at the implications of that, but he thought about doing it.

"Sorry," Hayes said, wincing as he glanced over at him. "I know you're going to hate that."

And it was absolutely not okay for Hayes to think he hated doing media with him. Sure, he hadn't really enjoyed it on the first day, but that had nothing to do with Hayes the man and everything with the inane questions they always peppered him with.

"If they asked better questions, I would hate it less," Morgan said.

"But," Hayes asked, nudging him as he sat back on the edge of the bed, "if the questions were actually decent, if they were all insightful and shit, would you even *answer* those questions?"

Morgan laughed, so fucking charmed. Way too fucking charmed. "No. No. Goddamn you."

Hayes just grinned at him knowingly. Still naked. Still gorgeous. And he was apparently now living rent-free in Morgan's brain and not only did he *not* hate that, he actually thought he . . .*God,* he thought he might really like it.

"I should go," Hayes said reluctantly. He reached down and grabbed his jeans. His henley.

"Yeah," Morgan agreed, hoping that his reluctance was equally as obvious. He didn't want Hayes thinking that he just wanted him gone. The opposite, actually.

If he was admitting things—even to himself—he might mourn every inch of skin that got covered up.

When Hayes was dressed, he picked up his coat. Morgan was still naked, on the bed. Hayes' eyes swept over him, like he wanted to memorize the view.

"I'll see you tomorrow, yeah?" Hayes asked, and suddenly he didn't seem reluctant but awkward.

"Come here," Morgan said, holding out his hand and it was easier than it should've been to tug Hayes in, rough jeans rubbing against the bare skin of his inner thighs. Tipping his head back, he reached up and curled a hand behind Hayes' neck, bringing their lips together.

Morgan was utter shit at words. But he could say *goodbye* and *I already miss you* and *I wish you were staying* in a surprisingly tender kiss.

A minute later he pulled back and Hayes' eyes were a soft, lazy green.

"Breakfast?" Morgan asked.

Hayes nodded and then, a second later, he pulled away and Morgan let him.

Let him, but curled his fist into the blankets so he wouldn't grab him right back again.

CHAPTER 6

Practice felt standard enough—at least standard for this tournament, in that Hayes spent ninety percent of his time helplessly rotating around Morgan and the other ten percent staring at him, wishing he was—at least until Thompson called everyone together and said with the Canada game coming up tomorrow, he wanted to practice shootouts.

It wasn't even remotely farfetched that the US and Canada might go three periods and an overtime, before going to a shootout.

"We'll do half with Jacob and the other half with Bram," Thompson said.

Hayes told himself it was fine, that it wasn't a big deal, but he couldn't help himself. Before he could stop, he looked over at Morgan. He had a blank expression pasted on, a little rough around the edges, not looking at their coach, or at anything at all, tapping his stick against the ice like he needed to do something with his hands or he might explode.

"Hey," Hayes said, tapping Morgan's leg with his stick when Coach finished talking and they were setting up for the first run, Jacob skating down to one side of the rink.

Morgan glanced up at him, face still frozen. "What?"

"You okay?"

"Yeah. Course. Why wouldn't I be?"

Hayes shot him a look that said without him actually vocalizing it, *I don't know, you're kinda fucked up about Braun.*

"I play against him a couple of times a year. I can handle this."

Hayes wasn't sure he should say to him, *it doesn't seem like you can*, so he didn't. Besides what was *he*, Hayes Montgomery, going to say to *Morgan Reynolds* about a shootout, even against a great goalie like Jacob?

Nothing. That was what he was going to say.

Maybe things had equalized between them a bit recently. Maybe his crush had less hero worship qualities and more just regular worship qualities, but the last thing he was going to do was be dumb enough to give Morgan a hockey lecture.

"Daniels," Thompson called out, and Danny whooped it up, raising his stick in the air as he made lazy circles around the middle of the rink.

In the goal, Jacob had clearly locked in, assuming his position, gaze intent, as Danny grabbed a puck and began to skate towards him.

Danny wouldn't have been on Hayes' list of guys to use in a shootout, but he was probably a good-ish warmup for Jacob. Not a great skater or a particularly brilliant goal-scorer, but crafty, at the best of times.

"Come on," Morgan called out, "stop fucking around. Put one in on him, Dan."

Danny slipped to one side, but Jacob had already foreseen the move and easily blocked it.

"Oh well," Danny retorted, shrugging as he passed Morgan, who was already locked in for his turn.

Hayes didn't think Coach had even called his number, but clearly Morgan wasn't waiting any longer for his crack at Braun.

Morgan was skating harder and faster than Hayes had seen him do all tournament.

"He looks like he's going to will that puck past Braun," Danny said, skating up to where Hayes was leaning against the boards. "You think he'll get it in?"

"No," Hayes said, a second before Morgan tried a fancy dodging move, totally overthinking the whole thing, Jacob easily blocking the shot.

"Jesus," Danny muttered under his breath.

Morgan swept behind the goal, fury etched on his expression, looking like he was doing a lot more than muttering a few choice obscenities.

"Monty," Coach barked out. "Show them how it's done."

Hayes nodded and picked up his stick. As he skated towards the goal, he skimmed through his memory. Remembering his last few goals against Braun and what he knew of Braun's weaknesses—a damn short list, honestly—only deciding on what he was going to do a half-second before he did it.

Changing direction suddenly, he leaned hard on his edges and pushed in on one side, aiming the puck between Braun's leg pads.

It slid just inside.

Hayes skated in the rest of the way, giving Jacob a reassuring shoulder tap with his stick before heading back towards the mingled group at the boards.

"Absolutely fucking sick move, Monty," Danny crowed.

Morgan didn't say anything. Just gave Hayes a little nod, eyes narrowed.

Before Coach could say anything, could yell any other name, Morgan took off again, barely waiting until Hayes was back to the group before he was gone, skating hard and mean, leaning way over his stick.

Jacob didn't even flinch, didn't even call Morgan out for his repeated turn, even though Hayes could hear Thompson and Blackburn behind him, both yelling at Morgan to cut it out.

But Morgan, unsurprisingly, was not listening.

This time he waited until he was nearly on top of Jacob, practically in the crease before shooting, barely turning himself in time to avoid hitting the guy.

It was a shitty move—compromising the health and safety of both Morgan and Jacob—and Thompson barked out, voice carrying across the ice. "What the fuck are you doing, Reynolds?"

Of course, when Jacob lifted himself up, he had the puck in the cup of his glove and he let it drop to the ice with a pointed look over in Morgan's direction.

Hayes knew it was going to happen again the moment before it did.

"Oh shit," Danny murmured next to him.

But the words were barely out of his mouth before Hayes was off, skating as fast as he could, coming to an abrupt stop between a charging Morgan and a defensively postured Jacob.

"Get out of my way," Morgan grunted.

"No," Hayes said firmly. Put his hands out. "No fucking way. You're gonna lose it on anyone? It's gonna be on me. Not on that guy."

"I don't have a problem with *you*," Morgan said between clenched teeth.

"Exactly," Hayes said.

A moment later, Danny was there, next to him. "Come on, man," Danny wheedled. "You don't want to do this."

"Actually, I kinda do," Morgan argued.

"No, you really don't," Hayes said, frustration inevitably leaking into his voice. He moved closer to Morgan. Risked putting a hand on his arm. For a second, he was sure Morgan was going to shuck it off, and he was going to have to pretend that didn't matter, but to Hayes' surprise, he didn't. He tensed but didn't move.

Morgan didn't say anything.

And to Hayes' continued surprise, when Hayes risked wrapping a whole hand around his forearm and then the other around his waist, Morgan let himself be pulled away. All the way across the ice and then off it.

He was silent and easy all the way until they got to the hall outside the locker room. Then suddenly it was like he came to life, and the tables were turning and it was *him* dragging *Hayes* farther in, to the hallway they'd visited in the first game.

It was just as empty as it had been then. Emptier, maybe, because this was just practice.

"Seriously, Mo," Hayes huffed out under his breath. He unbuckled his helmet and pulled it off, letting it dangle from one hand by the strap.

Morgan still didn't say anything. Just wet his bottom lip with his tongue, and Hayes realized a second later that he was shaking a little, all over. Just straight-up trembling.

"Are you okay?" Hayes asked, leaning in a little closer. He unsnapped Morgan's helmet and pulled that off too, setting both of them on an equipment bin.

"I'm . . ." Morgan squeezed his eyes shut. "No."

Well, at least that was something. At least Morgan could see that his reaction had been completely unhinged and out of line.

Okay, so he didn't like Braun. Hayes couldn't say he particularly *liked* Braun either, but he wasn't going to go charging at him in the net during practice.

"You wanna talk about it?" Hayes asked gently, wrapping his fingers around Morgan's forearms and squeezing. Like he could somehow leech out by osmosis some of the ugly thoughts he *knew* Morgan was having.

"You get it—he just—*I* just—" Morgan broke off, hazel eyes wide and distressed. Then he looked away.

"I know you think he's got your number," Hayes said, probably too obvious about how careful he was being.

Morgan, even as spooked as he was, wasn't going to like being handled with kid gloves. He'd want the unvarnished truth, extra salt rubbed in the wound for good measure.

"You think?" Morgan's laugh was more a bark than an actual genuine laugh. "He got me *twice*. And you just slid one by him like it was fucking nothing."

Hayes winced. "Not like it was nothing. I play against him, too, you know? But I've got less . . ." He didn't know how to say it without reminding Morgan all over again that at one point,

Hayes had made him feel *old.* Hayes didn't have to ask to know that also meant *used up, washed-up, finished, done.*

"Less what?"

Hayes shot him a look. Morgan knew what he didn't want to say, and he was going to make him say it anyway. Nevermind the salt. It was more like he was asking—no, *begging*—for Hayes to pour vodka right on it.

"Pretending it's not happening doesn't change anything," Morgan muttered.

"No, but dwelling on it sure doesn't fucking change anything either," Hayes retorted with heat. "And you're fucking letting him—letting this situation—get to you."

Hayes gripped his arms harder. Not letting him pull away. Morgan was strong, but Hayes wasn't nothing. He could hold on. He could make Morgan face this, even though it was the last thing Morgan wanted to see.

"Oh, yeah, so I should just stop then? Why didn't anyone tell me that before?" Morgan's voice was as dry as the Sahara.

"Don't," Hayes warned sharply.

"What?"

"Don't do that shit. You're better than that. I'm better than that. You know I'm there. That I get it."

"No, you'll get it in ten fucking years," Morgan retorted without heat. "Maybe twelve, if you're really lucky."

Hayes sighed.

"Jacob Braun isn't the thing that's holding you back. There isn't anyone holding you back. Only this stupid assumption that you're . . . I don't know . . . on your last legs. You don't look on your last legs, not to me."

"You're sure that's not wishful thinking? You lookin' at me through those rose-colored glasses you like so fucking much?"

Hayes sighed heavier. "You are so fucking contrary, you know? Sometimes I just want to . . ."

"Want to what?" Morgan's grin was shark-like.

"Not what you're thinking. I want to knock some sense into you. I'm not looking at you like I'm idolizing you, still. I see you clearly. Probably *too* clearly." *Shut up, shut up, shut up.* But he couldn't shut up. Not now. Not when Morgan's edges were finally softening. "I see you, 'cause you're me."

Morgan didn't say anything. Just stared, wide-eyed at Hayes. Like it was finally hitting him. Or maybe that it was finally hitting him hard enough.

"You've got some time left," Hayes continued, because he couldn't stop now. "Your legacy's already defined. These last few years are just gonna buff it to a real good shine. That's all. It's there. You did it. And when it's over, you can put it down and not carry it around with you all the time."

Morgan's eyes slid away now. Like he couldn't look any more. And Hayes got it. This had morphed into something else, gone totally sideways. "You really believe that?"

"I do," Hayes said. "Because I don't want to carry it either, when I'm your age. I want to believe that I can put it down if I want to. That being a first overall doesn't define who I am forever."

"That's wishful thinking, right there," Morgan grumbled, but he seemed lighter and easier when he met Hayes' gaze again. His hazel eyes finally softening, some of that pain in them loosening and shaking free.

"Yeah, maybe. But it's still wishful thinking I wanna keep," Hayes said firmly.

He wasn't lying. The idea of being Morgan's age, of being older than Morgan and still trudging around with the weight of that first overall pick on his shoulders sounded excruciating.

"You're . . ." Morgan's tongue flicked out, licking his bottom lip. "You're something else."

"In a good kind of way, right?" Hayes chuckled, a little nervously.

But before Morgan could answer, a voice interrupted them.

"You two done in here? Practice's over," Danny announced loudly, striding towards them, still in his full gear and skates. He paused, still a few feet away. "It was really over the moment Mo here lost his shit. You good, bud?"

Morgan shrugged.

"Getting there," Hayes said.

Danny nodded. "Dude, I get it. Sometimes Braun's so good I wanna punch him in the face, too."

Morgan made a frustrated noise in the back of his throat.

Hayes wanted to punch *Danny* in the face for muscling his way into this conversation.

"Danny," he said, as patiently as he could, "can you give us a minute?"

"Oh, is this like a whole first overall thing then?"

Hayes rolled his eyes. "You were taken, what sixth?"

"And it's not the same. Can't pretend it is. Glad I don't get it, though."

"You should be," Hayes said, a little too honestly.

"Alright. Well, bus is leaving in thirty so you better get your asses in gear." Danny marched off.

Even after he was gone, Morgan didn't say anything. Hayes put a hand on his arm, squeezed gently.

"Are you okay?" he asked.

"I . . .I'm never going to like him. It's been too long thinking he's . . .knowing that I'm . . ." Morgan bit off with a muttered *fuck*. "You get it. *You get it.*"

"I don't have a goalie I want to cut off at the knees, yeah, but there's players I don't love playing against. Who make me feel like a little kid again, wondering if I'm ever gonna be good enough."

Morgan relaxed another fraction. "Only one you can ever beat is yourself."

"You ever gonna take that advice?" Hayes raised an eyebrow.

Morgan laughed, the last of the tension draining out of him.

He wasn't fixed—not because he wasn't broken, because living for so long with that kind of pressure always broke you, somehow—but because there was no fixing something twenty plus years in the making in five minutes.

"I'll try," Morgan said, and Hayes nodded, knowing that was the best he could expect.

"Good," he said. Patted him on the arm. "Come on. Let's get showered."

After they got back to the hotel, there was a team lunch, then the team and the coaching staff spent hours breaking down film of the first two games the Canadian team had played in. There were a few guys who were normally on teams with their players, and slowly but inevitably, they'd speak up, giving insights and advice, trying to do everything they could to get an edge. Everyone knew it was going to be that close.

By the end of the afternoon, Hayes was mentally exhausted, begging off the dinner plans some guys were making and retreating to his room.

He took a long nap, woke up, ordered room service for dinner, and while he waited for it to arrive, called Zach. That was better than looking at his texts, at the group chat for the US guys, wondering if Morgan had said anything or reached out.

"Hey," Zach said brightly. "You caught me right before I went out for dinner with some of the other guys. How's it going?" For the bye week, some of the Mavs not going to the tournament had found an all-inclusive in Cabo and Zach had gone with them.

"It's going." Hayes knew he sounded tired, even after his nap.

"You ready for the Canadians?"

"I don't know if you're ever really ready for the Canadians," Hayes muttered, "but we're gonna do our best, that's for sure."

"Your line looks good."

"It's got Morgan freaking Reynolds on it, of course it's great," Hayes said before he could snatch the words back.

Zach just laughed. "Not over your crush, huh?"

"It's . . ." Hayes wanted to say it was just a crush, still, but even he, with all his delusions, was having difficulty believing it.

He knew he should have texted Zach days ago and said, *hey guess what, it's not just a crush anymore and he isn't straight and we're having sex and it's even hotter than my fantasies.*

There'd been a part of him that wanted to. Another part that had held back, mostly because it hadn't felt right to tell Zach about Morgan's queerness but also because Zach would argue this was a terrible fucking idea.

"Oh come on, he can't be that great," Zach muttered. "He's probably a huge asshole, and you're in deep denial."

"He *is* kinda. But not . . .not because he wants to be." Hayes hated how earnest he sounded as he defended Morgan. "He's just got a lot of pressure, you know? Pressure I understand."

"Yeah. We know. First overalls." Zach didn't even sound bitter about it, just matter-of-fact.

"Yeah," Hayes agreed.

"Somehow you're not an asshole, though," Zach pointed out.

Hayes thought about what Morgan had said earlier. *You'll get it in ten fucking years. Maybe twelve, if you're really lucky.*

"Maybe not now, but who knows what I'm gonna be like when I'm at the end of my career and everyone's parsing what it means, where I fall. If I only *met* everyone's expectations, didn't even exceed them."

Zach sighed heavily. "I'm not sure whether you spending this much time with Morgan Reynolds was a good or a bad thing, honestly."

He had to tell him. Hayes hated it, but he had to tell him.

"Well, about that . . ." Hayes dangled the sentence.

Zach was not stupid. It didn't take him that long. Or very long at all. He inhaled sharply. "No. *No.* You and Reynolds?"

"Yeah."

"What happened?"

Any other guy, even another player, Hayes would've given all the details. Given Zach the whole picture. He knew why he was holding back, but Zach was discreet; he wouldn't tell anyone.

Still, Hayes found himself clamming up. "We've just been spending a lot of time together and one thing led to another . . .you know how it goes."

Zach laughed incredulously. "No. *No.* I do not know how it goes. This is *Morgan Reynolds.* You don't just fall into bed with him like some regular ass hookup."

"Why not?" But Hayes knew why not. Knew why it was dangerous. Knew it was the same reason he hadn't told Zach before tonight. It was the same reason he hadn't checked his texts. He wanted Morgan to have asked him what he was doing tonight—and he *didn't* want Morgan to be asking, either.

"Dude, you have been obsessed about him *forever*," Zach said bluntly.

"Not *obsessed*," Hayes argued.

"A little," Zach insisted. "And now what, you're gonna hook up with him for a week *and* play with him for a week, the guy you've always worshipped, the one you've looked up to, the one who's *just like you,* and you think you're going to go back to your regular life, no big deal?"

"This is why I didn't tell you," Hayes said.

"Because I'd tell you the truth?" Zach scoffed. Then his voice softened. "Monty, the chances this is going to fuck you up—"

"I know," Hayes said calmly. He knew it. And if Morgan texted him, wondering if he was up for whatever euphemism Morgan wanted to use for sex, he was going to say yes.

Would Morgan be a "u up?" kind of guy? Couch it in a nice friendly, "you wanna hang out?" sort of way? Like they were theoretically gonna play cards or watch a bad movie on TV but realistically, they were going to make out.

Hayes didn't know, but he was pretty sure he was going to find out.

"What the fuck," Zach said, full of disbelief. He didn't sound angry, just dubious.

"I can't . . .I *want* him," Hayes finally said, because that was all there was to say.

He did want Morgan.

He'd wanted him before, but it was nothing like how he wanted him now, now that he knew how it felt to *have* him.

Morgan's eyes on him. Morgan's attention zeroed in. Morgan's hands touching him. Morgan's body pressed against his body.

"Okay," Zach said. "Have you talked about this?"

Had they? It felt like they'd said everything and nothing to each other.

"About what?"

"About what you're *doing*?" Zach exhaled in frustration.

"Not really. And that's okay—I get it."

Zach didn't say anything for a long moment, and Hayes knew he was being stupid but that didn't mean he wanted to hear his best friend say it out loud.

"Well, you seem sure about this," Zach finally said, cautious in a way he almost never was. At least never with Hayes.

"Yeah, I am," Hayes said.

The truth was, he wasn't sure of anything. Not Morgan. Not himself, even.

Half the time, he was wondering what the fuck he was doing—just like Zachy had—and then the other half, when Morgan finally turned his gaze on him, it felt like the most real, the most natural thing in the whole fucking world. They wanted each other; resisting the inevitable would've been either insane or impossible.

"If you're sure," Zach said again.

"Zachy," Hayes warned.

A knock sounded on his door.

"Hey," he said, before Zach could even protest, "I gotta go. Dinner's here."

They said goodbye, Zach sounding like he wanted to say more but holding back, and then Hayes dealt with room service.

He ate, flopping back on the bed. Knowing he should check his phone, but still afraid of what he might find.

He could've told Zach all this, but what would be the point? It would just worry Zach, who was supposed to be on vacation in Cabo, ordering pina coladas and not angsting about what Hayes was up to. And it would just worry *himself*, who had two games in four days, almost definitely both against Canada, who'd assembled one of the best lineups of hockey talent in the world for this tournament.

If the US had any chance of beating them, not just once, but twice, Hayes was going to have to be dialed in. They *all* were.

That meant he couldn't rock the boat right now. Just keep going along with what was happening and enjoy it while it was.

He lasted only halfway through an episode of *Love is Blind* before he gave in and grabbed his phone again.

Sure enough, buried under about a hundred texts in the US team's group chat, were two from Morgan to just him.

Hey, the first one read, **you around?**

Turned out that Morgan was a "u up?" kind of guy. Hayes wasn't all that surprised.

Then a few minutes later, a second one came in. **Went to dinner with the guys but I'll be back about eight, if you want to hang out.**

Turned out he was *also* the "hang out" guy.

It was fifteen minutes after eight, and he was just debating what to say. It wasn't a question of whether he was going to ask Morgan to come over—more like *how* he should ask him to come over. But before he could, Morgan sent a third text.

Is it embarrassing to text you a third time? Probably. But I'm doing it anyway.

Hayes fucking melted.

Yeah, a little, he texted back, not thinking anymore. Couldn't think anymore. **But yeah, come over.**

It was only two minutes—maybe even less—after he'd sent the text before there was a knock on the door.

When Hayes opened it, Morgan looked almost sheepish.

"Sorry if I was harassing you," Morgan said, following Hayes awkwardly into the room. Hayes sat on the edge of his bed. Morgan didn't join him though. Just stood in the middle of the room, looking five seconds away from wringing his hands.

"You weren't. I was asleep and then I was talking to Zach," Hayes said. He nearly added, *why don't you get over here? We both want you to.* But he didn't, because it looked like Morgan wanted to say something, and maybe he should let him get it out.

"I . . .we said we were doing this," Morgan said, even though they most definitely had. Hayes nodded. "And I just . . ."

Hayes didn't know where the fuck Morgan was going with this. But he was clearly into it and was here because he wanted to hook up. Because he wanted Hayes as badly as Hayes wanted him.

Why were they talking when they could be kissing and touching and so much more?

"It's okay," Hayes said and patted the spot next to him on the bed. "Come here."

Morgan rolled his eyes but he came, no hesitation whatsoever, settling next to Hayes, thighs and shoulders brushing.

Reaching up, Hayes cupped his cheek. Felt that scruff against his hand and felt his whole body roll over and straight-up fucking *yowl* at how much he wanted.

"I want you," Hayes said bluntly. "You're not bothering me if you want me back."

This time Hayes didn't know who kissed who first. It felt like they met in the middle, two people becoming one so quickly he immediately lost where he left off and Morgan began.

Morgan moaned into his mouth, fingertips digging into his shoulders, and it was so easy—way too fucking easy—to just let the drugging perfection of it carry him away.

CHAPTER 7

The game was just as brutal as Morgan expected it would be.

It was fast and hard and physical, two fights breaking out in the first period, including one where one of the Canadian assholes thought it was okay to push way too far into the crease and try to fuck up Braun.

Morgan could do it, but he sure as hell wasn't going to let some other guy try it. Not on his watch.

But Danny had it before he could even do anything, shoving the guy back, leaning over him as he went down to the ice.

The refs broke it up pretty quickly, separating Danny from the other player, but as they skated back to the bench, Danny leaned in and said, muffled through his mouth guard, "That fucking dick. I'm going to kick his ass."

"No, you're not," Hayes said, skating up next to them, swinging his leg over the wall to get to the bench. "You're gonna cost us a penalty and I don't want to fucking have to deal with killing their power play."

Danny grumbled, but he kept it together—something Morgan hadn't ever thought he'd be grateful for. During any other game, he'd have been pushing Danny's buttons, trying to get him to explode. Trying to get him a minor, or even a major, because he couldn't control his goddamn temper.

It was so weird to be trying to do the opposite now. Calm him down, not work him up.

"Hey," Hayes said, leaning over and nudging Morgan midway through the second. They were up 1-0, and Morgan was tense. It was looking more likely than theoretical that Canada was going to get something too, and then they'd be tied.

"What?" *His* temper was fraying now. He could feel it. From the tenseness of the game, being as close as it was, to the forced intensity of the game exhausting everyone, to the way the other team kept pushing and chipping at him. Not just him, but Hayes too.

They knew to beat the US team they had to get to the first line, and they'd been doing it all game. Danny had been a pretty decent defense mechanism, which was another reason Morgan had campaigned for him to be on the line with him and Hayes, but he was only one person and he'd been doing his utmost to fight back without actually getting a penalty for it.

It was inevitable. Danny would push back a fraction harder than he should and then one of the refs was going to call a penalty and then Canada would go on the power play.

"You gotta keep calm," Hayes said. "We have this. Freaking out about it isn't gonna make it any better."

"I know," Morgan muttered. "But they—"

"Let me handle them," Danny interrupted from his other side.

Danny probably saw the apprehension that crossed over his face and added. "Not like that, bud."

"Danny's fine," Hayes said. "You're the only one who looks like he's five seconds away from fucking imploding out there."

"Earlier—"

"Dude, it gets heated *once*," Danny complained.

"Nobody's blaming you," Hayes said, legit leaning right over Morgan like he wasn't even there to pat Danny on the thigh pad.

"Mo was," Danny shot back.

"For fuck's sake," Morgan complained.

"I saw the way you shoved TK. And then you did it to Bennett too," Danny said.

"Bennett's an asshole."

"Hey, I'm not arguing with that." Danny probably should. Sam Bennett was his freaking teammate normally.

"We're telling everyone to keep their shit together," Hayes said. "Danny *and* you."

"Fine," Morgan said.

He didn't lose his temper; he wasn't that kind of player. He wasn't Monty, avoiding fights like his life depended on it—which, that was probably fair—but he didn't usually seek them out.

To win this game, and he wanted to win it, so fucking bad, he could ignore TK's exaggerated protestations of faux-innocence and Bennett's shitty elbows.

Except then his next shift started and Bennett slammed him right into the boards before he could barely get his skates under him. The puck was all the way on the other side of the ice, Hayes threading his way between Makar and Toews, but Morgan wasn't going to be there to get the pass, because Bennett had taken him out at the fucking knees, leaving him reeling.

Then Bennett stood up and smirked, and all Morgan saw was red.

He didn't think; thinking was overrated. He swung once and then twice and felt himself get swarmed on all sides, blue and red melding into one swirling mass around him.

Someone yelled in his ear and he thought it might be Danny.

Someone else grabbed the back of his jersey and he fought back, arms flinging out as he tried to avoid being dragged out of the scrum.

Morgan saw a flash of blue and then the white of a number. Shit. That was Hayes. He'd dragged Morgan out with a surprising amount of strength and then instead of keeping both their distance, he was in there, gloves gone, doling out hits on Bennett like he fought all the fucking time.

"Holy shit." That was definitely Danny screaming, right into his ear.

"What the fuck are you waiting for?" Morgan growled. "Get him out of there!"

Danny shot him a strange look and shoved his way in, right next to the refs who were unsuccessfully trying to break it up.

Less than a minute later they had, and to Morgan's shock, they dragged only him and Bennett to the box.

Positive: his stupidity hadn't meant the Canadians got a man advantage. Negative: he had two minutes in the box to try to calm down which also meant two minutes for overthinking.

Yeah, Bennett's hit had been unquestionably shitty. Not surprising, but still shitty. He shouldn't have reacted. Clearly Danny and Hayes had noticed he was riding the edge of his temper on the bench which was exactly why they'd warned him.

But if that was true, if it was only *his* frayed self-control, why had Monty jumped in like that? Monty, who was known for avoiding fights, had pulled him out of it only to put himself in with gloves off.

Morgan didn't have a chance to say anything to him during the rest of the period, once he was out of the bin, because when their line wasn't on the ice, the trainers had him down on the opposite end of the bench, giving him ice for his knuckles and patching up a little cut on his cheek that seemed to be persistently bleeding.

He thought, *when we get to the locker room, I'm gonna read him the fucking riot act for that bullshit,* but then he couldn't because Coach was up there, diagraming out some new plays for them to try, to get that extra goal or two. Talking up the defense, reminding everyone that they *all* had to be two-way players to win this game.

On the way back to the ice for the third, he tried catching Monty's attention. "Hey," he hissed under his breath, but Hayes only glanced back at him briefly before turning his attention back to the end of the tunnel and the ice at the end of it.

"Don't be pissed at him," Danny said to him in passing as they skated on.

"I *am* pissed at him," Morgan said, but the truth was, his feelings were a hell of a lot more complicated than just anger.

Morgan wasn't stupid enough to bring it up once the game started again. They needed to be locked in, and Morgan didn't need to say a word about that, because he didn't think he'd ever seen Hayes' expression so intense.

Midway through the third, Danny passed Hayes the puck, and Hayes just put his head down, and Morgan, playing interference with Makar, saw exactly what normally made him such a stellar first line center. He just took the puck and made the play, skirting around another Canadian defenseman and then shooting it, maybe half a second before Morgan would've done it. But if Morgan had shot it, he was pretty sure Binnington would've blocked it, but the goalie wasn't in position yet, and Hayes slid it right past him.

It was a sick goal—the kind of goal people would talk about forever.

Didn't win them the tournament, but it won them the game, even when the Canadians managed to get a last-minute goal at the end of the third.

"That's fucking right," Danny yelled in the locker room, pounding Hayes on the shoulder. Hayes grinned up at him. Morgan knew he should go over. It had been a great goal, and the way he'd pressed against Hayes when they'd cellied about on the ice hadn't been enough.

But there was a part of him that was still pissed. *That,* that beautiful fucking goal, was why Hayes was on the fucking team. Not to take punches. Not to dole them back out, in Morgan's honor.

He was just about to go over to Hayes and say exactly that. *Good fucking job but what the fuck were you thinking?* when one of the PR staff showed up with a dozen reporters in tow.

Of course there was no way around it but to just do it. That wasn't his only job as captain here but it was a big part of it. As much as Morgan hated it, he couldn't avoid it. He had to wipe the sweat off his face and go stare down reporters. Answer their stupid fucking questions. Try not to say anything that would play into one of the annoying narratives they liked to harp on constantly. He couldn't stop them from making up shit, but he could make sure he never said anything that made it easier for them to do it.

By the time it was finally, *finally* over, Hayes was nowhere to be seen.

"Mo's gonna tear you a new one," Danny said to him as they walked to the bus.

"I think it's a little more complicated than that," Hayes said. Hoping that he wasn't lying to himself. He'd seen flashes of Morgan's face throughout the third, ever since he'd waded into that fight for him. Then after, when he'd scored the goal.

Danny shot him a dubious look. "If you think so."

"I *hope* so," Hayes said. If Morgan asked him what the fuck he'd been thinking in the second period, when he should've let Danny and the other guys who were much more experienced in these kinds of fights handle it, Hayes still didn't know how he was going to answer.

Danny sent him another baffled look and settled into his seat.

What *had* he been thinking?

The thing was, thinking had not really entered into the equation.

He'd seen Morgan go down after Bennett's nasty check against the boards. Had seen him barely manage to stagger to his feet, and there'd been no thinking involved.

Hayes had felt zero surprise when Morgan had gone after Bennett. Supposed he should have felt *some* astonishment when he'd dragged Morgan out of the scrum and then taken his place.

It wasn't his normal MO. Any other time, he'd have dragged Morgan out and done the Hayes Montgomery kind of job in a fight, which was keeping their skill players out of the thick of it.

Zach had sent him about a dozen increasingly hysterical texts during the game that he had yet to respond to. Culminating in: **What the absolute fuck, Monty.**

Hayes still didn't know how to parse what had happened, and even though he wanted to pretend otherwise, part of that was because he hadn't had a second to discuss it with Morgan yet.

How he felt about it shouldn't be reliant on how *Morgan* felt about it, but for the first time in a week since he'd shown up at the tournament, Hayes felt like he'd really fucked up.

This was worse than underperforming and needing a pep talk between periods. *Way* worse than accidentally coming out to Morgan Reynolds when all Morgan wanted to do was gently chastise him for acting like Morgan was a god, not just another hockey player.

The complex emotions on Morgan's face, emotions he normally kept under wraps, told at least part of the story and that was: Morgan was pretty fucking pissed.

There was no point in hiding.

He wasn't going to be that hard to find if Morgan really wanted to find him and yell at him.

So, when Danny dragged him to the raucous celebratory dinner, he went. Sat at the opposite end of the table from Morgan
and tried not to think of how Morgan might be so pissed everything that had been so good between them this week was dead
now. Ashes in his mouth, dread filling every single pore as he
waited for Morgan to finally corner him.

But Morgan kept not doing it. Hanging back. Hanging with
Bram and Noah. Barely even meeting Hayes' eyes when he
looked over at him.

"Are you sure he's more than just pissed?" Danny asked him
when they returned to the hotel and Morgan's group broke off
to go to the bar for another drink, leaving just the two of them
to wait for the elevator.

Hayes was pretty sure Danny wanted another drink too and
was just standing here because he felt sorry for Hayes and how
stupid he was, wanting to go to his room and sulk because he'd
fucked it all up.

"No," Hayes said, licking his lips, suddenly *not* sure.

"Buddy, you done fucked up, and that's the thing about
Mo—he doesn't like fuckups," Danny said sympathetically.

Hayes wanted to smack him in the face, but adding another
fight to his total wasn't going to solve this problem.

"Believe me, I know," Hayes said.

Danny patted him on the shoulder. "You see that quote making the rounds, the one he gave to the media about you?"

Hayes shook his head. He'd kept his phone in his pocket at
dinner. Didn't want to look at it. Feel like he needed to answer
the dozens of texts and messages he'd gotten about his fight and
then his goal.

"You should look for it," Danny said, patting him again as the elevator door opened. "I'm gonna go grab another beer. You sure you're okay?"

"I'm fine," Hayes said, even though he really fucking wasn't. Danny nodded and Hayes got on the elevator, pushing his floor button with more force than entirely necessary.

He'd had the nerve to lecture *Morgan Reynolds* about keeping a tight leash on his temper and then he'd lost his own so spectacularly, so publicly, it was a fucking wonder that wasn't all everyone was talking about. It was why he'd taken the shot in the third instead of passing it to Morgan.

He'd wanted to distract himself. The team. The media. The coaches. *Morgan.*

And it had worked really fucking well, except that Hayes was sure Morgan wasn't fooled at all. He didn't *seem* fooled.

Hayes got off on the seventh floor and was halfway down the hallway to his room when he realized there was a figure standing by the door.

His steps slowed when he realized who it was, but there was no way to turn around and avoid this. Morgan had seen him. That much was obvious from his steady gaze as Hayes approached.

"Thought you went for another drink," Hayes said after he reached the point of no return. He pulled the key card out of his pocket and toyed with it, not opening the door. If he did, he'd have to know one way or another if Morgan was coming inside, and he didn't want to face that answer.

"Took the stairs." Morgan huffed under his breath. And yeah, there was a sheen of sweat on his forehead. What an absolute fucking lunatic. Playing a whole ass hockey game and then running up seven flights of stairs. But Hayes shouldn't call the kettle black right now. Not when Morgan was staring at him like he'd analyzed every one of Hayes' molecules and found them all wanting.

"Wanted to talk to you," Morgan continued.

"Yeah, no shit," Hayes said under his breath.

Morgan shot him a chiding look. "What the fuck were you thinking?"

"Amazed you didn't unload that question hours ago," was all Hayes could say.

"I *wanted* to, but everyone got in the fucking way, and then I thought maybe it might be better to ask when I wanted to wring your neck less," Morgan admitted. He was actually almost smiling, the corner of his lips tilting up, and Hayes felt unmoored by it.

This wasn't *funny*.

He'd admonished Morgan about fucking up their game plan, and then he'd gone in and done it with gusto. Morgan should be pissed, *rightly*.

"Do you?" Hayes asked.

"Do I what?"

"Want to wring my neck less?"

Morgan did laugh then, but it wasn't as amused as Hayes thought it might be, considering he'd just almost smiled at the half-joke he'd made.

"Are we really going to do this out here in the hallway?" Morgan asked instead of answering the question.

"Maybe I want the possibility of an audience if you do wring my neck," Hayes said.

Morgan rolled his eyes. "Come on," he said.

It was not the "Come here," that they'd both been using on each other up until this point, but it was enough of an echo, reminding Hayes of everything that had been so good, of all the pleasure that inevitably came after one of them said it.

He opened the door but didn't make a move farther into the room. Like he was telling Morgan that whatever they had to say to each other in anger had to stay here, in this tiny ass hallway.

Of course, that didn't really help that much, considering only a few days ago, Morgan had kissed him right here and pushed him back against this wall, his tongue in Hayes' mouth.

"Better?" Hayes challenged.

"You don't get the right to be an ass about this," Morgan said, suddenly crowding him back against the wall, muscling him right into the same spot he'd done that first time. Arms on either side of Hayes' head, leaning right in.

Hayes' body reacted only because of the déjà vu. Or else that was what he told himself, mouth and thighs falling open.

Like it didn't even matter if Morgan was pissed, Hayes wanted him anyway.

"Are you even fucking sorry?" Morgan demanded.

"I'm . . ." He *was* sorry. But not that sorry. "Bennett took you down, tried to fucking take you out, and I'm supposed to apologize for being pissed about that?"

"I had it under control," Morgan said between clenched teeth. "I *do* fight sometimes—"

"Unlike me. I get it."

"We had a game plan, Montgomery, and you just went charging off it, like you were a white knight riding to my fucking rescue." Morgan's jaw was hard, his gaze unrelenting as he stared at Hayes.

Despite his long reputation, Hayes had always thought Morgan's hazel eyes were warm and unexpectedly soft. But they were not warm now. They were bone hard, pinning him like a steel beam.

"I wasn't," Hayes argued, even though that was exactly what he'd done. Morgan had gone down, and his heart had been in his throat, his stomach in his skates, and nothing could've stopped him in that moment. *Nothing*.

He'd have gone through the entire Canadian team to get to Morgan.

"Don't lie to me." Morgan pressed in harder. "You're not here to be my fucking rescuer, you're here to score goals, and sure you did—"

"I did," Hayes interrupted, raising his chin. Morgan could be hard, but that didn't mean he couldn't meet him there. "I fucking did."

For a long second, Morgan just stared at him, and then to Hayes' shock—even to Morgan's too, it seemed, considering the astonishment crossing over his face—he laughed. Scrubbed a hand over his jaw. "Yeah, you fucking did. You sure fucking did. Shut us all up. Made me crazy. I wanted to kill you and kiss you. I don't even know, Monty."

Hayes met that melting gaze. "So do both," he said.

Morgan laughed, unamused. "Don't tempt me."

"Why not?"

That was the point where Morgan pushed away from the wall, abruptly. "This is . . ."

There were so many ways he could end that sentence.

This is stupid.

This is foolish.

This is everything.

This is over.

Hayes couldn't take the risk that he might say a thing he couldn't bear to hear, so he grabbed Morgan's wrist and reeled him in. Kissed him hard and fast. Intense.

They stumbled into the room, onto the bed. Hayes tripped over one of his shoes. Morgan's hands wrenched his pants off, their mouths barely separating even for a second, even when Hayes pulled Morgan's T-shirt off.

They fell together onto the mattress, Hayes crawling over Morgan's body. He was shirtless, but still wearing jeans, no shoes, one sock half-off.

"God, I want you so bad," Morgan groaned as Hayes pulled his jeans off. The sock lost its fight and went with them. "So fucking bad." He panted, bare chest rising and falling. "Even when I want to wring your neck."

Hayes didn't trust himself to speak. He only wanted to feel. Pressed his lips against Morgan's stomach, feeling the muscles clench as he did, tongue trailing down to the waistband of his boxer briefs, saliva soaking the fabric as he shifted lower.

Everything narrowed in to just the feel of Morgan underneath him, the taste of him heavy on his tongue, the way his cock twitched as Hayes trailed his fingers up its hard length.

"Shit, baby, please," Morgan begged.

Morgan begged.

Hayes couldn't deal with that right now, couldn't even begin to contemplate what that meant now, and what that meant for the future.

So he didn't think about it at all.

Let his focus narrow down to just *Morgan* and making him feel good.

He finally pulled down his boxer briefs, and they both moaned the moment Hayes got his mouth on his cock.

It was so easy to lose himself in it, a tunnel vision of taste and touch and feel as Morgan's hands buried themselves in his hair, rhythmically clenching and releasing as Hayes took him deeper. He choked a little, unable to take it all but wanting to, so desperately.

"Feels so good, baby," Morgan murmured, voice rough. His hand slipped down, cupped Hayes' cheek, tender and affectionate.

Hayes groaned around his cock. The tenderness shouldn't be as much of a turn-on as the rest of it, but it was.

He was only seconds away from pressing a hard palm against his own dick, aching and desperate for something, when Morgan gave a little aborted groan, fingers tightening in his hair again, and he came down Hayes' throat.

Hayes swallowed around him, panting as he finally let Morgan's softening cock slip from his lips. Pressing his lips to Morgan's thigh, he tried to catch his breath.

Tried to re-orient himself back to the place where this was just a hookup, and Morgan wasn't staring at him like he was the moon and the sun and the stars.

The same fucking way you've always looked at him.

It was a problem, but it was an easy enough problem to push away, to pretend didn't exist at all, when Morgan was pulling him up, flipping them and tugging Hayes' underwear off. Hand hot and insistent on Hayes' dick as pleasure spiraled through him.

"That feel good?" Morgan crooned, his gaze so intent on Hayes' face.

Hayes nodded. It felt fucking incredible, and he still wanted more. Wanted to gorge himself, even if he wasn't sure he'd ever be full.

"Bet this would feel even better," Morgan said, dipping his head low, sucking just the head of his cock into his hot mouth.

"Yeah, yeah." Hayes knew he was babbling now, probably sounding nearly incoherent with it.

And then Morgan's thumb, wet with saliva, slipped lower, pressing right against his hole, and Hayes groaned.

He hadn't even wanted to bring up anything more than they were doing. First off, because the stuff they were doing was so excruciatingly good, and second, because there was a part of him, buried and shameful, that was afraid he'd scare Morgan away. That he'd make it "too gay."

But of course, Morgan had no qualms about this. Just lifted his head and met Hayes' eyes. "Do you like this?" he asked, direct with zero fuss whatsoever. No pressure, like Hayes had to, or like it would be a problem if he said yes.

Hayes nodded.

"You gotta say it, baby, out loud, okay?"

That shouldn't have been so hot either, but Hayes felt like he was burning up inside at how *good* Morgan was. Careful but pushy. Tender but strong. Everything he'd ever wanted in a partner, and there it was, in the last place he'd ever expected to look.

You can't think about that now.

He couldn't really, anyway, because Morgan was pushing a finger inside him, and it was lighting Hayes up inside.

"Wanna make you come so hard." It was unclear if Morgan was saying that to Hayes—or himself. Or if it even mattered.

The sentiment was enough, and then Morgan hit that spot inside him at the same time as he sucked hard on the head of his cock, and Hayes was *gone*. His orgasm surged through him with a strength that had him whiting out.

When he finally came back down to earth, slowly blinking his eyes open, Morgan was staring at him with a very smug look on his face.

"God, that was so hot," Morgan said. "*You're* so hot."

Hayes covered his face with his hands. It wasn't shame exactly. It wasn't even embarrassment at how much he'd enjoyed it. It was like he was broken open, everything exposed to the air now and to Morgan's perusal, and he couldn't hope to hide it anymore.

"Don't do that," Morgan chided gently and pried Hayes' hands off his face. "I like looking at you."

How was Hayes not supposed to melt into an absolute puddle of goo at that?

"I like looking at you, too," Hayes admitted.

Morgan propped his head up on his hand. "I don't want to make things weird . . ."

"You're worried about that *now*?" Hayes chuckled under his breath.

"Fair." Morgan licked his lips. Hayes wanted to lean in and kiss him again. Not think about whatever it was Morgan wanted to do that might make this whole thing more difficult than it already was.

"How much would you freak out if I said I didn't want to go?" Morgan finally asked.

"Tonight?" Hayes tried not to freak out, but he was, and it was hard to hide.

Morgan nodded. "I know it's not really a hookup kind of thing, but I don't want to go. I'm . . .I like being here with you. Like this. It makes it . . ." He took a deep breath. "It makes some of this easier."

It suddenly occurred to Hayes that as much pressure as *he* felt, in this tournament, it had to be tenfold for Morgan.

He hadn't been on a national team in years and now Morgan was here as the captain, expected to bring home the gold for Team USA. Nevermind all the baggage about how Morgan felt about nearing the end of his career and being forced to confront it, because of Hayes' presence here.

Honestly, because of that Hayes shouldn't even be that person for Morgan—the one who made the burdens easier to carry—but it seemed like he was, anyway.

"You make it easier too," Hayes said and he took a chance, half-nuzzling into Morgan's shoulder.

They weren't cuddling exactly but close enough.

Close enough that Hayes wasn't even sure what else he'd call it.

"That shouldn't be true," Morgan said softly, "but it is."

For the first time, Hayes let himself really seriously think about what this might have been if they didn't play on opposite sides of the country.

But they did, there was no reason to believe that might change anytime soon and, as a result, there was only so far it could go, unless they were considering long-distance a viable possibility.

"Yeah," Hayes agreed. Wondered, also for the first time, if he *should* say something. They'd both seemed happy enough to keep it just sex, a fun hookup, at first, but now things were deepening. Changing.

Maybe it was like Danny said—the first overall thing, rearing its head. Or maybe it was something else.

"You should stay," Hayes continued before he could stop himself. "If you want to."

"I want to," Morgan said.

And that something else reared up again, insistent and undeniable, at least until Hayes pushed it away.

Something else was a problem for a different day, for a Hayes who'd already been through the next game, the championship game.

Not a Hayes who just wanted to fall asleep to Morgan's steady breathing.

CHAPTER 8

Danny came up to Hayes after morning skate and leaned over him. "Hey," he said, "how are you doin', kid?"

Hayes shot him a look. "First off, we're the same age and second off, what did you do now?"

"Who said I did anything?" Danny asked, with exaggerated innocence.

Hayes rolled his eyes. "You're a terrible liar. And not subtle, either."

"Okay," Danny said, "fair. I wanted to know what you thought of some of these quotes going around about you."

"What quotes?" Once they were confirmed to be in the championship game, Hayes had inevitably had to do media yesterday. Some of the other guys had too. But he hadn't ended up paired with Morgan again, which he wasn't sure he was relieved or disappointed about.

"You haven't heard, then," Danny said with smug satisfaction and then pulled his phone out of his sweatpants. "Let me tell you what our illustrious captain is saying about you these days."

"Danny," Hayes warned him.

"No, no, it's good. And you should hear this."

"I specifically go out of my way *not* to read the press shit. Especially when it's about me," Hayes said. Even though if he knew Morgan was saying good stuff about him, he might've been very tempted.

But *no.* Because the *something else* was already taking up a part of him, growing with very single moment he spent in Morgan's presence, and he was worried that Zach might've been right after all when he wondered if this whole thing was going to fuck Hayes up, in the end.

"You're gonna want to hear this," Danny said. He put a hand on his hip and affected what he probably thought was a Morgan-like tone. Hayes didn't tell him it was a terrible impression, but he could have. "Monty's a vital part of this team. Maybe the most important piece we have. *Blah blah* something else about the goal you scored against Canada and then someone asked if that could really be true if Morgan's the first line center and he said, and I fucking quote, Monty, *I'm only here to make him look as good as he really is.* He fucking said that. About you. To the media. *Unprompted.*"

"Danny," Hayes said weakly, "I don't understand the point of this."

"Do you really not get it or are you in some serious denial?"

Serious denial. Digging my way in deeper every single day.

Hayes just shrugged. "It's . . .it's an honor to play with him too."

"The way Morgan's talking, it's more than just an honor to play with *you.* And you know, you have to know, he didn't like talking about you before this. Kinda went out of his way to avoid talking about you."

"I know," Hayes said. And he'd known why, objectively. Understood, even though it had sort of stung, deep down. He'd gotten it, and he'd gotten it even more when Morgan had admitted that Hayes made him feel old. Washed-up. Like his career was essentially over.

"I'm just saying, what are you two doing?" Danny questioned. "If you don't come out of this like . . .super committed, what are you *doing*?"

"That's not going to happen," Hayes said bluntly. "He lives in New York. I live in California. It's not . . .it's just not happening. It's been fun, it's been—"

"Bullshit," Danny said bluntly. "I see the way you two look at each other. I'm your fucking line mate. I have to see it. I can't *avoid* seeing it."

"It is what it is," Hayes said.

"And so what, Morgan extolling your praises before the game tonight is, what, just him being nice? Him having fun? You have *met* Morgan Reynolds, haven't you?"

Hayes leaned over and picked up his bag. He didn't have the emotional bandwidth for this conversation. It was hard enough keeping things light and uncomplicated around Morgan when his feelings felt increasingly involved without having to answer Danny's pointed questions.

"Yeah, I have. But we've got a game to play, Danny. You know that."

Danny shot him an incredulous look, but couldn't really argue with him, because it *was* true.

Right now, they had to head back to the hotel, take their nap, eat dinner, and then get ready for the championship game.

Tomorrow afternoon, he'd be flying back to California, and this whole insane interlude would—probably—be over.

He and Morgan hadn't talked about it. They'd specifically *not* talked about it. Not two nights ago when Morgan had stayed over, and not last night, when Hayes had ended up in Morgan's bed.

The sex was really good. The conversation was unexpectedly amazing, just talking to someone who *got* it. Who understood the very specific pressure cooker they both existed inside. But anything else was asking for a miracle that wasn't happening.

Hayes wasn't stupid enough to wish for it.

"When and if you wanna talk about it," Danny said as they made their way to the team bus, "you just holler, okay?"

Hayes didn't imagine he was *ever* going to want to talk about it. He was going to want to do the opposite, probably. Pretend it had never happened. Move on, somehow, and denial seemed the most likely avenue to make that possible.

There were a handful of texts from Zach on his phone when he woke up from his pregame nap.

I just saw Mo talking you up. Think you've made a fan for life, Monty.

Then, **Holy shit, he was REALLY talking you up. You recovered yet? You still alive, under all those crushing feelings?**

And finally, **Good luck in the game today, you're gonna freaking kill it. And that's not just the Morgan in me talking, it's the Zach in me believing it's true :)**

Hayes didn't know what to say. It was hard enough to have even twenty-five percent of this conversation with Danny, nevermind Zach.

Thanks, he finally sent as he headed downstairs, suit on, to have dinner before they headed to the arena.

It was better than him sending nothing, but there was no question it would tip Zach off that he was kind of a mess.

How many years had he wanted an acknowledgment from Morgan of his game and his skill? Too many. And now he'd finally gotten it and it tasted fucking bitter in the back of his throat.

He knew Morgan meant it. He wouldn't have said it otherwise, but the circumstances were fucking him up.

And like Morgan somehow knew it, he kept his distance during dinner, sitting on the other end, chatting with Bram and the coaching staff.

Hayes sat with Danny, who kept shooting him knowing looks, and Noah and Cal, and shoveled chicken and pasta into his mouth, not tasting a single molecule of it.

Morgan didn't approach him until they were in the locker room. He'd been making his rounds as everyone warmed up and then geared up, doing his good captain routine, dropping encouraging words and last minute advice into their teammates' ears.

Hayes *did* notice that Morgan saved him for last—or nearly last, because he'd also noticed that during Morgan's rotation he'd yet to head over to where Jacob sat in his stall, locked-in expression serious.

"Hey," Morgan said, gazing down at him.

"Hey," Hayes said, telling himself, *be normal, be normal, be normal.*

"You good?"

Hayes licked his lips. Dug his fingertips into his hip pad. "Yeah."

Morgan shot him a bit of a knowing look. "Really? You've been quiet."

And you've been hiding from me, from the moment you woke up in my bed this morning and kissed me like you meant it with your whole heart, and I kissed you back because I couldn't help it.

"Focused," Hayes corrected.

"Just remember that it's the three of us out there. We've got your back and you've got ours. It's not all on you."

Hayes nodded.

"And, it's . . .uh, a sixty-minute game."

Hayes raised an eyebrow. "Any more captain-ly platitudes you want to say?"

The seriousness in Morgan's face dissolved. "Fuck, I'm being weird, aren't I?"

"Has Danny been bothering you, too?"

Maybe it was weird to bring it up, but it felt even weirder to be talking around it.

Morgan let out a little groan, and Hayes flushed before he could force himself not to react. "Yeah, ever since he saw that stuff I said about you." His voice dropped even further. "I meant it all, you know? I should've said it a long time ago—"

"Don't," Hayes said, sharper than he'd intended. "I . . .you aren't obligated to say anything about me. About how I play."

Hayes hated and loved how earnest Morgan looked. "I meant it."

"Yeah, I know." Yeah, Hayes knew. Which was what made it so fucking awful.

"If Danny won't quit harassing you, just send him my way, okay?" Morgan said.

"He's not—is he harassing *you*?" Hayes asked.

As annoying as Matt Daniels could be, it was obvious he meant well.

"No, no of course not," Morgan blustered. "He was just giving me shit about that stuff I said yesterday. But it was all true, so I didn't really mind."

Hayes wasn't sure he really believed him, but he wasn't going to call him out on it. Not now.

They were going to have to talk about this, but it was going to be after the game, no matter how it went.

"Well, if that changes," Hayes said, giving Morgan the easiest smile he was capable of right now, "you just let *me* know, and I'll deal with him."

Morgan returned an even brighter smile. "Alright."

"And remember," Hayes said, reaching out and catching Morgan's arm before he turned away, "*you're* not alone out there, either. I know you've got the C, and like a whole fucking nation of *yee haw Americans* relying on you, but you've got us—Danny and me. The whole team, too, but *us*." *But me, most of all*, Hayes wanted to say. Didn't quite have the nerve to say it, but he felt it.

Morgan's expression softened into something tender that made the *something else* in his chest tighten and expand.

"Uh, yeah. Thanks." He shot Hayes a smile almost identical to the one he'd worn this morning, right before he'd leaned over and kissed him.

Hayes had to believe that they were going to be okay. That they'd figure this shit out. That this *something else* inside him would eventually be satisfied and calm the fuck down.

Morgan had heard the talk before the tournament started. That this was only going to be a slightly different, no less physical example of the yearly and very pointless All Star game. That nobody would want to play hard. That nobody would hit. That the games would be just everyone skating around, shooting the puck like it was going out of style.

But he'd always known every minute on the ice was going to be hard fought.

Their last game against Canada had been that way, and this one was even tougher.

It was still 0-0, midway through the third. No matter how hard their team had pushed—or how hard the Canadians pushed, it was like they both kept running up against the same fucking wall.

"Shit," Danny exclaimed as he climbed over the boards, sinking onto the bench. "They're fucking all over us. I can't even get a moment to breathe, nevermind to hold the puck. Forget about passing or shooting it."

"I know," Hayes said on Morgan's other side.

He looked as frustrated as Danny sounded.

"We just gotta keep pushing and keep being patient," Morgan said, even though he could hear the opposite in his own voice. "They're gonna make a mistake, eventually."

Danny made a grumbling noise, but Hayes nodded his agreement. "They're not perfect," he said. He met Morgan's gaze, and they both nodded.

Hayes' resolution and determination fueled his own.

They would get this done.

It was maybe their second to last shift, based on the four minutes left on the clock, and Morgan, despite Hayes' confidence, couldn't help but feel the pressure.

Even though it had seemed inevitable all game that they were going to go to overtime, he didn't want that. He wanted to finish the Canadians off *now*. Their team was tired, *he* was tired, and in two days, they all had to go back to their regular NHL teams. Playing extra shifts wasn't going to make any of that easier.

"Come on," he barked at Monty and at Danny as they went over the boards. "Let's get this shit done."

Hayes nodded at him and took off towards the net where the US defenders were trying to dig the puck out from behind it to get it away from where Braun was poised, ready to deflect a shot if he needed to.

Danny headed over, helping him out, and managed to muscle the guys out of the way, flicking the puck towards Morgan, who caught it and then, out of the corner of his eye, he saw Hayes sliding open. A lane opening up past the blue line. He passed it and then blocked one of the defenders from catching up with him, and that was all the time Hayes needed.

He took off so fast it was like Morgan barely blinked and there he was, already across the ice, more flying than skating, two defenders and one of the Canadian forwards behind him, scrambling to catch up and stop him somehow.

But Hayes wasn't going to be stopped. Not now.

Morgan could see the determination in every stride, in the tenseness of his shoulders under his pads, in the way he angled himself, Binnington bracing for the shot.

But Hayes wasn't going to waste this opportunity, and he slid to the left and then flicked the puck in barely a second before Binnington could react, launching it over his glove hand.

The arena erupted.

Morgan was pretty sure he was yelling, but he couldn't hear it, not over the sheer wall of noise. He was the closest to Hayes and hit him at full speed, Hayes' arms around him as they slid into the boards.

"You fucking did it," Morgan yelled. "You fucking did, baby!"

Hayes smile was as wide as he'd ever seen it. "I fucking did!" he crowed back.

Danny hit them then, followed by pretty much the rest of the team, even though there was still just over three minutes on the clock.

"We gotta focus up," Morgan said to the team when they finally all returned to the bench. "We can't let Monty's goal go to waste. Do *not* let them get around you. Do *not* let them get a free shot in, okay?"

But even that lecture didn't seem to dim Hayes' joy.

Or Morgan's own.

They'd made that play. Danny had started it, with his aggressive move against the boards, then getting the puck to Morgan, who'd only had a split second before he knew he'd be passing it to Hayes.

Hayes, who'd made the most out of the single opportunity he'd been handed.

Morgan had told him and Danny that their chance was going to come around, if they could just keep fighting and keep being patient.

It had, and Hayes had grabbed it with both hands. They *all* had, maybe, but Hayes most of all. Hayes who'd started out this tournament worried and pressured but had come into his own. Glowing now, with Morgan's gaze on him.

"Shit," Morgan said, leaning towards Hayes, his glove in front of his mouth. "That was just . . .when I said we were here to make *you* look good, that's exactly what I fucking meant."

Hayes flushed, a deeper red than his already pink-from-exertion face.

"You're so good, Monty," Morgan said, because he couldn't seem to stop running his mouth.

The look in Hayes' eyes was tender. Goopy. Not the look of a teammate. But of a lover. Morgan didn't hate it; he actually wanted to eat it all up, even though he'd known when they'd woken up this morning, wrapped up together, that there was no future here.

That no matter how much he wanted it, it just wasn't there. This wasn't a play he could make by muscling an opponent out of the way. A shot he could perfect by practicing long after everyone else had left the rink. It was immutable fate, and he couldn't change it, even if he was dying to.

Even if Hayes looked at him like he was thinking the same things.

He'd thought maybe he'd finally need to talk about this tonight, but maybe talk was the last thing they needed.

Maybe to say it out loud would just make it worse.

Hayes nudged him and Morgan turned his attention back to the ice. There was a minute and a half left now, and the Canadians had just pulled Binnington.

"Reynolds, Monty, get out there," Coach Blackburn barked. "Kill this."

The Canadians pushed hard, but the clock finally ticked down to the last thirty seconds, then the last fifteen. Morgan knew what they needed and finally managed to steal the puck and clear it past the blue line, time *finally* running out.

They'd done it.

Morgan met Hayes' eyes as he skated up to him, whooping the whole way.

And he knew, without a doubt, who he was passing the brand-new Four Nations trophy to, first.

Hayes felt like every molecule in his body had been electrified.

The celebration on the ice had sped by, but every so often a visceral perfect memory could cross his mind—the smile on Morgan's face as he'd lifted the trophy, the look in his eyes as he'd handed it to Hayes first, the heft of it in his hands and the taste of silver on his tongue as he'd tipped his head back and drunk out of it.

He'd showered and changed, but even then he felt the sticky sweet slick of cheap champagne and cheaper beer over his skin.

They'd been at the bar for at least an hour and Hayes hadn't had to buy himself a single drink, even though they were currently in Canada and Canadians in general weren't really thrilled about how their tournament turned out.

He mentioned this to Danny who just smirked and said he probably wouldn't have to buy a single drink for himself, ever again, no matter what country he was in.

The problem was that Hayes didn't want to get drunk. He wanted to float endlessly on this perfect, hazy river of uncomplicated happiness forever. Tipsy but not drunk, realizing that nearly every time he looked over that Morgan was gazing at him, the look on his face making it clear exactly where they were going to end the night.

Hayes decided nobody could blame him for wanting to end it *right now*. Making up his mind, he set his beer down and, not giving a shit, walked right over to where Morgan was chatting with a few of their defensemen.

It wasn't very subtle, but then 1) hockey players were a pretty obtuse bunch and 2) it wasn't like Morgan had been particularly holding back.

"Hey," he said to Morgan, "remember that thing I told you about?"

There had been no thing.

Morgan frowned, moving closer, his hand reaching up to steady Hayes even though he wasn't unsteady at all. "What thing?"

"The thing," Hayes said, nudging him.

Up until now, he'd been letting Morgan dictate this whole thing, but he was done doing that. This was happening tonight, and it was happening *now*. Hayes was practically a national fucking hero right now, so if he wanted to have Captain America fuck him? That only seemed like fair and adequate compensation.

It only took Morgan a second. Then he was on it. "Oh yeah," he said, nudging back. "The *thing*."

"Yep," Hayes said smugly. "The thing."

Morgan turned to their teammates and didn't even have the grace to look disappointed. "Hayes and I have something we need to take care of," he said.

They just nodded, giving Hayes another round of backslaps and congratulations, before Hayes could finally drag Morgan towards the door.

"You don't want to stay and celebrate?" Morgan asked, grinning at him like it was making his whole ego sing that Hayes couldn't wait a second longer.

"No," Hayes said succinctly. "I've waited long enough, don't you think? Besides, it's practically my party. If I want to leave it early, that's my prerogative."

Hayes grabbed his coat and handed Morgan his own.

Morgan's smug grin only grew as he shrugged it on. "Yeah. I take it I'm invited to this private party you're hosting, then?"

That *something else* was pressing hard and fast against his diaphragm, making it hard to even breathe as Morgan leaned in, using opening the door as an excuse to get even closer.

It shouldn't have felt more intimate to gaze up at Morgan as they headed out onto the sidewalk and say, "The only person I'm inviting," but it was.

They'd talked about other personal things, but they'd never talked about what *this* was. At first Hayes had felt like that wasn't necessary, since they both knew the score, and then it had felt like the opposite—like he couldn't have gotten the words out of his mouth even if he wanted to.

He wanted to say, *I want you to be the only person I'm inviting for a very long time,* but he didn't know if he could. If he *should*.

"Good," Morgan said, nodding once.

It was all they said to each other on the five-minute walk from the bar to the hotel. Morgan only broke the silence when they got into the elevator and he leaned over, pressing the button for the seventh floor.

Okay, Hayes realized, they were going to his room and not even talking about it. Just doing it.

Then Morgan turned to him, "That goal was something fucking else."

"It was a good pass," Hayes said.

Morgan laughed under his breath. "Take the win, okay?"

"I've spent the last few hours taking the win," Hayes pointed out.

"And somehow that's too much?" Morgan rolled his eyes but he didn't make any attempts to hide his fondness as he glanced over at him.

Hayes' throat felt tight. *Say it, say it, say it, say it.* "I can think of one more thing I want. That you can give me."

"Yeah?"

"Your dick." Hayes paused, realizing he needed to be crystal clear about what he wanted. "I want you to fuck me."

It was such a fucking cliche he was fully expecting Morgan to smirk knowingly the moment it was out of his mouth. But instead Morgan looked floored, blown away by Hayes' words.

And yeah, duh, it was probably the first time a guy had asked Morgan to do that. Possibly the first time Morgan had ever contemplated fucking a guy. Now that Hayes was thinking not *only* with his dick, he could see maybe he'd gone too hard. Not offered other, possibly easier, things, first.

Morgan turned to him, jaw still a little dropped. "You mean that," Morgan said.

Yes, Hayes could've worked up to it, but this was what he'd *wanted*. What he'd been half-afraid to ask for, before. What he'd definitely known was a bad idea, considering the number and sheer toughness of the games they had to play during this tournament.

He'd thought this through, though. At least as well as he could with the haze of the booze in his system. He didn't have a game for three days. Asking for this was allowed, and maybe if he was very lucky, Morgan wouldn't be turned off by the request. Maybe he'd even *like* it.

"Yes," Hayes said unsteadily. Resisting the urge to apologize. To snatch the words back and claim he hadn't actually meant what he'd asked.

The elevator doors dinged open and they headed down the hall towards Hayes' room.

Morgan didn't say anything else, not until Hayes got the door open. The moment it closed behind them, Morgan had his arms around him and he was half-pushing him, half-dragging him to the bed, lips pressed hard and insistent against Hayes'.

"God, yes, *please*," Morgan all but begged, pressing Hayes against the edge of the bed, tilting his head back as he kissed him intently.

Hayes broke off the kiss with a gasp. "You mean that?" he had to ask.

Morgan stared at him, the pupils swallowing nearly all the hazel of his eyes.

"God, yes, I want you. I want *all* of you," Morgan muttered. He was already shucking Hayes' jacket, then pulling at his sweatshirt, his T-shirt. "You make me crazy. When you scored that goal—I thought I was going to fall to the ice, worship you right there."

Hayes had a fleeting thought that they really *should* talk about this.

That *I want all of you* sounded just about as serious as the *something else* currently pressing so insistently against his breastbone.

But then Morgan was sinking to his knees, pulling down his jeans and his briefs, mouth and then teeth on his thigh.

It was too easy to get lost in the sensation of it, the pleasure Morgan pulled out of him, easy as breathing.

He was still floating, everything perfect and amazing and wonderful as he told Morgan the lube and condoms were in the drawer. He'd bought them yesterday, in a fit of optimism, thinking that whether they won or lost the championship game, he was going to want to experience Morgan inside him, just once.

More than just once. This is just the first time.

It was impossible not to ride high on the way Morgan looked at him. Touched him. Every bit of it reinforcing the idea in Hayes' mind that this wouldn't be happening just once. That they wanted each other too much to be that stupid.

"God, you're so sexy," Morgan murmured as he slipped a finger inside him. Hayes groaned at the way it felt, shifting backwards so he could have more of it.

"Another," Hayes begged, no longer even caring if he sounded desperate. He *was* desperate.

Morgan pressed his mouth to his inner thigh again, nibbling at the muscle there, then moving up, slipping Hayes' cock into his mouth, not sucking on it, just letting it sit on his tongue as he slid another finger in.

Hayes groaned around the stretch, already craving the heft and weight of Morgan's dick inside him. His fingers were so good, but he wanted—*needed*—more, the way he needed to take his next breath.

"I got you," Morgan murmured around his cock. "Let me."

And even though this was his first time, Hayes let him.

Kept floating on that easy, uncomplicated cloud of pleasure. Clenched up when Morgan gave him another slick finger, moaning when Morgan finally hit that spot inside him.

Ate up every single word of praise Morgan gave him. Every *gorgeous* and *hot* and *sexy*. Practically came when Morgan told him how good he was taking it.

Then Morgan was rising, pushing his knee up to his chest and a moment later, groaning as he fit the head of his cock to Hayes' hole.

"Shit, baby, you're so good like this. So fucking perfect." Morgan met his eyes as he said it, and it was like he saw inside Hayes, knew exactly what he needed to hear, knew exactly what effect those words had on him.

It shouldn't have been good sex. Morgan might be experienced with women, but he wasn't with men. It didn't matter. It was already the best sex of Hayes' life, Morgan filling him like he was built for him. His cock, for sure, the perfect length and girth and curve, making Hayes shout with how unerringly he hit every good spot inside him, lighting him up with pleasure. But it was more than that, too.

Like they were two puzzle pieces finding each other and finally nestling together the way they'd always been meant to.

Morgan leaned over him as he fucked him, kissing him on the lips, tender and gentle, at odds with his hard, firm strokes, and sent Hayes over the edge with just that.

A second later, Hayes felt him tense and he was following him.

They collapsed onto the bed, and Morgan slung an arm around him, like he couldn't quite bear to let him go.

This was the moment. Hayes should say something. Should break the silence, but it felt so weighted.

Instead, it was Morgan who did it. "Good?" he asked.

Hayes nodded, and Morgan groaned as he sat up. Headed to the bathroom and when he returned, he helped Hayes clean up, and Hayes knew *this* was definitely the time.

Especially when Morgan returned to bed, to his side, like he was a magnet and he couldn't possibly resist.

He started out half a dozen times in his own head.

What do you think?

Are you as into this as I am?

You felt that too, right?

We could do this, even if it's crazy?

Three thousand miles isn't that far.

Anything has to be better than being without each other, now that we've found this.

But before he could decide on a tactic, on a single approach, Hayes felt his eyes begin to slip closed, the game and the adrenaline and the booze and the sex all catching up with him at once.

He had one last thought before he fell asleep.

I think I know what this something else is.

And then he was gone.

CHAPTER 9

MORGAN DIDN'T FALL ASLEEP. Hayes knocked out almost immediately, combination of the game, the adrenaline rush and then fall, the booze and then almost definitely the orgasm.

But Morgan couldn't turn his mind off. He hadn't had nearly as much to drink as Hayes—almost nothing, other than the few sips of cheap beer and shitty champagne in the locker room and a single beer at the bar—because he'd somehow known he'd need his wits about him tonight.

That Hayes would want to turn him inside out, and he'd need to be able to think for that.

There was no question about it: Hayes had done it. Effortlessly, even, like it wasn't even hard. Like he'd been doing it, basically from the first day, when he'd spent too much time apologizing for him being Hayes Montgomery and for Morgan being Morgan Reynolds.

He hadn't apologized for it today. He'd leaned into it, and look what had happened. They'd won, and yes, it had been a team effort, but Hayes had also put them all on his back. Had said, like it was nothing, *I got this, you guys.*

He had. Hayes had been his most amazing brilliant self, all the more extraordinary because he didn't even see how brightly he shone.

And Morgan had never felt the resounding echo of that so much in his whole damn life.

He'd won two Cups, and neither of those wins had felt even close to what tonight had been, with Hayes. A stupid manufactured tournament and he couldn't say that he was the same person after that he'd been before.

But I don't want to be different. Morgan didn't want it, but the thought was impossible to ignore, screaming at him with flashing red lights.

Morgan knew he only had two or three years left, at most. Maybe he'd win another Cup. Maybe he wouldn't. Maybe he'd set some more records, maybe he wouldn't.

Maybe later, when it didn't feel like he was on his last fucking chance, he could lean into that difference. Maybe later it wouldn't *mean* anything, in the scheme of things.

But when he lay here and thought about what this thing between them could look like, he felt soft and happy and like a person, not a hockey player.

You're not ready to be anything more than a hockey player.

That was the unvarnished truth he couldn't seem to get away from. He wasn't ready. He wanted this. A part of him even craved it. Wanted to roll over and press as close to Hayes as he could, to soak up his warmth and affection and his sheer fucking brilliance, but he didn't.

Become second to him.

But he couldn't.

Morgan waited until the clock turned over to three a.m. and then four. Five.

Waited to change his mind. And it hurt—no question. The vague concept of getting out of this bed and leaving now, of only meeting Hayes tomorrow morning over his eggs and being able to give him a brief, friendly, bro-y hug as he said goodbye, made him want to hurl.

But the alternative felt worse. Too many years of ingrained habits. So many sacrifices. Believing, even when he'd been married and had a child, that hockey was enough, that it would always have to be enough.

The clock hit six.

He took one breath and then another and then slid out of bed. Gathered his clothes. Didn't look at the Hayes-shaped lump in the bed. Wasn't sure he'd really be able to say goodbye if he waited around to do it.

Shut the door as quietly behind him as he could.

Ran into Blackburn in the hallway, who looked at him oddly, but accepted the bad excuse he gave for being on a different floor. Went back to his room, took a shower, packed his shit and then an hour later he was downstairs at breakfast. Pretending like nothing was wrong.

He couldn't say he'd reassembled his armor, but at least he didn't react when Hayes walked in. Their eyes met and Morgan looked away. His chest ached, and his throat tightened. He *wanted* to be different. But they'd only ever been who they were and no amount of desire was ever going to change that fundamental fact.

Hayes probably knew it, better than he did, even, and he wasn't the one ghosting Morgan.

But Morgan was ghosting him.

Before this, Morgan would have proudly proclaimed he'd handle anything the world threw at him. Any amount of pain and suffering; he could handle it. But walking up to Hayes and acting like he was just another player and this was just another goodbye, it was taking him out.

It was shitty. *He* was shitty. He should tell Hayes the truth. But he wasn't sure he could choke out the words.

This was the only way.

Even when Hayes shot him a confused look, and Danny said, in a particularly pointed way, "Guess you aren't eating with Hayes this morning," he stayed strong.

He'd been strong his whole life, and it seemed that practiced strength was training for this very situation, because it was taking every single bit of it to pull it off.

Even when he left early, catching a ride to the airport, and Hayes texted him, wondering where he'd gone, he didn't turn around. No matter how much he wanted to.

This was the path he'd chosen. The path he'd always chosen, its ruts and grooves so natural to him it was almost like the path had chosen *him* instead.

He just had to stay on it, and it would take care of him. Morgan had to believe that, because otherwise, he didn't know what the fuck all this had been for.

Hayes knew something was wrong the moment he woke up alone.

Knew it was wrong, even more wrong, during breakfast when Morgan deliberately avoided him.

When he disappeared early, and Coach Thompson mentioned offhandedly when he asked that he'd gone to the airport early to catch his flight, Hayes knew it was more than wrong.

Not just wrong; the situation had catastrophically imploded.

Where'd you go? he sent Morgan. Aware he was being needy. Telling himself anyway that he was being totally normal, even if it was a lie.

But as he paced in his room, minutes ticking by without an answer, it was harder and harder not to face reality. *You should have talked to him sooner.* But what good would that have done? In that alternate vision of the future, Morgan would have been forced to tell him to his face that he wasn't interested in keeping whatever this was going, and that would have sucked even harder.

His throat felt tight when he called Zach twenty minutes later.

"I fucked up," was all he said.

Zach made a sad clicking noise. "What do you mean?" he asked, even though he had to know. Maybe not how exactly Hayes had fucked up, but he knew the end result. He'd known it when he'd warned Hayes a week ago. Told him he was playing with fire and he was going to get burned.

Hayes was scorched earth now, pain spreading through him in a nauseating wave of disbelief. Was Morgan really going to pretend they hadn't been anything to each other? Just a hookup? They'd both known it wasn't like that.

And yes, maybe it was essentially impossible to keep up a relationship when they played on opposite sides of the country, but if they both wanted this—if they both wanted each other, the way Hayes *knew* they did, deep down in a place where the truth shone like a fucking beacon—they could make it work. Anything had to be better than doing *this*.

"It's over," Hayes said dully.

Because in the end, he'd been right. It didn't really matter what had happened, what Hayes had or hadn't done, what Morgan had or hadn't done, only that the end result was that Hayes was alone and Morgan-less.

"Oh, Monty," Zach said sympathetically. "What did he say?"

Hayes swallowed. "Nothing. Just . . .nothing."

"What did *you* say?"

"Nothing." Hayes laughed, unable to deny how hysterical and unhinged he sounded. "Fucking nothing. I didn't think—I didn't think I *had* to say anything. I thought we were on the same page. No, we *were* on the same fucking page. We won, and he looked at me . . ." Hayes couldn't go on. It hurt too much, to think of how Morgan had looked at him yesterday. Like he hadn't even realized he was a key, but then he'd seen Hayes' lock, and it was magical the way they fit together.

On the ice, and off it, too.

"I saw," Zach said in a low voice. "I know what you two looked like yesterday. You didn't imagine it, Monty, I saw it."

"I know," Hayes snapped and then immediately regretted it. It wasn't Zach's fault that Hayes had been a monumental idiot.

That he'd trusted in the basic decency and good intentions of someone who self-professed to be an asshole.

"So you didn't try to stop him," Zach finally said in a quiet, resigned voice.

"He made it so I couldn't." Hayes froze. He was furious. Resigned. Hurting. And then suddenly, he felt something even worse, a feeling that had to be understanding.

Hayes hadn't even known what this thing between them would be like, and he had *some* kind of framework to fit into. Morgan clearly didn't, and had freaked out. It was hard to even be angry about that, even if he was.

Zach hummed in sympathy. "It sucks, Monty. No way around it. It really fucking sucks. When are you coming home?"

"In a few hours." He needed to pack. To get to the airport. Not discover sudden empathy for Morgan Reynolds.

"Good."

But it was inevitable. "I didn't even know what it was going to look like, between us," Hayes said, the words tumbling out. "How was he supposed to know?"

"He was supposed to not ghost you," Zach said sternly.

"I should've talked to him. I was just so tired last night—the win and the booze and then the sex—" He broke off. It felt weird telling Zach, who was his best friend, who he *trusted*, about him and Morgan. That should've been an indication from the first that Morgan was different.

"I just should've talked to him. I should've. Even if it felt unnecessary. Even if I was afraid." Hayes' voice broke. Because that was really what it had been. He'd been terrified if he confronted Morgan with the truth, that Morgan wouldn't pick him.

"You are not to blame here." Zach still sounded steely, tough. Like he was five seconds from kicking Morgan's ass. Like next time they faced each other on the ice, Zach was going after him.

Oh, *God*. They still had to play the Bandits one more time this season. Hayes didn't remember when, but suddenly he was scrambling for his phone, frantically searching for the Mavs' schedule.

"Shit," he exhaled hard. Six weeks from now. It could be worse. It could be better, too.

"What is it?" Zach asked, sounding less stern and more worried, now.

"We have to play them again. In six weeks."

Zach's sharp exhale said it all. Then he said, "You're gonna be fine, Monty. Six weeks. You're gonna be good in six weeks. Like it never happened."

Hayes wanted to believe that was true. Maybe in six weeks, Morgan would fade from his memory and from his heart, like he'd never wormed his way in in the first place.

CHAPTER 10

Six weeks later

Morgan had been through grueling stretches before. The end of the season always felt like a grind. Every Cup run felt like he was running on fumes, exhausted and worn to a shadow of his former self, at least until the puck dropped, and he found a new well of energy and drive—not just wanting to win, but *needing* to win.

This was not the same.

He was tired, but not sleeping. When he finally did manage to fall into a restless sleep, the dreams haunted him.

Hayes smiling, Hayes laughing, Hayes scoring unbelievable breakaway goals.

Hayes soft and tender next to him in bed.

But when Morgan woke up, he was always alone.

It was his own goddamn fault, so it was hard—no, *impossible*—to feel sorry for himself. He could only push through it, hoping that each morning when he woke up he felt less like death.

Less like calling up Hayes, fingers trembling as he gripped his phone, and begging for his forgiveness. For any pathetic crumb that Hayes felt like tossing his way.

Any time he felt like doing that, he called Danny instead.

Danny, who despite the fact that he had *never* liked that guy either on the ice or off it, had become a friend. "I'm only doing this," Danny had said the first time he'd called him, a week after Four Nations had ended, "because you are so fucking pathetic, and anyone with eyes can see you're dying inside, even on the ice."

Morgan had wanted to deny it, but he saw the emptiness in his gaze in the mirror. "Guess I got you in the divorce," he only said, hoping it came out light and funny, but instead it was flat and horrible, kind of how he felt inside.

"Yeah, and not because you deserve it. Hayes has people. That's because he's not a dick. You don't have anyone. So I guess you've got me."

Morgan had never told Danny how it had gone down. He hadn't needed to; Danny had guessed. Something about the inevitability of Morgan reverting to his natural asshole state and fucking it up, in the end. Morgan hadn't argued with this assessment because it was dangerously close to the truth.

They didn't usually talk about it. They usually talked about anything else but Hayes. Danny was always good for the latest hockey gossip, who was pissed at whom, who was on a scoring streak, even who was hooking up and who they were doing it with. But they never usually talked about Hayes.

Which was why Morgan couldn't even be pissed when Danny sounded completely fucking floored when he opened the conversation this morning with, "So, we're playing the Mavs tonight. I'm going to have to see Hayes."

"Shit, is it already that time?" Danny asked.

"Come on," Morgan said, rolling his eyes. "You knew this was coming up. You probably had it circled on your calendar. Bandits versus Mavs. The night when Morgan Reynolds totally—"

"Totally melts down, falls to his knees on the ice, and proposes hot gay marriage to Hayes Montgomery? White picket fence and cute yappy dog and sappy brunch dates and all?"

"I hate you," Morgan said between clenched teeth. He didn't want that. *He didn't want that.* Except that he did desperately want Hayes Montgomery. The white picket fence and dog and brunch dates appealed less, but in the face of having Hayes, he'd have accepted a hell of a lot worse.

"No, you hate that I'm right." Danny wasn't exactly sympathetic on these calls, which was why Morgan could tolerate them. If Danny had been *nice* about it, if he'd made empathetic noises about how much this sucked, Morgan couldn't have stomached it. He didn't deserve that kind of gentle treatment.

Morgan made a frustrated noise in the back of his throat. "How am I supposed to—just—you know? See him? Face off against him?"

"Pretend that he's someone else," Danny said promptly. "Oh! Pretend he's me."

"He's a lot better at faceoffs than you," Morgan grumbled.

"I'm so glad that love hasn't changed you; you're still a massive asshole."

"I'm . . . it's not like that," Morgan retorted weakly. Of course it was like that. Of course he loved Hayes. He'd known it the night of the championship game, when he'd looked at him and realized he never wanted to look at anything else.

When he'd have thrown it all away to never look away from him again.

Except that it turned out hockey was a bitch of a mistress.

"Bud, I thought you were depressed and pathetic, not stupid," Danny said. "So are you gonna go see him? Tell him how good you think he is at faceoffs?"

"Shut up," Morgan said.

"*Are* you?"

Morgan hadn't really thought about it. *Lie.* He'd thought about it basically nonstop the last six weeks, alternately dreading and counting down the days like a little kid with a birthday party. He wanted to just *see* Hayes, even if Hayes looked like he hated him. Even if Hayes looked at him like nothing had ever happened between them. It didn't matter, he just wanted to see him.

And *yes*, he wanted to talk to him. To apologize. To try to explain. To beg his forgiveness. To make things right.

To hug him and kiss him and touch him—*no*. Morgan cut that thought off hard and fast. If he showed up at Hayes' room and fucked him, it would destroy him.

But then, he was already halfway there. What was a little more destruction?

"I don't know," Morgan said slowly. "I shouldn't, right?"

"You ever want to get over this?"

"You know I do," Morgan bit off.

But that wasn't entirely true either, because as absolutely fucking miserable as he felt, *not* having that misery lodged tight under his breastbone, right up against his heart, meant that it was over. Really fucking over.

That actually sounded worse.

He didn't want to be the guy who'd fucked and left Hayes Montgomery. But he really didn't want to be the guy who just got over Hayes Montgomery like it was nothing, either.

"Then you gotta be strong, man," Danny advised.

That was a whole fucking trip. Danny *advising*.

"You're an idiot," Morgan said. "I can't believe I'm even considering taking suggestions from you."

"Hey, I'm a catch," Danny protested.

"Yeah, in that women catch you and then throw you back when they realize you're a fucking lunatic."

"And how is that any different than you and Hayes?"

It wasn't. Except he'd thrown *himself* away, because he'd already fucked up one marriage and that was when they'd lived together, in the same state, in the same *house*.

"Maybe if I see him, it'll be like closure or something."

"Yeah, okay, Dr. Phil," Danny said sarcastically. "That's not an excuse to like . . .fuck him one last time, or something?"

"Or something," Morgan admitted.

"Yeah, I'm going to go on record saying that's a bad idea. Don't try to see him after the game. They're probably not even staying in New York." Danny paused and when Morgan didn't answer, he made a frustrated noise. "Fuck, dude, don't tell me you figured out if they were sleeping over."

Morgan had already emailed their traveling coordinator, under the flimsiest pretext known to man, wondering if the Mavs would be staying over after the game or immediately leaving.

Turned out they weren't leaving until the next day, because they were only heading up to Buffalo. Morgan regretted sending the email the moment he'd gotten the answer he'd wanted.

"I . . .I might've asked." It was easier to lie to himself than to Danny. Morgan thought a therapist would probably have a field day with that particular realization.

"Dude," Danny said. "You cannot go see him."

"I should apologize. I *ghosted* him, Matt. I just fucking . . *.left*." Morgan hated the way his throat was choking him.

"And he's probably really fucking pissed at you for that. You want him to punch you in the face?"

If Hayes did, he'd *feel* something again. Something besides this all-consuming regret.

"Scratch that," Danny continued. "You'd probably love that, you sick fuck."

"I'm not that sick," Morgan protested.

"Not because you normally like anyone punching you in the face, but if that was all you could get from Monty? You'd take it, and you'd like it."

"I would not." It was embarrassing how right Danny was.

"Now that I'm thinking about it," Danny continued like he hadn't even spoken, "if you let him win all the faceoffs just because he's Hayes, and you're crazy about him—maybe just full-on crazy at this point—I'm flying to New York and personally beating some sense into you."

"I would not," Morgan repeated but firmer this time. Because yeah, if Morgan went to see him after the game, and Hayes was angry and justifiably punched him in the face, he'd probably take it. But he was not going to let Hayes win anything on the ice, just because he was Hayes.

"Okay, there's Morgan again. Remember that, okay? Remember who you are. You're Morgan fucking Reynolds."

He was. And Hayes was Hayes Montgomery.

It was important to remember that. Maybe if he did, if he reminded himself over and over again of their roles, not who they really were, underneath, but of the parts they played in the NHL, he could get through this game.

"Okay," Morgan said.

"Is that an *okay, you're an idiot and I'm going to see him anyway, fuck common sense,* or an *okay, yes, you're so right, Danny, thank you for always being a beacon of reason?*"

Morgan scoffed under his breath. "Neither, actually. I'm never gonna think you're a beacon of reason."

"That's fair. But still, don't go see him, Mo. Don't do it. Don't do *him,* either."

"That right there is why you're not a beacon of reason," Morgan retorted. But he knew no matter what he said, Danny had a point. If he went to see Hayes, even if he told himself he was only going to apologize, no matter how pissed Hayes was, they would probably end up doing something Morgan would only pretend to regret.

Something that would make this whole mess even messier.

"I mean it," Danny semi-threatened. "I'm gonna be watching. Put your game face on, Mo."

"Got it," Morgan said, and hoped to God that he actually could.

"If you ask me one more time if I'm okay, I'm going to break your nose," Hayes said to Zach under his breath during warmups.

"You're not looking over there."

"No shit," Hayes huffed out. "I'm not going to. I *can't*."

"You're not going to be able to pretend he doesn't exist the whole game. The faceoffs—"

"I'm going to pretend that it's seven weeks ago, and I barely even know the guy," Hayes said between clenched teeth.

It was the only way he thought he could get through this.

He'd woken up this morning in New York sick to his stomach. Yearning to see Morgan so badly he'd have traded everything for just one glimpse and also dreading that first look so epically it was a wonder he'd even managed to make it out of bed.

"That's smart. So smart," Zach said.

The problem is that Zach didn't sound convinced. Like he wasn't sure Hayes could actually pull it off, and maybe he couldn't.

"I'm trying to be reasonable about this," Hayes said, even though his heart was screaming out for the least reasonable course of action. "I'm expecting you're gonna be reasonable about this, too."

They'd touched on this subject a handful of times in the last week, Zach shrugging him off every single time.

But Hayes was not going to stand by and let Zach go after Morgan like he was his knight in shining armor and Hayes was a ruined maiden.

Hayes had gone into the hookup with his eyes wide open. Sure, the whole thing had gone sideways, but he'd known, *he'd known*, that it was probably not going to be some big epic love story.

He hadn't meant to fall in love; it had just happened. Almost by accident. That wasn't anyone's fault. Morgan didn't deserve to have his ass kicked on the ice just because Hayes hadn't been able to keep his feelings under control.

"I don't know what you want from me," Zach muttered, flicking a puck over to Hayes, who shot it back.

"I want a promise that you're not gonna do something stupid, just because you feel like you should."

"He hurt you," Zach said, jaw jutting out.

"Yeah, he did." Somehow it hurt even more to admit that was true. "But he never promised me anything—"

"He *ghosted* you, Monty."

Hayes pressed his lips together. "Yeah. He did. That was not his finest moment, for sure. But it was kind of inevitable he was going to freak out, wasn't it? I can't blame him for something that's absolutely in line with his personality."

"You sure fucking can," Zach argued.

"Zachy," Hayes said with resignation. "Please. It's going to be hard enough to face him out there. But if he knows how much he hurt me—if he *knew* . . . I don't know if I could handle it. Leave him alone, okay?"

Zach sighed. "Fine. He doesn't deserve it, but I'll leave his face unpunched."

"Think of it this way—losing this game will probably piss him off more than anything else, so let's win it, okay?"

Zach grinned at him. "Now you're talking like the Hayes I know. Go out and show him what he's missing, Monty."

Hayes repeated his pep talk over and over, as the Sentinels finished up their warmups and headed back into the locker room.

Then they were back out on the ice, the words a constant chant in the back of his head.

Show him what he's missing. Show him what he's missing. Show him what he's missing.

But the moment he skated over to the center of the ice and looked right at Morgan, right into those warm hazel eyes, it changed.

Show him how much you missed him.

But then Morgan looked right at him, but it was like he couldn't see him at all. His gaze was where it should be, but it was like he didn't see him. The hazel wasn't warm at all, but cold.

Like he was looking at a stranger.

Hayes' heart ached.

It was over. It was really fucking over.

He leaned in and let his focus engulf him. Hockey he could do; it was so much easier than feeling.

Hayes won the faceoff.

Scored a goal on his second shift by picking a puck right off Morgan's tape and taking it the other way.

Scored another goal before the end of the first period.

Each and every time they faced off, Morgan looked more and more pissed, but that could also be the score. First it was 2-0, then it was 3-0, and by the end of the second it was 5-0, and Morgan looked infuriated as he skated off.

But his gaze still slid right over Hayes like he didn't even exist.

A three point night already—two goals and an assist—and it was like he was still just another hockey player for Morgan.

That's all you're ever going to be to him, now.

Before tonight, Hayes had known that was probably true, but his heart was having trouble recalibrating. It wanted what it wanted, no matter how much of an unfeeling asshole Morgan had turned out to be. It couldn't forget those perfect intimate moments they'd shared; he'd been there and he couldn't believe they were a lie, even if it would've been so much easier.

He slunk into the locker room, collapsing on the bench in front of his stall, dragging his jersey off and grabbing a towel to wipe his face.

"You good?" Zach asked as he walked by.

"Yeah," Hayes said, because that was the only choice.

"Killin' it out there," Michael said, slumping down next to him.

"Yeah, dude, that last goal was freaking poetry," Zach agreed with him.

"We gotta stay focused no matter what the score is. Can't forget who we're playing," Hayes said, raising his voice. He wasn't the captain of the Mavericks, not yet, but he knew he was the heir apparent, and Gabriel, the captain of the Mavs, gave him an approving nod at his leadership.

"Hat trick watch," Zach murmured, nudging him as they headed down the tunnel for the third period.

"Don't," Hayes said sharply. Let him believe it was pure superstition. But it was something else entirely. The agony of knowing that no matter what he did out here, it wouldn't matter. Morgan still wouldn't *see* him.

The recalibration after having every insecure, every anxious, every unsure, part of him acknowledged and shared was brutal, but there was nothing Hayes could do but just accept it.

He couldn't force Morgan to love him.

He couldn't force Morgan to *accept* he loved him.

They met on the faceoff dot again. Hayes won that one, too, and flicked the pass behind him, to Michael, and they were off and running again. Setting up a play and then another play.

Hayes scored again and, since they were in New York, only a handful of hats rained down.

The game finally ended 6-1, and Hayes knew he should've felt better.

He did not feel better.

It turned out it didn't matter how many brilliant goals he scored, Morgan was never going to look at him like that again. It was over, and it was time for Hayes to accept it.

Since they were staying overnight before heading up to Buffalo, some of the guys tried to get up a group to go out and celebrate the win and Hayes' hat trick, but he had never felt less like celebrating.

Hayes shot Zach a look, but he probably didn't even have to. Zach spoke up for both of them, offhandedly mentioning this show they were watching.

They weren't watching anything particular right now, but clearly Zach knew he was not in the mood to go out.

They returned to the hotel. Zach nudged him in the elevator, but Hayes only shot him a tired smile. "You'll be okay," Zach said as they got off on their floor.

Would he? He imagined that yes, eventually, he'd find his way back to *okay* but right now he'd misplaced the map.

"Yeah," Hayes said, because that was easier than confessing the truth.

"Great game, though. Really. You were fucking amazing out there," Zach said. Hayes knew he was right, but he couldn't find it in himself to give a fuck.

"Thanks."

Zach paused as Hayes stopped at his door and dug into his pocket for his key card. "If you need anything . . ."

"I promise you. I'm going to order dinner, collapse into bed, and sleep until morning," Hayes said.

"Okay." Zach sounded worried, like he knew that was a lie, but at least he didn't call Hayes on it.

He opened the door and heard it shut behind him.

Then he was finally alone. Hayes felt his knees give out as he dropped to the edge of the bed.

He wanted to cry, because that might make him feel better—at least it might exorcise some of the nauseating pain rolling around inside him—but he couldn't.

For a long time he just sat there, looking at the room, but not seeing anything. It was the same kind of hotel room they always stayed in. He'd been in hundreds over the years. The ones he and Morgan had ended up sharing in Toronto had been just like this.

If he closed his eyes he could picture them. Could imagine that he was back there and everything was different.

But when he opened his eyes, he was still alone.

He'd just decided he should get up and get something to eat when a knock on the door echoed through the room.

Probably a teammate or a coach, wanting him to go out even though he'd made it clear he really didn't want to.

Groaning a little at how stiff he'd gotten, Hayes stood and after toeing his shoes off on the way to the door pulled it open.

He was wrong.

It was not a teammate or a coach.

Morgan stood in the doorway, a sheepish, ashamed look on his face, still in his suit, though he'd loosened his tie.

Hayes stared, shock tangling up his vocal cords.

"Hey," Morgan said, shifting uneasily from one foot to the other. "Can I . . . uh . . ."

Hayes wanted very badly to shut the door in his stupid fucking face, but he didn't.

"Sure," he said, which *really*? He couldn't believe he'd just agreed and stepped back so that Morgan could walk right in.

Hayes didn't know who he hated more right now: Morgan for daring to show his face tonight or himself, for just *letting* him.

"I wanted to talk to you," Morgan said earnestly.

"Oh, now you want to talk?" Hayes retorted.

Morgan's face fell. "Yeah. About that."

"About that?" Hayes prompted.

"I shouldn't have left like that. I . . .I sort of freaked out."

"Really," Hayes said, with faux-surprise.

"You're pissed." Morgan had the fucking nerve to sigh with resignation.

"Kinda think I've got the right here," Hayes said bluntly. There was a part of him who really wanted to fold like a soft hand of cards. To tell Morgan he understood. That he'd been afraid too. Terrified, really. What did this whole thing mean, anyway? They hadn't talked about it, hadn't known *how*. That wasn't just on Morgan; Hayes hadn't managed to find the words, either.

But then he thought about how Morgan had looked right through him only a few hours ago, like he wasn't the guy he'd shared his body and his bed and his heart with. Like he wasn't even Hayes Montgomery, who he'd shared ice and a line and a team with, less than two months ago. When he remembered that, it was easy to stay angry.

"You do. I fucked it up. I really fucked up." Morgan ran a hand through his hair.

"So that's why you're here? To apologize?"

"Yeah. Apologize. For sure. And to uh . . ." Morgan shot him a look, and suddenly his eyes weren't cold anymore. They were molten and full of heat.

Oh, he was serious, wasn't he? He really thought he could show up here, to Hayes' hotel room, after ghosting him for six weeks, and think Hayes was going to let him touch him?

"Are you fucking joking?"

Morgan had the nerve to take a step closer, like Hayes hadn't even said anything at all.

"Monty," he said, his voice low. "I *know* I fucked up. I'm sorry. I'm really sorry. I should've talked to you."

"So you're apologizing now cause you want me to suck your dick? Is that how it is?" Hayes demanded archly.

"What? No. I just . . .we're both here and you're here overnight and . . ."

"We should just fuck because we're both here? I don't think so." Hayes shook his head emphatically. Not just for Morgan's benefit but for his own. There was a very vocal part of him clamoring to just give in. It would be so good. Maybe he wouldn't get confused this time, because now, he knew exactly what the score was.

Whenever they saw each other, they'd hook up. His heart would stay out of it.

But no matter how much he might be tempted, Hayes couldn't, because his heart was already *in* it.

"You're telling me you really don't want to." Morgan sounded surprised, like of course Hayes should want him. Should want to take advantage of this opportunity.

Hayes rolled his eyes. "I don't want to. I'm not so pathetic I'm waiting around for whatever scraps you throw my way."

He was, actually, but the last thing Hayes wanted was for Morgan to realize that.

This whole thing was infuriating and humiliating enough as it was.

Morgan pulled himself up to his full height.

"I'm not trying to throw you a *scrap*," Morgan said, and he had the fucking nerve to sound offended. "I came to apologize."

It had been a shitty apology. Hayes wanted to tell him that. He'd only even bothered because he'd ghosted and nobody on the fucking planet, not even Hayes, who'd been freaking obsessed with Morgan, was going to get on their knees without one. Not necessarily because he really meant it.

"Yeah, you tried," Hayes said bluntly, crossing his arms over his chest. Wishing he'd never opened the door. Let Morgan stand outside and *rot*.

"I *did*." Morgan sounded almost desperate now, which should've felt better than it did, kind of like the hat trick he'd scored tonight. "I really feel bad about the way we left things—"

"The way *you* left things," Hayes corrected.

"Why are you being so pissy? What happened to the Hayes who apologized every other sentence?"

"You killed him off," Hayes retorted. "He's dead."

"Oh come on," Morgan said.

"No, you don't get to show up here and decide that you want me when it was clear you didn't." Righteous anger was bubbling inside him now. Morgan had hurt him, had hurt him over and over, the last six weeks, every moment of silence a knife to the gut, and now he just wanted to say he was sorry and that made it all okay? Fuck no.

"I was . . .fuck, baby, you know this is a lot for me. I'm . . ."

"Didn't seem a lot to you when we were doing it." Hayes was not going to listen. If he listened, he might be tempted to believe Morgan. Maybe he really had freaked out; maybe fear really had gotten the better of him.

"It was easy, you were there—"

But Hayes didn't want to hear it. "No. I was there that morning too. I was right fucking there, Morgan, and you just *left*. I was there at breakfast, when you wouldn't even look at me. I was there, the whole goddamn time, and you just walked away like it was nothing." He hated how his voice broke at the end. "Like I was nothing."

Morgan froze. "No, no, *no*, baby, you're not nothing, you're . . ." But he didn't finish the sentence. Like he *couldn't*.

And maybe Hayes might've listened, might've *really* listened, if he had. But he didn't.

He left it unsaid. Again.

"I know I'm not nothing," Hayes said in a hard voice. "I proved it tonight. And I'll prove it to you over and over again. I'm never going to stop. *Never*."

Morgan looked broken. Like Hayes had broken him. And that felt fair. Because he'd broken Hayes first.

"Baby—"

"Don't you fucking call me that. Not ever again," Hayes spit out. Anger was easier than bitter disappointment. Than realizing the man he'd thought Morgan was had never really existed. Had only been a figment of his imagination.

Morgan looked at him, really looked at him, and there was that warmth, again, but this time it was mixed with devastation. Even worse: it was a devastation Hayes recognized.

And maybe, *maybe*, there was still that Morgan inside him, the one that Hayes' heart had brushed up against and just *known*, but what was the point if Morgan fought against it so hard? If they spent eight to ten months apart every year? Hayes would never even have a chance to find that Morgan again, if he really did exist.

"So that's it, then?" Morgan asked quietly.

"That's it," Hayes said. He dug his fingernails into his palm so he wouldn't reach for Morgan at the last moment, as he turned away, towards the door.

"Alright," Morgan said, and a moment later, the door shut behind him.

Later, so much later, years and years later, Hayes couldn't help but wonder what would've happened if he'd actually let himself reach out for him.

If he hadn't been so full of bitter indignation and humiliation at being ignored.

If they hadn't played for teams on the opposite coasts.

But Hayes never knew the answer, because that was the last time Morgan ever really looked at him.

Every game for the two years after that—before Morgan retired—he didn't talk to Hayes. Didn't look at him. When he had no choice, he stared right through him like he didn't exist.

Maybe he didn't, Hayes would think. Maybe that Hayes, the one who had loved Morgan and then lost him, had never been real to begin with.

But if that was true, Hayes knew he'd have hurt a hell of a lot less.

CHAPTER 11

Six years later

Morgan knew he needed to relax, but if he was being honest with himself, relaxing was the last thing he was going to be doing during the next three hours.

Hyperventilating? Much more likely. And not just because Finn was in goal, either, about to warm up for his first NHL start, but because in a few minutes, Hayes was going to be right there on the ice, skating around like it was nothing, like this was just another game and Morgan wasn't up in the stands, currently losing his goddamn mind.

"Did you tell him about the way he's got to watch the loose puck around the net? The Pens are aggressive on that shit, and if Crosby—"

"You need to take a fucking breath," Jacob muttered next to him.

He wouldn't say that he and Jacob were *friends* now. He wasn't sure what he'd call them these days. Friendly acquaintances? Two guys who happened to both care about his son?

Two ex-hockey players both struggling with the way the game had moved on without them?

Regardless of what he called him, he and Jacob were . . . well, not a *thing*—that was Jacob and Finn, their committed relationship a life swerve that Morgan had *not* seen coming—but some kind of odd couple.

The first time they'd sat together at an AHL game, Danny had texted him, **Sitting next to Braun? You've officially lost what was left of your mind.**

Danny still thought he was funny, and he still wasn't.

"Fuck you," Morgan retorted. "This is important! He needs to know this."

You couldn't take Crosby, even thirty-seven-year-old Crosby, lying down.

"Finn knows this," Jacob said dryly. "I think if a puck and Sidney Crosby get near the net, he's going to be paying attention."

Ugh. Why had his son decided *this guy* was *the* guy?

It seemed like this was a Reynolds type of emotional shortcoming, because it wasn't like Morgan had done any better picking for himself.

Not that Hayes wasn't absolutely fucking perfect. He was. Every inch of him was stunning, inside and out. Hot as fuck. Charming. Fucking fantastic at hockey. A guy who had seemed, initially, like he'd been built with Morgan in mind. Except for one tiny, niggling detail: Morgan loved him utterly, completely, ridiculously, and Hayes had moved on.

Morgan wanted to hold it against him, but he couldn't even manage *that*.

He'd been such an asshole. Such a stupid, afraid, monumentally blind asshole it was impossible to even resent the guy for kicking him out and then ignoring him for the next six years.

"It's not that I don't think he's capable, right? Or that he doesn't know how to do this, but I just . . ." Between Finn's first start and the fact that Hayes was Finn's captain now, Morgan was definitely losing it. Evidence for the bench: confessing these sort of emotional vulnerabilities to *Braun*.

"You're just going out of your mind?" Jacob asked, the corner of his mouth tilting up, like Morgan's pain was funny.

And maybe it was, in a sort of ironic, *God-can-you-believe-cool-collected-calm-Morgan-Reynolds-is-like-this-now* kind of way.

"Don't tell me you're not." Morgan had seen too many of his own fears and hopes reflected in Jacob's eyes. He'd hate the guy more, but there was no question he genuinely cared a lot about Finn.

"Oh, I am," Jacob said with a wry chuckle as punctuation.

"Doesn't seem like it," Morgan said. Which was a total lie, but it wasn't like he could do a total one-eighty and decide that Jacob was great. At least to his face.

"That's because you're emoting enough for both of us right now," Jacob joked.

Ugh, he was probably right. But then Jacob didn't know about the Hayes half of Morgan's current meltdown.

He'd known this day was coming sooner rather than later. The Sentinels needed a good goalie. Finn was a good goalie. From the moment they'd drafted him four years ago, this had been in the cards.

Morgan had railed against this inevitability in his mind—and to Danny—more than he wanted to admit.

"Also," Jacob continued, "it turns out being amused by your total meltdown is a good distraction from my own anxiety."

Ugh. This guy, Finn, really?

Morgan considered saying that out loud, not for the first time, either. But he didn't, if only because he knew Jacob loved Finn and also because it was impossible to deny Jacob's mentorship and coaching was a big part of the reason Finn was starting in the Sentinels' goal tonight.

"I stayed up all night watching game tape." *Half of it wasn't even the Pens, it was the Sentinels, and if I jerked off to one of Hayes' pretty goals, nobody knows but me and my couch.*

"Yeah, that's really obvious," Jacob said.

Morgan didn't need to take this abuse. He shoved an elbow into Jacob's side, but Jacob only yelped and then shot him a grin. Like they were *actually* friends.

"What? You're being an unsupportive asshole," Morgan retorted.

"Sucks, doesn't it?" Jacob said unrepentantly.

Morgan had so many issues with Braun it was hard to know where to start, but it always began with Jacob reading him a little too well.

He shoved another elbow into Jacob's side, but he just looked amused.

"I'm supportive," Morgan defended himself. "I'm even wearing his sweater! I haven't worn one since—" He stopped abruptly. Frankly, the whole thing felt weird as hell, the Sentinels' logo splashed across his chest, not only because it wasn't the Bandits colors he'd worn his entire career, but because they were Hayes' colors. Like an outward manifestation of the hold Hayes still had on him. It said *Reynolds* on the back and not *Montgomery*, but it felt at least a little of the way Morgan had always thought it might, if he ever got lucky enough to publicly claim Hayes as his.

Jacob looked over at him and yeah, he got it, too.

Maybe not *all* of it, but most of it. Jacob couldn't get the Hayes' part, because he didn't *know* about Hayes. Or rather, he knew there'd been someone Hayes-shaped in Morgan's past, but not that it was Hayes Montgomery.

Thank God for small miracles. Danny knowing about Hayes was bad enough.

"It's gonna mean a lot to Finn that you're wearing it," Jacob said gently.

"And he's gonna laugh his ass off that we're sitting here, like fucking twins in a Sears photoshoot," Morgan grumbled.

Jacob grinned. Like he didn't even mind that, and this was why Morgan had semi-gracefully accepted Jacob's place in Finn's life. Because anyone who was good for Finn, who loved Finn like this, was worth something, at least.

"Yeah, probably." Jacob glanced over at him. "Don't you dare shove that elbow into me again. I *will* kick your ass if you do."

Like he could. *Ha.*

"No, you won't," Morgan said confidently. He paused. Still wanting to prove how committed he was to Finn and his future. Without being the worst version of himself, because he'd done that version enough and he was trying to be better. "Did I tell you I'm cutting back on some of my ESPN commitments?"

"No," Jacob said. Not sounding like he was about to throw a parade for Morgan, which . . .*unfair*. He was fucking trying, here.

He'd always imagined that when Finn eventually joined the Sentinels, he'd bury himself in New York and never leave, because that meant he'd never come face-to-face with what he'd lost.

But when it had finally happened, he'd been so proud and desperately wanting to be properly supportive for Finn—and miraculously Finn had actually *wanted* him around—that he'd buried all his misgivings and essentially moved to Tampa.

"Well, I am. I want to be present for this, for Finn. It feels important, you know? I'm still doing segments, but they said I can do those from my rental house."

"Good. Do more of those," Jacob retorted, and then laughed, like a total asshole, at the grimace Morgan hadn't been able to hold back.

"For the hundredth time, I don't want to hear about your sex life," Morgan said.

"Then stop interfering in it." Jacob barely blinked when Morgan shoved another elbow into his side.

"Do you . . .should I . . ." Morgan trailed off, suddenly feeling like he might vomit.

"Spit it out, Reynolds." Of course Braun didn't sound sympathetic.

"Should I not have come?" He'd worried if he was overstepping. If he was actually a distraction, a *drawback* even. More than once. Or a hundred times. No matter how many times Finn smiled at him and said, *I'm so glad you're here, Dad.*

"To this game? I don't think Finn would've ever forgiven you for missing it," Jacob joked.

"No, *no*. I mean . . .should I not have come down here? Rented the house?" It hadn't been easy. And not for the reasons everyone assumed.

Danny was the only one who knew why it would really suck for Morgan to basically move to Tampa. And he'd called him on it a bunch of times. Danny gave him plenty of shit for not being over Hayes, six years later, but it was when he got careful and kind that Morgan realized he was actually kind of pathetic.

Danny had been really mindful about the whole Tampa thing, even for Danny.

"Oh, well, no the house rental thing was a good idea. You'd have *really* cramped our style if you'd insisted on moving in," Jacob said.

Morgan made a face. Like he was ever going to live under the same roof as his son and *Jacob Braun*. That was not happening. There were limits. "I was never going to do that."

"Thank God for that." At least he and Jacob were on the same page about that. "But seriously, I think it's good you're here. Finn respects you a lot, and you give him a good perspective, and well . . .this is a big time in his life. You've been there, too. You get it."

"So do you," Morgan said, and yeah, this was the biggest reason he could stomach Jacob these days. He looked at him and occasionally saw the same pain in his eyes. It was hard to hate someone who was going through the same shit you were.

"Yeah, I'm his boyfriend. But you're his father," Jacob said. "It's okay that you're here. I promise. If it hadn't been, you'd have known."

For a second Morgan assumed Jacob was saying *he'd* have told Morgan to fuck off, but then he realized that *no*, Jacob meant Finn would be the one saying it.

His son was growing up, becoming a full-fledged adult with a backbone, and Morgan had never been prouder. Even when he ended up on the shit end of the stick. If he did, it was probably because he at least *partially* deserved it.

Kind of like the last six years of Hayes' cold shoulder.

"Good." Morgan looked out on the ice. Realized, as the lights went down, that the warmup was starting. Which meant the moment he'd been looking forward to and dreading in equal measures was about to happen.

Finn's rookie lap.

"Oh, look, it's . . .uh . . .it's starting."

When he'd been a rookie, this hadn't been a thing, but now it was a beloved tradition. He'd known this was coming, and he hadn't been sure he could get through it without embarrassing himself.

"Did you bring—" Jacob asked, voice sounding suddenly rough.

Morgan dug the item in question out of his pocket. He'd known *he'd* need them, but he hadn't realized Jacob would too. That had been a stupid assumption. The way they loved Finn was very different, but they both loved him.

He smacked the tissues into Jacob's hand. "Here," he said through a tight throat as Finn stepped onto the ice.

"Thanks," Jacob muttered.

Braun might not be the son-in-law he'd imagined having, but the truth was, Morgan realized as he and Jacob both tried to discreetly wipe the tears out of their eyes, he wasn't half-bad.

Two periods later, Morgan was re-thinking his casual acceptance of Jacob.

"God, Monty's on fire tonight," Jacob said, tilting the bottle of beer towards his mouth. "Nice he's giving Finn some great offensive support."

Yeah, he sure was. The score was 5-1, Sentinels, and Finn had played well, but his biggest advantage was how aggressive Hayes and the Sentinels' offense had been all night.

Morgan told himself not to tense because it would make it all way too obvious, but he was out of practice with Hayes Montgomery sneak attacks. When he had to talk about him on a segment, he almost always knew in advance. Could practice saying his name normally, like his whole heart wasn't yearning for something it hadn't figured out yet—or ever—that it couldn't have.

"Yeah," he said uselessly. The trick he'd used every time he'd faced Hayes on the ice did not work with Hayes still playing and him in the stands. He couldn't just pretend he didn't exist. Couldn't look right through him like he wasn't there at all. Like he was just any other player on the ice, even though he very much was *not*.

He definitely couldn't do it when Jacob kept insisting on bringing him up.

Jacob looked over at him. "Yeah? That's all you have to say? You're the biggest fucking yapper in the universe when it comes to hockey, and all you have to say about Montgomery's four point night is *yeah*?"

Morgan swallowed hard. "Um yeah. He's good." *So fucking brilliant I can't even look at him.*

Jacob's jaw dropped. "Are you joking?"

"What? No?" Morgan tried very hard not to sound defensive, but he was pretty sure he failed.

"Don't tell me you have a problem with him too," Jacob said. "From what I remember at Four Nations, you two were all buddy-buddy."

Shit. Fuck. *Abort, abort.*

"No, no problem," Morgan said.

"Why are you so weird about him then?"

"I'm not," Morgan argued valiantly. "He's a good hockey player—a great hockey player. And uh . . .he's playing great. So not that surprising? Not much to say?"

Jacob shot him a look like he was nuts and for a single heart-stopping moment, Morgan was afraid that he'd given himself away. Jacob knew too much already. That there'd been a guy, *once*, and he'd been a hockey player and that it hadn't ended well. He could *not* be allowed to put together the correct theory that the guy was Hayes. Jacob would never let him hear the end of it, and then he'd probably push him to tell Finn, and well, fuck that noise. Morgan was not ever doing that. Not when he was already so viscerally aware of how pathetic he was.

"The craziest part of that argument is it's actually believable that you'd think that." Jacob shook his head. "You tell him that after he scored that goal at Four Nations?"

No, he had not.

He'd said lots of other things—and yet nothing that meant Hayes was still in Morgan's life—but not that. Morgan might be an asshole, but he wasn't a total fucking dick.

What did it say about him that Jacob actually believed he might pull that kind of move?

He pulled his phone out of his pocket. Tilted it away from Jacob's prying eyes. Sent Danny a text. **This is worse than I thought it would be.**

He couldn't remember if Danny had a game tonight, but if he did, he'd get it after. That might actually be better. Danny coming in on the tail end of his meltdown was always better than witnessing the whole ugly thing.

But no dice. Danny's response came through instantly. **Yeah, I'm watching the game. Figured you were freaking out. Finn's playing great. Then there's Monty, putting on a show, just for you!!!!**

Morgan wanted to yell at him, but yelling was not very effective over text. Honestly, when it came to Danny, yelling was not very effective, *period*.

He's not doing it for me.

Lie to yourself if you want, but don't fucking lie to me, Mo!!!

"Who's that?" Jacob asked.

"Uh, Danny," Morgan said, slipping his phone back into his pocket as Hayes' line headed back onto the ice. "Matt Daniels."

"Didn't know you played with him," Jacob said.

"I didn't, actually. He signed with the Bandits the season after I retired. But he's a friend," Morgan said.

Morgan was not going to go into the details of when and why. That all edged too close to the truth of what had happened at Four Nations, and as much as Morgan wanted Braun to be stupid and oblivious, he definitely wasn't.

"Finn really did this," Jacob said a minute later, thankfully changing the subject, tone of voice warm and proud. Full of love.

"Never doubted for a minute."

Jacob shot him a commiserating smile. "Me neither. Just really fucking proud of him."

Morgan had worried, but not doubted. Any goalie could have a bad game, and the Penguins could still bring it. He'd just wanted this one game, his *first*, to go right for Finn. Set him up on the right trajectory.

But as time ticked down, it seemed that a Penguins resurgence, even with Crosby on the ice, wasn't going to be happening.

The Pens pulled their goalie with two and a half minutes left, which considering they were down four goals seemed to be an exercise in pointlessness to Morgan, but Hayes went over the boards, along with the penalty kill, and they provided Finn the extra boost of defensive power they needed to keep the four goal lead.

Morgan was the first on his feet in their suite, cheering as the game clock hit zero, Jacob half a second behind him.

Jacob persuaded him to come to the locker room to congratulate Finn, despite the fact that he had two very compelling reasons not to go: 1) Morgan knew he pulled attention and he didn't want to distract in any way from Finn, not tonight and 2) even the concept of seeing Hayes in his natural habitat, gear half-on, half-off, sweaty hair and victory smile on his face, made him break into a cold—or maybe a hot—sweat.

But somehow, despite everything, Morgan found himself trailing behind Jacob as they walked into the locker room.

Luckily, Finn's locker was at the far end, next to the other goalie, and with the media swarmed around Hayes' stall, it was easy enough to avoid the second problem.

As for the first, Finn's face lit up even more when he and Jacob approached.

Morgan wasn't stupid; he knew that smile was a solid seventy-five percent for Jacob, and only twenty-five for him, but Morgan didn't mind that. There'd been a time when he wouldn't have even gotten five percent of Finn's joy and he'd take what he could get.

"You absolutely killed it out there," Jacob said as Finn flung himself into his arms.

"Thanks," Finn mumbled into Jacob's shoulder. Then he glanced over at Morgan.

"Great job," Morgan said, and to his surprise, Finn turned to him and gave him a tight hug too.

"I couldn't be prouder," he added when Finn let go.

Finn's smile only grew. "It was a great game. Helps to have such great guys to play with."

Jacob started rhapsodizing about the Sentinels' defense and even their offense being defensive, most of which seemed to have something to do with Hayes, and Morgan tuned it out, because it was already hard enough being in this room. Knowing Hayes was only just over there, a dozen feet away. Morgan could hear the lilt of his voice, and the happiness in it. He sounded a lot pleased about how the game had gone, and frankly, Morgan couldn't be angry at him for that.

It was the kind of NHL debut he'd wanted so much for Finn.

His distraction was why, when Jacob nudged him a minute later, he had no idea what he'd just been volunteered for.

"We're heading out in a bit," Finn said to him.

Morgan felt like he'd missed something vital. "Heading out where?"

Finn grinned. "Celebratory drinks, what else? You're both coming."

Panic raced up Morgan's spine. "Oh, no," he said with an awkward shrug. "Jacob yeah, he should. He's your boyfriend. I'm just—"

"Just my dad," Finn said softly, so proud and happy when the opposite had been true for so fucking long. How was Morgan supposed to say no to that?

He couldn't.

Even if it meant that an hour later, he was sitting in a dark bar, music pulsing around them, as he tried his best to avoid Hayes.

Hayes was doing his captainly duty, rotating himself through the various knots of players and their partners, which meant that at some point, the chances of him stopping by their open booth to personally congratulate Finn was high.

"You're being weird, even for you," Jacob said, nudging Morgan.

What he *was* doing was tracking Hayes like he was a starving hunter and Hayes was a particularly tasty morsel of an apex predator.

Not because he wanted him. Nope. No way. Morgan just wanted to avoid him.

Danny would have told him he was being stupid, and that was probably true, but it was easier to be stupid than to look right at Hayes and try to figure out, six years after everything had gone to shit, what the fuck he should say to him.

"I'm gonna go to the bathroom," Morgan said, ignoring Jacob's comment and instead eyeing how Hayes had now arrived at the next booth.

He could slip out, take a piss, grab another beer at the bar, and by the time he was done, Hayes would have done his duty and left.

It all worked perfectly, until he was washing his hands at the sink, staring at his reflection, at the way his hair had gotten a little long, curling over his ears, and the wrinkles he was trying to pretend didn't exist, when the door opened.

Everything inside Morgan froze.

Hayes met his eyes in the mirror.

It had been six long years, but he didn't look older. Hair perfect. Face perfect. Green eyes widening as he stared at Morgan.

Fuck my life.

Hayes swallowed once and then twice. Wondered wildly how he could have made such a stupid mistake when he'd been so careful all night.

He'd been tracking Morgan as he'd made his way around the bar, sharing drinks with his teammates and congratulating them on a great game, timing his arrival at the table where he'd been sitting with Finn and Jacob exactly when Morgan slid out, holding his empty glass like he needed a refill.

But no. He hadn't headed to the bar for a fresh beer.

He'd come to the bathroom, and so had Hayes.

You knew this was going to happen eventually.

Hayes just hadn't been ready for it. Maybe it was delusional to think he would have *ever* been ready.

His heart ached, a steady, pervasive hurt that never seemed to go away, no matter what.

He'd told Zach last summer he was working on moving on, not using someone else as a distraction or to make it easier, but instead focusing on learning how to be happy just being Hayes Montgomery.

Annoyingly, he'd have told anyone who cared to listen that he'd done it. That he *was* happy just being Hayes.

But now, he wasn't sure. Not with Morgan's hazel eyes staring at him, wide and shocked and *affected*.

The total fucking opposite of the blank-eyed stare Hayes had gotten every time they'd played each other after.

This time Morgan's stare wasn't sliding over him like he didn't even recognize him. The opposite, in fact.

Hayes cleared his throat. "Hey."

Morgan blinked hard, like he was astonished Hayes had said anything to him. "Uh. Hey."

Hayes gave himself a brief pep talk consisting of *you can do this* and *you have to fucking do this.*

"Finn had a great game."

"Yeah." Morgan didn't seem capable of more than single words, which . . .Hayes *got* that, a little too well. But then he'd also seemed perfectly fine leaving the morning after and ghosting Hayes and then barely eking out an apology before disappearing again for the next six fucking years.

So maybe single words were all he was capable of, when it came to Hayes. Like that other Morgan, the one who'd opened up to Hayes, like deep down, they were made from the exact same material, had been the mirage.

Hayes steeled himself. Decided that he didn't care if he was an asshole, because Morgan was a self-professed asshole *and* he'd been the asshole first.

"You're not going to hang around Finn all the time, are you?"

Morgan had the nerve to look both worried and guilty. Picking at Hayes' heartstrings like it was his new fucking job.

"No," Morgan said.

"He's gonna be a great goalie. Deserves more light than your shadow provides."

Morgan opened his mouth and then snapped it shut, fingers tightening on the edge of the sink, knuckles going white.

"Just saying," Hayes said, shrugging. "I'm his captain now. I gotta look out for him."

"I didn't expect that you wearing the C would also turn you into a dick," Morgan drawled. And okay, turned out he *was* capable of more than one word answers.

Hayes regretted even engaging. He should have left it alone. Left Morgan alone. Should have left it at *Hey*.

Shouldn't have gone out of his way to have a four point night, too. He'd told himself it was for the Sentinels, but was it really? He'd known Morgan was out there, watching, and as much as he hated to admit it, maybe that had driven him harder than normal.

"Watching out for Finn isn't being a dick," Hayes said, far too aware how bitchy he sounded now. Zach had always told him he shouldn't end up a bitchy, bitter gay, but if he had, could anyone blame him?

"Well, tell *him* that, then, cause I'm only here because he asked me to be." Morgan let go of the sink and took a step closer. Hayes told himself to move back, too, but his limbs suddenly didn't seem to work. "What the fuck, Monty? You're really not like this."

"You don't know what I'm like anymore," Hayes argued. *You haven't been around to see what the C did to me.*

Actually, he thought it had grounded him and turned him into a better, more generous player. No way it wasn't a good thing, a *great* thing. It hadn't turned him into a dick.

That had been Morgan.

But if he said that, Morgan would know how much he'd hurt him, how much he was *still* hurting him, and that was intolerable.

Morgan took a deep breath and actually had the nerve to look vaguely upset that he hadn't been around. When he'd been the one to leave in Toronto! To ghost *Hayes*.

"No," he said, softly. "I don't know what you're like anymore."

"And let's keep it that way," Hayes said brusquely. He walked over to the urinal. Had a momentary loss of feeling in his toes as he unzipped and pulled his dick out. He'd really had to pee before this moment, but now he was suddenly terrified that he'd freeze up, just because Morgan was staring at him.

Morgan waited silently until he was done, moving to the side, next to the sink, so Hayes could wash his hands without being in any danger of them touching.

For a single hysterical moment, Hayes considered not just mentioning this out loud, but *thanking Morgan*. Luckily, he came to his senses before he actually said it out loud.

He shook the water off his hands, turned to look for the paper towel dispenser, but of course Morgan was between him and it.

Morgan still didn't say anything, just grabbed one and held it out for Hayes to take.

"You're my son's captain," Morgan said quietly. "You can hate me. But don't punish him for the crime of having the wrong last name, okay?"

"I don't—I *wouldn't*—" Hayes broke off abruptly as he snatched the paper towel and dried his hands. Compressed it into a tight ball in his palm.

"No, of course you wouldn't. You'd never do that." Morgan sighed, his gaze sliding away from him again. Not the same cold, calculated disassociation as during all those faceoffs post-fling, but *different*. Hayes wanted to believe it was because looking right at him sucked too much. Reminded him of too many things he wanted to forget, just like Hayes.

But there was no evidence whatsoever, except this single moment, that Morgan had spent the last six years thinking about him and regretting, just like Hayes, how it had ended between them.

"I wouldn't," Hayes repeated. Didn't promise, but hoped that Morgan could hear the vow in his voice. "I like Finn a lot. He's a great guy and a great hockey player."

"I'd say thank you, but not sure I had much to do with either of those," Morgan said.

This was so ridiculous, Hayes could only stare at him in utter disbelief. "You? Being modest? What the fuck, Mo?"

Morgan chuckled. "Can't say I didn't try to fuck it up, like everything else. But I'm trying." His eyes met Hayes' and for a solid moment, Hayes was sure he was going to say something else. Like, *tell me it's not too late to try with you, too.*

But he didn't. Of course he didn't. They weren't practicing that kind of idiocy still. At least Hayes wasn't.

"All we can do," Hayes said, trying for a light, casual tone, and he wasn't surprised he failed utterly at it, because one thing they had never been was light or casual.

Morgan nodded once. "See you around," he said, and then he was gone, the door swinging shut behind him.

Hayes let out a shaky breath and leaned against the sink, trying to steady his suddenly wobbly knees.

He'd tried for so long and so hard to exorcise him, to forcibly remove Morgan from his brain and his heart, but the truth was, there was no getting rid of him. Morgan was a fact of his life, same as being drafted first overall.

Once, he'd told Morgan he thought he'd be able to put that baggage down, someday. But now, a few years further down the road, he was beginning to see why Morgan had thought that was impossible.

CHAPTER 12

Hayes' agent, Bartholemew Smith III, was a jerk, but he was *Hayes'* jerk. It was the only reason he'd kept Barty around as long as he had. And, because it was impossible to deny that the guy was the best agent in the NHL.

That didn't mean he hadn't worked Hayes' last nerve more than once.

Or that he wasn't working it now.

"Come on," Barty wheedled. "Don't tell me this isn't the fucking life."

Hayes looked around, and it was hard not to be impressed—they *were* on a fucking boat, a boat possibly big enough to be characterized as a yacht, even—but there was no way in hell he was going to give Barty the satisfaction.

"It's the life. Good to know my blood and sweat bought this for you," Hayes retorted.

Barty rolled his eyes, his blond curls ruffling in the breeze, Ray-Bans covering his eyes. You could take the guy out of Massachusetts but you could never fully exorcise the Masshole out of the man.

"Bit egotistical to think it was *just* your blood and sweat," Barty said. "It was lots of guys' blood and sweat. But I'm glad you brought that up, because we should talk about your contract."

"Do we have to?" Hayes took a sip of his virgin mojito. He tried not to drink much during the season, though every time he saw his agent, he was reminded of why that was a really shitty idea.

And every time he thought about running into Morgan again? Even shittier.

"It's what you pay me for," Barty said pragmatically. "We've opened negotiations. You want the dirty details or just the summary?"

"God, just the summary." He knew the Sentinels had every intention of signing him again. They wouldn't have given him the C three years ago if they didn't want him to stick around. If he was lucky—and he was pretty sure he'd done what he needed to do to make his own luck these days—he'd play out the rest of his career here in Tampa.

But the details, those were why he had Barty.

"Okay, they're low-balling me, but that's to be expected," Barty said, not sounding overly concerned as he sipped his pretentious espresso martini.

"Isn't that how it always works?" Hayes asked.

Barty shrugged. "Yes and no. They wouldn't want to give away that they want you wrapped up, but obviously they do. But I didn't expect them to start so low."

A frisson of worry shimmered in his stomach. Hayes set down his drink. "Is that concerning?"

"Not necessarily. You want to win another Cup. So do they. That takes money. Cap space. Draft capital."

"Right." Hayes knew that, which was why he'd never cared if he was the highest-paid player or whatever. He'd take a little less, to keep playing for a contender.

"But I didn't expect them to start this low. It's fine. They're going to come up. They're going to throw in sweeteners. Did you know you're top five in jersey sales?"

Hayes shook his head. "Not bad for a gay guy not from Canada," he said, chuckling self-deprecatingly.

"I'm not trying to freak you out," Barty said, which was *always* what he said when the news was not good, "but if things continue this direction, we may need to test out free agency."

"Isn't that months away?" Hayes tried to keep the panic out of his voice. "The season just started! It's not even November yet."

"I know," Barty soothed.

"I thought you told me it was going to be fine. Last time we talked, you said, *it's gonna be just fine, Monty. They want you. We're gonna keep you here.* And now all of a sudden I have to go on the open market?"

"It's gonna be fine. I expect they'll see reason. This is why you pay me. But I thought you should know," Barty said calmly.

Hayes wanted to be pissed off, but it wasn't Barty's fault. This wasn't exactly a "dirty detail."

"I'm glad you told me." He was trying to be diplomatic, but it wasn't easy. Didn't he have enough on his plate with a captainship and a rookie goalie and a rookie goalie's father that he couldn't seem to avoid?

"No, you want to yell at me," Barty said knowingly, laughing now like this whole thing was actually funny.

Hayes shot him a faux-glare as he stood up, walking over to the deck railing. "Kinda, yeah."

"Listen. I'm gonna do my job, you do your job." Barty paused and actually set his drink down and got to his feet, joining Hayes at the railing. "And you're already doing it, man. You keep these kind of numbers up, they're going to be slobbering all over themselves to re-sign you."

Hayes didn't tell Barty that his hot start to the season probably wasn't sustainable because Barty had been doing this long enough he knew it wasn't. But leading the league in points and being top three in goals sure didn't hurt.

"Okay," Hayes said, trying to calm the panic that was bubbling away inside him.

Barty patted him on the shoulder. "There *is* something else we can do."

Hayes was immediately suspicious. "What is it?"

"Own the court of opinion."

Yeah, he was really going to hate whatever came out of Barty's mouth next. "How?"

"As I'm sure you know, your new goalie's dad is on ESPN practically every other day. We should get him on your side."

Yep. Hayes pretty much fucking hated it. "No," he said flatly.

"Are you joking? You have a solid fucking gold opportunity to have *the* biggest hockey player in the last few decades talking you up, telling everyone how you've taken Finn under your wing, how good of a captain you are, how well you lead this team, and you're not going to take it?"

Common wisdom said you were supposed to tell your agent everything—all your dirty secrets, all the shit you'd done that you wanted to stay under wraps, every mistake you'd made, starting at the age of twelve. Every stupid tweet. Every scrap you'd ever gotten into with a teammate.

There wasn't much dirty laundry in Hayes' closet. With the exception of the Morgan Reynolds affair. And that was, of course, the one thing he'd never told Barty about.

"This is non-negotiable," Hayes said in a tight voice. "No Morgan Reynolds."

At the time, and directly after, it had hurt so much, been so humiliating and painful that Hayes hadn't been sure he could even talk about it. By the time he thought he might have some objective space from the whole mess, it hadn't made any sense to tell Barty. It was over, it was *so* over.

Even when fate had decided it hated him and Finn had been drafted by the Sentinels, Hayes had known it was years before he'd possibly end up on a team with the kid. And even that was hardly a guarantee.

Barty stared. "Why the fuck not? Hayes, I don't have to tell you—"

"You don't have to tell me," Hayes interrupted. "But we're not doing it." Hayes could tolerate a lot of things—and he had a feeling that this season would probably test the limit—but he couldn't stomach asking Morgan to talk him up to the press.

"What's your issue with Reynolds? I thought all first overalls were all buddy-buddy and shit? And what about Four Nations, when you played on the same line?"

"No," Hayes said steadily. He knew the risk of being so hard-assed and circumspect about his reasons why. Barty could be insatiably curious with a stubborn streak developed over way too many years working with professional hockey players.

"I feel like there's something you're not telling me." Barty sounded testy now. "We've always been honest with each other, Monty."

Hayes *had* been honest, otherwise. Barty hadn't been the first person he'd told he was gay, but he was the fourth—after his parents, and Oscar Garcia, who he'd hooked up with when he played for the Otters.

"You of all people know how fucking weird it gets, being seen as the heir apparent," Hayes said. "I don't want to give that story any more fuel than it already has."

Barty shot him a look. "Are you joking? It *already* has fuel. The fact that Morgan's son is on your team has given it new life."

"And I don't want to give it any more," Hayes said, closing the door with as much certainty as he could.

"You're going to change your mind," Barty warned.

"I really don't think I will," Hayes said.

⤜⤜⤜ ⋘⋘

Zach called three times before Hayes finally picked up.

He'd been outside, lying on one of his loungers by the pool, sulking, since he'd gotten home from the marina.

Plausible deniability, he was taking advantage of a rare day off by working on his tan in the late afternoon sunshine.

Reality was a whole different kettle of fish, which was why he'd avoided Zach's calls.

But finally Zach texted him, **I'm pretty sure you're avoiding me, and that says more than you telling me the goddamn truth about how you're doing.**

The last thing he wanted was for Zach to be proven right so he dialed his number, hitting the video button.

Zach was in his office when he picked up. "Hey," he said, leaning back in his chair. "You okay?"

Hayes rolled his eyes. "I'm fine. It's my day off. Slept in. Worked out. Had a lunch meeting with Barty on his yacht. Now I'm relaxing by the pool. I promise I'm not putting up a murder wall with Morgan's face in the middle of it."

Not actually, anyway, but he might've constructed one—or ten—in his mind.

"If you ever do snap, please call me. I will *gladly* help you get rid of the body," Zach said earnestly.

Hayes wanted to protest, but he was touched, always, by how much Zach cared about him. "Thanks, Zachy."

"I mean it, he fucks with you at all, I'm there."

"You've got a job and a hot boyfriend. I'm fine." *So fucking fine.*

"A hot boyfriend who happens to be my boss and the head coach, who would totally let me leave," Zach pointed out.

"I appreciate the concern, but again, I am *fine.*"

Zach frowned. "Except your face is doing that thing where it doesn't match your eyes. Is it really terrible? You didn't tell me what happened after Finn's debut. Did you run into him? Was he an ass? Did he pretend he didn't even know you?"

It might have been easier—and a blow to the ego, too, though it wasn't like Hayes hadn't been taking those regularly for the last six years—if Morgan had pretended that they didn't know each other. Instead, he'd looked sad and torn and almost regretful.

And that was way fucking worse.

"No, he was . . .he wasn't bad," Hayes said.

Zach's frown deepened. "What does that mean?"

"It means, he's trying to be a good father to Finn and I don't know . . .generally not an asshole," Hayes said.

"Did he tell you that?"

"Yeah." Not in as many words, but it turned out that being fluent in Morgan Reynolds wasn't something you forgot, even after six years.

"You're not gonna—" Zach stopped abruptly. "You *wouldn't*."

Hayes knew exactly what his best friend was worried about. That Morgan might express just enough regret that he'd start to look really good again.

But what Zach didn't know was that he'd *never* stopped looking good to Hayes. Not ever. Not even when they'd played each other and Morgan had stared right through him, like he wasn't even there. No matter how acute the humiliation was, that he *loved* this complete asshole and he could still pretend that Hayes didn't even exist, nobody had ever looked better.

Maybe it was because Hayes knew who Morgan was, deep down, better than anyone else. He'd seen further inside him than anybody Morgan had ever allowed before. Morgan didn't have to tell him that was true for Hayes to *know* it was true.

He'd picked hockey over Hayes, and Hayes couldn't even hate him for that, because if you knew Morgan, nothing about that decision was particularly surprising.

"Am I going to hook up with him again? No. Of course not." But he'd wondered, after their run-in in the bathroom. He hadn't seen Morgan in person since he'd retired, and he'd been . . .different two nights ago. Retirement, especially when you were as committed to a career as Morgan had been, was bound to change you, but Morgan had seemed fundamentally altered.

Softer and more vulnerable, yes, but it wasn't like Hayes hadn't known those parts of Morgan existed. Six years ago, he'd dug down deep into him then put his hands on them and tested their veracity. But two nights ago, they'd seemed a lot closer to the surface. Easy to spot, if you were looking. Hayes was stupid, so of course he was looking.

"Hayes," Zach warned. "I know you—"

Yeah, they were not going down this path. It was hard enough not thinking of the attractive qualities it might possess without Zach insisting they talk about it. Hayes changed the subject, instead. Sort of, anyway.

"Barty is worried about my contract extension," Hayes said.

Normally, this would not be a subject change he welcomed, but beggars couldn't be choosers.

"What?" Zach sounded shocked. "Why?"

"They low-balled him initially. He says it's gonna be fine, but if he's worried, then I'm sort of worried."

"Shit. Monty. That's ridiculous. Of course they want to keep you. You're their captain."

"Yeah, so was Marchand, and look what the Bruins did to him," Hayes said.

Zach made a frustrated noise under his breath, and his eyebrows pushed together, eyes narrowing. "And you're in your fucking prime."

"Thanks," Hayes said dryly.

"What's Barty's plan? I know him. He's got one."

And of course, like everything else, even a subject change circled back to Morgan.

Hayes sighed. "He wants me to convince Morgan as Finn's dad to talk me up."

"Are you fucking kidding me?" Zach choked out. "You're not going to let him?"

"No. *No.* Hell no. Just . . ." Hayes had been sitting out here, watching as the sun skimmed across the sky and eventually dipped past the horizon, thinking of this the whole damn time. "Just, what if he's right and it would help? I want to stay here, Zachy. What if it helps me do that?"

"And he *owes* you," Zach said, more than a little self-righteously.

Hayes didn't know if he'd go that far. "I guess."

"You guess? He fucked you up, Monty."

"We fucked each other up," Hayes said heavily. That much had been obvious, from the way Morgan had looked up at him in the mirror when he'd opened the bathroom door. "It was probably never going to turn out differently. Even if I hadn't kicked him out in New York, it was always going to end badly."

Zach pursed his lips, looking like an overly concerned grandmother, even though he was a year younger than Hayes. "You should do it, Monty. I bet he'd agree, no question. I still remember the shit he said to the media about you at Four Nations. He knows just how good you are. And you've only gotten better."

"It could turn into a circus, all over again," Hayes said, still not convinced. He wanted to stay in Tampa, but he didn't want to do it at this cost.

He'd tried so hard to distance himself from Morgan and Morgan's legacy, over the years. He didn't want to erase all that work just because he was desperate and it was Barty's first idea.

He'd find others. He'd find a way to make it work. He always had, before. It was why he'd never considered switching to a different agent. Barty was the best. There was a reason he had a freaking yacht.

"Just think about it," Zach said, echoing what Barty had said himself, when they'd said goodbye a few hours earlier.

Hayes wanted to say that he wouldn't, but he knew himself. He was a self-professed obsesser. There was no way this question wouldn't linger. That he wouldn't turn it inside out dozens of times in the safety of his own brain.

"Sure," Hayes said.

"And maybe they'll come to their senses without it. I'm sure they will. The Sentinels love you," Zach said loyally.

Nobody was as loyal as Zach; it was one of the many reasons they were still friends, over ten years after they'd met for the first time.

"This is a business, Zachy," Hayes reminded him and Zach made a face.

This was why Zach had retired early from the NHL. He hadn't liked being a *thing*, a pawn to be moved around on the board as management saw fit.

Hayes couldn't say he loved it either, but even though he'd been traded across the country once, it had always seemed like a decent tradeoff to play the sport he loved.

The millions of dollars didn't hurt, either.

"Well, let me know if there's anything I can do," Zach said. "I can talk you up, too. I'm not nobody, not anymore."

Hayes smiled. "You've never been nobody."

"Yeah, but now I've got a national championship under my belt and it turns out that people take that really fucking seriously."

Hayes laughed, because of course Zach would just now be realizing this. He could be so jaded and bitter about hockey, but also incredibly naive.

"Imagine that," Hayes teased.

"I mean it," Zach insisted. "And I'm sure Gavin would say something too. You know they're always trying to get him on podcasts and to give quotes."

"I know," Hayes said softly. It meant a lot that they both had his back, even though Hayes felt like he'd only ever earned Zach's loyalty. Gavin's came because he was in love with Zach and if Zach told him, buckle up, we're going to space, he'd ask how many nights they should be packing for.

A minute later, Gavin's head ducked into the frame and Hayes said a quick hello before he let them both go.

His head hit the back of his lounger as he set the phone down next to him.

He'd known, from the moment management told him that Finn would be coming up to the Sentinels from their AHL affiliate, that things were going to get weird.

But he'd never imagined they'd already be at *this* level of weird.

His phone dinged again then again, and again. Hayes groaned and rolled over, glancing at the screen. The team group chat, quiet for hours because of the off day, had suddenly come to life.

Jasper, one of Hayes' A's, and the second line center, was trying to get a group to go out to dinner. Several of the single guys had replied in the affirmative. Including Finn.

Hayes groaned again. He should go. This was part of his responsibility. Not just to keep an eye on things but to make sure the rookies felt included in team activities.

He typed his affirmative and hoped, really fucking hard, that he wasn't going to regret this.

"I didn't think you'd come out tonight," Jasper said as he leaned back in his chair, looking at Hayes with a watchfulness that made him sort of uncomfortable.

Made him wonder if, at any point in the last month, he'd given himself away.

"Why?" It was stupid to ask but Hayes had to know.

"You've been quiet this month." And then Jasper glanced down the table at where Finn was teasing Noah, one of the older vets who'd just had a nasty breakup. "And I'm sure that's pretty weird for you too."

Hayes froze. He hadn't thought anyone knew about him and Morgan—especially Jasper, who hadn't even been at the tournament six years ago. "What do you mean?" he asked carefully.

"How many times have you been compared to his dad? Hundreds?" Jasper shrugged. "And now he's here and everyone's gonna be bringing that shit up again. You don't need that *next one* or *chosen one* shit in your life."

Jasper was not wrong.

"A lot," Hayes said wryly.

"And that's gotta be uncomfortable."

It was even more uncomfortable than Jasper knew.

"It sucks, sometimes," Hayes admitted. "But I don't want to take it out on Finn. Not his fault, you know?"

"No, no," Jasper said, leaning forward and dropping his voice. "You don't. You're great with him, but then I don't have to tell you that. You know how to be a C for this team. But I'm not surprised it's kind of a burden. That you've got a lot on your mind. All that plus the contract shit and everything."

"Barty's getting the contract done." It was one thing to tell Zach, who wasn't even in the NHL anymore, about his contract fears, but he wasn't going to put Jasper in a difficult position of knowing too much about it. That was one of the things he'd learned about being the captain in the last few years—he occupied a particular position of leadership, and he couldn't let even friends like Jasper in too close.

"Not surprised." Jasper smiled. Like of course Hayes was going to get an extension, and he'd stay with the Sentinels. That felt good, and it might have even been reassuring, if Barty hadn't told him how it was *really* going.

"Lars thought," Jasper continued, referring to Hayes' other alternate captain, after the waitress arrived to drop off their drink orders, "that maybe you were dating again."

"Me? Nah. Not during the season."

Jasper shot him a shrewd look. "Not ever, really. Not since that last guy. Alexander, that was his name, right?"

Yep, that had been his name. Hayes would always be a little pissed that their names would be connected together forever, because he was essentially the reason Hayes had come out. Then less than four months later, after Hayes had blown up the closet to make him happy, Alexander had decided that he didn't want to deal with it anymore.

Maybe if you really loved me, he'd thrown in Hayes' face, when it had finally ended.

Hayes couldn't even blame him for that. He'd loved Alexander as much as he could, which, admittedly, hadn't really been enough. It wasn't Alexander's fault that he wasn't Morgan. That Morgan had taken all of his heart and hadn't ever given it back.

"Nobody since him," Hayes said. He took a long drink of his iced tea. "I don't know if I'm really cut out for dating."

"What about a hot hookup?" Jasper grinned.

Hayes shot him an incredulous look. "How do you even have the energy to troll for those?" Jasper was the textbook definition of a chaotic bi, and he had plenty of hot hookups under his belt.

Jasper's jaw dropped. "You're kidding, right?"

"No?"

"Dude. All you have to do is post a thirst trap and you'd probably have thousands of offers in your inbox. *Legit* offers."

Hayes brushed that off, even if Jasper was probably right. "Why would I want someone like that? Who only wants me because I'm Hayes Montgomery?"

"It's a *hookup,* man. Who cares why they're there if the dick is good?" Jasper shook his head incredulously.

"This is why I'm bad at hookups." He hadn't used to be. Pre-Morgan, he'd been perfectly okay with them. But falling in love with Morgan, alongside growing older and maturing enough to deserve the A and then the C, had changed him.

"A fucking waste," Jasper said, laughing now. "God, I can't imagine the ass I'd get if I was you."

"I guess the city of Tampa should preemptively thank me that you're not," Hayes joked weakly.

Normally, these conversations with Jasper made him laugh for real. Hearing all about Jasper's insane exploits and poking fun at him for how ridiculous he was could be a really good time.

But it didn't feel particularly good now.

Maybe, Hayes thought morosely, Jasper was right, and since the season started he'd been too far up his own ass and far too lost in his own head.

He did his job, even on an off day, finishing up chatting with Jasper and then making his way down towards the end of the table. Making sure everyone was having a good time.

And who's making sure you're having a good time, Monty? That voice might normally belong to Zach, but now, it uncomfortably reminded him a little too much of Morgan.

Hayes brushed it aside as he approached where Finn was flopped down at the end of the table. He took the chair opposite him—vacated by Noah, who'd gone to talk to Jasper, probably about what kind of hot hookups he could find now that he was single.

"Hey," Finn said, nodding at Hayes. "Having a good time?"

Like father, like son.

"Of course," Hayes said, far too aware his answer sounded rehearsed. Perfunctory. Like something he said without even thinking about if it was true.

Did he mean it? Well, he *wanted* to mean it. Surely that counted for something.

Finn's hazel eyes narrowed. He looked a lot like Morgan, but the younger, easier, less-complicated version of him. The *softer* version. His curls fell, untamed, over his forehead, his ears.

"Anyone actually believe that?" he asked.

Hayes made a face. "Usually, yeah."

That knowing look on Finn's face eased. "You can be honest, you know? Is it weird?"

"Why does everyone keep asking me that?" Hayes complained.

"Probably because it's a little weird," Finn said sagely. "My dad's a lot to deal with. I know exactly what that feels like. How he can eclipse everyone in his vicinity."

"He's not normally in my vicinity," Hayes said, hoping that his voice sounded at least semi-normal. It was probably too much to ask to never discuss Morgan with his son.

"He doesn't have to physically be around to make an impact. I know that. And I bet you know it too."

Hayes shifted uncomfortably in the chair. This was not the easygoing conversation full of teasing bullshit he'd expected to exchange with Finn Reynolds. They'd kept it pretty light before this, and Hayes realized that had been all him. Finn had been letting him set the tone, and now he was turning the tables on Hayes.

God, he really kind of hated everyone with the last name of Reynolds. It was like they had a perpetual boner to overcomplicate everything.

"That's not *not* true," Hayes allowed.

"I should've asked you if it was okay if he hung around," Finn said, full of sincerity. "I just . . .I guess I wasn't thinking."

"You don't need to worry about me," Hayes said and meant *that*, one hundred percent. Finn was a rookie; he had a lot more burdens on his plate than just trying to deal with all Hayes' weird fucking history with Morgan.

"We just . . .we haven't always been close," Finn confessed. "He can be kind of shitty." *Understatement of the fucking century*, Hayes thought.

"But he's been better? If he's still shitty—"

"No," Finn interrupted, "he's a lot better these days."

Hayes was glad Finn didn't let him finish that sentence because if he did, Hayes would probably make a promise he wasn't sure he could keep. *Could* he tell Morgan to get out of Tampa? If it helped his rookie, then yes, he would. But he really didn't want to. It would mean getting too close again, and Hayes was operating under a very strict *No Morgan* policy.

"Uh, retirement agrees with him, then?" Hayes told himself he didn't want to know. That he was just making the kind of casual conversation he'd intended to have with Finn, but he didn't even believe it himself.

Finn barked out a laugh. "No, not even remotely. But he and Jacob keep themselves occupied. Mostly by fucking around with each other."

"It's kind of bizarre they're friends now," Hayes said.

Finn laughed again. "I know, right? I wouldn't believe it if I didn't see it every day. But it's good for them. I think my dad needed someone who understood what it was like, you know, to be him."

He had someone, kid, and he ditched me, at the first available opportunity.

"Of course," Finn continued, "not that he'd ever actually admit that. He still whines about Jacob all the time. We just don't believe him anymore."

At one point, right before camp had started, Hayes had wondered if Morgan had told his son about the fling. But it was clear, from the moment Finn showed up, that he hadn't. That he was in the dark, like everyone else.

It was better that way. Easier, for certain.

But there was still an annoying and perverse part of Hayes that wanted Finn to know. To understand when he said shit like that, for him to *really* know what he was saying.

"Yeah," Hayes said. He should get up. Make a smooth, easy exit. Not keep talking about Morgan with Finn. No matter how tempting it was. *Especially* because it was so tempting.

Like getting a little glimpse of who Morgan had been these last six years. What Morgan was like now, three years after retirement.

"But really," Finn said, all earnestness, "it's okay that he's around?"

Finn had so much natural confidence, an easy way of conducting himself, so used to being the center of attention his whole life because of his last name, that sometimes it was easy to forget that he was also a rookie.

"It's cool, as long as it's cool with you," Hayes said, meeting his earnestness.

"Don't worry." Finn grinned at him. "The moment he pisses me off or fucks up, I'll be the first person to tell him to get out."

Part of Hayes was screaming, *what about me? What about me? What about fucking me?* But he ignored it. It wasn't that hard, because he'd been ignoring that voice for six years now.

"Good," Hayes said and even managed to dredge up a conspiratorial smile.

CHAPTER 13

"You're being weird, even for you," Jacob claimed as they sat next to each other at the bar down the street from their rental houses.

It was honestly kind of a shithole dive, but it was quiet and neither of them had ever been bothered by the regulars there, who probably wouldn't know a hockey player—even a famous hockey player—if he smacked them on the side of the head with a stick.

The Sentinels were on a three game road trip, and both of them were going out of their mind with the inherent boredom of not even having the distraction of Finn and Finn's schedule to keep them occupied.

Thus, drinking at this shitty ass bar.

"I am not," Morgan retorted.

Jacob was like his son. Way too intuitive for his own good. All those fucking mysterious goalie powers. At least Finn seemed to be using his for actual goalie-ing. Jacob didn't have any good hockey reasons to use them anymore, so now he was just deploying them willy-nilly on people who he claimed were friends.

Like Morgan.

Morgan considered telling him he didn't want to be goalie-ed, but that would give Jacob too much proof that he was right, and that was no good, either.

"You forget I know you," Jacob said, putting his beer down with a click on the stained bar top. "You're normally edgy as hell, like you don't even know how to turn it off, but ever since we got to Florida, you've been even more of a fucking mess."

"Lie," Morgan declared, hoping that the single word encompassed his disdain for all the accusations Jacob had just made.

"Finn even mentioned it the other day," Jacob said casually, but there was a knowing glint to his eyes that Morgan didn't like.

"Finn should be focusing on what's important right now. Not me."

"I'm just saying, if he noticed it, even with everything he has going on . . ." Jacob trailed off, shooting Morgan another meaningful look. "And then there's the way you looked when we were out with the team for Finn's first win."

"I didn't look like anything." But Morgan knew what he'd looked like. What he'd *felt* like. There'd been no hope of keeping that much feeling off his face. He was a hockey player, not a fucking robot.

"I have a theory," Jacob said.

"Oh, that's fucking great," Morgan muttered. Desperately trying to figure out how to play this. They'd only been here for fifteen minutes. It would look guilty as hell if he demanded the check from the bartender and scurried off, no matter what excuse he gave. The only way forward was to just to brazen it out and tell Jacob that he was full of shit. That wasn't that different than normal for them, so maybe it would work.

"I think your guy—your hockey player—is on the Sentinels, and it's making you weirder than normal."

Morgan had been very afraid that Jacob was going to say that, and now that it had happened, there was nothing else to do but *deny, deny, deny.*

"I don't know what you're talking about," he said primly, draining his beer and waving his hand at the bartender for another round.

"You sure do," Jacob said, leaning in. "And we can even talk about it. We *should* talk about it."

"Oh, thank you. So generous," Morgan retorted.

"It's true then?" Jacob prodded.

Morgan barked out a laugh. Not feeling very amused, but trying to play it off that way. "I don't know what you think you've noticed—"

"Morgan," Jacob said seriously. "You came back to the table a week ago like you'd just seen a ghost. Who is it?"

Like he was going to tell *Jacob* any of it. First off, he'd immediately go tell Finn, no question. The fact that Jacob hadn't already told Finn what he knew was a fucking miracle. Second off, it was too humiliating to confess. Especially to Jacob of all people.

Especially after he'd given Jacob so much shit for dating Finn.

"Even you wouldn't be stupid enough to pine after Hayes Montgomery, so it can't be him," Jacob continued when Morgan didn't answer.

Oh, that was fucking hilarious. Jacob Braun, missing his calling as a stand-up comedian.

"Stupid," Morgan echoed numbly. "You're writing fanfiction now, and I don't like it. You're like one of those shippers on Twitter or whatever the fuck it's called now."

"*You* said there was a guy and it ended badly."

He had. And he'd never regretted that more than he did right now.

"That was a weak moment."

"And *then* you admitted it was a player," Jacob retorted mildly.

"You said that," Morgan argued. "I never admitted shit."

"Morgan, cut the crap," Jacob said.

"I can't even tell you how much I don't want to talk about it," Morgan said. "I didn't want to talk about it then, and I really, *really* don't want to talk about it now."

"Is it Jasper Brandt?"

"Oh, fuck off," Morgan said, grateful that the bartender finally set his next beer in front of him. He'd gone out of his way to *not* get drunk with Jacob, not after the one time they did not talk about, right after he'd found out about Jacob and Finn dating. But maybe it was time to break that self-imposed rule, especially if Jacob kept up this line of questioning.

"He's cute and I know he's bi," Jacob mused. "If it *isn't* Jasper, you could do worse."

"For the love of God, please do not attempt to matchmake. You'd be terrible at it," Morgan said between clenched teeth. He was so tense he thought he'd never get his shoulders to loosen.

They'd come here specifically to relax. Or at least that was what Jacob had claimed. But the truth was, he'd set this whole thing up, trying to get *Morgan* relaxed, so he could interrogate him.

Morgan was not a fan, and if Finn wasn't so head over heels in love with Jacob, he would seriously consider beating his ass right about now.

Punching him right in the mouth so he would finally shut the fuck up.

"Or I'm sure we could find you a nice girl." Jacob glanced around the bar like they were going to find him a "nice girl" here, which was a total joke.

"I don't want *anyone*," Morgan said.

Jacob's gaze was sympathetic. So fucking nice. Caring. Affectionate. Morgan could almost see why Finn loved him so much. *Almost.* "Sure, you love being alone. It's super fun."

"I'm not *alone*." But he was, and he'd never felt it more than he had in the last year.

When he returned tonight to his big empty rental house, different but so painfully similar to his big New York penthouse, the walls would echo around him with silence and he'd turn the TV up louder, hoping that ESPN might drown out all the thoughts he didn't want to hear.

Jacob raised a dubious eyebrow. "You're not? You're hanging out with me out of your own free will? Not because you don't have any other choices?"

"You're actually the worst," Morgan said, with feeling.

"I know." Jacob was grinning now, way too pleased with himself that he'd caught Morgan out. "We gonna talk about it now?"

"Yeah, it's . . .it's someone here." He was definitely *never* telling Jacob who it was, not after that whole *even you wouldn't be stupid enough to pine after Hayes Montgomery* bullshit. If he wanted to be stupid, there was nobody to stop him. And if anyone deserved being pined after, it was Hayes.

"Jasper?" Jacob said expectantly.

"No. *No.* And I'm never telling you. So stop asking." That would probably not be the end of it, because Jacob was Jacob, and even though they were friends now, he'd never really stopped being a pain in Morgan's ass. But he could hope.

"Do you want to talk about it?"

"I said it before and I still mean it. *No.* It . . .ended. That's the best, the *only*, thing I can say about it."

"Because you're Morgan?"

Morgan rolled his eyes. Took a long drink of his beer. "Why would you just assume it was me?"

"Because you're Morgan," Jacob repeated. "And you never saw a good thing you didn't want to fuck up by overcomplicating it."

Seriously, fuck Jacob. Fuck *everything*.

"It was never meant to last," Morgan admitted morosely. He'd long since come to the conclusion that even if Hayes hadn't kicked him out of his hotel room six years ago, if by some insane miracle, he'd let Morgan stay, their end was always inevitable. Two people had never been less meant to be.

Morgan desperately wanted to believe that was true. But then, if it was, it was beyond unfair that they had fit together like that. Like Hayes had been made for Morgan and Morgan for Hayes. Fate was a bitch like that.

"Well, that's just depressing." Jacob nudged Morgan with his shoulder.

"You don't know anything about it," Morgan said. He'd thought he'd sound prickly and defensive, but instead it came out sad and miserable.

"Then tell me," Jacob said persuasively.

"I . . .I don't know," Morgan said. How could he tell Jacob about any of the details without Jacob guessing who it was?

"You worried I'm going to tell Finn?"

"If you were going to tell Finn, you'd have already done it."

Jacob nodded. "We're friends, Mo. You know that, even when you try to deny it. And it *does* help to talk it out."

"It's been over for a long time. I should be over it. But I'm . . .I'm not." It was hard to admit that, and he'd imagined when he came down to Florida that it was natural for some of the feelings to rise to the surface. But it was even worse than Morgan had anticipated.

"You really cared about this guy."

Morgan had to give Jacob credit. He did not say *God, Morgan, I'm so shocked you were even capable of it.*

Sometimes Jacob could be a good guy, and sometimes, even, Jacob could be a good guy about things that were not related to Finn.

"Yeah." Morgan swallowed the rest of his beer. "I loved him. 'Course I didn't really realize that at the time. No. Actually.

That's a lie. I knew I . . .I knew I did. I knew if I let myself, I'd pick him over hockey. And so I . . ." Morgan nearly slipped and said, *and so I left*, but that was too close to the truth. "So I ended it, before I could fuck up the end of my career."

"Some of us manage to have hockey careers *and* a relationship," Jacob said, but his voice was kind. Probably kinder than Morgan deserved. "You even did it."

"Not well," Morgan said. He knew what an asshole thing it was to say, *but those were other players and I'm Morgan Reynolds.* But that was the truth.

Jacob shrugged. "So you dumped him. Let me guess, he hates you now."

Morgan thought back to the bathroom, a week ago. The hardness in Hayes' voice, in his green eyes, sharp like a cut emerald. "Yeah. I think so. And I can't even be pissed about that. 'Cause I'm the one who fucked up. But then I ask myself, did I even fuck up? Would I go back and make a different decision? I don't know. I got what I wanted."

For a long moment, Jacob didn't say anything, just looked at Morgan. Like he was really seeing him. Even all the ugly parts Morgan usually tried to hide under bluster and cockiness. "Did you, though?" he finally asked.

Morgan sighed. That was the million dollar fucking question. "I don't know." He'd thought he had. But seeing Hayes again had pulled all the old wounds back open, and now he was full of doubts, again.

"Something to think about," Jacob said, patting him on the shoulder reassuringly. "You could always tell him that."

"Yeah, right," Morgan said, barking out a laugh. If he got too close to Hayes, he'd chop his balls off. *Deservedly.*

"I'm just saying, it's never too late to try to make something right. Look at us," Jacob said.

"It's not the same. But I did think about it . . .once. I thought maybe after I retired, things had changed enough, I really considered pulling some epic romantic shit. Showing up at his doorstep, telling him I wanted him. That I'd never stopped wanting him."

Jacob's jaw dropped. Like he'd never expected *epic romantic shit* and Morgan Reynolds to exist in the same thought—and he'd be right. But Morgan had still been this close to doing it. He'd even bought the plane ticket. Had prepared a whole speech.

"Then what the fuck happened?" Jacob asked.

He'd been too late.

That had always probably been true, and regardless of who Hayes had been with, chances were he'd have slammed the door in Morgan's face.

"He started dating someone. Or I found out he was dating someone. Pretty seriously. I wasn't going to get in between that." And Morgan hadn't had any faith that if he threw his hat in the ring, Hayes would ever pick him. Maybe he was in love, but he was still Morgan Reynolds in love, and he wasn't sure his ego would survive that kind of rejection.

"That really fucking sucks," Jacob said.

It had. Morgan had crawled into bed and spent a solid week there, staring at the TV but not seeing a single image.

It hadn't mattered that Hayes and his boyfriend broke up only a few months later. Morgan's hope had died its final death that week and it wasn't ever coming back.

Morgan shrugged, trying to do an imitation of *it did suck, but I got over it,* even though he never really had. "It was what it was. A reality check, of a sort."

"No wonder you were a fucking mess when you showed up in Portland and found out Finn and I were dating."

"It wasn't . . .I wasn't a *mess.* And that wasn't why I was pissed."

The corner of Jacob's mouth quirked upwards. "No? Well, maybe not. I remember some long, drunken rant about how I was just using him to feel young again." He paused. "So the guy was also younger than you, huh?"

"Yes," Morgan said crisply, "but *no,* I was not using him to feel young." *I was just using him to* feel, *period.*

"I get it, not everything is about your broken heart," Jacob teased kindly.

Morgan wished that was actually true.

"And," Jacob added, patting him again, "I want you to know I'm very deliberately not putting all the hints you keep dropping together and coming up with a name."

Morgan rolled his eyes. "Thanks?"

"Your secret's safe with me," Jacob said.

There wasn't a hockey player on earth that didn't love a routine. Hayes knew he wasn't the only one, but over the years in Tampa, he'd created a fairly detailed one.

Wake up. Breakfast from his meal service. Smoothie in his travel cup, head to the practice facility, and get his workout in early before practice started and the place was overrun with other players. He loved those guys, but they always distracted him.

Game days had other routines, but this was his standard non-game day routine.

Morgan Reynolds was not supposed to be part of the routine.

He was definitely not supposed to be in the gym, lifting weights in an old, decrepit New York Bandits T-shirt, the 20 faded on the shoulder, sweaty fabric clinging to him for dear life.

Hayes opened his mouth and then snapped it shut again, fingers tightening around his protein shake. Glued right to the floor just inside the doorway. Fucking staring as Morgan lifted weights like he was planning to take the ice tomorrow.

He could work out in the same gym as Morgan. He could do it. *You can do it*, he repeated to himself weakly.

Despite the pep talk, he still didn't move. Seriously considered turning on his heel and marching right back out again.

But the *routine*.

Of course, before Hayes could decide which was worse—continuing to watch this wet dream torture or skipping the routine, or God forbid, making a *new* routine—Morgan spotted him.

The bar with its weight clanged down on its holder and Morgan lifted his T-shirt, wiping his face. Hayes flushed hot, tongue too big, too clumsy in his mouth. How did he look even better than he had six years ago?

Fuck Hayes' life. Fuck *everything*.

"Hey," Morgan said casually. Like Hayes wasn't a surprise interloper in Morgan's gym routine. Like he'd actually expected him to show up.

That was a thought Hayes shoved away, hard and fast. Morgan wasn't here because he knew Hayes would be here, too. That would be . . .well, stalking first off, and second off, definitely not hot. Not at all.

"You're here," Hayes said very stupidly.

"Oh yeah. Well, Roger told me I could drop by whenever I wanted." Morgan flashed him a little grin as he referred to the Sentinels' GM. "I've got credentials and everything. Wanna see them?"

Morgan pretending that Hayes didn't recognize him was not cute. Hayes was not endeared.

"No," Hayes said. "I . . .I trust you." He didn't. Not at all. But had Roger told him he could work out in the Sentinels' gym? Probably. Because apparently not only was he going to lowball Barty on the contract negotiations, he wanted to make Hayes' life as difficult as possible, too.

Morgan's smile widened. "Yeah? Good."

"Not like—I didn't mean—"

"Chill, Monty. I get it. You hate me on sight, you wish I was a thousand miles away. I know."

But Hayes didn't like that either. How easily Morgan accepted those things as the truth. Should they be true? Probably, but they didn't feel that way.

Morgan re-racked the weights and wiped down the machine, moving onto the treadmill as Hayes set down his shake next to the leg press. Tried to get his shit together as he prepared for his workout.

Even though Morgan clearly didn't agree, turning away from him like the conversation was over, Hayes couldn't shake the persistent thought that Morgan's comment deserved some kind of answer, but fuck if he knew what it was.

He agonized over it *and* every moment they were in the same gym, breathing the same goddamn recycled air, doing his utmost to ignore the sweat dripping down the side of Morgan's face. How it soaked into the collar of his ancient T-shirt. Made the curls at his temples darker.

Hayes finished his leg reps and was profoundly annoyed he hadn't managed to use his normal focus and the physical exertion to block Morgan out.

Tugging his ear pods out, he finished his protein shake and turned to Morgan.

"I'm only thinking about how you being around so much impacts Finn," Hayes finally said. Ignoring how Finn himself had told him only a week ago that he was okay having Morgan around.

Morgan hit a button on the treadmill and slowed to a steady jog. Shot him a dubious look, which smarted somewhere deep inside Hayes. He'd thought he'd done a fairly decent job at not seeming *that* bothered by Morgan's presence in Florida.

"That's all it is? You're worried about Finn?"

"Of course," Hayes said self-righteously.

"I'm not trying to be in your hair," Morgan said apologetically. "Or in Finn's hair." And what the fuck. *What the fuck.*

Morgan had never even *sounded* apologetic in his whole life. Why was he starting now? And could Hayes erase it from it from his brain so he wouldn't over-obsess about what it meant during his next sleepless night?

He said he was trying.

Hayes pushed that thought right the fuck out before it could take root any further.

"You're doing a very good job of acting like a real human father," Hayes muttered.

That was kind of shitty but he was *feeling* kind of shitty.

"Isn't that what everyone wants?" Morgan retorted dryly.

"It isn't *you*," Hayes burst out.

"Well, you said it yourself. You don't know me anymore," Morgan said mildly. Like the fact of it didn't hit Hayes right where it hurt.

Hayes shoved a hand through his damp hair. Maybe this conversation was inevitable. They'd only had half of it in the bathroom at the bar. Morgan had left before they could do anything more than bristle at each other. At the time, that had seemed like the smartest idea, but from Hayes' years as a captain, he'd learned that leaving shit unsaid only guaranteed that it would fester and then infect everyone.

They could not afford for this cold war to affect Finn.

Not when Hayes wanted a new contract and another Cup. Not just for him, but for every guy on this team.

"Listen, I'm glad you're here for Finn."

Morgan slowed the treadmill further, down to a walk, and then hopped off. Further ruined Hayes' day by lifting his T-shirt up again, wiping away more sweat. He didn't come any closer to where Hayes was leaning against the bench press, but his gaze was intent. *Interested.*

"What about you?"

It was not what Hayes had expected him to say, and he floundered.

"I'm not—this isn't about me. This is about Finn."

"I told myself that when I showed up, you'd be cold, unfriendly. Unbothered." Morgan wet his lips. "But you're not."

"That's ridiculous," Hayes said. *Unbothered*? Honestly, what the fuck. Yes, it had been six years, but surely Morgan had understood how into him he'd been. Head over heels, logic thrown right out the window, building dream castles in the hotel rooms they'd shared.

"No, it's not. You threw me out—"

"I kicked you out, because you were a total asshole at the end of the tournament, and because then you showed up like you could just get in my pants because I was convenient," Hayes interrupted. Nevermind him being stupid, nobody was as stupid as Morgan Reynolds, *verified.*

"*Convenient.*" Morgan had the nerve to actually look floored by this. "I can't believe you think that. You were literally the least convenient option I could come up with. I was there because I . . ." He hesitated, and Hayes mentally begged him to finish while simultaneously hoping he never uttered the rest of that sentence. "Because I missed you. I knew I would. But I missed you more than I ever expected."

"What the fuck," Hayes said, because that was exactly what he was thinking, nothing else.

"I meant it back then. I came to apologize. Ditching you at the end of the tournament was totally shitty."

"You freaked out," Hayes corrected in a hard voice. If they were really going to talk about this, they weren't going to dance around it. Not like they'd done in that hotel room doorway, six weeks after. Hayes had been too sad and still half-hoping that it could end differently to be as blunt as he should've been.

"Yeah. And I . . ." Morgan swallowed hard, his Adam's apple bobbing, and he looked away. "I might've freaked out again, when I saw you again."

Morgan had said before that he'd expected Hayes to be angry when he showed up in Florida, and Hayes couldn't say he'd been particularly angry before this. Maybe he'd wanted to be, because anger at least felt productive, unlike all this endless sadness. But now he actually was angry. So angry it burned through him, a shaft of pure righteousness spearing right through his middle. It made him strong. Gave him purpose, *finally*.

"Yeah, no fucking kidding," Hayes retorted, letting that feeling fill him. He'd been miserable for so long it felt *amazing* to feel something else.

"Hayes—"

"No," Hayes said, hand clenching around his empty plastic cup. "No, you don't get to show up and do this now. I was sad for *so fucking long*. And you were just . . .what, freaking out? Panicking? Having your big gay panic?"

Morgan frowned, but Hayes had a full head of steam and nothing was stopping him now. He'd lived too long with all this shit inside his head.

"You were a total asshole, on that last day. And then you never texted me back? It wasn't just sex, and you knew it. I should've said something, I should've called you on it, but I was so fucking . . ." Hayes' throat went tight, just thinking about how much he'd *felt* during those ten days. Less than two weeks and they'd been everything. "I was so fucking into you. Terrified that you might not feel the same. More terrified that you would, because what were we going to do about that?"

He knew it was true, the moment it came out of his mouth. He'd known it was true for some time now. What *could* they have done about it?

Morgan's gaze was painfully understanding, like he'd just seen Hayes get it. Poison finally draining out of the wound.

"You were a total asshole," Hayes repeated, but now the righteous anger was gone, evaporated like it had never existed in the first place. "You *were* a total asshole about it. You didn't need to do that. You could've been . . ." What could he have been though? Morgan had never pretended to be anything but what he was. He'd never lied to Hayes.

"And you kicked me out," Morgan said.

Yeah, he had. At the time, it had felt like the safest possible choice. The only way he could get Morgan back, hurt him the way he was hurting. Hayes had told Zach that he couldn't stand to get just the scraps that Morgan felt like tossing him, and that *was* true. It was still true. But it had been more too. Morgan had left. So when he came crawling back, trying to apologize, Hayes hadn't listened and then he'd slammed the door shut in his face.

An eye for an eye.

Hayes nodded. Not sure he trusted his voice now.

Well, they'd finally hashed it out. Everything was in the open now.

Maybe this was what he'd always needed to finally move on, but as Hayes stared at Morgan, that didn't feel right either.

But it was all he had.

"I don't want you around," Hayes said. "But I don't think I have a choice but to accept it. For Finn."

Morgan didn't look hurt by Hayes' admission; he didn't look like anything at all. He just nodded. "For Finn," he agreed.

He didn't know where that left them; laid bare by honesty, but no better off than they'd been before. It seemed impossible they could co-exist like this, but what other choice did they have?

Hayes finished his workout. Left without looking over at Morgan, and believed—hoped, maybe—that Morgan ignored him too.

He was in the locker room, taping his stick, gear half-off, half-on, when Jasper plopped down next to him. "Hey," he said.

Hayes nodded at his friend, pretty sure that he didn't have to tell him the last thing he felt like right now was making small talk.

He wanted to go to practice, then head home. Lick his wounds in peace. Maybe call Zach when he'd finally rehashed all the layers of that conversation and felt like he could actually talk about it.

But Jasper looked at him expectantly. "You alright?"

"Why wouldn't I be?" It was so much easier to turn the whole thing onto Jasper than to tell him *no, I'm not alright.* He was the captain, he couldn't afford to not be alright.

Jasper shot him a look. "I told you, you've been weird and quiet. You can talk to me, you know?"

He knew it. But nobody on the team had figured out about him and Morgan yet and he wasn't about to start telling anyone now. He couldn't actually imagine admitting the truth to Finn, but if he was ever going to go there, Finn kind of had to be the first person to know.

"Yeah, of course," Hayes said.

Not Jasper, even as tempting it was to blurt out in the middle of the locker room, *I used to be in love with Morgan Reynolds and having him around is kind of killing me.*

It would probably feel better if Jasper at least looked at him with sympathy *and* understanding, not just sympathy.

Jasper made a frustrated noise. "You don't have to shoulder all the burdens alone, you know? I'm your A. I can be there for you. I *want* to be there for you."

"I know, and you are," Hayes said, patting him on the knee. "We're good, I promise."

It's just me that isn't good.

But Hayes had to believe that someday he might be able to say it—to Jasper, to any of his other teammates—and actually mean it. Maybe today had been the first day in making that possible.

CHAPTER 14

It never occurred to Hayes that when, on the way back from a game in the Midwest, he'd texted Barty back and agreed to a late afternoon tee time the next day after practice, that Barty might feel inspired to bring guests.

Hayes tried not to gape as Barty walked up to where he was standing, golf bag in front of him, with Jacob Braun.

He liked Jacob—he'd always liked him, even when Morgan had hated him, probably *especially* because Morgan hated him—and he'd gotten a chance to know him in the last two months as more than just the Vezina-winning goalie he'd been and more as Jacob, Finn's boyfriend. That had been cool.

What was probably not cool was that it seemed inevitable that a half a step or two behind the pair of them, Morgan was probably lurking somewhere.

Could he not even golf in fucking peace?

"Hey," Hayes said, as Barty pulled him into his signature half-handshake, half-hug. That done, Hayes turned towards Jacob and offered him a quick handshake. "Barty, you didn't tell me you were bringing a friend." He paused. Tried to be subtle about how he was craning his neck around Jacob's bulk, attempting to figure out if Morgan was around without having to flat-out ask. "Friends?"

Jacob had the nerve to laugh. Did he know? Hayes didn't think there was any way he did, because *Finn* clearly didn't know. "Don't worry, I didn't bring any Reynolds with me," he said.

"Nope, you insisted that you didn't want their help," Barty said, sounding smugger than Hayes would expect, considering how their last conversation about Morgan had gone.

"I don't," Hayes said firmly.

"Our cart's over here. They were just getting it stocked up," Barty said, gesturing over to where, no big surprise, there was a golf cart with a cooler strapped to the back, taking up half of the rear seat. He strode over and talked to the attendant, glancing in the cooler and peeling off a few bills from his clip as a tip for the guy after he'd finished loading their bags.

"So," Jacob said, gaze opaque behind his sunglasses, but Hayes swore there was a knowing edge to his voice.

There was no way he could know the truth, but it seemed that somehow, impossibly, he knew *something*.

"So," Hayes parroted back. He should be working harder at being friendly. Jacob was a good guy and one of his rookies' partners. They'd played each other a number of times. This *should* be easier, but faced with a guy who, if all things had gone radically different, would've ended up as an in-law of sorts, Hayes couldn't seem to dredge up even the most basic of small talk.

Jacob raised an eyebrow. "You any good?" he asked, gesturing towards the flawless emerald green course spreading out in front of them.

"Not really," Hayes admitted. "I only said yes because if I said no, Barty would harass me into doing something worse."

"I'm pretty good these days." Jacob's expression did something complicated. "Got more time on my hands to practice and walking the course tends to keep my hip pretty loose."

Barty, finished with the attendant and climbing into the cart's driver's seat, beckoned them on. It was kind of a tight fit, but he and Jacob were both hockey players. They were used to close quarters.

"I didn't know Barty was your agent, too," Hayes said, still trying to dredge up another topic of conversation. They'd covered their golf skills and skipped the weather—it was Florida and even though it was November it was still way too fucking hot.

"Barty's actually my agent's partner," Jacob said dryly. "Mark Clifford is my agent. Mark works with him."

"And I'm still annoyed you picked Cliffy over me," Barty complained. "My ego might never recover."

Hayes didn't have to see behind his sunglasses to know Jacob was rolling his eyes. "I think your ego's plenty inflated," Jacob muttered under his breath.

"It was too bad Mo couldn't come," Barty said as he pulled the cart alongside the first hole.

"He had some ESPN commitments," Jacob said. He shot a glance in Hayes' direction, then added, "He was real sorry to miss it."

"Barty," Hayes said with exasperation, "I told you I didn't want to go that direction."

"And he's not here, is he?" Barty said in a tone full of faux-innocence. "Just Braun."

Hayes didn't even bother rolling *his* eyes because it wouldn't have done any good.

"What direction is that?" Jacob asked Hayes as Barty strode out onto the green with driver in hand.

Hayes didn't particularly want to tell Jacob all of this. He'd tried to keep his contract negotiations away from the team, and Jacob, while not technically a member of the Sentinels, was as good as one these days. But he was out of small talk subjects, and he didn't know how to shut Jacob down without sounding like a real asshole.

"We're negotiating my extension, and the Sentinels low-balled Barty. He had some brilliant idea that Morgan could go on ESPN and talk me up. Sway public opinion to convince them to settle this early and not force us onto the open market."

Jacob nodded. Like most goalies, he had a great poker face, but the corner of his mouth tilted up. "And you said no."

"It's . . .no. I mean, *yes,* I said no. I told Barty no." Hayes might've been surprised he'd tripped over his words when discussing this, but he wasn't. Nothing about Morgan surprised him anymore. "For good reasons," he added.

"Not because you thought Mo would turn you down," Jacob guessed.

Hayes watched as Barty took a practice swing and then an-other. He was absolute shit at golf, but it almost didn't matter, because he always played like he had both the lowest handicap and the biggest dick on the course.

"I don't know if he would or not," Hayes answered honestly. He had given up understanding Morgan Reynolds a long time ago, and he couldn't claim, even after their conversation three days ago, that he'd gotten any additional clarity.

"Seriously?" Jacob asked.

Hayes looked over at him. "I mean, *yeah*. We're not friends, Braun. I can't say we're enemies, like you two were, but it's not . . .we're not close."

Barty took a big swing and his ball sailed off wide right, landing on the far edge of a sand trap. He shrugged and headed back to the cart, grabbing a hard seltzer out of the cooler then motioning to the pair of them. "Who's up next?"

"I'll go," Hayes said. If Jacob was as good as he'd hinted at, he didn't want to go last.

He was just going through the motions, brain still stuck on the conversation he'd been having with Jacob. He couldn't figure out Jacob's surprise—or what he knew. And he sure as fuck couldn't *ask* him. Hayes swung and his ball soared along the fairway, straighter than Barty's, and avoided the sand trap.

"Great job," Barty exclaimed, patting Hayes enthusiastically on the back as he and Jacob switched places. Hayes rooted around in the cooler, finally settling on a plastic bottle of unsweet tea.

Jacob was true to his word and his shot was by far the best of their trio. His putting game, both long and short, was solid, too.

"Not a lot going on down here in Florida. Didn't get to golf much in the winter in Portland," Jacob admitted with an easy shrug, referring to the Pacific Northwest city he'd lived in after retiring. Where he'd ended up meeting Finn, who'd been playing college hockey.

"Much better setup here," Barty enthused on the third hole.

Hayes was half-focused on the game and half-worried that Jacob would bring up Morgan again.

He should've known Jacob was just biding his time, in typical goalie fashion.

Jacob struck on the ninth hole.

"You two were pretty cozy at Four Nations," he said, nudging Hayes, as they watched Barty hit his ball out of another sand trap.

"Me and who?" Hayes asked, pretending ignorance even though he knew perfectly well who Jacob was talking about.

Pushing up his sunglasses, Jacob shot him a look. "You and Morgan."

"Oh. Yeah. Of course. Um. Yeah, I suppose."

"And he's been around quite a bit since the season started. He's only had good things—great things, really—to say about you and the way you've mentored Finn during his rookie season."

"I didn't have to do much," Hayes protested. "He has you, and he has his father. I'm just here as a last resort."

"Not true," Jacob said steadily.

"Alright, well, it's what I'd do for any rookie on this team. Not just rookies with famous hockey players as fathers." Did he sound a little bitter? Hayes thought it was possible, but he couldn't help it, not entirely. Besides, what could Jacob possibly extrapolate from some bitterness? Maybe he'd guess that Hayes was actually bitter that all the stupid talking heads kept saying that he was a really, really good hockey player but that he'd never be Morgan Reynolds' caliber.

Lots of people would be plenty pissed about that. Nevermind everything else.

"I get it, you know? Morgan can be a total dick," Jacob said in a low voice as Barty crushed his third White Claw and tossed the empty into the trash. Hayes had a feeling he was going to have to confiscate Barty's keys if he kept up this pace. "But his heart's in the right place. If you needed help—he'd help you out."

Hayes' tongue felt too big for his mouth. What would he even say to that? Maybe it was true. But it would kill Hayes' pride to ask.

"We don't need him," Hayes said firmly.

Jacob nodded. "Sucks that they're low-balling you," he said. "That's bullshit, honestly. You're wonderful for this team. A great player and a great leader. I told Finn the other day you're going to win him a Cup."

"Finn's gonna be part of that," Hayes said honestly. They'd needed goalie help last year. But Finn was putting together a Calder-worthy season for a rookie goalie, and that hadn't happened since Dustin Wolf.

"I sure hope so," Jacob said with a nod.

They finished up their eighteen holes, returning to the clubhouse, Jacob actually the one to pluck the keys from Barty's fingers and drive them back, ignoring his whining.

"I need a drink," Barty announced when Jacob pulled them up in the shaded roundabout in front of the clubhouse entrance.

"Do you really?" Hayes asked skeptically.

Barty nudged him. "You're gonna need something more than that iced tea, for what we need to talk about."

"Ugh," Hayes said.

"And that's my hint to duck out," Jacob said. He turned to Hayes. "I'm not Morgan, but I'm happy to do what I can."

"No, no need," Hayes said, shaking his outstretched hand. It meant something that Jacob, who was fairly private, would be willing to talk publicly about Hayes' position on the Sentinels. But Barty was—annoyingly—probably right. If anyone was going to move the needle, it was probably Morgan, and Hayes would rather die than ask him.

"And if you need me to play interference with Morgan, you just say the word," Jacob added, smirking. "He sort of listens to me now."

"Kind of like having a rabid dog on a leash," Barty observed.

Hayes laughed because he was supposed to. Not because he wanted to.

Ten minutes later, they were in the bar, ceiling fans swishing above them, a beer in front of Hayes and another one of those godawful espresso martinis in Barty's hand.

"So, how bad is it?" Hayes asked. It had only been a few weeks since they'd talked last—surely Barty had been able to work some of his magic.

"They're dragging their feet," Barty said succinctly.

Hayes groaned under his breath.

"Doesn't mean they *won't* budge, just that they're trying to prolong this whole thing, like they believe that'll give them the upper hand. That you'll just take what they give you."

Hayes made a face. "Can't I just do that?"

"No," Barty scoffed.

"I don't care if I get paid ten million a year or eleven. You know that. I'll pick up another sponsorship, make up the difference."

Barty leveled him with a serious look that scared Hayes more than he wanted to admit. "The number per year isn't the issue. It's the number of years."

"What?" Hayes wasn't proud but he straight up yelped it.

"You and I talked about potentially a five or six year deal, to finish out your career. They're on three, and not budging."

Hayes' jaw dropped. "You're serious. They think, what, I'm gonna be fucking washed-up in four years?"

"They didn't say that, not in those exact words, but they had a bunch of data they trotted out, analysis of how production declines in the mid-to-late thirties."

Hayes sank back in his chair. Disbelieving. It hadn't felt like so long ago when he and Morgan had this same conversation. Morgan telling him that he'd understand someday, about the complicated nature of legacy when you kept getting older.

And yet it *had* been six years.

He'd deliberately avoided thinking about it. Some days—a lot of days, in fact—it felt like he had all the time in the world. But he didn't feel like that now.

"We both know you're not the average player," Barty continued, "and they know that too, when I pressed them. But they're trying to use it as leverage. I can break them down, but it's going to take time."

"So, don't expect to have an actual contract on the table for awhile," Hayes interpreted.

"Not any time soon. We can get there." Barty paused. "We could get there faster if you used Reynolds, but you've made it clear you didn't want to."

"I don't," Hayes said firmly. "And don't even suggest Braun. The situation's different there, but that's not his kind of thing, and we both know it."

"I wasn't going to." Barty held up his hands like he was being unjustly accused.

"So, he just happened to come golfing with us, total co-incidence," Hayes said wryly.

"He's one of Mark's clients, and you know Mark and I are partners. Felt right to invite him," Barty defended.

"Cut the shit."

Barty sighed. "Okay, fine. You caught me."

Hayes picked up his beer, contemplated the light shining through the window as it caught the glass. "You know I don't want to test free agency."

"You'd get a lot more money. Probably any contract length you wanted," Barty said.

"And I might end up having to play for a different team."

"You wouldn't be the first to do it at the end. Patrick Kane did it. Marleau. Marchand. There's a long list."

"It was never going to be me, though. I know I started out playing for the Mavericks, so it's not even like I've only ever played for the Sentinels, but in some ways, that's the way it feels. When I got traded, it was like, I don't know . . .I grew up."

Barty tilted his head, like he was considering this. "I'd actually say it started before that. Like . . .six months before?"

Ouch. It was annoying that someone as stupid emotionally as Bartholemew Smith III noticed how fucked up Hayes had been in the wake of the Four Nations tournament.

"Okay, but it was *in process*," Hayes argued. "I just . . .I don't want to play for anyone else. That was my one requirement."

"You had two actually. You wanted to play out your career for them, too. And unless you're planning to retire early . . ."

"You know I'm not," Hayes said with a huff.

"Okay, yes, I do know that. But we could take the three-year deal as a bridge. Hope they give us another one. That'll take you to thirty-seven."

"You actually think they'd give me another three-year deal then?" Hayes heard the skepticism in his voice. They didn't want to give him one now, even after all the ways he'd proven himself. So what if he won another Cup. They'd just be looking for an excuse to claim he was too old. Washed-up.

Hayes didn't often feel jealous of Morgan, but whenever he thought of how the Bandits had let him retire a Bandit on his terms, he felt an unpleasant jolt of it.

"No," Barty admitted. "No. Probably not."

"So then I'd be thirty-four, and the offers wouldn't be as good as they'd be now." It was unusual that Hayes had to push Barty to be this honest. Usually he loved being brutally frank about a situation. That told Hayes it was serious. That Barty was genuinely not convinced he *could* get the Sentinels to come around.

"No," Barty said, shaking his head. Finally not offering any kind of qualifier.

It was shitty. There was no way around it. In some ways, they had him by the balls and they knew it, which was why they were acting this way.

Hayes took a long swig of his beer. Barty had been right. It sort of helped.

"What do you want me to do?" Barty asked.

"Give me the best-case scenario—not the one where they come to their senses and give me six years, eleven million a year," Hayes said. "The *other* best-case scenario."

Barty drummed his fingertips on the table. "We push them the whole season and then see where we're at. You've got a locked down no-trade clause. They can't move you. They know that. So, we get them as far as we can, re-assess at that point, and if we have to move to the open market, come back with whatever juicy offers we get. Which will be a lot." Barty paused. Tipped his martini glass in Hayes' direction. "Especially if you keep on this tear you're on. Point and a half per game? Thirty goals so far? You're killing it. Then maybe the Sentinels want to match that, want to keep you, but maybe they don't. We cross that bridge when we come to it."

It was still shitty. There was no erasing that. Part of Hayes felt angry. Unwanted. Rejected. Even though he knew, better than most, how the NHL was a business.

He'd learned the hard way, being sent across the country practically in the middle of the night.

Traded for a whole bunch of draft picks, so the Mavericks could start *another* rebuild. Hayes had ranted to Barty, to Zach, to literally anyone who would listen to him, that if the Mavericks had just done the rebuild right the *first* time and put the right pieces around him, they wouldn't have had to start over.

Eventually Hayes had been forced to accept that this was just how things were. It was almost pointless to get angry about it, because there was nothing you could do to change it. Even your performance on the ice sometimes didn't matter.

In the end, it had been fine. Good, even. And then great. The Sentinels had become his team. They'd won a Cup together.

But the lessons he'd learned hadn't faded.

He'd only forgotten them for a little while.

"Okay," Hayes finally said. "That's the plan then. We push them as far and as hard as possible. I'll give you all the ammunition I can. The rest is . . ." Hayes shrugged. He didn't have to say it. Barty knew it.

"Not up to us," Barty agreed.

CHAPTER 15

MORGAN HAD LEARNED, PRETTY early on in the season, that if he sat in the regular stands or too far to the front of the management's box, he would spend half the game worrying that the camera would catch him at the worst possible moment—or that the media would spend the whole game trying to interpret every single one of his expressions.

Now he hid deep in the box. The view wasn't as good, but it was better for the whole fucking world not to see every single one of Morgan's lovestruck expressions as Hayes continued to play like he was ten years younger, out-skating and out-shooting and just plain fucking out-*thinking* everyone else on the ice.

Six years ago, he'd been reluctantly in awe of Hayes' hockey.

Now, he couldn't miss it.

"Dad, you don't have to come tonight," Finn told him very seriously as he'd caught a ride with his son to the arena. Jacob was in LA for a few days, doing some work for his foundation, so Morgan would be on his own tonight. "I'm not starting."

Morgan knew that was true. He didn't *need* to be here, but it was even better watching Hayes in person, even if he had to do it from the back of the box.

But he couldn't tell his son that.

"What if Silov gets hurt? What if he gets pulled?" Morgan questioned.

Finn only made a face. "Then I go out there without you or Jacob watching in person. It's fine. I can handle it."

"You've also won five in a row," Morgan pointed out. "That's not nothing."

"It's not even the longest win streak in the league this season," Finn said.

"Doesn't matter," Morgan said. "I'm around, and besides, what am I gonna do instead? Sit at home and watch the game?"

The look Finn shot him was concerned. "Dad, you don't have to completely change your life to be here. To support me. You know that, right?"

Morgan wanted to laugh. Wanted to cry, too. Embarrassing that his son actually thought he'd *had* a life in New York. "I know."

But when Finn shot him an even harder look, Morgan caved. "If I was in New York, you know what I'd be doing?"

"No?" Finn pulled into the player section of the parking garage and turned off the car.

"Staying in and watching probably two to three games on TV."

"Dad," Finn chided, meeting his resigned expression with one of his own. "You *could* date, you know. You don't have to be alone. Mom moved on. I don't mind if you do, too. In fact, it would make you look less pathetic if you did."

Ha. *Moving on.* That was a fucking joke. "I know," Morgan said testily.

"You're not that old, and you still look good for your age," Finn pointed out more softly this time, like this whole conversation didn't make Morgan wish he *had* stayed home.

"Not that old," Morgan muttered. "God, it's a good thing I have a decently sized ego, still."

"Hey, it's a compliment," Finn retorted, because he was twenty-three and everyone who was forty was practically ancient. "I'm sure that a lot of women would go for you. Not just because you're Morgan Reynolds, either."

It would be nice if that was true, but even post-divorce and pre-Hayes, Morgan had discovered that was a pipe dream. One of a very long list of reasons why Hayes had been so perfect for him. He hadn't cared who Morgan was—or he *had*, but only the parts that Morgan actually *liked* being wanted for.

"Thanks, but no thanks," Morgan said dryly.

As he made his way to the box, stopping to talk to a few of the arena staff that he'd gotten to know over the last two months, he wondered, not for the first time, if it would ever be worth telling Finn the truth.

He couldn't see himself confessing the whole story, not if Hayes stayed Finn's captain, and with the way he was playing, the Sentinels would be really fucking stupid to get rid of him now.

But maybe he could tell Finn *part* of the truth. At least enough that he'd stop nudging him towards only women, who were all invariably interested, who he then had to extricate himself from. But mostly so he'd stop making noise about how Morgan wasn't quite dead yet.

It was a five p.m. game tonight. Maybe he'd take Finn out for a late dinner, to his favorite steakhouse in Tampa, and explain enough of the story that it got Finn off his back. Jacob knew, and as much as that stuck in his craw, he didn't want to keep Finn in the dark forever or force Jacob to keep all of Morgan's secrets.

Morgan settled in the suite, not happy about the plan, necessarily, because it was hard to imagine that Finn wouldn't push just as hard, if not harder, than Jacob, to find out the mysterious ex's identity. But it was time. It was probably *long* time. If Finn hadn't been drafted to Tampa, Morgan imagined he might have actually confessed the truth sooner.

As always though, Hayes was there, inserting himself, making it impossible for Morgan to move on, impossible for Morgan to do anything but pine hopelessly over him.

Wish things had been different six years ago. Wish things were different now.

Warmups started. Jacob wasn't here, and the rest of the box was mostly empty, and for once, nobody was actually paying attention to him, so he could stare goopily at Hayes as he rotated around the ice, checking in with his players and warming himself up.

Finn was over with Silov at the Sentinels' bench, and every so often, Morgan *would* glance over at them, but it was honestly hard to tear his eyes off Hayes.

Maybe he should be ashamed or even humiliated that he was still stuck on this.

Hayes had told him, without really mincing words, that he'd missed his chance. *I don't want you around, but I'm going to have to accept it, for Finn.*

That had hurt, but in a way that at least Morgan expected, and it *was* better than if Hayes had been totally unmoved and apathetic about Morgan's presence in Tampa.

Morgan could imagine both Jacob and Finn ganging up on him if he actually admitted Hayes' hate was better than nothing. Danny, too.

They'd tell him he was pathetic. *Check.*

They'd tell him to get his head out of his ass. *I've fucking tried.*

They'd definitely tell him it was time to get over it. *Don't you know if I could have, I would have?*

The Bandits did have a game tonight, but they were on a west coast roadie, so Morgan pulled his phone out and sent Danny a text.

Am I pathetic?

Danny texted back almost immediately. **Woooo boy!!! Don't tempt me with a good time, Mo.** And then before Morgan could even get pissed, **Kinda, sorta, but it's okay because the rest of the world thinks you're really fucking cool. HAHAAHAHA!!!!!**

Morgan groaned under his breath.

Thanks for the brutal honesty.

You're welcome!!!!!

Morgan generally ignored Danny's exclamation point addiction. He couldn't ignore the next message that came in.

You know, crazy AND wild thought, you could DO something about it.

Like what?

Like get him back, you idiot.

It wasn't like Morgan hadn't considered that once or twice or a hundred times.

He hates me now. How would that even work?

You really are an idiot. It's called groveling, dipshit.

Morgan didn't know what to say to that. He just stared at the screen, at Danny's blunt words. He'd thought about it. Of course he'd thought about it. Never thought it could work, so why bother?

Since you don't seem to get it, I'm gonna do you a solid and tell you: he wouldn't hate you still if he didn't give a crap.

Warmups ended with Morgan still staring at his phone. Only when the game started did he put it away, sliding it into his pocket, wishing that he could forget Danny's advice that easily.

But it haunted him throughout the game.

Every time Hayes went over the boards, his line coming onto the ice, Morgan thought, *what if he was mine? What if the name and the number on my back were his? What if when he did something fucking amazing I didn't have to hide my awe? What if, after the game, I knew he'd be coming home to me?*

Morgan's heart clenched.

It would be hard. Hayes was angry and had no reason to trust Morgan.

And that was just getting him to consider it. Nevermind what came after.

In Toronto six years ago, they'd never had a chance to have a real relationship. In some ways, even though he'd been married and had a child, Morgan wasn't sure if he'd *had* a real relationship. But Hayes wouldn't accept less. Hayes didn't *deserve* less.

Morgan wasn't delusional; he couldn't imagine even wanting to try for anyone else, but this was Hayes. He was special, not just to the rest of hockey, but specifically to Morgan.

Hayes scored midway through the third, a beauty of a goal, sealing the Sentinels' two goal lead and the win.

The video scoreboard flashed out, *Sentinels win!!! Six in a row!!!!*

Clearly, the operator knew Danny and they shared an affection for exclamation points.

Morgan tried to avoid going into the locker room, even though Finn had told him before that he was always welcome. But now he tended to linger in the hallway just down from the door.

Finn hadn't played, so he didn't get pulled for media, and he was out of the room, tie loosely slung around his neck, shirt partially unbuttoned, fairly quickly after the game ended.

"Hey, I was thinking we could grab dinner. That steakhouse you like so much." Morgan didn't say, *because Jacob's out of town and you might actually have time for your pathetic dad,* but he was thinking it.

They included him—enough, that he really shouldn't complain—but when the three of them were together, it was hard to shake that third wheel feeling.

"Actually," Finn said, "Monty's hosting a win streak thing at his house tonight."

"Oh." It made sense. Six games.

"You should come," Finn said.

Hayes would definitely not want him to be there. Morgan knew that without him ever telling him. But Morgan wanted to go. Wanted to see Hayes' house. Wanted to see Hayes not just on the ice.

Maybe he could even start to soften Hayes up. More receptive to Morgan's groveling, anyway. Morgan tried to remember the speech he'd composed the last time he was going to do this, but couldn't. Maybe that was better anyway. That time felt so dismal and brutal he tried not to think about it. He couldn't say he'd ever hated himself, but he'd come damn close those weeks.

"I don't know." Morgan hesitated as they walked out towards the player parking lot.

Finn smacked him in the arm. "Seriously?"

"It's for your team—"

"And the families of the team. All the WAGs are gonna be there."

"Too bad Jacob won't be then." It usually filled him with some kind of amusement that Jacob Braun was now a WAG, but could he even make fun of Jacob for that now? When he wanted to be one, too?

Correction: he'd considered being one for awhile now. He was just contemplating actually doing something about it now.

Finn smacked him again. "That's mean. And that term is ridiculously outdated."

"They come up with another one yet?"

Finn shook his head. "But they should. Anyway, you should come."

Morgan wasn't stupid enough to ask if Hayes had invited him specifically.

Obviously, Hayes kept Morgan's name out of his mouth unless he had a very good reason to say it.

"I—"

"Don't say you don't know. You're coming," Finn announced.

"I always wondered how you wore Jacob's good intentions down. This is how you did it, isn't it?" Morgan grumbled as Finn grabbed his keys from his hand.

Finn just laughed. "I thought you never wanted to know the details."

"I don't," Morgan said, climbing into the passenger seat.

"Yeah, sort of. It's not like you don't know how to be persistent about something," Finn said, shooting him a sideways look.

There was a certifiably insane part of Morgan that considered telling Finn at least part of the story on the way to Hayes' house. But he hadn't been sure he'd work up the nerve during an entire three course steak dinner. It was never going to happen on a short drive.

"True," Morgan agreed. "It's sort of a Reynolds trademark." It was. Why had he forgotten that? He'd never let anyone tell him no, not when it came to something he wanted. Of course, those things had all been hockey related.

"Exactly," Finn said, shooting him a grin. "Jacob didn't stand a chance."

It was an even shorter drive than he'd anticipated, and way less time than he'd needed, to work up the determination to not let Hayes just brush him off again. Less than ten minutes later, Finn was pulling the SUV down a side street lined with palm trees and gates. Discreet outdoor lighting, shining on impressive Spanish-inspired facades and spotless landscaping.

One gate was open. A few cars had already parked on the street. But there was one spot left on the big driveway. Finn pulled in and parked. Turned off the car.

Turned to Morgan, who was really trying not to panic.

Was showing up uninvited the best way to begin getting on Hayes' good side? Morgan was suddenly unsure.

His fingers twitched, nearly reaching for his phone. He could ask Danny, but Danny would tell him to just go for it, probably with a hundred exclamation points.

"Come on," Finn said, shooting him a look that said, very clearly, *what the fuck is your problem?*

Morgan wanted to laugh. Maybe cry. But he followed Finn into Hayes' house, anyway.

He'd been to enough of these that the kitchen full of rowdy hockey players, joking and jostling as they descended on the pizza boxes laid across the countertop, didn't faze him. Hayes stood in front of an enormous stainless steel refrigerator, handing out bottles of water and beer and laughing.

He hung back, letting Finn go ahead and greet Hayes. Grab a few slices of pizza. But then after he'd done that there was nothing in the way, no reason for them not to look at each other.

Morgan knew the moment their eyes met, and he wanted to pretend he imagined the complicated look that crossed Hayes face, before it was wiped clean. But he didn't think he had.

"Hey," Morgan said, shoving his hands into his pockets so he wouldn't be tempted to reach out and touch. "I . . .uh . . .Finn said I should come."

Hayes looked at him, his eyes annoyingly opaque, not giving anything away. "You want something to drink? I've got some beer. Water. Um. Gatorade?"

"A beer's fine."

"Lars will be around in a minute. He stopped by his house for more supplies. I don't drink much in the season." Hayes pulled a beer out of the fridge and then swiped a hand through his loose, damp hair.

Morgan's fingers tingled. He'd done that once. Remembered, too well, tangling his hand in Hayes' hair. With desire and desperation. And with fondness.

"Smart." Guys today were so much smarter than they'd been even fifteen years ago.

"Em—Lars' wife—helps me out a lot. Since you know . . ." Hayes made a face. Another one of those complicated looks passed over his face. Morgan wanted to tell him it was okay. That nobody cared if Hayes didn't have a partner to take on the traditional head WAG duties. "Since I've been single basically forever."

Hayes' voice was wry. Almost pained. He opened the beer and slid it over the counter towards Morgan.

"You weren't once." God, they weren't going to talk about this now, were they? With half a hockey team ten feet away, including his son, eating through a small pizzeria's worth of takeout?

Apparently yes.

"Yeah, that didn't exactly work out the way I hoped." Hayes pushed his hair back again and sighed.

"If he wasn't willing to stick around when it was hard, he wasn't worth you."

Hayes looked shocked. "Are you really—no, actually, I *can* believe you'd be the one saying this."

Morgan shrugged, picking up the beer. If he was using his own rubric, then *he* didn't deserve to be within a hundred feet of Hayes. But he could be better. He *would* be better.

Yes, he'd fucked up, but he was smart enough to realize he'd done it, and he was going to make it right. That asshole who'd dumped Hayes hadn't been bright enough to realize what he'd lost.

Morgan had spent every moment of the last six years knowing.

"You're unbelievable," Hayes said, not even sounding mad.

"He was an idiot." Morgan lowered his voice. "I was *also* an idiot."

Hayes stared at him, like he couldn't believe what he was hearing. A second later, he turned back towards the fridge and pulled out a second beer. Opened it, took a very long drink.

"I thought you didn't typically drink during the season," Morgan said.

Hayes' gaze was hot. With anger? With something else? Morgan didn't know. But it was *still* better than that flat expression Morgan couldn't interpret. "I decided to make an exception."

Morgan nodded, like it all made sense. Like he was used to driving people to drink.

Danny would have told him right now that he *should* be.

Jacob would've agreed with him.

God, why did all his friends suck?

"Makes . . .uh . . .sense," Morgan said.

Hayes wet his bottom lip. Just a flicker of his pink tongue, and it made Morgan hot all over.

He wished that he could remember even a line from the groveling speech he'd planned, but all coherent thought was wiped clean from his brain with just that glimpse of Hayes' tongue. Besides, he wasn't going to be able to deliver any of it here. Not right now, anyway.

"You used to be more contrary," Hayes observed neutrally.

"I know," Morgan said.

He'd been kind of an asshole most of his career—most of his life, honestly. But this was part of *trying*. To keep to the sideline. To the back of the suite. To not waltz into the locker room like he still owned hockey. He was mostly doing it for Finn. But also for Hayes.

Hayes didn't deserve to be overshadowed on his own god-damn team.

"It's weird." Hayes' nose crinkled, adorably. "I don't know if I like it."

"Oh." Clearly Hayes didn't see it as Morgan proving his loyalty. His affection. His endless fucking love. But in so many ways, that was what it was.

Fucking figures.

Before Morgan could correct him, Lars and a petite blond woman Morgan recognized from seeing her around the facility walked in, carrying boxes. "Hey, guys," Emily called out, "a little help, please?"

And there was no question she was in charge, because half the team leaped up, filing out the front door to help her bring more boxes of booze in.

"Guess it's good we've got an off day tomorrow," Hayes said, shrugging. He met Morgan's eyes and then he looked away.

Hayes was in heaven and in hell.

Morgan was here. In his house.

In his house.

Drinking his beer. Eating pizza he'd bought.

Chatting with Jasper and Lars and Em, with Finn and Silov, rotating around to several of the groups of players. Laughing with them. Not being Morgan Reynolds, the chosen one, but someone else.

Someone Hayes wasn't sure he quite recognized anymore.

Hayes tried to distract himself. Did his usual captain routine. Made sure when he did his own rounds, he went the opposite direction of Morgan. Always kept at least one group in between them at all times.

He wasn't going to make the same mistake of the bar bathroom. When he did have to pee, several beers and a tequila shot in, he retreated to his suite, going to the bathroom and splashing cold water on his face, giving himself a pep talk in the mirror.

It didn't really work. He still felt flushed. Partly from the booze, sure, but also because it felt like Morgan was slotting into his life, into this team, gently and insistently, like he was meant to be there.

They'd agreed that they'd do what they needed for Finn.

But this didn't feel like it was for Finn. Not when every few minutes, Hayes would feel a particular burning between his shoulder blades, and when he'd look back, his gaze would intercept Morgan's.

It felt too much like it had been in Toronto.

Like they were both just biding their time before they got to be alone again, finally.

This night isn't ending that way, though.

Except that Hayes was pretty sure he was the only one who'd gotten that memo.

Because he looked up, a few hours into the party, and realized that Morgan was one of the few guys left.

Lars and Emily had just taken off, to relieve their babysitter.

Jasper had left five minutes earlier with a contingent of the younger guys, including Finn and Silov, to go to some hot new club in town. Hayes had been pretty sure that Morgan left then, too, not to go clubbing, but back to his house. Alone. Thank goodness.

But when Hayes grabbed a garbage bag and started going around, filling it with empty bottles, he emerged from the back patio.

Still very much here.

And, Hayes realized with growing horror, the only one who was still left.

"Hey," Morgan said, like it was totally normal and fine that they were alone together in Hayes' house. Like it wasn't weird. Like he hadn't spent too many years and had too many unhinged fantasies about this very scenario. "There were some empties outside. You want me to grab them for you?"

Hayes shoved the trash bag at Morgan's hands. "Sure."

Morgan shot him a confused look. "Weren't you using this?"

"I . . .uh . . .yes."

"So just come with me," Morgan said, gesturing to the big open doors that led to the patio. "Bring your bag."

Hayes considered arguing, but it was clear from the way Morgan turned and started walking outside that he just expected him to follow.

So fucking typical.

"You're so bossy," Hayes complained as he trailed after, stepping through the wide-open doors.

"I thought you were just complaining that I was too nice," Morgan said, his tone gently teasing.

"I take it back," Hayes grumbled under his breath. Morgan leaned over and picked up several bottles in one of his big hands and Hayes tried not to remember what that hand had felt like on him.

Maybe Jasper was right and it had been too long since his last hookup.

Walking over, Morgan dropped the bottles into the trash bag but didn't move away the way Hayes expected he would.

He could say a lot about Morgan Reynolds, but since he'd arrived in Tampa, he'd given Hayes his space. Hayes hadn't even run into him at the gym again.

He'd told himself that was fine and good, better than the alternative, for sure, but maybe he'd been a little disappointed.

The view really had been top-notch. Distracting, yes, but excellent.

"When are you going to the gym now?" Hayes asked, the booze making his tongue loose, and the thought just popped out.

Morgan paused, a slow smile spreading across his face. "You noticed."

"Kind of hard to forget," Hayes bitched.

"Late at night. Seemed the best time to avoid . . . um . . . anyone who I might be bothering."

Morgan didn't have to stumble over his words for Hayes to know who exactly Morgan was avoiding. *Him.*

"You didn't have to do that," Hayes said softly. It was so hard to think of Morgan as the guy who'd broken his heart when he was staring at him with those soft, warm hazel eyes. When he was trying to be nice, just to be nice. When he'd avoided Hayes just because Hayes had been shitty and told Morgan to his face he didn't want him around.

"You asked me to." Morgan took a step closer. His jaw clenched and a second later, he glanced over Hayes' shoulder. Like he'd given too much away.

And maybe he had. Maybe . . .

No. *No.* That would be insane. It would be insane to forget how the last six years had felt, how he'd missed Morgan every single fucking day.

But you missed him every single fucking day.

He had. And he'd had what, three beers and two shots of tequila, when he'd barely drunk for the last three months? He was allowed to make a stupid mistake when three beers and two shots were involved. And if that stupid mistake felt as good as it seemed, before it could even happen yet?

Well, that said it all.

Hayes set his free hand on Morgan's shoulder. "I shouldn't have said that." He'd meant it, one hundred and ten percent, at the time, because it had felt like sheer fucking torture, to have to face Morgan and *not* want him. But looking at it now, Hayes wished he hadn't been so blunt.

"Did you mean it?" Morgan asked. Soft. Intimate. It brought back so many memories, visceral and hot, of dim hotel rooms. Morgan's voice murmuring in his ear. They'd only had ten days, but every single minute of their time together felt like it was scribed onto his heart.

"At the time, a little. But not enough." Hayes' fingers curled into Morgan's shoulder as he tugged him a half inch closer. He felt as big and broad and firm as he'd felt then. Hayes wanted to gorge, to fling himself right at Morgan and hope he'd catch him, but he held himself back, *barely*.

Morgan huffed out a little laugh. "I want to argue with you but that would be stupid of me."

"Yeah?" It was so easy to tilt his head up, to look Morgan right in the eye. He could already taste Morgan's mouth.

There was an inevitability about this, same as there'd been six years ago. He was fated to want Morgan. Fated to lose him. Fated to pine over him. Fated to get another taste, when he'd been so sure he never would again.

"Well, duh. I told you I was an idiot, I told you—"

The last thing he wanted was for Morgan to ruin this with another shitty apology. "Shut up. Stop talking," Hayes said and kissed him.

Morgan gasped into his mouth, like that was the last thing he'd expected. But then before Hayes could pull away and demand to know if that wasn't what he'd fucking meant by saying in that wry, regretful tone, *I was an idiot, too*, Morgan wrapped one of those big, warm hands around his waist and pulled him flush against him. His tongue dipped between Hayes' lips.

Hayes dropped the trash bag with a crash, barely hearing the sound as he slid his other hand onto Morgan's opposite shoulder.

He kissed him like he'd dreamt about for so fucking long.

Like he'd thought about doing this every day for the last two thousand plus days, and *missed* it for every one of those days.

And Morgan? Gave back as good as Hayes was giving. Like he'd been there, too, and now that he was getting another chance, was not going to waste it.

They stumbled, hands gripping each other, lips moving together fiercely, over to one of the pool loungers.

Hayes felt his knees hit the edge, and then Morgan was pushing him down. Hovering over him. His big, hard body covering his, cock noticeably pressing against Hayes' thigh.

"Fuck, baby," Morgan groaned out. "You feel so good?" His voice was full of incredulous disbelief.

Like he'd never imagined he'd ever get to feel it again.

Hayes wanted to tell him that he'd never intended to let him, but that wasn't just a punishment for Morgan, but for him, too.

And he was so fucking tired of punishing and denying and pretending.

He curled a hand around Morgan's shoulder and pulled him more tightly against him, relishing the feel of Morgan's body caging him in, pressing him down.

It felt like déjà vu and a hallucination. An echo of what it had felt like then, all those old memories clashing and blending with the new.

Hayes tucked a calf around Morgan's and swallowed another of his groans. Their mouths moved against each other, slick and so eager, and for a single delusional second, Hayes thought, *this could be enough. This could be enough forever.*

But of course it wasn't. It wouldn't ever be.

He'd seen Morgan's big hand earlier tonight and imagined how it would feel against his bare skin. And when it rucked up Hayes' shirt, he nearly short-circuited at the feel of it, heat pressed into heat.

"Good?" Morgan murmured into his mouth.

"The best." For a second, Hayes felt a flash of embarrassment. Because that was true. It was the best, and he'd never wanted Morgan to know that.

But then Morgan was straight up groaning harder, hips making tiny little aborted thrusts as he ground his cock against Hayes' thigh.

Turned out it was impossible to feel any kind of way but insanely turned on when two simple words had that kind of effect on a man like Morgan Reynolds.

"Want you," Morgan gasped out. "Let me."

Hayes didn't know what he was letting him do, but he nodded mindlessly. Morgan could do anything he wanted. No questions. No hesitation.

Morgan reached down and tugged Hayes' T-shirt over his head, his fingertips pressing into his pec, thumb reaching down to brush his nipple.

Keeping the noise in was impossible, but Hayes tried.

"No, no," Morgan argued breathlessly. "Let me hear you, baby. I wanna hear you. Imagined you like this so many goddamn times."

Morgan's words were like a shock to his spine, to his skin, to his cock. Bowing him, remaking him, *unmaking* him.

He slid down Hayes' body, tugging his shorts and his briefs as he went, and Hayes only had a brief moment to prepare for the white-hot heat of Morgan's mouth before it was closing over his dick.

Hayes knew he should take advantage of the view. Should *look*. Even if the sight of Morgan's mouth closing over him and sucking him down was another, nearly unbearable, jolt of electricity.

He pulled off for a second, hand closing around the base, tapped the head of his cock against his tongue and that was definitely a move Morgan hadn't had six years ago.

Hayes didn't even give a fuck if he'd learned that from someone else. He only cared that he was doing it to *him*, now.

"So eager I didn't even ask if it was okay out here," Morgan murmured in a hushed voice. "Can anyone—"

"No, it's private. There's walls."

Hayes wouldn't have even cared if there wasn't. Let the world see Morgan sucking his cock. He'd wear even the shame of it as a badge of pride.

"Good," Morgan said. "Then they won't hear you scream."

The haughty, sure-he-no-longer-gave-a-shit part of Hayes, that wanted to be more over him than he clearly was, scoffed at Morgan's presumption.

The other part rolled over and hoped, desperately, that Morgan would take pity on him and make it that good. Give him everything he'd wanted on all those lonely, silent nights.

"Come on," Hayes begged.

Morgan didn't even hesitate. Didn't make him ask again. Just swallowed him in his mouth, tongue flicking out, curling around the head. Making Hayes sweat.

He'd definitely been tipsy before the kiss. But now he felt stone-cold sober. Sober and desperate, like he was already holding on to control by the tips of his fingernails.

It probably wasn't even the best, most expert blowjob he'd ever gotten, but none of that mattered. It was lighting him up that this was Morgan. That for once, he didn't have to imagine and fantasize and pretend. It was Morgan's hair he was curling his fingers into. Morgan's face lifting towards his, the heat in his eyes searing Hayes.

Then Morgan curled a hand around Hayes' thigh and squeezed, drifting lower. Brushed a thumb against his hole. Hayes made a garbled noise full of nonsense.

"What's that, baby? You want something?"

Hayes knew what he wanted.

He'd have died of shame before asking for it even six hours ago, but he'd not only run out of give-a-fucks, he'd decided to embrace the crawl of humiliation up his spine.

What did it matter, if he could feel *this* again?

"I want you to fuck me," Hayes slurred out.

Morgan froze, mouth curling around the tip of Hayes' cock, thumb barely nudging his hole.

"You heard me," Hayes said when Morgan said nothing. Just stared at him with shock.

Not *bad* shock. Just . . . *shock* shock.

"You mean that?" Morgan whispered.

Hayes laughed, a little hysterically. "Yes, fuck, *yes*. God, let me up. My bedroom—" He broke off. Laughed again.

Morgan lifted himself with a curse and held out a hand to Hayes. They both stumbled a bit as he finally came upright. "You okay?" Hayes said, still chuckling under his breath. He didn't let go of Morgan's hand as he dragged him into the house. Then through the living room, the kitchen, down the hallway.

Until he opened the door to his suite and tugged Morgan inside.

Pushed him down onto the bed.

Having his whole body covered by Morgan's had felt fucking unreal. But climbing onto him, perching on those incredible thighs, getting to see his face as he gazed at Hayes? That was resolve-melting.

He was right back at *anything Morgan wants, he can have.*

"Shit, baby, you look so good. Like . . ." Morgan gusted out a sigh. Sounding in awe or something very like it. It made Hayes' dick twitch. His heart clench. "Like an angel, right here for me."

"Yeah?" Hayes wiggled on his cock, feeling it hard and eager beneath him.

"God, so good. So beautiful. Imagined you like this. Feel heavenly. Look even better. Better than I could've thought. Meant it. A fucking angel."

It was overwhelming. Hayes rucked up Morgan's T-shirt and pressed a palm against his abs, his ribs. Wiggling harder. He was going to end up coming against Morgan's shorts, when that wasn't what he wanted. But if Morgan kept running his mouth, his dirty talk so unbelievably hot and unexpectedly romantic, he wasn't going to end up having a choice.

"Want you just like this." The words slipped out of Hayes' mouth like a prayer. So serious. Too serious, probably.

But it was impossible to consider the implications of that right now. Not when Morgan was settling one hand on his hip and the other was gripping his cock. Giving it a much-needed twist of his wrist.

"Fuck, so good," Morgan had the nerve to say. Like he was the one getting touched. The one getting dragged to the edge.

"Want you to be naked," Hayes said and tried to shove Morgan's pants off without even bothering to get off his lap.

It was hard and more than a little frustrating and Morgan kept half-laughing, half-marveling at him as he did it.

But then he let out a solid moan when Hayes had finally accomplished it, leaning forward, pressing his mouth against Morgan's collarbone and then lifting his head to meet his mouth.

Their cocks brushed, precome making the slide a little easier, and Hayes swallowed Morgan's groan.

"Need to see you," Morgan begged against his mouth. "Let me see you, angel. Gonna come, just watching you like this."

The sex they'd had in Toronto had been hesitant, initially, but still hot. Hot enough to think about six years later. But this was a whole other level of honest mixed with a good dose of unhinged insanity, and Hayes' head was spinning with it.

Hayes propped himself up again, missing Morgan's mouth but this was good too. Not just to see Morgan's face, no longer just in his head, but in *reality*, but more because of the way Morgan looked at him. Like all the polite indifference he'd worn since arriving in Tampa had been stripped away, and what Hayes was seeing in his eyes was how he really felt.

That look was almost enough to get Hayes all the way there. Then Morgan reached up and spit in his hand, and wrapped it around both of their cocks, and Hayes groaned at the feel.

At the way the pleasure pulled him right under, sent him reeling.

He was so close.

Then Morgan reached up and kissed him hard, murmuring against his mouth, "So beautiful, angel," and that was the last piece he'd been missing.

His orgasm hit him hard, and a second later, Morgan tensed underneath him, and they were practically coming together.

Morgan fell back onto the bed, white streaks of come decorating his partially exposed torso.

For a moment, Hayes just stared.

That had really happened.

He wasn't in a dream. He was really sitting here, on Morgan's thighs, and they'd just both come their brains out.

Morgan was staring too, like he couldn't quite believe it either.

Hayes wondered if he was going to have to be the one to break the silence, but then Morgan opened his mouth. "I didn't . . ." He trailed off.

Well, it was too much to hope for him to say something that meant *anything*.

"Didn't what?"

Morgan chuckled, then, his chest vibrating. "I didn't come here for this. But this . . ." The look in his eyes was deadly earnest. "It was more than I could've hoped for."

It was hard to stay still and see that look. Hayes was pretty sure he *had* to mean it, but then if that was true, why had it taken them six years to get here? Why had he ever left in the first place?

And what was going to stop him from *not* meaning it in a week?

Gingerly, Hayes slid off, not saying anything. He padded to the bathroom, not bothering to flick on a light. It wasn't hard to clean up—only took a few swipes of a wet washcloth—and he came out with another one in his hand for Morgan.

If it had been six years ago, Hayes might have wiped him up himself. But there was a chasm between them still. A careful distance that he'd just crossed, but now he wasn't sure. He handed it over to Morgan instead.

"What did *you* hope for?" Morgan asked, after he finished and then tossed it in the open hamper. He didn't have to point out that only a week ago, Hayes had insisted—and wanted to *mean* it—that he didn't want Morgan around.

Hayes shrugged. His heart felt too close to his throat; like he was five seconds away from word vomiting everything he'd spent all these years thinking.

That would be bad.

Lifting himself onto his elbows, Morgan shot him a look full of uncomfortable honesty. "Aren't you going to tell me you regret it?"

He *should*. Zach was screaming in his ear that he absolutely, one hundred fucking percent regretted it. But he didn't.

"No," Hayes said. Realized it was the first thing he'd said since it ended. Since he'd supposedly lost his mind.

"I don't," Morgan said.

Hayes considered repeating what he'd said six years ago, that he couldn't take scraps, but these had been *very* good scraps, and it wasn't like he hadn't regretted saying that a thousand times after the words had left his mouth.

Instead, he turned out the light. Pulled the covers back and settled onto the bed. Morgan didn't exactly cuddle up close, but Hayes could feel the heat of him, impossible to ignore.

"You gonna kick me out?" Morgan asked, in a low voice.

"No," Hayes said again. Apparently that was the only word he knew anymore.

And he fell asleep like that. Morgan, closer than he'd been in years, but still far away.

CHAPTER 16

When Morgan woke up, it was still dark.

For a second, he was confused and unsure where he was.

The bed felt foreign. Firm and big, an acre of mattress. Cool sheets against his naked skin.

Then he remembered, his memory coming back in flashes. *Hayes. Him.*

They'd slept together, again.

Morgan rolled onto his back and realized a moment later that he was alone.

Was that why he'd woken up?

He never slept next to anyone, not for years and years, so it didn't make sense that he'd woken up when Hayes slipped out.

For a long minute, Morgan waited. Expecting him to come back from the bathroom. Maybe even the kitchen. But that minute turned into five, counted down in his head, and then Morgan realized maybe he wasn't coming back.

Hayes had been quiet after they'd had sex. He'd barely said a handful of words, and Morgan had wondered if he should say *more*, but then he'd been afraid to. What if he said too much?

Said it wrong, again? Scared Hayes away before he could ever make it right?

But then he hadn't kicked Morgan out of bed, either.

That had to be enough.

Morgan lifted himself out of bed and went in search of Hayes.

Found him a few minutes later, outside, face lit by the dim blue pool light. Curled up on one of the loungers—not the one they'd nearly fucked on—a blanket wrapped around his naked shoulders even though it was south Florida, so it was hardly cold even though it was the middle of the night.

"Hey," Morgan said, and Hayes looked up at him in surprise. Like he hadn't been expected to get caught. "You okay?"

Hayes picked at the corner of the blanket. "Yeah," he said.

He was regretting not grabbing any of his clothes. Not because it was cold, but because he felt exposed. Weirdly vulnerable in a way he never did, even after spending so many years naked in changing rooms.

There was a moment he thought he should leave Hayes to his two a.m. mental gymnastics, but there was no way the mental gymnastics were not about him.

Morgan settled down on the next lounger over.

Glancing over at him, Morgan saw the corner of Hayes' mouth tilt up. "You gonna sit out here, too?"

It was not a hard question to answer. "You're here. So I'm here," Morgan said, shrugging.

Hayes opened his mouth and then snapped it shut again. But before Morgan could elaborate, he was turning his whole body in Morgan's direction.

"Honestly, what the fuck," he said, not really asking and not really sounding pissed either. Just incredulous. "What the fuck, Morgan."

"I was an idiot. We established that." But it was more than that too. "You know it never could've worked. We didn't talk about it, back then, because it was impossible."

Hayes didn't say anything but the look on his face told Morgan that the same thought had crossed *his* mind.

"And after . . ." Morgan had promised himself he'd never tell Hayes this, but there was no way to make this right without complete honesty. "After I retired, I was going to come see you. Had my ticket booked and everything. And then you came out."

It was hard to watch Hayes as the bomb dropped on him. He sat there, shocked into silence for a long moment.

"Alexander." He looked drawn and white, blue light playing over the angles of his face.

"I thought you were happy. For a crazy moment, I thought, I could go ask him still. Maybe he'd want me instead, but then I thought, you're happy. That's all I wanted. Better that I leave you alone—"

"I wasn't," Hayes interrupted. Leaning forward. "I wasn't fucking happy. Not happy enough, anyway. He dumped me because I was still in love with you."

Morgan froze. Couldn't imagine what his expression looked like.

Should he apologize? Should he grovel? *Keep* groveling?

Immediately fall to his knees, like Danny constantly kept suggesting, and say he loved him too? That he'd loved him for six years?

None of the options seemed good enough. So he just sat there in stunned silence, instead. *Totally better*, Danny told him in his head. *Faced with* the *moment, you fucking freeze.*

"I know, pretty pathetic, isn't it?" Hayes said, with a self-deprecating smile. "I tried to get over it. But from what happened tonight, you can see how well *that* went."

Morgan finally managed to unstick his tongue. "I . . .I never got over it. I meant it, I was an idiot."

"Not a wrong idiot though," Hayes pointed out gently. "You were right about it not working then. How would it have? And I knew it, which is why I didn't say anything, either. I only wish you hadn't . . .just . . .*left*."

Morgan wished he hadn't either. He hadn't been able to be as honest as he should have during that piss-poor apology six years ago, but he could do it now. He'd practiced the confession enough times. "I shouldn't have handled it that way. It doesn't make it right, but . . ." It was hard—terrifying, actually—to meet Hayes' gaze but he did it anyway. "But I didn't think I'd have been able to do it, if I waited, if I said goodbye. If I . . .if I did it right."

"What are you saying?" Of course Hayes cut right through his nebulous bullshit.

Morgan stood, still feeling that vulnerability creep up his spine. Walked over to Hayes. If he fucked this up now, he wasn't going to get a second chance.

Hayes stared at him.

"If I'd had to say goodbye, I wouldn't have said goodbye."

"But—"

But Morgan shook his head. He had to get through this. "Hockey was the most important thing, forever. My entire life. More important than my marriage. God help me, more important than my kid, for a long time. I'm trying to fix that now. But that time, with you, it made me want more than just hockey for the first time ever. I wanted to feel that way every single fucking day. I'd have done something crazy to keep it."

He'd lain there, insane thoughts going through his head. Like demanding a trade to a California team. Like refusing, like a lovestruck fool, to play if he couldn't play with Hayes.

"You wouldn't have," Hayes argued, because of course, even now, he was being contrary.

But Morgan wouldn't take him any other way.

"I would have," Morgan said. If he'd fallen in any deeper, there was no way he wouldn't have.

Finally, Hayes moved his legs back. Morgan sat at the edge of the lounger. Maybe he'd screwed this up so many times. Maybe they'd gone past the point of no return. But he could at least be honest.

"I loved you, so I absolutely would have," Morgan said quietly. "Never felt that way about anyone else. Not before. Not since."

Hayes' breath went out of him in a big whoosh. He leaned back on the lounger. Eyes so green, even in the blue light of the pool. "Loved?" he questioned quietly.

Digging his fingers into his thigh, Morgan knew he was doing the right thing, even though it felt like the scariest leap he'd ever taken. "Love," he corrected. "I love you."

"Oh. *Oh*." Hayes actually sounded surprised. Shocked, in fact.

"What did you think? That I said all that stuff during sex because I . . ." Morgan didn't know how to finish that sentence. Decided maybe it was better that he didn't.

"I thought it was . . .I don't know . . .sex. You talking with your dick."

"I *was* talking with my dick. It's always been a little obsessed with you. But it wasn't just my dick," Morgan admitted dryly.

Hayes sighed. "We're both idiots. Clearly. It *wouldn't* have worked then. We can agree on that, I guess. But what about now? Do you even want—"

"Yes," Morgan said quickly. Before Hayes could change his mind.

Hayes smiled and, for the first time in a long time, definitely for the first time since Morgan had come to Tampa, Hayes looked *happy*. Really fucking happy. He reached out and poked Morgan in the thigh with a fingertip. "You don't even know what I was going to ask."

"Whatever you're going to suggest, I'm gonna want it."

"You seriously mean that?" Hayes rolled his eyes, but he looked absolutely delighted. So surprised and unexpectedly thrilled, Morgan knew that he'd work, just as hard as he'd worked at hockey, to make sure Hayes looked like this *every single fucking day* for the rest of his life.

"I wouldn't have said it if I didn't."

"But . . ." Hayes *looked* happy, but he still seemed like he was hesitating.

Morgan wanted to lean in and kiss *him* this time, but like before, he didn't want to be the one pushing. As tough as it was to put everything in Hayes' court, that was where the final decisions needed to stay.

"But what? I'm crazy about you, angel. I love you. I want everything you'll give me," he murmured. He could prime the pump though, so to speak. And felt no guilt about leaning in closer, tucking his hand under the burrito-ed blankets, and squeezing Hayes' knee.

Butterflies fluttered in his stomach. He hadn't known what that was, before, but he knew now.

"How would this even *work*? It wouldn't have before."

Morgan wasn't sure he was following Hayes' logic. "You're playing, but I'm not. I'm . . .well, half my time is spent playing third wheel with my son and Jacob, a quarter pretending that I know what the fuck I'm talking about on TV, and the last quarter . . ." It was painful to admit this, too, but Hayes *had* to know. "The last quarter, I'm alone. How do you *think* it would work?"

Hayes' gaze was serious. "You know how much time I have to give to the team."

"Angel, believe me. I know. I've spent the last two months watching you."

"You were around, sure—" Hayes began to ramble, but this was just ridiculous. Morgan couldn't let this stand.

"No," he corrected gently, squeezing Hayes' knee again. It felt delicate under his hand, which was insane, because he knew how tough Hayes was. He was beautiful and sexy and he was also so good at hockey, at twisting D-men around his little finger, it made Morgan want to cry. Made him want to drop to his knees and worship him the way he deserved.

"No," he continued, firmer this time. "No, I've been around for Finn, sure, and I've been watching him, but you know who I watch every single goddamn game? *You*. Every time Finn mentions your name, it's like something inside me lights up. I've been paying attention. I know how much time you spend. You're a great captain of a great hockey team. I'm not asking to take from that. I just . . .I just want you. However much of you that you're willing to give me."

It kind of killed Morgan how shocked Hayes increasingly looked. With every word he said, his mouth dropped open a little bit more. Like he couldn't even believe what he was hearing. And yes, absolutely, Morgan knew he was an asshole. That he'd been an asshole to Hayes, for sure, but it really fucking sucked that Hayes didn't know just how *much* Morgan cared.

He was going to make sure, no matter how this turned out, that Hayes never had a reason to doubt, again.

"You . . ." Hayes wet his lips. Morgan really, *really* wanted to lean in. Chase that tongue. Taste him again. Take him to bed, *again*. Once had not been enough. A million times would not be enough.

They'd barely gotten to take the edge off their mutual hunger six years ago, and ever since, Morgan had never found anyone who'd ignited his own, not like Hayes had.

"Me what?" Morgan murmured, leaning in another inch closer. He knew what it had looked like, when he'd shown up after that first game. The last thing he wanted was for Hayes to think he was doing or saying any of this to get laid. He'd meant it then, and he meant it now. Hayes was the *least* convenient choice in the world.

But that didn't mean he didn't want him, desperately.

"I didn't know you could talk like this. Say this stuff. You're going to . . ." He laughed, sort of self-consciously. "You're fucking me up, Mo."

"In a good kind of way, I hope?"

He laughed again, but easier this time. "Yeah. It is good. But it's scary. I don't know. I don't . . . I've spent a long time believing this was never going to happen. That you didn't feel the same way I did."

"And that's my fault." Morgan didn't have to ask. He *knew*.

"Yes, but no. Maybe I should've listened to you, after the game. Instead I just kicked you out."

"You were brave. You were smart. You made the right choice." It killed him to admit that, but it was true.

Hayes shot him a hard look. "Seriously?"

"You did what I couldn't. Which was take a stand. I wanted you too badly to do the non-crazy thing."

Hayes tilted his head closer. A mischievous look on his face. Morgan wanted to eat it up. "Can we do the crazy thing now?" he asked.

"*Yes*," Morgan said and kissed him.

This time, he wasn't going to let them get carried away without giving Hayes the thing he wanted. The thing he'd asked for. Morgan slid his hands up Hayes' thighs and then settled his legs around Morgan's waist. Then picked him up, Hayes giggling adorably into his mouth, and carted him right back into the house.

"Wait, your back, your *knees*," Hayes laughed as Morgan carried him into the bedroom.

"Angel, I'm forty-one, not a hundred and one, *and* you're really not that heavy." He set Hayes on the edge of the bed, and it was impossible to resist leaning in and kissing him, gentle and soft.

They'd shared so many passionate kisses. And those were amazing. But somewhere in year two or three, he'd started thinking about it, not just when his dick was hard or when he was horny. What it might be like, when his bed felt particularly lonely, how it would feel if he could turn over and Hayes would be there, a tender look in his green eyes. Morgan would just press his mouth carefully against Hayes'. Not to start something. Not so he'd eventually get his dick wet. Just because he wanted to. Just because he could.

"I like this," Hayes said, curling his fingers around Morgan's shoulders more insistently, pulling him in closer between his legs. "I like *you*."

"You might be the only one." At one point, that thought would have filled Morgan with a nihilistic apathy, like it didn't even matter if he was universally hated, as long as he was still Morgan Reynolds. It mattered now, only for *one* person. Okay, two maybe. Three if Jacob was in a good mood. Four if Danny texted him back—and Danny always texted him back.

The point was: Morgan's circle of people who tolerated his shit, who he actually *liked* back, was extremely small.

But Hayes had always been at the top.

"Jacob likes you now. And you like Jacob now," Hayes teased, bare foot hooking around Morgan's calf, even that simple touch electrifying.

"Can we not talk about him now, not when we're about to . . ." Morgan trailed off as Hayes used his considerable leg strength to pull him in even tighter, until he could feel Hayes' hard cock against his stomach.

"When we're about to what?" Hayes pretending innocence should not be sexy. But it was unbelievably sexy. Kind of like every other part of Hayes.

It was insane how at one point, so long ago it was nearly impossible to remember, he hadn't liked Hayes. Had barely ever let Hayes cross his mind. When he'd actively had to work not to resent him.

Those days were long gone.

"When I'm about to finally fuck you again, angel." Morgan leaned down, let his lips brush against Hayes' ear, then his neck, drifting down towards his collarbone. Felt his shiver. "You want that?"

"Wanted that before," Hayes murmured. "Lube's in the drawer by the bed. There's condoms, too, but . . ."

"But?" Morgan prompted, hearing the rough gravel in his own voice. They'd used condoms before. It hadn't even occurred to him to think they didn't have to.

But that had been a fling. Maybe neither of them knew exactly what shape this took now, but it was definitely not a fling.

"But I haven't with anyone, not in a long time, and I'm on PrEP and I've been tested too, recently. Start of the season." Hayes gazed up at him. "What about you?"

He'd had sex exactly twice since Hayes.

Once, about a year after Toronto, when he'd picked up a woman at a bar on a road trip. It had been mechanical and awful, and he'd thrown up in the bathroom sink after she'd left.

Then, the second time had been a few months after Hayes had come out—before he'd released the blunt press release that he and Alexander had broken up—and he'd picked up a guy that time. Let him suck his dick. Had given him a hand in return. Had stared at himself in the mirror after, hating his face, hating the crawling feeling of *not right, not right, not right* all over his skin.

But he couldn't tell Hayes any of that right now.

"I . . .there hasn't been anyone." That much was true. "And I was tested a year ago."

Hayes had been kissing down *his* neck, then, but his head popped up.

"In a *year*?" he asked incredulously.

"It's not that surprising," Morgan argued.

The look on Hayes' face said that the opposite was true. And okay, before Hayes, he'd never struggled to find sex when he wanted it.

"Um, yeah, it is," Hayes said.

"We're not talking about this right now," Morgan said firmly and wrapped his hand around Hayes' thigh and squeezed. "Does that mean you want me to leave the condoms in the drawer?"

Hayes nodded, gazing up at him like he was finally really seeing *and* believing what Morgan had said before.

Good.

He gave Hayes another long, leisurely, deep kiss, feeling his chest begin to rise and fall faster and his cock twitch against his stomach, smearing precome all over his skin.

Made sure he was nice and distracted first, before he went off to grab the lube.

Hayes had scooted up on the bed, moonlight falling over his skin, when Morgan returned.

"God, I want you," Hayes sighed as Morgan opened the lube, trying to ignore how his fingers were shaking. It was lust, pure and simple. It was also nerves. It had been six years, and there had been times, more times than he liked to admit, when he'd imagined doing this again. How good he'd make it. So perfect that Hayes would never leave him again.

But now he knew Hayes loved him too. Could see it in his eyes, in every curve of his gorgeous face, as he leaned over, kissing him as Hayes' legs opened for him.

He'd have to trust this would be enough. That he'd eventually say all the right things, in the right order. That Hayes would believe him, would trust him again.

That they could fully mend this thing between them that they'd broken, before.

"Want you too, angel. So gorgeous just like this," Morgan murmured into his mouth as he slid a finger inside him.

Hayes groaned. Head falling back. Spine bowed. Neck exposed. Morgan felt lightheaded with it. Maybe other men had seen Hayes like this before, but he would be the last. The most important.

The only one Hayes loved.

He nudged another finger alongside the first, taking his time not only because it felt good even to do this to Hayes. To feel his heat and his tightness around his fingers. But because Hayes had said it without saying it—it had been awhile for him, and Morgan wasn't going to rush him.

"Please, *please*," Hayes begged, when he finally gave him a third. Slowly pushing in and out, wanting to absorb every moment of this. Never forget it.

"You gotta be patient, angel," Morgan warned. His cock was throbbing, insisting that it didn't want to be patient either. But he could do it, still. He could be anything Hayes needed.

"I'm done being patient," Hayes complained, hot green eyes meeting Morgan's. "*Come on.*"

And okay, maybe they *had* waited long enough. Hissing as he wrapped his lube-covered fingers around his dick, getting himself nice and slick so that all Hayes was going to feel was melting pleasure, Morgan positioned himself.

"Just like this," Morgan told him. Hayes' eyes fluttered closed in pleasure as he began to push in.

His fingertips dug insistently into Morgan's shoulders. He was probably leaving marks, the bite of pain a counterpoint to the pleasure spreading through him at the hot clasp of Hayes' body. But it was obvious from the look on Hayes' face that he was loving every second of this. Then there were the little punched groans he kept making, like he'd never felt anything as good in his life as Morgan's dick.

And Morgan's dick agreed right back, because Hayes was an angel and he felt like straight up heaven inside.

So good, Morgan was probably not going to last.

"Faster. I know you can," Hayes groaned, kicking at the back of Morgan's thigh with his heel. "Fuck me like you mean it, baby."

"I'm not gonna," Morgan panted. Hayes felt way too fucking good, and then it was *Hayes*. Under him, around him, the taste of him on his lips, on his tongue.

"Me neither," Hayes said, pushing himself up and kissing Morgan insistently.

Morgan lost it then, thrusting over and over like he could lose himself and that would be okay. It would be better than okay. It would be them, together, finally, and even though maybe their window of opportunity might've closed, it *hadn't* because they were here right now.

"God," Hayes cried out, angling his hips. Morgan pressed down harder, the slick head of Hayes' cock rubbing against his abs, and then he clenched up and that was it. He was falling, falling, *falling*, but this time he wasn't alone, Hayes was here, to catch him.

When he opened his eyes, still panting, there was something weirdly metallic on his tongue, and oh yeah, that was blood.

He glanced down and barked out a laugh. His teeth were imprinted right into Hayes' perfect shoulder.

And Hayes was laughing too. Straight up giggling, like he was never going to stop.

"Baby," he said breathless, "don't worry, I'm definitely yours."

"Sorry," Morgan said, flustered. God, he'd just bitten Hayes.

"Don't be." Hayes grinned. "I liked it."

"Yeah? It's not gonna be a problem in the locker room?"

"I can't exactly fine myself, right?" Hayes smirked.

"You could. Maybe you *should*." It was shockingly easy to joke about it. Easy because he felt light and easy, filled with helium.

If he wasn't pressed to Hayes, neck to thigh, he might just float away.

"Maybe I should," Hayes mused, tucking his face into Morgan's sweaty neck. "Can I . . ."

Morgan didn't know what Hayes was asking for but the answer was straightforward. "Anything."

Hayes chuckled again. Sounding just about as light as Morgan felt. "You don't even know what it is!"

"Only because you didn't tell me," Morgan joked, running a hand up and down Hayes' flank. "You gonna tell me?"

"Can I . . ." Hayes huffed out a laugh. "I feel stupid even asking. I love you, okay? I wanted to say it again."

Morgan's heart tripped again. He wasn't used to hearing it. He definitely was not used to believing it. And he couldn't do anything else, not when Hayes said it all breathless and eager and perfect like that.

"Why wouldn't that be okay? I love you, too." It was a fucking miracle, about a hundred miracles, one piled on top of another one, to be able to say it and not get immediately punched in the face for it.

Danny was going to tell him he'd used up the rest of his lifetime of luck on Hayes, and Morgan was going to tell him and *believe it*, that it was worth it. That Hayes was worth it, and if he'd had more, he'd have spent that luck, too.

"You just . . .I didn't know if it was your kind of thing, but then you were so romantic before, saying all that stuff. I couldn't even believe it was coming out of your mouth." Hayes made a face and then buried his mouth in Morgan's shoulder again. "Ignore me, I'm sex stupid. Maybe I'm just stupid."

"No," Morgan said. He pulled back a little, not letting Hayes hide from him. "Give me five. I'm gonna clean us up, and then we're going to talk about this."

"Do we have to?"

"Yes," Morgan said firmly.

He didn't want to leave either, but they were sweaty and covered in come and blood, too. Because apparently Morgan doubled as a caveman. Groaning under his breath, he finally pulled out and scrambled over the bed on the way to the bath- room.

Washed out his mouth. Did his own cleanup and then came back with a washcloth, not letting Hayes take it from him.

He'd made this mess, he'd clean it up.

When they were finally clean and tucked back in bed—and Morgan had insisted on finding some first aid cream and smear- ing it across his teeth marks on Hayes' shoulder—Morgan said, "I know I was a shithead in Toronto."

"Just in Toronto?" Hayes teased sleepily.

"Okay, not just in Toronto. After too, definitely. When I came to see you in New York, for sure."

"I kicked you out, though." Hayes nuzzled into Morgan's shoulder.

"I was an ass before that," Morgan muttered. They could spend the ten years going over every ass-like thing he'd done.

The list was long. They might not ever exhaust it, but as long as he got this, it didn't matter.

"When you stared at me like I didn't even exist. Like you could see right through me, yeah," Hayes said quietly. "Every time we faced off that game, I thought I was going to die. Just crawl off the ice and hide forever."

Shame and guilt choked Morgan. It was hard to say anything, but he needed to. *He needed to.* "It was the only way I could do it. The only way I could get through the game without, I don't know . . ." Danny had said he might fall to his knees at center ice and propose gay marriage, with dogs and picket fences and late brunches. And maybe he'd been right. But that seemed like a *lot* to say, when they were still trying to figure out exactly what this looked like. It was still fresh. Delicate. Newly repaired.

"Doing something crazy?"

"Yeah." That sufficed. Hayes *understood*. Morgan took a deep breath. "Exactly."

"That . . .that makes sense. I hated it at the time. Every time it happened after that, but I get it."

"You don't think you did it, but you did. After that game, you did it to me, too."

"Thought I could give you a taste of your own medicine. But I didn't mean it." Hayes tucked his face into Morgan's bicep. "Never meant it."

"I didn't either, angel."

For a long moment Hayes was quiet, and Morgan thought maybe he'd fallen back asleep. Which would be perfectly okay with him. Falling asleep with Hayes in his arms would be the best thing that had happened to him in forever.

But then he said, so quietly Morgan barely heard it, "You were really going to come to Florida tell me you wanted me?"

"Had the trip booked. The speech rehearsed."

"What *was* the speech?"

"Something along the lines of *I'm an asshole, but I'm your asshole*," Morgan said.

Hayes laughed, which had been exactly the idea. "Seriously?"

"It was something like what you heard tonight. Probably this was a little better. Had more time. Was more desperate."

"I'm flattered."

"You should be."

"Also . . .you're not an asshole."

"Not to you."

"Not really at all, you just like to say it, probably because everyone always says it to you," Hayes said. "But even then . . .I don't want you to change. I like you just as you are."

"Really?" It felt too good to be true, but then Hayes as an entire entity had always felt too good to be true.

"Always," Hayes murmured and a second later, Morgan heard a gentle snore rumble through him.

He tightened his arm around Hayes and let sleep take him, too.

CHAPTER 17

When Hayes woke up, he ached. The general all-over ache of playing a hockey game the day before sure, but two specific aches.

First off, his ass. He could tell he'd had sex last night, and that it had been awhile.

And then there was his shoulder, where Morgan had straight-up *bitten* him.

God, Morgan.

Claimed him mind, body, and fucking soul.

Hayes lay there, very still, for a moment. Not wanting to roll over, worried that if he did, that space next to him in the bed might be empty.

He knew last night had happened. There was no way he could've even dreamt up how it felt, or how he still felt from it. A little bit like he'd been hit by a truck, physically and emotionally.

It had most definitely happened. There was no taking it back now, even if Hayes regretted it. Which he didn't.

It wasn't regret. Even if he turned over and where Morgan had slept was empty now, Hayes wouldn't call that feeling regret. Morgan had too obviously meant everything he'd said.

He'd promised he wanted to make this work, and Hayes believed that he meant it.

It was exhilarating, and he hadn't been happier in a very long time. But it was also fucking scary and he couldn't remember the last time he'd been more terrified.

He'd never *had* Morgan before. He'd lost him, before he'd ever gotten a chance to enjoy what that meant, how that *felt*, and it had fucked him up for six years.

How much would it fuck him up now if they couldn't make this work?

Morgan had seemed very sure. Almost flippant about it. But Hayes didn't think he could be.

Took a deep breath, then another, and slowly turned over.

Morgan wasn't lying there, but when Hayes put a hand out, the sheets were still warm.

A moment later, Morgan appeared in the doorway, just his shorts on, and he had two cups of coffee in his hands.

"Hey," he said, holding out a cup for Hayes. "I took a guess that you drink it the same as you did six years ago. Still had half and half in your fridge anyway."

Hayes took the cup with hands that almost didn't shake. 'Thanks. Yeah . . .uh the same. For sure."

Morgan bringing him coffee in bed. Wearing only shorts, chest bare, hair messed up from Hayes' hands. He was *never* going to be able to go back from this. He should be fucking terrified. It was so much reward, the most unbelievable upside of all time. But the risk . . .

"You're freaking out, aren't you?" Morgan asked bluntly. He didn't get into the bed, but he settled a hip on the edge. Close but not too close. Like Hayes was a horse he didn't want to spook.

"No." But if Hayes lied, if he wasn't honest, if they *both* weren't honest, how would this ever work out? There was a narrow window here, a path through a whole maze of defenders stacked up between Hayes and the net, and if he was very good—no, if he was *the best*—he could score the goal.

Win the guy.

Maybe even be happy like this for the rest of his life.

"Okay, maybe a little," he corrected, trying not to grimace. "It's . . .it's a lot. A *good* lot, but I still don't know how this all works. It was . . .well, it was really easy in Toronto—"

"So easy," Morgan agreed.

That almost stopped Hayes in his tracks, because he hadn't expected Morgan to be on the same page. But it was stupid to think that, because yes, back then, all the way up until the moment Morgan had ghosted him, they'd felt so in sync.

"And then nothing was easy," Hayes said. "Not even hard, just impossible. I love you . . ." God, he hadn't mean to say that again, so quickly, even if it was true. He'd meant to be a bit more circumspect, at least. You didn't *start* a relationship by declaring your undying love. But here Hayes was, launching himself right into the sun. "I love you," he repeated, because he'd committed now. "But we've never really been together. Not in any way that matters."

"You're still stuck on that." Morgan sounded indulgently sweet, and Hayes made a face.

"Don't be an asshole," he complained. "I *mean* it."

"We're gonna figure it out."

Hayes shot him a hot look. "You say that but what does that even *mean*? That's so freaking nebulous. Easy to say we'll 'figure it out' when we just don't."

Morgan didn't look so casual now. "That's not what I meant."

"Then what, you'll show up here after a game and we'll fuck? Like last night?"

"No," Morgan said steadily. He didn't look upset, but he was clearly serious. "Drink your coffee. You're grumpy and freaking out. That's not what we're doing, and it's *especially* not what we're doing if you think that's what I'm here for."

Hayes took a sip of coffee. Annoyed, in spite of himself, that it *was* perfect. Exactly as he'd taken it six years ago and still how he liked it now. That fact shouldn't have calmed him down, but it did. And Morgan must have known it would mean—would *do*—something, because the corner of his mouth turned up in a smile.

"What do you mean it's not what we're doing?"

"If you think I'm just going to fuck you and jet, we'll skip that part."

Hayes' jaw dropped. "You want to skip having sex?"

"Angel," Morgan said earnestly, and that should not have been so hot, but it was. So fucking hot. Normally, Hayes hated pet names. Once Alexander had called him *honey* and he'd iced him out for a full twenty-four hours. "I don't *want* to. But if it's the only way to prove to you that I'm serious, that we're going to build something together, then sure. I can live without sex." Morgan's earnestness melted into smugness. Because of course it did. "I know you can too."

Yes, stupidly Hayes had told him just last night that it had been awhile since he'd had sex. Maybe not Morgan's year, but close to that long.

"Fine, okay. We can do that." Hayes gave Morgan a ten percent chance of actually pulling off abstinence.

"And," Morgan said, "I fell asleep before I could ask you what you were doing tomorrow night."

"Not tonight?" Hayes asked archly.

"I have a work thing tonight. Or else you know I'd be yours." Morgan was not a charming person, normally. He'd not been particularly charming in Toronto either. Definitely not any other time they'd met since then. But the earnest honesty he was bringing to this conversation was charming Hayes even when he didn't particularly want to be charmed.

"I don't know that, actually." Hayes was not this easy. He was *not*.

Morgan grinned. Didn't even look like Hayes had hurt his feelings. "Don't you?"

"I don't," Hayes insisted.

"Okay, well, that's the first order of business then." Morgan set down his coffee on the table next to the bed and leaned in. Didn't kiss Hayes but the look on his face was as good as one. Hayes felt it all the way down to his toes. "Proving to you that I'm yours."

Hayes shouldn't be melting right back into the sheets.

But when Morgan crowded him into them, he couldn't help it.

And when Morgan rolled over ten minutes later, both of them breathing hard, Hayes couldn't help it, again. "Are you joking?" he whined.

"Hey, *you* said you thought I was just going to hit it and quit it." Morgan smiled, but it was more half a grimace.

Hayes faced him, amused, despite some epic blue balls. And from only ten minutes of making out! "I don't think anyone says that anymore," he teased.

"Well, I wasn't going to be doing it," Morgan grumbled. Looked over at Hayes and then made a groaning sound in the back of his throat. "Can you stop being so . . .so . . ."

"So?" Hayes questioned. The only positive of this sex-less path was how much Morgan seemed to regret suggesting it in the first place.

"So . . ." Morgan waved a hand, encompassing Hayes' entire self. "So completely, totally irresistible. Good at kissing. Good at hockey. Good at just lying there."

"Nope," Hayes said, but he felt good. Yes, the fear was still there. It was going to take more than two rounds of exemplary, life-altering sex, some love confessions, and Morgan's earnestness to banish it completely. But he could imagine that someday, he'd look over at Morgan and Morgan would look back, and he'd be *sure*.

Sure beyond any reasonable doubt.

"You don't have to sound so delighted about it," Morgan claimed.

"Actually, I do. Feels good. Seems good. What isn't there to be delighted about?" Hayes could think of one thing, but he wasn't going to say it.

He shouldn't have worried; Morgan said it, anyway. "Could be a little less delighted I'm not gonna stick my dick in you," he said gruffly.

"I'll cry about it in the shower," Hayes promised. Sliding out of bed. He grabbed his coffee, then pressed a kiss to Morgan's cheek. "And the answer is that no, I don't have any plans tomorrow night. I'm all yours."

Half an hour later, Morgan was gone after giving him one last, long, entirely perfect kiss, and he was showered, scrambling eggs in a pan on the stove while he debated whether Zach would be awake yet.

Decided this was momentous enough that Zach could deal with an early wake-up call.

He'd just finished pouring himself a second cup of coffee, humming under his breath, when he dialed Zach.

It rang once, twice, then three times. It was just after six a.m. west coast time, in Portland, where Zach coached now with his boyfriend and head coach of the Portland U Evergreens, Gavin Blackburn.

"What," Zach answered flatly, sounding three-quarters asleep still. "You okay, Monty?"

"Oh, I'm just peachy," Hayes trilled.

"You sound way too happy for it to be—" Zach paused, mumbling to someone next to him. Gavin, definitely. "Six fucking a.m."

"Don't you have early class today?" Zach was still working on his master's.

"No," Zach said petulantly. "Are you going to tell me what's going on or are you just going to act annoyingly awake and mysterious?"

Hayes took a deep breath. He wasn't naive enough to think Zach would be happy about this, but he needed to tell him. Zach was not only his best friend, but he would tell him the truth. About his joy, and about his fear.

"I saw Morgan last night. We uh . . .talked. A lot. Then we um—"

"You slept with him," Zach said, sounding incredibly non-judgmental. There was a reason he'd always loved Zachy so much.

"Yeah. But—"

Zach interrupted again. "It's okay. I'm not surprised."

"What?" Maybe Zach wasn't all that shocked it had happened, but Hayes couldn't parse his reaction.

"You were back in his orbit. He was back in yours. It was bound to happen."

"Sort of inevitable, honestly." This was a comment provided by a second, deeper voice. Gavin. "Was he at least not an asshole about it?"

"Not at all, in fact." It was ridiculous to be afraid of Morgan and the chaos he could bring to Hayes' life and also feel compelled to defend him to Zach and Gavin.

"Well, that's something," Zach said wryly.

There was rustling, and then Gavin asked, "What happened?"

"Well, uh, like I said he came over. Most of the team came over, actually. Earlier game, and the win streak and all. But Finn brought him. Jacob's out of town."

"Yeah, we had dinner with him last night," Zach said. "He flew up to Portland from LA, before he heads back to Florida."

"So, Morgan came over. Ended up the last one here."

"Accidentally," Zach said, and Hayes could hear the impossible-to-see air quotes he was absolutely making.

"Hey, he was helping clean up. Being not an asshole," Hayes retorted mildly. "Then um, one thing led to another and . . .well, you get the picture."

"So just sex, then." Zach sighed heavily. And there was the fucking judgment.

"It wasn't just sex. It's . . .he told me he loved me. And you know I love him."

There was silence on the other end of the line. "Seriously?" Zach sounded shocked.

"We cleared the air, too. We didn't *just* fuck," Hayes said and couldn't deny just how defensive he sounded. "I wouldn't have done that. Not again."

"Okay," Zach said. "So you talked."

"We're uh . . .well, we're doing something tomorrow night. A date?" Hayes realized that Morgan had not defined it, but it had to be, right? They weren't having sex. So what were they going to do? Sit around and *talk*. Suddenly, Hayes' breath went short with panic. To distract himself, he added, "And, *and*, he's decided we can't have sex, so I'll believe him that he's not just around to hit it and quit it."

"Do people even say that anymore?" Zach wondered skeptically.

Hayes was pretty sure he heard Gavin murmur something like, *what's wrong with that?* Zach laughed, and then Gavin did too, teasing and full of joy.

Before this morning, even inadvertently overhearing that exchange would have filled Hayes with a bitter regret he'd swallow down because it wasn't Zach's fault he was in love with someone who didn't want him. Who didn't love him back.

But Morgan *did*. He'd said it, earnestly and with feeling, more than once. Even if Hayes was understandably nervous, that didn't change the fact it *had* happened.

"Regardless," Hayes said confidently. "It's not just sex. It's not really sex at all." It was hard to be optimistic about that, but somehow even *not* having sex with Morgan was better than not having Morgan at all.

He could imagine Zach telling him that he was pathetic.

It was not a hardship to omit that particular thought process. Zach didn't need to know *everything*.

"It's weird you sound so happy about that," Zach said suspiciously. "Was it bad?"

Of course Zach had figured out how weird that was without even being told.

"No! Of course not," Hayes squawked.

"We believe you," Gavin said dryly.

"It's a *commitment*," Hayes said with pride.

"And he's taking you out? Wow. Maybe he really has turned over that asshole leaf for good."

"He's been pretty good with Finn, too," Hayes said.

Morgan had always been tough—on others, sure, but mostly on himself. Unrelenting, even, and nobody had ever really understood how so much of that "asshole" behavior sprang from that drive. But then, they'd never understood, either, what the pressure of being drafted first overall was like. Almost nobody understood, but Hayes always had.

"He's not as bad as you always make him out to be," Hayes said.

Zach sighed. Or maybe that was Gavin. Or both of them, actually. "No, he's absolutely as bad as we make him out to be. Everyone knows it. *You* just like him for all the reasons everyone else doesn't."

Hayes wasn't sure that was true, but he wasn't sure it was *not* true, either.

"We understand each other," Hayes said quietly.

"Right. So you're going out on a date, and not sleeping together?"

"Yep." But Morgan *hadn't* called it a date. Hadn't said anything about what it was, only that it was happening.

Maybe he'd just go over to Morgan's soulless rental house or he'd come back over to Hayes' and then they'd what? Hayes tried not to panic and failed. They'd only ever done sex and hockey. He imagined them putting a game on and breaking down the play like the Sentinels were facing off against one of the teams next week.

"You're freaking out, now," Zach said knowingly.

"Shut up, no, I am not," Hayes argued, even though he totally was.

They couldn't even Netflix and chill, because the chill part was officially off the table.

"A little," Zach insisted. "At least admit that."

"Fine, a little. What are we even going to do?"

"Guess he's going to have to figure that out."

"Guess so," Hayes said.

He supposed Morgan could take him out, but Hayes was out of the closet and Morgan was not—and he couldn't imagine him wanting to do that anytime soon. Hayes couldn't even be mad about it. He got it. Legacy was everything to Morgan, and while he'd been ready to tell the truth—hadn't wanted to continue living a lie, anyway—would Morgan want that asterisk next to his name, forever? Hayes wasn't sure.

So they wouldn't be going out.

Maybe with anyone else, Hayes wouldn't have liked that, might have even resented it, but maybe Zach was right, and he *was* easy for Morgan. Always had been, really.

"Keep me updated," Zach said. "And Monty?"

"Yeah?" Hayes pushed the rest of his eggs around his plate, appetite dwindling. He didn't want to text Morgan—he'd *just* left—and demand to know what they were doing tomorrow night, but it was the first test, wasn't it? And he was suddenly afraid, like before, that they wouldn't even pass this one. Wouldn't even make it out of the gate.

"I'm really happy for you. And you know what else?" Zach's voice was soft.

"What?"

"You should be happy for you, too. Don't freak out. Don't flush this down the drain before it even starts."

"I wasn't—"

"You were freaking out."

"It's kind of a lot," Hayes argued.

"Yeah, it is. But it's a *good* kind of a lot. Maybe it's not perfect, right away. But you said it yourself, you love him, and he loves you. I think that kind of love deserves a little patience and understanding, don't you?"

Hayes hadn't thought about it that way. Had been so uber-focused on getting it right, immediately. But maybe Zach was right.

"Did you and Gavin?"

Zach laughed. "Fuck no. We're still figuring it out. As long as you don't shut down or shut him out, you will too."

CHAPTER 18

Morgan couldn't remember the last time he was nervous.

If he'd *ever* been nervous.

Even before games, even before *important* games, he was filled with a sense of edgy anticipation, but it had never felt like he was going to be sick and puke all over the shoes that Finn had declared to be "better than that crap you normally wear, Dad."

He pulled up in Hayes' driveway. Took a deep breath and then another. He was going to do this right, but *right* felt like a particularly narrow balancing act.

If he fucked up again—if he was too earnest, or not earnest enough—Morgan wasn't stupid enough to think Hayes would give him another chance.

This was his one shot.

Before, with hockey, he'd had the skills and the capability to make that happen. But now, he was just stumbling around blind in the dark. He'd gotten Finn's advice on his outfit, refusing to tell his son what it was for, and he *could've* told Danny and then asked for his advice, but it was *Danny.*

Danny had never wooed someone before. Danny had probably never even considered the possibility, and if Morgan had asked him, he could only imagine the bullshit suggestions he'd get in return.

Obviously, he couldn't ask Danny. And Jacob had been equally off-limits, only because he didn't trust the guy to not be his normal wily and too-observant self and finally guess once and for all who Morgan was hung up on.

So he'd white-knuckled his way through these plans all on his own.

Freaking out when he'd texted Hayes, rewriting it at least ten times, when Hayes had asked what they were doing. It shouldn't have been so hard saying, **we're going to dinner,** but he'd practically needed to workshop it.

All on his fucking own.

Freaking out over the place. Freaking out over his outfit. Freaking out when he'd needed to text Hayes and say he'd be happy to pick him up.

Hayes had only sent back a thumbs-up.

What did that even *mean*?

There was a distinct lack of emotion attached to emojis. The last time he'd tried to make that argument—and for once Jacob had actually been on *his* side—Finn had told him he was old, decrepit and nobody would ever want to date him if he couldn't figure out the emotional resonance of emojis.

Great. He was on his own, on his way to Hayes' front door. They couldn't have sex—the *one* thing he felt confident he could ace—and according to Finn, he didn't even speak the right fucking language.

Morgan rang the doorbell and hoped he hadn't sweated through his shirt too badly.

God, he was so fucking nervous. He *was* going to puke, right on these too-expensive and too-tight shoes.

Hayes opened the door a second later. He looked cool and equally as expensive. White linen emphasizing his tan and a green shirt making his eyes so bright Morgan felt words dry in his throat. Stared and didn't even try to hide it.

"Hey," Hayes said, smirking a little. He knew exactly what he looked like, the effect he hoped to have, and he'd succeeded. Morgan couldn't blame him for doing a victory lap about it.

"Hey," Morgan said and leaned in, reminding himself that he could deal with only a single kiss now and a nice long goodbye kiss after dinner. That he'd *promised*. Not just to Hayes, even though that was important, but *himself* too. "You uh, look really nice."

"So do you," Hayes said.

Morgan cleared his throat. Hayes smelled so good, looked so good, it was actually nearly painful to pull himself back. Remember that they weren't doing this.

You did it before, a whole bunch of times. But that had been before Hayes had said in that tight, almost sad voice, *He dumped me because I was still in love with you.*

"Should we . . .uh . . .go?"

"So we *are* going out to dinner?" Hayes' voice was teasing, but there was no mistaking the interested glint in his eyes as they made their way to the car.

"Yes," Morgan said. He debated opening Hayes' door for him, but would that be romantic or just make him look old-fashioned and stuffy?

But before he could make up his mind, Hayes had opened his own door, so Morgan detoured around to the driver's side.

Morgan had spent an hour last night brainstorming conversational topics. As he pulled out onto the street, he wished he could remember what any of them were. He should've written out flashcards and memorized them.

Luckily for both of them, Hayes seemed to have no issues talking. "Caught your segment yesterday," he said.

"Oh yeah?"

The earlier smirk was back, in spades. Morgan concentrated on his driving so he wouldn't drive right off the road. Crash the car and not even give a shit, because then if they weren't going to the restaurant, he could get his hands on Hayes *now*.

Except that no, he couldn't.

"It was good, except when you picked the Stars to win the Eastern conference," Hayes said.

"Uh, well, didn't want to look too biased," Morgan said. Finn had sent him more than a few pointed texts about it. Jacob had only shot him a look when he'd seen him this afternoon.

"Biased would've been picking the Bandits," Hayes countered. He shot Morgan a wild grin. *Stay on the road, stay on the fucking road.* "'Course you're not doing that, because I think it'd be a miracle if they make the playoffs."

"Ouch," Morgan said weakly. But Hayes was not wrong. His old team was struggling a bit. He'd been trying to give Danny advice, but shit was hard. It was entirely possible they'd end up in the draft lottery.

"Hey, just being honest." Hayes shrugged, adorably. "Just like you were being, I'd imagine."

"Wanted to pick you," Morgan admitted.

"I know," Hayes said, shooting Morgan a look that said it all.

Yes, he knew, and yes, he was enjoying giving him shit about it.

It was a short drive to the restaurant he'd picked. He'd been there with Finn and Jacob a few times, and he knew Finn and Jacob liked to go there on date nights. Knew they had a semi-private back room. Private *and* romantic.

Still, Hayes looked a little surprised when Morgan pulled up to the valet station.

"We're going here?"

"Have you not been here before?" Morgan frowned as he handed the keys over to the attendant. He'd been sure that this place had originally come as a recommendation from Hayes.

"No, I have. I just . . ." Hayes looked at him strangely.

Morgan had no idea what he was trying to say. Bluntness was probably not the best choice for a date, but he never wanted to do anything Hayes didn't like.

"Do you not want to go here?" He'd made all the arrangements. The private table. The flowers. The candles. The special dessert. But he'd pivot, if this wasn't what Hayes wanted.

"No, no, it's perfect." Hayes smiled, looking flustered. "Just . . .not what I expected."

They were going to have to dig into whatever *that* meant, but *after* they were at their table. And maybe after he'd buttered Hayes up with the flowers and the candles.

"Alright," Morgan said and gestured towards the doorway. Hayes shot him a look a little sweet and a little baffled still but went. Morgan had told himself he wouldn't go all caveman, *dragging-his-catch-back-to-the-firepit,* but it was impossible not to at least put his hand on Hayes' lower back, fingers brushing the fabric of his shirt, feeling the heat of his skin underneath, as he walked into the restaurant.

The hostess recognized him and took them to the back of the room. It was cozy, intimate, and they'd pulled the screen partially over, as he'd requested, not because he was afraid of people seeing them together and drawing the correct conclusion, but because he didn't want to create a sensation.

And he and Hayes together tended to create a sensation. Even their names linked together was all it took.

The hostess brilliantly made herself scarce after showing them to the table.

Morgan watched with apprehension and a still-twisting gut as Hayes looked at the low arrangement of trailing ivy and white gardenias in the middle of the table. The candles scattered across it, illuminating his face.

"Um, is it okay?" Morgan asked. Then kicked himself. He was supposed to be charming Hayes, not constantly worrying about whether he'd screwed up. *Have some fucking confidence, Mo,* he could imagine Danny telling him.

"It's . . ." Hayes laughed, a little hysterically. "I thought you'd want to stay at one of our houses. Then when you said we were going to dinner, I imagined, I don't know, some kind of very obvious bro-dinner." Hayes collapsed into his chair. If he was anyone else, it wouldn't have been graceful, but he was Hayes Montgomery so it looked like a work of performance art.

"What the fuck is a bro-dinner?" Morgan sat down across from him and resisted the urge to reach out and take Hayes' hand.

"Like, I don't know. Wings and beer. Slapping each other on the back. Talking about hockey."

Morgan told himself he had prepared for every eventuality. Every single thing that could go wrong. He'd even prepared the conversational topics list, even if he couldn't remember a single fucking one of them.

But he couldn't have ever prepared for this.

His jaw dropped. "You thought I was going to take you to beer and wings? I'm not saying I wouldn't *ever*, but on our first date? *Seriously*?"

Hayes was flushed now. "I don't know. It sounds stupid when I say it like that, but you're not out. I *am*."

And oh. *Oh*.

Fuck everything, they were not doing this. They were *not*.

Morgan gathered himself and prayed he didn't sound like a lovestruck, *dick*-struck, idiot of a caveman in the next thirty seconds. "I don't give a flying fuck if you're out and I'm not. I don't care. I don't care if everyone in this restaurant takes a photo of us and spends the next week of their lives speculating on . . .Instagram. Or Tok or whatever."

"TikTok," Hayes said, the corner of his mouth beginning to tug into what Morgan hoped was going to be a very big smile.

"Whatever," Morgan said, waving a hand. "I don't give a fuck. I really, really don't. I want to be here with you. I want to take you out. Spoil you. Treat you the way you deserve. And that includes romantic dinners. It probably *also* includes beer and wings at some point. But not tonight."

"You really don't care?" Hayes said. And there was the smile Morgan had hoped to see.

"I really, *really* don't care," Morgan said. Didn't know how else to prove it other than the fact that he was here, right now, and they weren't hiding that they were about to enjoy a pretty romantic dinner.

But Hayes didn't seem to need more proof. He smiled again, more gently this time, and it was he who reached out and squeezed Morgan's forearm. "This is honestly so great. I didn't . . .I didn't expect it, and that makes it even better."

"Stupid." Morgan smiled back at him. "You *should* expect it."

Hayes tilted his head. "Guess you aren't afraid of setting the bar too high."

He was actually sweating about it, already, but he wasn't going to tell *Hayes* that. "Of course not. Have I ever been afraid of setting the bar too high?"

He knew what Hayes would think; that Morgan was the same about this as he was about hockey. But he was not. He was absolutely fucking not.

Hayes actually giggled, clearly delighted. "Never."

"Exactly."

He wanted to say, *actually, you scare the shit out of me, because I've never aced you, not like I've always aced hockey.*

Morgan would, someday, but not tonight. He picked up his menu. "So what's good here?" he asked. Even though he'd spent the hour after assembling the conversational topic list examining the online menu and trying to decide what would be the best "first date" entree to order.

This was actually why he hadn't told Danny, because Danny would tell him that he was a freak and that he couldn't control everything.

But so far, he was doing a pretty good job of it, and Hayes was smiling, still, lit up from within, and if Morgan could make him look like that at least seventy-five percent of the time—one hundred was an impossible standard he knew not to wish for—he would take it.

"Oh, the mahi-mahi's really good, and so is the sea bass," Hayes said. "Do you want to get wine?"

"Are you going to get wine?" Morgan had done his research. Despite his behavior the other night at the party, he knew Hayes rarely drank during the season.

"Probably not, but *you* can," Hayes offered generously. "I was going to suggest some pairings, if you wanted to get the fish. I know a few of their whites are good."

And this right here was why Morgan had gone out of his way to plan this date. If he hadn't, if they'd done the same shit they had back six years ago, hockey and beer and sex, he'd never have known this about Hayes.

He wanted to know *everything* about Hayes. Not just the obvious things. Not just the things that everyone else knew.

"Sure," Morgan said, even though he wasn't really a big wine guy. He just wanted to hear Hayes ramble on about it.

And he did, for the next five minutes, sounding knowledgeable enough that Morgan was both charmed and took one of his suggestions, ordering a glass of the sauvignon blanc from New Zealand when the waiter arrived.

Morgan also ordered the shrimp cocktail and regretted it when it arrived, because watching Hayes de-tail it with his fingers and then lick them clean of cocktail sauce made his pants tight.

Made him wish that he hadn't been quite so quick to declare they weren't going to be having sex, especially when he caught a glimpse of Hayes' pink tongue, darting out to lick sauce off his thumb.

Morgan remembered, a little too well, exactly what that tongue felt like.

He couldn't regret it too much, though, not when this dinner seemed to be going so well. After its inauspicious start, they'd actually had no trouble talking. Morgan had told himself firmly, when he'd compiled his conversational topic list, that he wouldn't focus too hard on hockey. And they did talk about it, both Morgan's work with the media, and the Sentinels, but it felt natural. Right. Avoiding it would have been weirder.

It had been going so well, Morgan had almost gotten lulled into a state of complacency. *Almost.*

Then, after they finished their dinner, Hayes took a long drink of his sparkling water, pinned Morgan with the most earnest look in his green-eyed arsenal and said, "I guess you didn't ghost me because you were afraid of looking too gay, then."

"Is that what you thought?" Morgan heard the shock in his voice.

Hayes crossed his arms over his chest and leaned back in his chair. "It wasn't a wild assumption that you might've freaked out about it."

Morgan could not believe this. Of course, they'd both screwed up the end of their fling. Mostly him, but not entirely him. Still, that hadn't even really been a thought that crossed his mind.

"Did I *seem* like I freaked out about it?" Morgan pushed back.

"No . . .but then you *did* ghost me."

"Not because I was worried about the closet," Morgan spluttered.

"You were worried about hockey. About legacy. That could've been part of it." Hayes tilted his head. "And the way people act behind closed doors, in the bedroom, doesn't necessarily mean they're willing to be upfront about their desires in public."

Morgan wondered if anyone had ever been shitty to Hayes like that. Happy enough to fuck him in private, but just bros in public. If that was true, he was going to kick that person's ass.

"What I did on the ice stands on its own," Morgan said firmly. "If they want to think less of me because who I want, who I love, then that's their own problem."

Hayes' face softened. He was almost smiling again.

"And," Morgan continued, "my son is gay. I've never been anything less than fully accepting of Finn."

"Finn isn't you, though," Hayes pointed out.

"I do get why you might've thought that," Morgan said, wondering when he would ever stop kicking himself for just *leaving* instead of being honest. But honesty had felt so impossible six years ago. "But no. *No.* That wasn't part of it. I knew I only had a few years left, if I was lucky, and you threw me for a major loop. I said it before, and it was true. I'd have done something insane. That was the issue, not that you were a guy."

"So what you're saying is that if I did this . . ." Hayes reached out and slowly took Morgan's hand, squeezing it. "It'd be okay?"

"Anytime you want to touch me, I'm not ever going to argue," Morgan scoffed. "I know you don't believe me, but I'm *yours*, angel."

"You can't say shit like that." Hayes flushed.

"Why not?"

Hayes shot him a knowing look. "You know why."

"I'm just being honest." Morgan lifted their hands and pressed a kiss to Hayes' knuckles. "You ready for dessert?"

"Dessert?" Hayes perked up, then schooled his expression into something more serious. "I shouldn't, though, it's not on the meal plan . . ."

"Don't worry about that. I ordered something special, in advance."

Hayes looked floored, again. "You did?" he asked incredulously.

"Angel, I keep telling you—you can't be surprised when I spoil you. You *deserve* spoiling."

From the way Hayes' mouth tilted up in a warm smile, Morgan hoped that he was starting to believe it.

The waiter brought the dessert, a dark chocolate mousse, fruit scattered across its glossy surface, and two spoons.

Morgan had patted himself on the back for thinking in advance of a dessert that Hayes could enjoy without guilt. What he hadn't anticipated was how painful it was going to be watching Hayes lick chocolate mousse off a spoon, knowing that when he dropped Hayes off at his house, he was only allowing himself one goodbye kiss.

"You alright?" Hayes asked in a teasing voice as Morgan settled the check.

The brat knew exactly what he'd been doing to Morgan, and he was *enjoying* it.

Morgan huffed out a breath, reminding himself that, if he did things *right*, if he was good and thoughtful, he would get to have sex with Hayes Montgomery for the rest of his life.

When he thought about it like that, it was easy enough to swallow hard, put his lust away, and lead Hayes away from their table, their hands intertwined together.

There'd been a second where Hayes nearly dropped his, but Morgan had hung on, shooting him a look.

Hayes shrugged, like, *if you insist*, and yes, *yes*, Morgan insisted.

By the time they made it back to Hayes' house, Morgan's palms were sweating. The nerves were back. He'd kissed Hayes plenty. But he'd never imagined that a kiss would have to be *A Kiss*, enough to make Hayes want more.

Enough to make Hayes want to do this again.

To give Morgan another chance and another and another.

He pulled into Hayes' driveway. Hayes shot him a little coy glance. "You wanna come in?"

Oh, he wanted to. But he knew if he did, there was no way he was stopping at a single kiss.

"I . . .uh . . .I probably shouldn't."

Hayes laughed softly but didn't move. Okay, they were doing this. Morgan psyched himself up, unbuckling his seat belt and walking all the way around the car to open the passenger door.

Of course opening Hayes' door for him and reaching out with a hand to help him up only made him think a whole bunch of inappropriate caveman thoughts.

Then Hayes glanced up at him, affection and desire in his green eyes, and the thoughts screamed insistently.

"Unfortunately, I don't have any keys to twirl," Hayes said in a low conspiratorial voice as they reached his front door. "Do you think—

Morgan didn't let him finish. Tugged him in by his arm and kissed him.

Hayes' mouth was hot and sweet on his, the remnants of chocolate on his tongue, and Morgan groaned at the back of his throat as he backed them into the door.

He'd told himself he'd get one *really* good kiss, and maybe if he just kept kissing Hayes, if one kiss just spun out and out and out, it would still count as only one.

Hayes' fingers dug into his shoulders, one hand slipping up to the back of his head, tangling in Morgan's hair and holding him in place.

Made it easy to think they were on the same page.

But sooner than Morgan wanted, Hayes tilted his face away and broke the kiss. Morgan was addicted to how breathless he sounded and the way his pupils swallowed all the green in his eyes. The unmistakable press of his hard dick against Morgan's thigh.

"Are you *sure* you don't want to come in?" Hayes asked.

"No," Morgan said, laughing. "But I really shouldn't. You know it, too."

"It was *your* idea," Hayes protested, chuckling too.

"Yeah, but I was right. We . . .we can do the sex thing. Really, really well. No issues on that front. The rest of this . . ." Just because tonight had gone well didn't mean all their dates would go like this. Morgan wasn't naive enough to believe that was true.

"Zach made me promise that I wouldn't freak out if tonight didn't go well, but . . ." Hayes smiled up at him. "I shouldn't have worried. You spoiled me. Made me feel special."

"Just doing what I should've done six years ago," Morgan said self-consciously, the honesty flaying him open. He wasn't good at it, but he was *trying*.

"I like to think of it as we're starting over," Hayes said. "What do you think?"

Morgan considered this. Also considered if he could get away with kissing Hayes a second time.

"I like that," he agreed.

Hayes patted him on the cheek. "Doesn't mean you're off the hook."

"Wouldn't dream of it," Morgan said earnestly. He knew exactly how much he had to make up for. He never wanted Hayes to look at him with that cold, dead-eyed stare ever again.

"Give me one more kiss," Hayes said, batting his eyelashes and grinning.

"I—"

"I know," Hayes said. "But bend your rules for me, baby."

Like Morgan was ever going to be able to resist *that*. He leaned in and kissed Hayes again.

When they finally broke apart a second time, the leash on his self-control was tenuous and he already knew he was going to be tasting Hayes on his tongue for the rest of the night—and he wasn't even bent out of shape about it.

"Well," Hayes said breathlessly. "Goodnight."

"I'll call you," Morgan promised.

"I know," Hayes said and slipped through the door before they could throw the whole goddamn rulebook out the window.

CHAPTER 19

HAYES WASN'T ALL THAT surprised that during warmups against the Bandits, Matt Daniels skated over, just crossing the blue line to nudge up right next to him.

"Hey, Monty," Danny said. "How's it hanging?"

"Danny," Hayes said, nodding at his ex-teammate. "Going pretty good. Better than you, at any rate."

Danny grimaced. "Better not let Mo hear you say that. I know he's wearing a Sentinels jersey these days, but he'll always be a Bandit at heart."

"Oh he knows," Hayes said lightly, smiling probably a hair too brightly to be playing it cool, but it was unclear if he was supposed to. He'd heard, through the rumor mill and from Danny himself, twice a year, that he and Morgan had stayed in contact. It was highly possible that Danny knew everything that had gone down in the last week.

But he and Morgan hadn't discussed who exactly they were telling. Obviously the top of the list had to be Finn—and not just because he was Morgan's son, but because Hayes was his captain, and he wasn't going to do anything to jeopardize this team.

"He told you?" Danny looked astonished, which for such a chaos gremlin was saying something.

Okay, so Danny didn't know. That was interesting, though not very surprising, because Morgan had told him that he was going out with Danny tonight after the game to "catch up." Maybe he was waiting to tell Danny until then.

"We do speak," Hayes teased, unable to help himself. And he was rewarded when Danny's jaw literally dropped open.

"Seriously?"

Hayes just shrugged, gaze back to his side of the ice, scanning the group as they finished their warmups. "He *is* around a lot."

"Yeah, but I thought you two were in the middle of the world's coldest war," Danny spluttered.

Hayes shot him an amused look. "Couldn't stay ice-cold forever," he said, skating off before Danny could demand to know exactly what that meant.

Finn was in goal tonight, and that meant that Morgan was up in his usual suite, Jacob next to him. Hayes couldn't see him, but he knew they were there. Knew Morgan was there, his gaze prickling on his shoulder blades as he took the first faceoff.

The Bandits were not very good this year, but they always fought hard, regardless, and Hayes had no intention of resting back. They had a win streak on the line, and that mattered the most, of course, but there was also his own personal stats, which Barty kept telling him would change the Sentinels' minds about the contract.

Lars, his right wing, had gotten the puck, and they pushed into the Bandits' side of the ice, Lars passing the puck to Hayes, who took it behind the goal. Danny's hit was mis-timed though, and he took off, unscathed, looking for a shooting lane.

He passed it back to Curtis, one of their starting defensemen, and skated up closer to the net, brain alert as it scrolled through what he knew about the Bandits' goalie. He was good low, but shit high. Middling on the rebound.

Lars knew it too, because he slid over, closer to the other side, obviously getting ready to slide the puck behind the goalie's backside if he got a chance at the rebound.

A second later, the play materialized.

Curtis passed back to Hayes, who took the shot, knowing it was probably going to bounce off his kneepad, and sure enough, it did.

The puck hit Lars' tape and then it was in the net.

Hayes hit Lars' side, patting him on the helmet with a glove as they celebrated the goal.

Swore he still felt Morgan's gaze burning into him even after he was off the ice, sliding down the bench.

Wouldn't even be surprised if when he got to the locker room during the first intermission and looked at his phone, Morgan would've been unable to resist sending a text about that play.

It was the kind of classic misdirection that Morgan loved more than anything else, the sort of move he'd made his bread and butter as he'd gotten older and wasn't the fastest or the strongest guy out there any longer.

But he'd always been the smartest, and his brain had only gotten sharper as he'd grown older.

Hayes hoped that he could do the same. Hoped that the Sentinels could see it, too.

At thirty-one, he didn't want to start over. He wanted to stay with this team and continue building.

Hayes pushed the thought away and re-focused on the game. What mattered was this team and what Hayes could do for them right now.

Not in a year. Not in two years or four or five from now.

"Sick fucking play," Morgan enthused. He was probably not being very subtle, but he had a feeling it was only a matter of time—probably not weeks, but *days*—before Hayes sat him down and told him that Finn, and by extension, Jacob, needed to know about them.

Jacob looked over at him, a knowing glint in his eyes. "It sure was. Reminds me of someone—"

"Me," Morgan crowed, "totally me. That was a classic Morgan Reynolds play."

"And you wonder why people say you're insufferable."

"I think I even got that one by you a few times," Morgan said, even though if he'd managed it once, he'd have been shocked.

"You really think that?" Jacob asked, leaning his elbows against the front wall of the suite.

"Well, maybe once," Morgan blustered.

"I'd never fall for that," Jacob said. "You see the way Monty angled the puck when he shot it? If the goalie was paying attention, he'd have seen that Monty was practically aiming for the pad. Not to score, but for Lars to get the rebound."

"Still a great play," Morgan grumbled.

"Finn and I should work on that this week," Jacob mused. He turned to Morgan. "You meeting up with Danny after the game?"

Morgan nodded. Over the last few days, he'd gone back and forth on what he was going to say to his friend, but if he was being really honest with himself, there was no way he was going to hang out with Danny tonight and *not* tell him what was going on with Hayes.

"You mind me tagging along?" Jacob asked. "Finn and the team are flying out to Raleigh tonight, right after the game."

Morgan knew that, because Hayes had told him, but he couldn't tell Braun that.

He also really wanted to tell Braun hell no, and that he could fuck off. Eighteen months ago, he could've. But that had all changed after Finn and Jacob had gotten together. And since he and Morgan had buried the hatchet.

It was a perfectly normal request, but if Jacob came, then Morgan couldn't tell Danny about what was going on with Hayes.

"Uh," Morgan hesitated.

Jacob rolled his eyes. "Are you serious right now?"

"Sure, I don't see why not," Morgan said, because he clearly didn't have another choice. Maybe he could corner Danny when Jacob was at the bar or in the bathroom and tell him the truth.

Honestly, he wasn't even against Jacob knowing about him and Hayes, but he couldn't tell Jacob before Finn. Morgan would be the first to say he was an idiot, but he wasn't *that* much of an idiot.

"Awesome," Jacob said, tapping Morgan's hand with his fist. "I like Danny. He's fun."

"And here I thought you didn't know the definition of that word," Morgan grumbled.

Jacob shot him a look. "You really want to know about what I do for fun?"

"No, *no*," Morgan spluttered. "How many goddamn times do I have to tell you that I am *off-limits* when it comes to you and Finn?"

"Just checking," Jacob joked.

"God, you're the worst." Morgan couldn't say he wasn't a little worried about Braun finding out about him and Hayes—he'd given Jacob kind of a lot of crap when he'd gotten together with Finn. And if there was one thing he knew about Jacob, it was that he could take it, but he could also dish it right back.

"Where are we going? Don't tell me you were gonna take Danny to that bar by your house."

Morgan made a face. "What's wrong with that place?"

"It's a shithole."

"Yeah, exactly. Why I like it."

What he actually liked was that he didn't get bothered there. That nobody cared that he was Morgan Reynolds.

"If you insist," Jacob said, shrugging.

Of course, when they were at the bar, two hours later, and Danny shot him a look full of semi-outraged disbelief, Jacob didn't bother holding back.

"It's Mo's favorite," Jacob said.

"You've really changed," Danny said.

Morgan made a face. He'd expected Danny, at least, to understand. He wasn't going out for status or to be seen. That had changed when he'd retired. Now he just wanted to slide under everyone's radar.

Hayes had said it best. Sometimes Morgan just wanted to take all this shit he was carrying around and *put it down*.

It was easier said than done, but coming to this shitty, hole-in-the-wall bar, with its sticky tables, floor littered with peanut shells, and completely disinterested clientele was one of the best ways.

"You bring Hayes here?" Danny asked under his breath when Jacob leaned over the bar and grabbed the bartender's disinterested attention.

"Uh, no."

"Oh, right why would you? He hates your guts now." Danny shot him a knowing look.

Jacob turned back to them with three bottles in his hand. "We're all set," he said, distributing the beers. "Who hates Mo?"

"Nobody," Morgan said quickly. "And everyone, honestly."

Danny laughed as they made their way to a booth in the back of the bar.

"I was just wondering who Mo's brought here from the team."

"Finn came here once and then refused to come back. Said he'd rather not get rabies," Jacob said chuckling.

"Definitely not Hayes then. He's got taste." Danny eyed Morgan again, like he was mentally finishing that sentence with *God only knows what he was doing with you.*

"Right," Morgan said weakly. Trying desperately to come up with a reason to get Danny alone so he could 1) remind him that Hayes was off-limits as a conversational topic and 2) explain exactly why that still was.

Sipping his beer, Jacob leaned back in his chair. "Hayes isn't all that snooty, though. He's a great guy. Real chill, honestly, but a leader. Finn likes him a lot."

Danny waggled his eyebrows suggestively and Morgan wanted to murder him. "You worried about Finn liking him too much, Braun?"

"No," Jacob said, rolling his eyes.

"They're very happy. Totally domesticated. Just don't ask him to go into more detail," Morgan said, while he tried to decide which subject was potentially worse: Hayes in general or how loved up his son was with Jacob Braun.

"Well, now we gotta make Mo here squirm a bit. Tell me more," Danny said, leering as he leaned in.

Jacob laughed, the asshole.

"Hey," Morgan said, clutching at straws, "you should go order us some mozzarella sticks. And um, a basket of fries."

Jacob looked at him like he'd just grown a second head. "You don't eat that shit. And you definitely don't eat that shit *here*."

"I'm hungry," Morgan lied unconvincingly. "Didn't eat enough at the game."

Shaking his head, for a second Jacob didn't move and Morgan was pretty sure he was going to be forced into grabbing Danny's arm and dragging him to the bathroom like they were two girls needing to check their lip gloss.

But then he groaned and lifted himself up. "Maybe you are human after all, Reynolds," Jacob said and then wandered back over towards the bartender.

"Quick," Morgan said under his breath. "I wanted to tell you something."

"Yeah, 'cause I can't imagine you actually want to eat the food here. What is it?"

"Jacob doesn't know, because Finn doesn't know yet." Morgan took a deep breath. Then told himself to get on with it. Jacob wasn't going to be ordering for that long. "Hayes and I are dating."

Morgan was expecting some low-level shocked surprise. Or maybe a snarky comment about how Morgan had finally gotten his shit together.

Danny just gave him a lazy once-over. "And?"

"And? *And?*" It was hard not to be butt hurt that was all the reaction his pronouncement had gotten him.

"Did you really think you were going to end up here in Florida in his proximity and *not* win him back? You did grovel, right?"

Morgan clenched his teeth and then forced himself to relax. This was a good thing. Crap from Danny meant that all was right with the world. "You say grovel like it was a one-time-only occurrence, but really, it's more like a frame of mind."

Something that looked suspiciously like pride and approval crossed Danny's face. "You really got your shit together, didn't you?"

"Trying," Morgan admitted. "It's still pretty new. But um . . .it's good."

"You're happy? You *look* happy," Danny said. "I wondered if something had happened, because you seem . . .lighter. For you, anyway."

Morgan couldn't remember the last time he'd considered—seriously or otherwise—if he was happy. He couldn't say it didn't matter because he wasn't dumb enough to think otherwise, but he'd been on the same path, one foot in front of the other, for so long he'd never really thought about how the path made him feel.

Except maybe one time: six years before when he'd lain next to Hayes in bed and thought, *if only I could do this every night for the rest of my life.*

The answer back then was he couldn't.

He could now.

"Yeah, I think . . .I think I am."

"You think you're what?" Jacob settled back down in the booth.

"Uh, happy here. In Tampa," Morgan said, trying not to stammer over it.

Jacob tilted his head, thoughtful expression on his face. "Yeah, I can see it. Maybe if you were less alone, though."

"You and Finn are both obsessed with my singleness," Morgan argued lightly, sending Danny a strong message with his eyes that if he knew what was good for him, he was *not* going to break and declare that Morgan was very much not single anymore.

"For good reason," Jacob muttered.

"You'll find someone," Danny said, his knee nudging Morgan's under the table.

"Maybe if you ever get over yourself," Jacob said, reaching over and patting him on the arm. "And if you're willing to bend and eat fried food more than once every decade."

"I'm not that bad," Morgan argued.

He almost wished Jacob already knew about Hayes because then he could declare, proudly, that Hayes had definitely seemed to enjoy all the work he'd put into his body, even after retirement. But Jacob didn't know, and until they told Finn, Jacob *wasn't* going to know.

"You're totally that bad," Danny said pointedly. Like he knew the argument Morgan wanted to make and was trying to shut it down. "I'm tired of talking about how pathetic Mo is. Let's talk about how pathetic my team is."

"That Barnes kid is going to get you somewhere," Morgan said, at least a little grateful for the subject change.

"Charlie's coming along," Danny agreed. "Just his second year. He's gonna get even better."

"You need to put some better pieces around him. A decent defense, for one thing," Morgan said.

"Doesn't he have a brother?" Jacob asked.

Danny cackled. "Have you been living under a rock? He has *two*. Avery plays for Monty's old team, out in LA. And the other brother, the youngest one, is about to declare for the draft, I think. But he's the only one who plays defense. Charlie and Ethan are both forwards."

"Get Avery then," Jacob said, and everyone laughed. There'd been two brothers on teams before, but there'd never been three.

"Yeah, I'll just snap my fingers," Danny groused. "*Make it happen*. You were a fucking goalie, Braun, not a wizard."

"Thought that was practically the same thing," Jacob said smugly.

Morgan smacked him in the arm and that set the whole table off, all three of them laughing.

There'd been a part of him that hadn't thought he'd ever have this again, this easy camaraderie, once he'd retired. That it was something he'd had, that he hadn't even appreciated as much as he should, and then he'd lost it.

But when he'd come to Portland eighteen months ago, ostensibly for Finn, and discovered him shacked up with the newly retired Jacob, he'd found out that part of his life wasn't as over as he'd imagined.

Maybe it wasn't quite the same. Danny had played today, but neither he nor Jacob had. But it didn't matter.

In ten years, he could imagine him, Jacob, Danny, maybe even Hayes, all sitting around, giving each other shit and simultaneously reminiscing over old times and looking forward to everything in the future.

And he was, Morgan realized, *happy*.

CHAPTER 20

HAYES WAS IN THE middle of his first round of reps, breathing through the strain, when the gym door opened.

They'd gotten back from Carolina late last night after the quick one-game road trip, and he'd considered suggesting to Morgan that they grab a late lunch today, but he hadn't decided yet if he wanted to put the ball back into his own court.

Besides, Morgan's semi-begging texts were enjoyable, and Hayes hadn't decided if he wanted to put him out of his misery yet.

But he hadn't needed to do that, because here Morgan was, crashing his early morning gym time again.

"Are you going to be that kind of boyfriend?" Hayes asked mildly, glancing over at where Morgan was setting down his gym bag and a bottle of water.

It was presumptuous, maybe, to call Morgan his boyfriend. They'd been on one date. Possibly another today. They weren't even currently sleeping together—again—by Morgan's own choice.

But his hazel eyes darkened as he looked up, his gaze colliding with Hayes'.

"What kind of boyfriend?" Morgan's voice was rough around the edges.

Hayes had known he would like it; that wasn't particularly a surprise. It was *how much* Morgan liked it.

"Hmm, like the possessive, creepy, stalker-y kind," Hayes said casually. Though he might be into it, honestly, if it was Morgan. He was into a *lot* of things, as long as they were related in some way to Morgan.

Morgan didn't say anything right away, just headed right over to where Hayes was sitting up on the weight bench.

They were alone in here. But it was still a little bit of a risk for Morgan to lean in and brush his mouth over Hayes' lips. It was a brief kiss, but that was all it took for Hayes to be panting and thinking about putting a hand on Morgan's neck and pulling him right back.

There was the evidence right there that even the risk was sexy because it was Morgan.

"You want me to be?" Morgan asked, his mouth still close to Hayes'.

"A boyfriend or a stalker boyfriend?" Hayes questioned.

Morgan hummed, not answering right away. He pushed Hayes' hair back with his fingers, his touch lingering. He didn't have to say anything, because the desire was written all over his face.

"Whatever you want," he finally said.

What Hayes wanted was for Morgan to press him down against this weight bench, screw who might walk in, and kiss him deep until he didn't care who might see. Make him so desperate he'd throw all his fears and worries and logical rules right out the window.

It wouldn't be very hard. Hayes already wanted to do it.

"What about what *you* want?"

Morgan laughed. "You know the other night, when I went with Danny and Jacob for a drink?"

This was not the answer Hayes had been anticipating, but he nodded anyway.

"Danny said I looked happy, and I realized, I didn't really think about that before. I hadn't thought about it in years. But when he said it, I knew he was right. I'm happy, and I'm happy doing this with you."

Just when Hayes thought he'd re-aligned his expectations with the blunt truth of what Morgan was capable of, Morgan blew everything right out of the water.

He leaned into Morgan's shoulder, into his touch. "I'm happy too," he admitted softly.

"Where's that leave your question?" Morgan wondered. He took a step away, and even though it was safer, definitely smarter, Hayes hated it.

Stupid, just invite him to lunch.

"I think just a regular kind of boyfriend," Hayes said. "Maybe a boyfriend who'd go to lunch with me today? After I'm done with practice?"

"Sounds good," Morgan said with a knowing grin.

Hayes returned to the weights. He was off schedule, and that was okay, but he didn't want to throw it out completely. Even after Morgan stripped out of his old, worn-out Bandits' sweatshirt, the 20 on the chest nearly worn off, and was only in a pair of low slung black athletic shorts clinging to his thighs, he tried to focus on what he was supposed to be doing.

Morgan had looked really fucking good six years ago. So good that Hayes had pretty much lost his mind the first time he'd gotten him naked. But he looked even better now. Maybe because it was becoming clearer every single day that he *had* Morgan, no questions, no exceptions, no distractions.

He'd been unsure how this thing between them would look and feel and *be*. It had made sense a week ago to pump the brakes. It could still make sense, if they ran into more potholes, but so far everything had been fairly smooth sailing. As concerned as Hayes had been before, hurt and afraid and needing him so much it was difficult *not* to reach for everything he wanted, it was impossible to doubt how all-in Morgan was.

They texted now. Hayes had even called him when he'd had a little downtime in Raleigh, after morning skate and before his pregame nap. They'd talked after the game briefly, even though it was really late last night when they'd gotten back to Tampa. Morgan had still been up though, dim light in his bedroom, moonlight streaming across his bare chest.

He'd nearly said *fuck it* and driven to Morgan's house instead. Curled up against him in bed, instead of going back to his empty house. But it was so soon. Too soon, maybe.

Hayes finished his set and then went on to his stretches.

Felt Morgan's gaze on him the whole time as he walked over to the treadmill.

"We should talk at lunch," Morgan said unexpectedly as he started out with a gentle jog to warm up.

"I wasn't expecting to spend the meal in silence," Hayes teased, trying to tamp down the sudden spike of worry that there *was* something wrong and he'd missed it.

"About telling Finn," Morgan said.

"Oh." Hayes should have seen this coming. He'd known it was, of course, but he'd pushed it aside, thinking they'd make sure they were on very solid ground first. No timetable on that. But he had a feeling Morgan was going to tell him he didn't feel comfortable lying to his son for longer than he absolutely had to. Frankly, as Finn's captain, he didn't really feel all that comfortable lying about it, either. So far it had just been lies of omission, not actual denials of what was happening right under Finn's nose. But Finn was not stupid; he was going to sense something was going on sooner rather than later.

"Yeah," Morgan said. "Think about it. And we'll talk about it."

Hayes hummed in acknowledgment and met Morgan's gaze across the room. "I gotta get to practice."

Morgan gave him a single nod, and it *was* nice to not have to explain to Morgan that he couldn't stick around, just to flirt and to talk. That he knew Hayes had responsibilities and obligations that he couldn't flout even if he wanted to. Didn't argue, or complain, just watched him leave the room with that unique combination of hunger and acceptance and obstinacy that Hayes recognized so well.

Alexander had never played team sports, even T-ball as a kid, and had had difficulty understanding all the things that he felt Hayes had to put above their relationship.

It was that, and the shards of Morgan still lingering in his heart, that had doomed them. Alexander hadn't been capable of understanding, but Morgan had practically been born understanding.

It felt good to know that problem wouldn't be following them. They had others, of course, but not *that* one.

Maybe he and Morgan hadn't always been close, but they'd always spoken the same language. Had the same pressures bearing down on their shoulders. Understood the particular weight that first overalls faced.

It was why Hayes hoped, with a fervency that scared the shit out of him, that they could make this work. Because while he had friends—he and Zach had been sharing secrets since they were teenagers—he'd never met anyone who *got* him the way that Morgan did, and he'd never imagined understanding anyone the way he could Morgan. Just by looking at the expression on his face, the guarded shadows in his eyes.

Even if that meant possibly tempting fate and telling Finn barely a week after they'd gotten together.

Hayes didn't avoid Finn during practice. He couldn't. And he didn't even want to. But he would admit that he felt less inclined to head immediately over in his rookie's direction. He'd spent a lifetime not letting secrets slip, so he didn't think he'd let *this* one slip now, but there was still enough of a concern that there was a noticeable pause every time it would make sense for him to interact with Finn.

That alone made him want to agree with whatever Morgan suggested at lunch.

Still, he was a little taken aback when Morgan leaned in, just after they'd sat down at Hayes' favorite sub shop, only a few blocks from his house, and said, "I want to tell Finn that we're together."

Hayes had absolutely known it was coming. Had even thought about it, as requested, and still, his first gut reaction was to ask Morgan, "Are you sure we're really together?" Even though he had *just* gone out of his way to call Morgan his boyfriend not four hours ago.

Morgan clearly agreed, because he shot him a hot look. "I thought we established that already."

"We did," Hayes said. Why was he being so weird about this? He'd been way less freaked out about bringing Alexander around, even about telling the team that he had a boyfriend. "What if I hadn't brought it up today?"

"Why you always gotta ask the hard questions?" Morgan asked wryly. But he didn't give Hayes a chance to answer—no doubt because he already *knew*. "I would've wanted to talk about it, regardless, but it helped to know we were on the same page. That it wasn't going to freak you out."

"You don't want to lie to Finn." *See*, Hayes wanted to crow smugly, *I can read you, too. I know you, too.*

"No. And I'm gonna assume you don't like it either."

"Of course not," Hayes said.

"It's just . . ." Morgan sighed deeply. "And this is not *your* fault, it's mine, but I haven't been a great dad to him. I didn't even realize I was being shitty. Well, scratch that. I didn't care, and that's worse, actually. Anyway I'm working on it. Being better. Lying to him now feels like I'm taking a step in the wrong direction."

"I get it," Hayes said. "So you want to tell him."

"And Jacob too, by extension." Morgan hesitated. "Though Jacob already sort of knows."

"*What*," Hayes hissed.

"Not that it's you, but that there was a guy. Who uh . . .fucked me up," Morgan admitted. "And then he figured out it was someone on the Sentinels."

Hayes didn't know what he wanted to unpack first.

"You were fucked up about me?" It was inevitable he'd choose that one before anything else.

Morgan laughed. "Uh, *yeah*. What possibly gave it away?"

"I just . . ." Hayes knew he was flushed red. Couldn't quite meet Morgan's eyes. "I guess I didn't think about it that way. Only that *I* was fucked up about what had happened. Never knew whether to be pissed at you or miss you so much my teeth ached."

"Didn't know whether I missed you or hated myself more," Morgan agreed, eyes soft.

Hayes didn't think he'd ever seen him look like that, before. He'd believed everything Morgan had said. Every part of it had seemed to resonate with truth. This was still hitting him hard, though. Like it hadn't felt real until this moment, and now it felt very, *very* real.

"And you told Jacob?"

"I . . .I did not handle finding out about Jacob and Finn, very well."

Hayes couldn't help but laugh at that. "No shit," he said. "Did you totally lose it?"

"Yeah. And then I got day drunk about it. Though . . ." Morgan winced. "We probably couldn't say that was *entirely* about them."

Hayes raised an eyebrow. "You got day drunk?"

"Not my proudest moment. Jacob had to come drag my ass out of the bar. We had . . .uh . . .a heart-to-heart. He figured out that you were a hockey player. I didn't *tell* him anything, not really, but you know how it is."

"Yeah for sure. *Goalies*," Hayes commiserated.

"Exactly. Anyway, he knows about some of it. Not all of it."

"How has he not guessed it was me?" Hayes said incredulously. Because he was the clear and obvious choice. Maybe he wasn't the only queer guy on the team now, but it wasn't like Jasper was the kind of guy you'd spend six years pining after. Jacob had even been around in Toronto six years ago. Of course, he and Morgan had hated each other back then so they'd steered clear of each other, but *still*. Looking back, they had not really been all that subtle about what they were doing.

"Honestly, I don't know." Morgan frowned now, like it was just now occurring to him how obvious it was.

"Maybe he's just been preoccupied by Finn," Hayes said.

"Maybe." Morgan didn't sound convinced.

"So how did you want to do this?" Hayes asked.

Morgan made a face. "I don't *want* to do it." He paused, probably realizing how that sounded. "No, no, not like that. I'm not ashamed of you. I want people to know we're together, it's just—"

"Babe, I get it," Hayes interrupted with a smile. "It's gonna be weird. Does Finn know you like guys?"

"No," Morgan said. "And that's gonna be part of it. He might—he probably *should*—be pissed that I didn't tell him. But I never met anyone else that I wanted. Never as much as I wanted you. And if I couldn't have you . . ."

Privately, Hayes thought he probably *should* have told Finn. If he was Finn, he'd have wanted to know the way he and his dad were alike, but he wasn't going to tell Morgan that. Especially not when he was baring his soul like that. Not when he was laying his heart so bare, and it was obvious how all of it belonged to Hayes.

"I get it." Hayes reached out and squeezed his forearm. "It's probably going to suck a little. But Finn loves you, and he wants you to be happy. That's gonna eventually overrule everything else."

"I hope so." Morgan rarely looked apprehensive. But he clearly looked it now. "I guess we should just . . .do it. I'm having dinner with them tonight. Maybe you should come with us, and we'll just . . .rip the band-aid off."

"You want me to be there?" Hayes asked cautiously. He'd hoped so, but he hadn't wanted to shove himself in, uninvited.

"Of course I want you to be there. You're—" Morgan broke off. "You're important. You're the whole reason this is happening at all. And also, you can help keep Jacob off me."

Hayes laughed. "Don't want to be outnumbered, huh?"

"Thinking I'm never gonna be outnumbered again, angel," Morgan said, and happiness spun through him, clear and true and perfect.

"I didn't know you were so close to Hayes," Finn said as he finished tossing the salad.

"Yeah," Jacob said as he came in from the patio, holding a platter of grilled chicken. "I always thought you two sort of kept your distance. All that *chosen one, next one* nonsense."

"It's not nonsense," Finn said with faux-sternness to his boyfriend. "Dad was totally great. And Hayes? He's got it, too."

"Yeah," Morgan said weakly.

It had been the first step in a long line of awkward steps to tell his son and his son's boyfriend that they were having a fourth to dinner. Extra awkward to dodge the immediate reaction that he was finally not third-wheeling it. Technically they were right, but he couldn't tell them that yet.

Then there were the pointed questions about why Hayes was coming to dinner. And the questions about how he even knew Hayes well enough to ask him.

On and on and on. Until Morgan wanted to scream, *because I love him and we're together now.*

But he wasn't going to do that, no matter how tempting it was.

The doorbell rang, and Morgan jumped up and said, "I'll get it," ignoring Finn and Jacob exchanging confused looks.

"Hey," Morgan said after ushering Hayes inside. He was in a T-shirt and shorts, same as all of them. He'd texted Morgan an hour ago questions about what he should wear, and even though he'd tried to phrase it casually, Morgan could hear the panic underneath his words. They were both kind of freaking out about this. That shouldn't have made it easier, but it did. Sort of.

"How's it going?" Hayes asked under his breath.

"The interrogation I've already been subjected to about why you're coming to dinner almost made me break twice," Morgan hissed. Hayes slipped out of his shoes and then he handed Morgan the bottle of wine he'd brought.

Morgan gave it right back. "Give it to Jacob. He likes wine. It'll make you look good with your future step-son-in-law," Morgan advised.

Hayes flushed. "Don't you think—"

God, Morgan wanted to kick himself. Two dates in, and Hayes thought he was *proposing*. "No, no, I mean, they're going to get married, aren't they?"

Hayes nodded enthusiastically. "I'm sure they will." He patted Morgan on the shoulder. "They're great together."

Morgan straightened up. "I guess...no choice but to do this," he said.

"I'm following your lead," Hayes said under his breath before they walked into Jacob and Finn's kitchen.

Both Finn and Jacob greeted Hayes with enthusiasm and hugs. Jacob seemed pleased by the wine, and Hayes let himself get pulled into a conversation about different New Zealand varietals and vintages. Morgan helped Finn finish setting the table.

"This is nice," Finn said, tilting his face towards Morgan as he set the salad onto their kitchen table. "It was a good idea to invite Monty."

"Good. I thought so, too," Morgan said, trying to sound normal and not like a man wildly in love who desperately craved approval on his life choices.

"He's a good captain," Finn said. "Different than you, but good, still."

"I might've been pretty tough on guys, sometimes. There's more ways to go about things than just being a hard-ass all the time," Morgan said. Ten years ago, he'd have never said that—wouldn't have even *thought* it. But he'd mellowed. Learned that there were more things out in the world than just hockey.

Sometimes he thought what would have happened if he'd had that realization sooner. But he'd won two Cups with the Bandits because he'd been hard on everyone—starting with himself, but definitely not ending there.

"Dad, look at you," Finn teased. "It's like you're a real person now!"

"Shut it," Morgan said, reaching over and messing up Finn's curls.

He'd thought maybe he should save the big revelation but he'd also had the perfectly legitimate concern that it would be awkward to keep it until after dinner. That they wouldn't have anything to talk about without it.

But he shouldn't have worried. Hayes was too good, natural and practiced and also ridiculously charming, drawing Finn and Jacob into the conversation effortlessly, probably like he'd done with dozens of rookies since he'd become captain. Morgan always thought he was amazing, but watching him laugh with Finn and Jacob, he was reminded again of how goddamn lucky he was that Hayes had forgiven him, that Hayes was still willing to give him the time of the day.

They were nearly all the way through dinner when Hayes shot him a meaningful glance under his long eyelashes.

Morgan knew what it meant.

It's time, baby.

Also, *good fucking luck.*

God, Morgan loved him.

"So . . .uh . . .Finn, you asked why I asked Hayes to dinner," Morgan said. He wasn't nearly as good at this as Hayes was. Another reason he was grateful Hayes was around.

"Yeah?" Finn barely looked like he was paying attention. Morgan was pretty sure he was playing footsy under the table with Jacob. Normally he might've thrown a fit about this gross disrespect—or at least given Jacob shit about it—but he didn't want to get derailed now that he'd finally decided it was time to confess everything.

"You know we knew each other."

Finn shot him a look. "Yeah, Dad. We all know. The fucking saviors of US hockey. We're aware."

Morgan ground his teeth together. "Right. Yes. We played together at the Four Nations tournament six years ago." He risked a glance over at Hayes. His expression was perfectly neutral. Maybe a little too neutral, like he was holding something—or everything—back. "The only time we've ever played together."

"And I was there too. Let's not forget that," Jacob said, laughing.

"True," Morgan said, even though Jacob's presence on Team USA was not why they were having this conversation.

"Still," Finn said innocently, "it's not like you've spent the last six years talking about him."

Morgan let out a weak gasp of a laugh. "Also true," he said.

Someone nudged *him* under the table. It had to be Hayes. He was the only one who knew what Morgan was really trying to get at.

And yes, he really did need to get on with it.

"We . . .uh . . ." Morgan cleared his throat again, eyes glued to his plate. He couldn't lift them up or look Finn in the eye, even though he should. Hayes kicked him under the table again and he managed to get his shit together. *Eyes up. Mouth open.* "We spent a lot of time together at that tournament."

Finn still looked vaguely bored and totally uninterested in this journey to the past. "Okay?"

God, he was going to make Morgan say it. Out loud. *Out loud.* "A *lot* of time."

Finn's eyes narrowed. "What does that mean, exactly?"

"Are you saying what I *think* you're saying?" Jacob asked.

Finn looked over at Jacob. "What *is* he saying?"

He hated all of them. They could all fall in the ocean, as far as Morgan was concerned. Except Hayes. He was an angel and deserved only the best things.

"I'm saying that we spent a lot of time *in bed*. Hayes and I hooked up at the tournament." There he'd said it.

"I wouldn't have put it exactly like that," Hayes said mildly.

"You're—" Finn looked at Morgan, then at Hayes. Like this news was taking a brain recalibration. And yeah, Morgan understood that. He'd gone through one of his own, six years ago. "And *you*."

"How *would* you have put it?" Jacob asked. He put his elbows on the table and leaned forward, clearly interested.

Hayes glanced over at Morgan. "At the tournament, we did have a fling where we spent a lot of time in bed, but that's not all it was. We fell in love."

Morgan nodded rapidly. Hoping that this might clear up a few things and not require him to make any more personal confessions.

But Finn was apparently still stuck on the fact he wasn't straight. "I'm sorry *what*," Finn said bluntly. "Dad—you've *never*."

"Well, clearly not *never*," Morgan said self-consciously.

"And all these times I kept pushing women at you?"

Morgan winced. "I should have been honest that I like both."

"Yeah, no shit," Finn said, crossing his arms over his chest. He had the Reynolds glower down pat.

"Truthfully, I wasn't interested in dating *anyone*. Not after Hayes." Hayes' gaze was warm on his face as he said it. Warm and approving and encouraging. It was easier to look at him than to look at Finn, who still looked—justifiably—pissed off.

"Still," Finn said with a pout.

"What's the point of this history lesson, anyway?" Jacob asked, a little too casually.

"We both regretted how it ended. We . . .well, it was never going to be anything. How could it have been? We were on separate teams, separate coasts—"

"And you were an asshole," Hayes added, still smiling.

Morgan couldn't even be mad that he was being forced to grovel in front of his son. Jacob, that was a little tougher to swallow, but he'd dealt with far worse.

"*And* I was an asshole," Morgan agreed. "But now that I'm retired, and you're here, and *I'm* here, we started talking again. Turns out we both—well, we both regretted how it ended. And we decided to give it another go."

Finn burst out laughing. Not the best reaction to the news. Laughter had not even been in the top five when Morgan had considered how this was going to go.

He squirmed in his chair, unsure if he was embarrassed or angry or some other emotion that defied definition.

"Are you joking?" Finn demanded.

"Uh, no?" This was the worst. Morgan was now officially on record as regretting being the one to suggest this.

"You're telling me you're in love with Monty and that you've *been* in love with him for six years, and now you're finally back together or whatever, and the words you're gonna use are, *give it another go*?"

"Your father is painfully unsentimental sometimes, you gotta forgive him for it," Hayes said and *smiling* about it.

"Not that unsentimental," Morgan yelped defensively. "I've said lots of romantic things to you. So many romantic things."

"Yeah, we don't need to hear those," Jacob said dryly, taking a long sip of his wine.

"Good," Finn said. "Monty's a great guy. A *catch*. Don't forget it."

"I have zero intention of forgetting it." God, he wanted to drop through the floor. Finn lecturing him on how to romance his boyfriend. There was no way this could get any worse than it currently was.

"As long as you're happy, Dad, I'm happy for you." Finn grinned at him and paused, expectantly. "Though, there's only one question I have for you."

Morgan tried not to cringe. "What?"

Finn gave him a hard stare. "Did you really think I didn't know?"

Morgan's jaw dropped. "What? *What?*"

Finn waved his hand. "The first time you saw Hayes this summer, you literally froze in your tracks."

"I did not," Morgan muttered. Though he had, a little. But not obviously! He'd been more subtle than that.

Finn shot him an unamused look. "And then there was all the times you stared at him like he was a full buffet spread and you were starving."

"I definitely did not do that, either," Morgan said, feeling a flush creep up his chest from under his shirt collar.

"Oh, you did. The opposite of low key. I know what yearning looks like, and you were like front and center definition, Dad. It wasn't that hard to ask Jacob if you'd hung out with Hayes at all, six years ago, and it was even easier to put the pieces together." Finn looked unimpressed. "I just can't believe it took this long for you to get your shit together."

"It did—I didn't want to—" Morgan gave up. Turned to Jacob. "You told him!"

"I did not," Jacob said, laughing now. "But yeah, you were not very hard to figure out, bud. I knew the moment we showed up at Sentinels camp that he was the guy you'd told me about."

"Oh my God," Morgan said. "All those times—"

"Which times?" Hayes and Finn interrupted at the same time with the same words. They exchanged glances and burst out laughing.

"You literally said, and I swear it's a direct quote, *even you wouldn't be stupid enough to pine after Hayes Montgomery.*"

Hayes grinned. "You said that?"

"He said that." Morgan glowered. "You couldn't have thought it *then.*"

"Oh, I was convinced by the time I said that," Jacob said. He leaned back in his chair and pinned Morgan with the kind of hard-assed look that had *always* made Morgan want to kill him when he was in the net and Morgan was trying to slip a puck past him. "Did you really think I wasn't going to give you crap about this? After what you said about me and Finn?"

Oh, he had. It was half of why he'd been so nervous. "I didn't react well, then."

"No shit," Finn retorted. "You accused Jacob of being a pedophile!"

Hayes shot him a soft look full of reprimand, which shouldn't have been hot, especially not in front of his son and his boyfriend, but the skin under the collar of his T-shirt prickled.

"Not my best parenting moment," Morgan allowed.

Finn snorted.

"Or what about when you accused me of sleeping with Finn in an attempt to get my youth back?"

Hayes raised an eyebrow. "You did that?"

"I didn't *mean* it."

"No, you did, and that *was* a good parenting moment," Jacob said, suddenly serious. "Made me wonder if your guy was younger. And lo and behold . . ." He gestured at Hayes.

"You trying to do that too?" Hayes said, leaning over and teasing him in a low voice.

That was the easiest accusation of all the whole night to dodge. "No way. You know I love you because . . .because we're the same. We get each other. Wouldn't matter what age you were."

"Wait, you are *not* the same," Finn said, frowning.

Morgan straightened and met his son's eyes. Wishing, not for the first time, that they were alone, and he could kiss Hayes.

"Actually," Hayes said, shrugging, "we kinda are. Underneath." He leaned over and was the one to press his mouth to Morgan's. It was a brief kiss, barely a press of his lips, but Morgan's heart fluttered anyway.

"Ew, gross," Finn said.

"Be good," Jacob said sternly to Finn. "How much PDA have we subjected your dad to over the years?"

Morgan wanted to say *too much*, but it was impossible to care, when Hayes was looking at him like that, heart in his eyes, happiness written across every line of his face.

CHAPTER 21

"You know, you could've stayed over last night," Hayes said when Morgan walked into his kitchen after letting himself in with Hayes' door code.

He'd only left a few hours before, after they'd shared a few plates of food from Hayes' meal delivery service and made out on the couch with a Sharks-Knights game playing on the TV that neither of them bothered watching.

It had been a week since they'd told Finn and Jacob and two weeks since they'd started dating, and if Hayes was being honest, he hadn't ever anticipated that Morgan could hold out on this celibacy thing this long. If he had, he never would've suggested that Morgan was just in it for the sex.

Because sex was not happening, and Hayes very much wanted the sex to be happening.

"I know," Morgan said, setting the tray full of coffee down on the counter.

Hayes moved closer. Tipped his head against Morgan's shoulder. "We could've woken up together and *then* you could have brought me breakfast in bed."

Morgan's arm slid around his bare back, his touch warm and reassuring. "I told you why I wasn't staying."

It was impossible not to pout about it. Because he *had* asked last night, too, practically grinding on Morgan's lap as he'd done it, and apparently Morgan was made of stronger stuff than that.

Or Hayes had somehow become less appealing.

But no—that couldn't be true. Because Morgan's fingers shook against his skin, then, and he turned his head away, taking a deep, shuddering breath.

"Don't be unfair," Morgan said.

"My turn," Hayes said. "If you want me to say it, I'll say it. No shame, whatsoever. Let's go to bed. Right now."

"You have to fly out in less than two hours."

It shouldn't have been so cute—or make want Hayes to drag Morgan to the bed, tie him to the headboard, and torture him sexually—that Morgan had apparently memorized Hayes' schedule.

"Less than two hours? Plenty of time." He could do a *lot* with that kind of time.

Morgan detached from him. Plucked his coffee from the tray and skirted around the island, like a dozen feet of marble was enough to deter Hayes from seducing him.

"Drink your coffee," Morgan said mildly.

"It *is* sweet that you came back this morning," Hayes said, picking up his own cup. Sipping it, feeling the warmth flood him when he realized it was made perfectly.

If you'd asked him a month ago if Morgan Reynolds would be a good boyfriend, he'd have laughed and said no fucking way. But he was.

Other than the fact he kept refusing to fuck Hayes.

Morgan drummed his fingers against the countertop. "You're welcome."

"In case I haven't said it, you trying to be romantic is *also* sweet," Hayes said.

Morgan huffed out a laugh. "Then why do you keep going for my dick?"

"Oh, baby, you know why."

"And you know why I gotta stop you." Morgan's face did something complicated. Hayes probably knew him better than anyone else, even after all this time, and he still couldn't figure out what *that* look meant. Morgan could be a prickly, difficult creature, but that was okay, because he was *Hayes'* creature.

"Supposedly," Hayes said, pouting. "What's it gonna take? I promise you, baby, I didn't mean it. I *don't* mean it, now. You wanna love me and romance me. I get it. But I also want you to hit it, *desperately.*"

Because Morgan was apparently determined to discover if you could die from blue balls, he changed the subject. "You're home in two days?"

"Yeah," Hayes said, nodding.

"Text me when you've landed, alright?" Morgan asked casually.

"Baby, you know I'm gonna be texting you all the time." He was also planning on sending at least one picture that, if it was as effective as Hayes hoped, might soften Morgan's determination to keep their relationship PG.

"I hope so," Morgan said, smirking a little smugly. "I know how it can be on the road."

He would, and clearly they had disliked the same parts of it, because just having these little intimate moments in between games and practices and flights, moments when he'd normally have been alone, was something Hayes could get used to.

"You're actually a really great boyfriend." He hadn't really meant to say it. After all, Morgan was making the effort now, to prove he could be better. What would it be like in six months? In a year? In three?

Would Morgan still be texting him first thing so he never had to get out of bed alone? Bringing him coffee? Grabbing lunch? Meeting up at the gym? Late night dinners, where Morgan didn't even mind if Hayes was so tired he didn't want to talk, just rested his head on his shoulder?

Hayes hoped he would.

Honestly, Hayes hoped it would be even better than the last few weeks had been.

"What am I always telling you, angel? You deserve it. Every single bit of it," Morgan said. His gaze had been warm, but now, it heated up.

And when Hayes rounded the island and set his cup down, kissing him hard and deep and insistent, Morgan didn't pull away. Didn't shift his hips away when Hayes rubbed his cock against his thigh.

Yes, Hayes thought, tasting the coffee on Morgan's tongue and beginning to tug him in the direction of the living room. If he detoured them to the bedroom, Morgan might change his mind, and at this point, Hayes wasn't picky.

"Hey, hey," Morgan said, lifting his mouth off Hayes before they collapsed together onto the couch. "Not this morning."

"Why?" Hayes wanted to believe he was above whining about it, but he wasn't.

Morgan's gaze darkened, sweeping over Hayes' bare chest, his ratty old basketball shorts. He'd definitely looked hotter, better. He'd even looked hotter and better in the last two weeks for sure. "Because you have to get on a plane and we don't have enough time for what I want to do to you. Wanna keep you in bed for a week."

Hayes flopped, alone, onto the couch. "I take it back. You're the worst."

Morgan grinned down at him, hands braced on the back cushions as he gave Hayes a series of too-brief pecks on the mouth. "No, you don't. You think I'm the *best*, you just said so."

"Well, don't be so smug about it then," Hayes complained. But he couldn't stop smiling, even as Morgan kissed him.

"You love it when I'm smug about it," Morgan pointed out, still smiling.

It was true and Hayes couldn't even deny it.

It was a back-to-back, up in Philly and then to New Jersey.

The Sentinels took the Flyers, four to one, and then went to a shootout against the Devils, ultimately losing because Jasper couldn't quite sneak the puck past Markstrom's kneepad.

By the time the team boarded the flight back to Florida, Hayes was tired, but it was more than physical exhaustion—though there was plenty of that, too.

It was unbelievable, sometimes, how he could be surrounded by so many people, people he *liked*, even, and still feel alone.

It was the C he wore on his jersey, but it was more than that, too. The specific pressure of his reputation and the expectations resting on his shoulders. Sometimes Hayes didn't feel like he could take a breath.

But every time Morgan replied to a text or sent him a stupid picture—this last one of his blurry and out of focus bare feet up on his coffee table—Hayes could breathe a little easier.

"You good?" Jasper asked as he settled down in the seat next to Hayes.

"I should be asking you that," Hayes said, pulling his earbuds out of his pocket.

Jasper shrugged. "It was a good shot. I'm not torn up about it."

"You shouldn't be," Hayes reassured him. "It was a good game. Tough but we hung in there."

"Yeah," Jasper agreed, nodding. "You gonna sleep?"

"I think so," Hayes said, slipping his earbuds in and pulling his phone out.

What he'd just said to Jasper was almost the exact same thing, word for word, that had been waiting on his phone after the game. Turned out Morgan was the sort of boyfriend who would, most of the time, give encouraging pep talks. But he was *also* the sort of boyfriend who wouldn't hesitate to call out anyone on Hayes' team or even Hayes himself if he thought they could be playing better.

Just yesterday, he'd seen a whole string of texts from Morgan after the Flyers game, when they'd been down 1-0 for the first two periods. He'd certainly had a lot of opinions about the lack of offensive drive and Hayes hadn't even been able to tell him that he'd been wrong.

In fact, that was exactly what he'd told the team during the second intermission. He'd led the way, right out of the gate, scoring in the first minute of the third period to tie it up, and the Sentinels hadn't looked back after that.

But Morgan had called him out on it. Hadn't let him slide.

Hayes hadn't expected *that* would feel good, but it actually did. Like Morgan was a good boyfriend *and* Morgan was still Morgan. It was becoming easier and easier to trust that the version he was seeing now was the version he might get forever, if he was lucky enough.

He sent Morgan a test balloon text. **U still up?** he asked.

I'm not that old, he got back almost immediately.

That was all the motivation that Hayes needed to send the picture he'd taken a few days back, in anticipation of this road trip. Early morning light streaming in from the windows, making him look tanner and younger, eyes half-lidded, hair messed up from sleep, chest flushed with arousal, hand wrapped around the base of his hard cock.

It was a damn good picture.

Feel like I should do a blood pressure check, just to be sure, he sent and then the picture.

Hayes squirmed in the seat in anticipation, ignoring how Jasper elbowed him half-heartedly.

He clicked over to his white noise, thumb hovering over his usual settings. Wanting to read Morgan's reaction before he fell asleep.

Morgan never disappointed and he didn't now.

No fair, angel.

Never promised to play fair. Hayes hesitated, then decided, *fuck it*, he wasn't trying to play games here. **You like it?**

Like it? I fucking love it. You're the most gorgeous thing I've ever seen in my life.

Hayes couldn't help the grin that overtook his face. He knew he looked good, but it felt better than he'd anticipated to have Morgan say it, especially like that.

Hope to see you tomorrow, he wrote back. **Breakfast in bed?**

Think we can arrange that, Morgan said.

Satisfied that he'd worn Morgan down sufficiently that he had a good chance of getting sex along with his coffee in the morning, he turned on his white noise and let it carry him to sleep.

It was long past midnight when Hayes finally turned into his driveway.

The outside lights were on, which he expected, but after pulling into the garage and grabbing his duffel from the back seat, he was surprised to see one of the kitchen lights, the dim one over the sink. He was pretty sure he hadn't left it on, but maybe his housekeeper had, accidentally. As he toed his shoes off, he considered it. Couldn't remember if she'd been scheduled to come by while he was gone, but between the season and

Morgan distracting him, it wasn't a stretch to think he'd just forgotten.

He grabbed a bottle of water from the fridge and dragged his tired ass towards his bedroom, stopping in his tracks, sure that his exhaustion was playing tricks on him.

Because the room wasn't dark and his bed wasn't empty.

Morgan grinned at him, in that smug way of his that might've been more annoying if he wasn't mostly naked and currently waiting up for Hayes to come home. Like he *belonged* here.

"Hey," Morgan said, like his appearance was nothing. Like Hayes had known he'd be here. And maybe he should have. He'd sent the picture, hadn't he? And heavily hinted that he'd wanted Morgan to let himself in in the morning and find Hayes in bed.

This was *so much better.*

"Hey," Hayes tried, trying to keep his voice even. But he probably looked overwhelmed with the surprise of it. Thrilled about it, too.

"Surprise," Morgan said, patting the bed next to him. "You wanted me to come over tomorrow morning . . ." He paused, checking the nonexistent watch on his wrist. "And *technically,* it's morning."

"It is." Hayes gave up on keeping anything steady. He was still standing halfway between the doorway and the bed. Was afraid if he took one step, he'd take half a dozen and crawl right onto Morgan, refusing to take no for an answer.

"And," Morgan said with a shrug that was clearly supposed to be casual, but looked way too practiced to *actually* be, "I always hated coming home from a road trip, late at night, to an empty dark house."

Hayes did not fall to his knees. He did not. But he thought about it.

He did drop his bag to the floor and finally cross over to the bed.

"Come here," Morgan said, and he didn't need another invitation.

He'd thought about taking a long hot shower and falling into bed, but all those thoughts were wiped from his brain. Hayes wanted only one thing.

Shucked his sweats. Crawled right over Morgan's body, gasping a little as Morgan tugged his T-shirt off, and they pressed together, skin to skin.

"Hey," Morgan said, cupping his cheek as Hayes leaned close. He still looked smug, but how could Hayes even be annoyed about that when he had *this*, when Morgan was in his bed?

"Already said that," Hayes teased.

"Missed you, glad you're back," Morgan said. Pressing a soft kiss to his lips.

They could talk about how bone-deep happy Hayes was that he'd found Morgan here tonight, but right now, Hayes only wanted to do one thing.

He gripped Morgan's sides with his thighs and rolled their bodies over. Morgan got the memo, and his next kiss was insistent and deep. Hayes gasped into his mouth.

Kissing was so good, and it was especially incredible between them, after so long missing Morgan's mouth on his, but they'd *been* kissing. Hayes didn't just want more, he *needed* more.

But he didn't have to say so. Morgan knew, because he *always* knew. A moment later, his lips meandered down Hayes' neck and then his collarbone. Drifted farther, giving him a nip right above his nipple, and then lower still, licking up his abs.

"Fuck," Hayes ground out as Morgan pressed a palm against his twitching hard-on.

"Feel good, angel?" Morgan murmured into his skin. "You want more?"

"God, yes," Hayes breathed out unsteadily.

He was almost dizzy from how quickly they were going, the transition between the assumption he'd be going to bed alone to Morgan tugging off his briefs, hot mouth finally sliding down his cock.

He dug his heels into the mattress and tried to think unsexy thoughts, because Morgan between his legs, sucking him down like he'd spent the last six years dreaming about doing it, was making him lose it way faster than he wanted.

"So good," he groaned as Morgan's tongue did something ridiculous. His mouth was so hot and wet it was fucking heaven. Morgan liked to call him angel, but Hayes wasn't sure the opposite wasn't closer to the truth.

This was all he'd ever wanted; it was impossible to put on the brakes even when he knew he should. He just wanted to dive right into the deep end and never come up for air.

It was *that* good, and then Morgan slid a wet finger behind his balls and up against his hole.

"I . . ." His voice wavered, which might have been embarrassing if he hadn't looked down and seen the look on Morgan's face, equally as overwhelmed.

"You want that?" Morgan's voice was fucked out too. Rough around the edges and desperate.

They had practice tomorrow, but no game. He could deal with it.

"Please," Hayes said, and Morgan groaned, like *Hayes* was actually the drop-dead sexy one here.

Saliva wasn't going to be enough to open him up, not for Morgan's cock, but Morgan didn't seem to be in any hurry. Toying with just one finger and then finally another, making Hayes squirm and swear.

"Come on," Hayes finally begged, "get the lube. I'm *dying* here."

Morgan muttered a curse under his breath as he got to his feet. His cock was hard and red, wet at the tip. Clearly he was just as turned on as Hayes was, and Hayes hadn't even touched him.

Something he *should* remedy, and he was in the middle of thinking about how he would—get his mouth and his hands on Morgan's dick—when Morgan slid three wetter fingers into him and brushed right up against his prostate.

"Fuck," Hayes screeched. Probably not in a very attractive way, but it felt so good he might be going out of his mind. "Get in me *now*."

"One minute," Morgan said, annoyingly.

"We've waited long enough," Hayes said, wiggling his ass. "Come *on*."

"So fucking impatient," Morgan complained, but his fingers were shaking as he rearranged Hayes' hips, angling him just right before sliding inside.

Every time Hayes had thought of how it had been six years ago, he'd tell himself that it had to be a mirage of some kind or he was just plain misremembering how good it was. Usually he gave himself a pep talk like, *you've had good sex before and you'll have good sex again.*

But sex with Morgan wasn't just good; it was like he freaking rearranged the fabric of Hayes' universe.

Morgan gripped Hayes' knee, sliding it up to his thigh, leaned into him and fucked him deaf, blind, and stupid. Hayes was aware he was probably making some really dumb noises, saying a lot of nonsense, but none of that mattered. All he cared about was the fucking flawless slide of Morgan's cock into him, over and over again, his dick brushing against Morgan's abs, catching a little on the skin. He was going to come just from this, and that was insane, but Hayes could only hang on and beg for more.

He came, and Morgan let out an equally unsteady groan before his own hips stuttered and he fell right onto Hayes.

They were both panting heavily, Hayes' fingers slipping along the sweaty curves of Morgan's shoulders. Morgan *was* sort of crushing him, but Hayes decided he didn't care. It had been too good to worry about things like messes and dirty sheets and breathing.

Breathing, totally overrated.

"I'm probably killing you," Morgan mumbled into his neck.

"Yeah, but it's okay. I'd die happy," Hayes said, pressing his mouth to the side of Morgan's sweaty hair.

Morgan sighed, a happy content sound that Hayes would never have imagined he could make. And *he* was the one who'd made Morgan feel that good.

"Give me a minute, and then we'll get up. Clean up."

"Shower?" Hayes offered. "I was going to wash the airplane off, anyway."

"Always with the best ideas." Morgan sounded dick-drunk. Love-struck. Blown away by it. Hayes understood. How was he supposed to go about his normal life when this was waiting for him at home?

It was a fucking miracle he was still playing hockey games.

There'd been a point when he'd been sure that Morgan was exaggerating when he said he'd have done something stupid in Toronto to keep this, to keep *him*. Hayes had gotten it then, but he'd never understood it more than he did right now.

"I love you." He'd told himself he wouldn't go overboard saying it all the time, but what else could he say to possibly express the way his heart felt like it just kept expanding, growing and growing until it felt like it could contain all the mysteries of the universe?

"Love you too." Morgan kissed his shoulder. Then groaned and finally pulled out, rolling over. "Come on, angel. Shower time."

They were quiet in the bathroom, waiting for the shower to heat up. Hayes stepping in first and Morgan following him.

They got clean and then Morgan crowded him against the chilly tile, kissing him soft and sweet.

They made out lazily and then finally got out, drying off.

Hayes got out new sheets and threw the others into the washer.

By the time he got back, Morgan had the bed made. Hayes raised an eyebrow.

"You're probably exhausted," Morgan said, cheeks flushed. Like it was something to be embarrassed about.

"Thanks, babe," Hayes said, pressing a kiss to his mouth. "And if I didn't say it sufficiently, I'm really, really glad you were here when I got home."

"It wasn't overstepping?"

"I literally invited you to let yourself in tomorrow morning."

"Yeah, but it wasn't tomorrow morning," Morgan said because of course he was that literal.

Hayes shot him a look as he climbed into bed. "Don't be ridiculous. I wanted you to stay the night before you left. I even gave you crap about it. I sent you a naked picture, even. I was surprised, but it was the best kind of surprise."

"Good." Morgan settled in next to him, pulling him in close. Hayes went easily, resting his head on Morgan's chest, enjoying the way Morgan's hands played with the edges of his still-damp hair.

For a long moment, Hayes thought he'd go to sleep, but then Morgan said, "You talk to Jasper?"

"After the game? Yeah."

"It was a good shot," Morgan said.

It had been. But they'd split the road trip, which wasn't easy on a back-to-back.

"Yeah, I told him that," Hayes said.

"You guys are playing lights out right now." This wasn't *that* much different from the compliments Morgan gave Hayes over text during the games, but it felt a little more pointed. Like there was something else he wanted to say.

"Yeah?"

Hayes shouldn't have even wondered if Morgan would say the rest of what was on his mind. This *was* Morgan, after all.

"The Sentinels should be falling all over themselves to give you whatever contract you want."

Hayes should have guessed this was what Morgan was getting at. He supposed it was inevitable that they were going to have to talk about it. Maybe Jacob had even mentioned their conversation during golf to Morgan. They were friends now, after all.

"They don't want to give me the years I want," Hayes said. He wanted to pull back, to get a little distance, suddenly, but he had a feeling Morgan wouldn't let him squirm out of this.

"The money's good?"

"Hm, yeah, basically. Just not the years." Hayes tried to remember the last text Barty had sent about their negotiations. It had annoyed him so he'd tried not to dwell on it.

"Would you take less?" Morgan wondered.

Every time he'd tried to say something like that to Barty, Barty had freaked out. Ranted about how Hayes was worth more, and Hayes should know his own worth. And he did. He didn't need the Sentinels to tell him what he was worth. He knew it already.

But this was Morgan, not Barty, and Morgan would understand, probably better than anyone else.

"Yeah," Hayes said softly. "I don't want to leave. I don't want to test the market. I want . . .what I want is to stay here. To win another Cup, *here*. Not somewhere else."

"They should want that too. They probably *do* want that too," Morgan said and his words were gentle but fierce. Full of belief.

"I want to retire here." It felt good to admit it out loud. "Like you did with the Bandits. You never played anywhere else."

"I wasn't going to," Morgan said bluntly. "And you're good enough, Monty, you shouldn't either."

"I know," Hayes said, and that was the pebble in the shoe of the whole argument. He knew how good he was. How many other teams would want him and want him still.

Morgan stroked his shoulder, reassuringly. "I don't need to say it, but I should. Doesn't matter where you end up. Even if you're not on this team. Even if you're not playing with Finn. I'm with you, as long as you want me."

Hayes nearly said, *so, forever?* But that was insane. They hadn't even been dating a month yet. But still. He'd loved Morgan for six years now, and apparently Morgan had felt the same for just as long. They'd made it through the horrible desert of separation, so how could being together screw anything up? It seemed impossible that could ever happen.

"I know," Hayes said, instead.

"I've been thinking I want to say something about your contract during one of my segments," Morgan said.

Hayes should have seen it coming. He *had* seen it coming. "No," he said, but even he could hear the indecision in his voice.

"I don't want to do it without your blessing, but I'd do it if I was in your bed or not," Morgan said with that ringing certainty only he possessed.

"Did Jacob talk to you about it?"

Hayes could feel, not see, Morgan's frown. "What does Jacob have to do with this?"

"Just . . .that day we golfed together. Barty brought it up to him." Hayes paused. He was still feeling out this friendship between Morgan and Jacob. It didn't always make sense to him, but he was slowly beginning to see how it worked. "Barty thought maybe if I didn't want you to do it, I'd be willing to have Jacob give it a shot."

"Jacob doesn't even do media," Morgan said, sounding a little dumbfounded.

"I know, which is why I turned him down."

"Angel," Morgan said earnestly, turning towards Hayes so he could look him right in the eye, "if anyone should talk you up and make the Sentinels feel wretched for not believing in you, it's *me*."

Hayes could agree that it made a certain kind of sense. "Yeah," he said.

"I get why you might not have wanted me to, before. You were pissed."

That was definitely true. "I'm not pissed now."

"Right, which is why I'm confused that you're not jumping all over this idea."

"Who says it'll even change anything?" Hayes waved his hands. "It's not like you're going to knock some sense into them."

"You don't think management on all thirty-two NHL teams gives a shit about how they're perceived by the media and the fans? They sure fucking do."

Morgan didn't have to add, *and the media and the fans always think I know what I'm talking about*, because it was a given. He was Morgan Reynolds. His word was hockey gospel.

"I . . ." Hayes sighed heavily. "You'd do it even if we weren't fucking? Even if you didn't love me?"

Morgan made an outraged noise. "I can't imagine a world in which I wouldn't love you—you're made for me. I've known it since the first time we stepped on the ice together—but yes. *Yes.* This isn't me doing you a solid 'cause you let me stick my dick in you." Morgan grinned.

Hayes squawked and smacked him on the shoulder. "God, why *do* I love you?"

"Good question, but don't ever stop."

It wasn't *so, forever,* but it was enough to say, "Don't plan to."

"Good," Morgan said. "It's decided then?"

"Ugh, I'll text Barty in the morning. I'm sure he has some specific talking points he'll want you to cover."

"Like Barty would ever have a list I wouldn't have already thought of," Morgan muttered but gave a little nod that told Hayes he'd wait at least until he and Hayes' agent got on the same page.

"Thank you," Hayes said, resettling back into the curve of Morgan's arms. "You didn't have to offer to do this."

"Yeah, I did. I'd do anything for you, angel," Morgan said softly.

And Hayes was slowly beginning to believe that was true.

CHAPTER 22

Morgan didn't dislike Bartholemew Smith III, but he didn't *like* him either, particularly.

Barty had spent at least two years when he'd first started gaining bigger clients attempting to convince Morgan to switch agents. But Morgan hadn't wanted to leave Natasha, who'd been his agent and a certified ballbuster since he'd been drafted into the league. He'd had his choice of agents; they'd practically lined up begging for a chance to represent him.

Natasha had been the dark horse, the only woman, and he knew she would be the hungriest. The most aggressive negotiator. It wasn't only because she'd be perennially ignored and dismissed, but because he looked into her eyes and recognized the same feeling he'd always carried in himself. A feeling that had less to do with everyone else doubting him and more to do with him *knowing* what he was capable of.

"When Monty called me and said he'd changed his mind, I didn't believe him," Barty said, leaning back in his chair.

They'd spent the last eighteen holes on the course making small talk and exchanging hockey gossip. But Hayes hadn't really come up until now.

Jacob had offered to come with him, because he knew he didn't really like Barty and that he really didn't like golf. But he'd turned him down, because he didn't want Barty to know how much he annoyed him.

Also, only a small handful of people knew how much Morgan disliked golf.

It was too slow, too much standing around and waiting. He'd only gone out of his way to get good at it because hockey players loved it and he wasn't going to embarrass himself on a course in front of any of them.

"He was that against me saying something publicly?" Morgan said casually. But it didn't surprise him at all. Hayes had his share of pride, similarly shaped to Morgan's own.

"Adamantly against it." Barty took a sip of his beer. "So against it I thought I must've missed something over the years. Like you two secretly hated each other and you've been fooling the world for the last decade."

"No," Morgan said. He'd believe that Barty didn't know the truth if he didn't see the knowing edge to his normally sly expression. If Hayes hadn't told Morgan himself that he'd finally confessed the entire story to his agent.

"Clearly." Barty was grinning now. "You planning on doing any kind of public statement?"

Morgan shook his head. "I don't give a shit what anyone says about me, even if people speculate about us."

"They're going to, you know," Barty said. "Especially if you go on ESPN and say what Hayes claims you want to."

Morgan knew what people were talking about. He'd seen the posts and the screenshots and the pictures because Natasha had sent them to him. The positive was that almost everyone believed that this was a new thing and the overriding consensus was that their relationship made a weird kind of sense. *Like the universe is righting itself,* one video claimed, after a bunch of sappy lyrics appeared over two dozen photos of him and Hayes over the years.

Morgan had been a little embarrassed he'd watched it and even more embarrassed that he'd ended up watching it *twice*.

"I know," Morgan said. "And they can speculate all they want to. I'm not much of a public figure these days."

Barty shot him a look that was eerily reminiscent of the one Natasha had given him the last time they'd discussed this. Was that particular combination of reproachful doubt something they taught in agent school?

"That's bullshit," Barty said bluntly. More bluntly than Natasha had. But then, she'd always known how to handle Morgan, and Barty hadn't. Which was why he'd never once been tempted to make the change.

"Okay, probably. But it's still not their business. I'm not affiliated with a team these days. No nosy and paranoid PR to force me to do whatever they want."

Barty chortled. "Right. Hayes is, but Hayes also—"

"Hayes is out. He's dated guys publicly. It's less of a deal for him," Morgan said. He didn't want Barty to force Hayes into making some big issue out of it, because Hayes had seemed perfectly okay with them not confirming or talking about the gossip surrounding them.

He'd only made one request and tonight, Morgan would be taking that first step. He wouldn't have done it unless Hayes had asked him to, specifically. And he was a little nervous about it. It wasn't like he was getting up on ESPN and addressing Hayes' contract, like he'd be doing in a few days. That would be a cakewalk in comparison.

"It is, and if I'm being honest, the whole thing with Alexander sort of burned him out on that public parading of his relationship," Barty said.

Morgan didn't say that the *Alexander* part had been the issue with that, but he had a feeling he didn't have to, if the way Barty's gaze went cold when he said his name was any indication.

"Can't blame him for that," Morgan muttered. Fought against his own inclination to apologize for his inadvertent role in that whole mess.

"As far as I'm concerned," Barty said, like he hadn't said anything, "you two are free to live your lives the way you want to. Hayes said he's taking care of the team, like the actual players on the team, and he said Finn knows." Morgan nodded. "The only thing left I want to say about this whole thing is you'd better not fucking break his heart again."

Morgan had always thought Barty was a bit of a buffoon. All flash and no substance. Had wondered more than once why Hayes kept him around. But now Morgan was wondering if that had just been a convenient and clever act, and *ugh*, if he'd fallen for it, he was a little embarrassed.

Natasha would have a good laugh if he ever decided to tell her.

"I won't. I wouldn't." He nearly stuttered in surprise, suddenly too eager to lay that killer expression in Barty's eyes to rest.

"Good," Barty said, leaning back in his chair again. He picked up his beer. "Now, do you want to go over the talking points I'd like you to cover in your segment?"

"I can handle it," Morgan said, annoyed again. He'd told Hayes he didn't need this meeting. That he knew exactly what to say. But he supposed he couldn't be mad or annoyed, even, that Barty and Hayes wanted to cross every *t* and dot every *i*.

"It's not about you not handling it," Barty said, proving again that he might actually be a good agent. Morgan should be happier about this than he was, because he needed Hayes to have the best, always.

This was going to be Hayes' last contract, hockey fates willing, and Morgan wanted what he wanted so badly he was nearly burning with it.

He knew, too, that if he channeled even a fraction of the burning indignation he felt, the actual words he used wouldn't matter.

But he'd tolerated eighteen holes of golf and now this interminable lunch with Barty already. He might as well listen to what Barty had to say.

"Then tell me," Morgan said.

Six years ago, he'd have rather died than be a parrot for anyone, especially Bartholomew Smith III, but he'd learned a lot in that time. How to be less of an ass. How to mostly listen to what others wanted. How to make an attempt to deliver it, instead of ignoring it entirely.

But most of all, he'd learned what it was like to live without Hayes Montgomery, and he'd jump through a hell of a lot more hoops than this to never have to live like that again.

The last time he'd done this, it had never felt right and, not surprisingly, the relationship had completely imploded after that. Hayes told himself it was totally different this time around.

Not just because he couldn't even *sense* an implosion on the horizon, and with Alexander, things had always felt one bad fight from falling apart completely, but because Alexander hadn't been a hockey player. He'd been a marketing exec, completely removed from the team.

Morgan was one of the most famous hockey players of all time, *and* the father of their rookie goalie.

"Hey," he announced to the locker room as they got changed after morning skate. They had a home game tonight against the Leafs. "Can I get your attention for a sec?"

"Sure yeah, Cap, what's up?" Jasper asked, glancing up after he tossed his balled-up sock tape into the garbage and totally missed.

Hayes sighed as he walked over, bending over and picking it up, depositing into the trash. "As you've noticed, Morgan Reynolds has been around some this season."

"Yeah, 'cause he's the rook's daddy," Lars said.

"Uh, yes, that is true," Hayes said. "But he's going to be around, um, more, too."

"Why is he *your* daddy too, Monty?" Someone—Hayes thought it might have been Silov—teased.

He went bright red. "Uh, no. *No.* But we are uh, dating."

The locker room fell silent.

"No shit?" Jasper was the one who broke it, like a plate crashing to the floor. "Wow. Way to get it done, Cap. Aiming for the stars there."

If it was possible, Hayes flushed redder and focused his gaze on the opposite side of the locker room, on the blank white board that Coach sometimes used to break down plays between periods.

"Personally," Finn piped up from his stall, "I think it's my dad that's lucky."

"Thanks, Finn," Hayes said. This was worse than he'd imagined it might be. Way worse than it had been with Alexander. But he'd needed to do it, because he'd extracted a promise from Morgan that he'd come around the locker room more after home games—not just for Finn but for *him*, too—and the first time Hayes indulged in even the faintest hint of PDA, the team would freak out if they didn't already know the truth.

"Honestly though, Monty, way to pull," Lars said, starting a slow clap that made Hayes want to die and fall through the floor.

"You guys are serious?" Silov asked.

"I'd say so, yeah," Hayes said. "We've . . .uh . . .liked each other for a long time. Just finally was the right time to get our shit together."

"Congrats," Silov said, nodding with approval.

"I don't want to make a big deal out of it—"

"But it's a big fucking deal?" Jasper interrupted, grinning.

"I guess, just because he's him and I'm me, but otherwise, no," Hayes said. "Just wanted to give you guys a heads-up."

There were a few more interested nods and Lars and Jasper were, of course, still slow clapping like they thought they were fucking hilarious, but otherwise everyone went back to shedding their equipment.

Hayes let out a breath then another. There was less relief than there'd been after they'd successfully told Finn and Jacob, but it felt similar. He hadn't expected anyone to really care, because they already knew Hayes was gay and had already met one of his boyfriends. But then, the boyfriend hadn't been Morgan Reynolds, either.

Still, Hayes' eyes had been wide open when he'd started this. He knew what kind of a heat score it was going to be. Barty had been sending him texts ever since the rumor mill had started up. There were pictures of their dates floating around. Them going to romantic dinners, sharing desserts. Holding hands. Going for a run together on the beach, Morgan's shirt off, him grinning over at Hayes like he was the best thing he could ever imagine. Some people were stupid and kept insisting they were just friends, but most people had taken a look at the situation, put two and two together, and had correctly gotten four.

That, Morgan had said, was good enough for him, and it turned out, that was plenty good enough for Hayes, too.

"You good, Cap?" Finn said, catching him after changing and as Hayes was making his way out to the parking garage.

"Yeah," Hayes said. Wondering if he should be asking Finn that question, but Finn was generally pretty rock steady. Morgan had made a few comments about how that hadn't always been the case, but it seemed those days were over.

"You know I'm happy for you two, right?" Finn asked.

In between his shrieking complaints about PDA, Hayes had gotten that impression. "Good. We wouldn't want—neither of us—" Hayes broke off, giving up. "Just…that's good."

Finn grinned knowingly. "I hope you realize how you two are basically made for each other."

Hayes did, but he didn't know that *other* people had realized it. "Um, yes?"

Finn patted him on the shoulder. "Don't forget it, okay?"

As Hayes made his way to his car, he realized he'd just gotten the shovel talk from his rookie and it was hard to even be mad about it.

Impossible not to smile all the way home about it, still grinning to himself as he tucked himself in for his pregame nap.

That good feeling followed him all the way through warmups, into the game, and it was hardly like winning 4-3 against a really good Toronto team was going to dim it at all.

Hayes was riding the highs of a pretty damn good day even before Morgan showed up in the locker room.

Finn had played really well against a very good team, and Hayes had contributed a goal and an assist. There was nothing to be sad about, especially when he spotted Morgan making his way over to where Finn sat in his stall.

Hayes got distracted by something Jasper asked him about the game, and he didn't look back over to where he was talking to Finn, anticipating that eventually Morgan would make it over to him.

"Hey," Lars said, nudging him. "Is it a total fucking trip that Morgan Reynolds is basically your WAG, now?"

Hayes choked on the Gatorade he'd been drinking. "What? He's not—he's . . ."

"Yeah, your boyfriend, we established that this morning. But then he shows up like that, and what else are we supposed to think?"

Hayes craned his head. He'd only noticed Morgan in his typical Sentinels jersey. He'd been wearing Finn's number since the opening game. Twenty-nine. No big deal.

But then he realized, like a lightning bolt to the chest, that Morgan was not wearing Finn's number tonight.

He was wearing eighty-six and there was a *Montgomery* plastered across his back. A C nestled right where Morgan's heart beat.

Holy shit. *Holy shit.*

"You okay, bud?" Lars asked, patting him on the back.

No, he was not okay. He'd died and gone to fucking heaven. He wasn't on earth; he was currently levitating a few hundred feet above sea level.

Morgan chose that moment to turn around and, meeting Hayes' eyes with a shit-eating grin, sauntered over.

Like he knew exactly the kind of sensation he was causing. Like he *loved* it.

"Great game," Morgan said, leaning in, not kissing him on the mouth but on the cheek, even though Hayes hadn't made it to the showers yet.

Hayes opened his mouth and then snapped it shut again. He had absolutely no thoughts in his head except *Morgan-bed-now.*

He already knew that when they finally made it there—hopefully as soon as possible—Morgan wasn't going to be taking that jersey off.

Though from the way Morgan was gazing at him, smug and superior and so fucking pleased with himself, it seemed very likely that he wouldn't get a single argument out of him about that.

"Uh, nice jersey," he finally said.

"Oh, you like it?" Morgan had never been innocent a day in his life, and he was absolutely not innocent now, but the way he sounded made Hayes want to push him down to his knees and see just how dirty he was willing to be.

It was wrong to think about Finn just now, not when he was desperately trying not to get a hard-on in the middle of the locker room, but Hayes couldn't help but think of what he'd said earlier today. *You two are basically made for each other.*

There was no *basically* about it.

"I . . .I fucking love it," Hayes said in a low voice. Hopefully just loud enough for Morgan only to hear.

"I love *you*," Morgan murmured. "You gonna take me home and fuck me wearing it?"

Hayes choked on air. "Is that what you want?"

It should be impossible for Morgan to look innocent still. But of course, he managed it, barely looking like he was breaking a sweat. And then there was Hayes, who was breathing hard enough it felt like he'd just finished a double shift.

"I said it was," Morgan said. "Do you even know the kind of shit I had to tolerate all game from Jacob, wearing this? Even though he *regularly* wears Finn's?"

But he didn't sound mad about it. More like proud, actually.

That was a whole different thing that Hayes couldn't wrap his head around.

"I gotta—" Hayes broke off, feeling strangled by the hard punch of desire wrapping itself around his throat. "I gotta take a shower. Uh. And then we can go?"

"You go do that, angel," Morgan said. "I'll be waiting."

He was as good as his word, waiting by Hayes' car in the players' parking garage. Of course he was not alone, though. Jacob and Finn were there too, hanging out next to him.

"If this is some kind of kinky sex game, I don't want to hear about it," Finn said.

Morgan just rolled his eyes. "Like I haven't tolerated more than two years of your kinky sex games with this idiot." He jabbed an elbow in Jacob's general direction. Jacob just laughed.

"Yeah, it's our turn," Hayes said, deciding that plausible deniability had probably gone right out the window. And why should he not get all hot and bothered about his boyfriend wearing *his* name and *his* number? It was really fucking hot.

"Don't worry though," Morgan said, shooting Finn a look. "This is just for special occasions."

"Gross, gross, *gross*. Enough. We're leaving. I'd say have a good time but I really don't want to think about it at all," Finn exclaimed, grabbing Jacob by the arm and literally dragging him off.

Morgan was still chuckling as Hayes leaned in and kissed him, more thoroughly this time. The way he hadn't in the locker room.

"Special occasion, huh?" Hayes murmured against his lips.

Morgan didn't bother even answering that. He just wrapped a big hand around Hayes' hip, warmth leaking through all his layers, and said, "Yeah, let's go home."

Hayes didn't need a second invitation.

"Fuck, you look fucking amazing like this." Hayes might've been embarrassed at how overwhelmed he sounded, but he had a feeling this had been Morgan's plan the whole time.

He was definitely the kind of guy who topped from the bottom and Hayes wasn't even annoyed about it. In fact, every single bit of it was so fucking hot, Hayes felt like he was trembling.

He had Morgan on his hands and knees on the bed, jersey still on, *Montgomery* still plastered across his back, the eighty-six going blurry in his vision every so often until he blinked hard.

One hand pinned Morgan's hip and the other, two fingers slick and deep inside of him as Morgan pushed back, demanding and eager.

This was the first time they were doing this—though Morgan had told Hayes he'd done it to himself a number of times. Which . . .that was something they were going to have to discuss, and Hayes was going to have to *witness*, when he didn't feel like he was already going hazy around the edges with desire.

"Come on," Morgan ordered. "Give me another one."

Hayes screwed his fingers in hard and fast, finding the spot that kept making Morgan squirm. "So pushy," he murmured, leaning over and brushing his lips against Morgan's neck, right above the jersey. "You'd wonder who you actually belong to."

"You. *You*." Anyone else would sound soft about that, but Morgan only sounded more arrogant than ever. Like Hayes owning him only made him stronger. More powerful. More *everything*.

Honestly, that was hot too. How could Hayes *not* give him a third finger after that?

By the time he finished getting Morgan loose enough, he was so hard. Dizzy with the desire to just shove in and fuck Morgan until he was reduced to only two words. *Angel* and *please*.

But he held back. Pushing his fingers in deeper. Making Morgan cry out. Pushing him close to the edge, until Morgan was nearly shaking with it.

"I'm gonna—you can't. *God*." Morgan begged about as well as he did everything else. It was one of the sexiest things, if not *the* sexiest thing, that Hayes had ever heard.

"You're not gonna come until I do," Hayes told him.

Morgan groaned again.

Hayes pulled his fingers out finally and slicked up his cock, sliding it in one hard push.

He'd been sure Morgan could take it. And he could. There'd been no resistance, only Morgan's body opening up to him like he'd been born to take him.

But Morgan dropped down to his elbows, panting with it.

"Shit, baby, you okay?" Hayes asked, leaning in when his balls brushed against Morgan's ass.

"Fine, *fine*. God if you don't fuck me now, angel, I'm gonna—"

"I got you," Hayes said, relief and new desire pumping through him.

He pulled back and thrust hard, caution and restraint going right out the window when he realized that Morgan had tensed up not because it was too much, but because he liked it so much he was afraid he'd come too soon.

Setting a brisk pace, Hayes knew he'd found the right angle when Morgan clenched, and he barely reached down, getting a hand around Morgan's cock, nearly dripping with precome, before he shuddered and his body tightened impossibly around Hayes.

Hayes couldn't do anything else but follow him right over the edge, grinding deep and feeling his own orgasm overtake him.

They slumped down to the bed, and for a second all Hayes could hear was the sound of their labored breathing, mixed together.

Then, something else. A low sound, half-muffled by the covers.

Was Morgan *laughing*?

"You okay?" Hayes asked. He didn't want to move, but if Morgan wasn't okay, then he needed to. He pulled out and rolled over, tucking a clean hand underneath Morgan's chin and lifting up.

Morgan looked blissed out and happy. "I'm good. Great, honestly. Happy one month anniversary. One month and six some-odd years," he said, still chuckling. "That special occasion enough for you?"

Hayes had to laugh then too. "You ever gonna request it the other way around?"

"Angel, I've got my jersey in my closet just over there, waiting for the right moment to pull it out and get me so hot I'm probably gonna die before I even get inside you."

"Good." Hayes leaned in and brushed a kiss across his lips. "I wouldn't expect anything less."

CHAPTER 23

Hayes didn't watch the segment when it aired. Barty emailed him a YouTube link to it after it went live, adding in, *Not that you won't get a complete rundown from the source.*

Technically, Morgan did text him when he was done recording. **It's done,** was all he'd said. He hadn't needed to go into more detail. Hayes could imagine what he'd said. Could still feel the phantom flush of being *known* and *seen*, from six years ago when Morgan had told the media at Four Nations how incredible he thought Hayes was.

It was too much to think he could duck it forever, because that day at practice, everyone was buzzing about it.

"Hear your man went to bat for you," Lars said, patting him on the back. "He's not wrong."

"Thanks," Hayes said, trying to ignore that squirmy feeling in the base of his stomach.

"Think he loves you a lot," Lars added.

"Maybe he just thinks I'm a good hockey player," Hayes claimed. Even though both of those things were true.

"Listen," Lars said, ducking his head down. "I love you, man. I think you're fucking brilliant. And he put me to shame."

Okay, maybe he was going to have to watch it.

He didn't have a moment, though, because practice was starting and he thankfully was too distracted for the next two hours to angst about just how effusive Morgan had gotten about him.

Then when practice ended, he had a meeting and then another, and it was nearly dinner time by the time he checked his phone. Surprised, but he supposed he shouldn't be, by the sheer number of notifications he'd gotten while it had been sitting in his locker.

Barty had called three times and sent him half a dozen texts, most of them a variation of *call me now*.

Morgan had sent him another text. **Glad it helped,** was all he said.

Had it helped? What was happening? Hayes plugged in his phone and dialed Barty on his drive home.

"Oh my God, there you are," Barty said when he answered on the second ring. "*Finally*."

"I had practice and meetings," Hayes said semi-defensively. "I take it things are going well?"

"Like your boyfriend is causing a sensation? Fuck yeah he is. I've got like five standing invites for all the big podcasts, and everyone wants to talk about it."

"Ugh," Hayes said.

"What is this *ugh*? You should be thrilled. This is majorly softening up the Sentinels' brass. They already sent me an email, wanting to meet this week again. I've had to be the one to push for every single of our meetings in the last month, Monty."

"They could just tell you to fuck off," Hayes said, afraid to get his hopes up.

"Are you fucking kidding? They're not going to do that. They're not stupid." Barty paused. "Well, they are pretty stupid, but not *that* stupid."

"I'm glad to hear that," Hayes said dryly.

"They're gonna want me to come in with what you really want. So think about that, okay? And between now and then we're gonna soften them the fuck up."

"The podcasts?"

"Yeah," Barty said excitedly. "And so much more, too. Couple other guys picked up the convo, too, after Reynolds started it."

"Oh, that's good."

"You've got a game tomorrow, right?" Barty asked.

"Yeah. A home game. And then we're taking a short trip to Nashville." Hayes drummed his fingers on the wheel. "Why, what's up?"

"You're gonna get asked about it when you do media. I want you to be prepared. Watch the segment, I know you didn't—"

"You don't know that," Hayes complained.

"Yeah, I do. I know you. You hate it when people say good shit about you, which, for the record, is weird, Monty."

"It's not weird." He also really didn't want to promise to watch it when he got home, because he knew Morgan would be there, waiting for him. And the only thing that would be worse than watching Morgan praise him would be watching Morgan praise him while he was right there.

"I love you, but it's totally fucking weird," Barty said. "Watch it. Be ready for tomorrow, okay? I'm going to send you the talking points."

"I know what the talking points are," Hayes protested.

"You *think* you know," Barty said, sounding exasperated.

"Okay, fine." He could hide in the bathroom or something and watch the video, volume cranked down with the subtitles on. He pulled into his driveway. "I gotta go."

Barty sighed. "Say hi to Morgan for me."

"How do you know—"

"You're joking, right?" Barty interrupted with a bark of laughter. "Seriously, though, thank him for me. I'm gonna send him a huge fruit basket. Or maybe some wine. Oh—that new bourbon I tried—"

"Goodbye, Barty," Hayes interrupted, before he could start laughing.

Sure enough, Morgan was on his couch when he walked in, a Predators-Hurricanes game on the TV.

"You scouting for me now?" Hayes asked, leaning in and resting his chin on Morgan's shoulder.

"Jacob and I are arguing about Forsberg," Morgan said distractedly as the player in question went over the boards for a line change.

"Yeah?"

Morgan made a frustrated noise. Debating Forsberg and how his and Jacob's opinions on the guy differed was vastly preferable to discussing the segment that had aired this morning.

"You know Jacob does unofficial scouting for Finn."

"I didn't know but it makes sense," Hayes said. Morgan hadn't been doing that for Hayes, yet, but he figured it was only a matter of time.

"Anyway, he mentioned one of Forsberg's moves and I'm trying to prove him wrong." Morgan sounded very proud of this.

"I'm gonna leave you to it and take a shower," Hayes said. It would be fun to sit here and listen to Morgan get annoyed about Jacob's take on Forsberg, but he could also use the distraction to watch the segment in peace in the bathroom.

Morgan barely glanced back, nodding absently.

He flipped the shower on—he'd actually showered at the rink after practice, but Morgan didn't know that. He could take another quick one, before they went to dinner.

Pulling his phone out, he clicked the volume way down until he could probably hear it but it was doubtful Morgan could. Not with the shower on and from the living room.

The video started playing, Hayes recognizing the setup from Morgan's living room at the rental house. Morgan did several different segments regularly on ESPN but this was the show he did every week with a couple of other retired players. It was billed as a series of hot takes.

"I've got a real good one for you today," Morgan said, looking laid-back and relaxed if you weren't looking closely, but Hayes was always looking closely and he could see the excitement brewing in his hazel eyes. "The question I keep asking myself, over and over, is why the Sentinels are hesitating to give Montgomery the contract he wants."

"You're always so high on him," Anderson, one of the other commentators, complained. It almost made Hayes want to look up what Morgan had been saying about him over the years. *Almost.*

"Nobody else is his age and playing at that elite level right now. He's leading the whole team and third overall in points, fourth in goals. He's going to drive the Sentinels to a second Cup. Why aren't they falling over themselves to give him a five-year contract?"

"'Cause he's thirty-one," Reilly retorted.

"He's not falling off," Morgan argued. "He's a freaking star. A *stud.* If you look at his numbers, he's brought it every year. I'd actually argue that sure, he's a hair slower than he used to be, but his vision is better, his IQ has never been stronger. I'd take him over any of those young guns out there right now."

"I meant it too."

Hayes looked up and flushed guiltily.

Morgan sauntered in. Mimicked Hayes' lean against the counter. "You didn't watch it?"

"I . . ." Hayes pressed pause as Reilly and Anderson started analyzing his last five years of stats. "I didn't. I knew you'd say what you needed to."

Morgan chuckled under his breath. "You really think I said all that because you needed me to?"

"Well . . .yeah?"

"Angel, I meant every fucking word." Morgan tugged him into his arms. "I'd have said more, if I thought it would make a damn bit of difference. It's so shitty what they're doing to you. I hate it."

"Because you're crazy about me," Hayes said. He'd almost said, *because you love me,* but that was a step further than he felt quite comfortable with. Morgan could say he loved him, but there was still a half a second of hesitation when Hayes thought about just casually assigning him those feelings.

Morgan pulled back a fraction, frowning. "Seriously?"

"Well, you wouldn't lie on TV, I guess."

Morgan laughed.

"Okay," Hayes said, poking him in the side and unable to help the smile that blossomed across his face. "You'd totally lie on TV."

"But I didn't today. If anything, I downplayed how I felt about it." Morgan sounded painfully earnest now.

Hayes decided this was a good time to change the subject. "Barty says they asked for another meeting. Them this time, not him."

"A good sign," Morgan said. "My phone's been blowing up all day. They want me to do some more interviews about it. I didn't commit to anything else yet—didn't want to before I talked to you."

"What does Barty think?"

Morgan made an exasperated noise. "Hayes, I don't give a fuck what *he* thinks. I only care how you feel about it."

"Oh."

"I know too much praise makes you weird."

Hayes wet his lips. "Not exactly."

"Oh, angel, it absolutely does. You were *hiding* in the bathroom to watch the good stuff I said about you."

Hayes was annoyed. He didn't want to admit the truth and Morgan was going to make him do it anyway. Zach would probably have told him this was what love really was; knowing someone so well you wouldn't let them get away with crap.

"Okay, fine, yes, I was hiding in the bathroom."

Morgan ruffled his hair. "You showered at the rink. You always do."

"Here I thought you were too distracted by Filip Forsberg to think about when I showered," Hayes muttered.

"Are you kidding?" Morgan laughed. "Forsberg doesn't have shit on you, angel. You gonna tell me about it?"

"It's . . . it's hard to watch *you* praise me," Hayes admitted. "It was hard six years ago. And it's still hard, now."

"Not because you don't believe me, right?" Morgan looked worried.

"No, of course you mean it. I know you mean it." Hayes squirmed. "Maybe it's that you mean it too much. I don't always know that I deserve it. Feels like I haven't earned it, yet."

Morgan cupped his cheeks in his palms, gaze deadly serious. "You've earned every single bit of it, angel. Take the compliments, okay?"

Hayes swallowed hard and nodded.

"Now, you really want to shower?" Morgan raised an eyebrow, gesturing towards the shower.

"With or without you?" Hayes asked in a teasing voice.

"With me," Morgan said, curling a hand around his wrist and tugging him in the direction of the water. "We can be late for dinner."

Morgan had been waiting in bed for Hayes to come home for almost two months now.

There'd been a time when doing this, just lying here, *waiting,* would have been enough to make horror and resignation crawl along his skin, but he'd made his peace with so many things. Maybe if he'd shown up when he'd initially intended, six months out from retirement, still fucked up about it, even though he'd known it was time, he couldn't have done this. Couldn't have been chill about it.

But three years after retirement, Morgan had learned a lot of tough truths about himself, including, but definitely not limited to, that he'd carried the burdens of being Morgan Reynolds for much of his life, and that it was not only okay to put them down now, but it was encouraged.

Right now, he wasn't Morgan Reynolds, the chosen one, but just Morgan, waiting for his boyfriend to get home.

He still had the rental house, and when Hayes went on longer road trips, he often retreated to it, still not quite comfortable in Hayes' space when he wasn't around for days at a time. But he had a feeling that when next season rolled around, he'd let the lease expire.

Honestly, Morgan had spent so many years traveling, even when he'd been living in New York, nothing ever felt like home. Not until he'd gotten together with Hayes.

Turned out home wasn't a place, but a person.

A person he was currently missing.

Morgan shifted in bed, glancing over at his phone. Still dark. No texts. Hayes was pretty good about telling Morgan when they'd landed and when he'd be home. It should be soon. He'd watched them beat Columbus, and with the time difference and the flight time, Hayes *should* be getting home soon.

He'd just about given up waiting and reached for his phone to text Hayes and make sure everything was okay when he heard a noise—the garage door opening and then closing.

He sat up, suddenly alert.

A second later, Hayes was walking into the bedroom, hair messy like he'd just taken a hat off, eyes tired, but the brightest smile on his face.

"Hey," Morgan said. "Is that smile all for me?"

Hayes flushed and set his bag down on the floor, next to the laundry hamper. Then wasted no time crawling into bed, wrinkled suit and all. "Not *all* of it," he murmured softly, leaning in and pressing a hot kiss against Morgan's mouth.

"Then what is it?" Morgan hoped it was the news they'd both been waiting for. The final contract between Hayes and the Sentinels—everything he'd wanted, that he deserved, finally within grasp.

Hayes inhaled and then let out a disbelieving laugh. "It's all done," he said earnestly. "I can't believe it, but it's done. Barty had to tell them to not post until tomorrow because I wanted to be the one to tell you."

"Yeah? Angel, I'm so proud of you."

Hayes grinned. "Not as much money as we'd initially discussed, but it's for the five years, option for a sixth."

"You're gonna retire a Sentinel." Morgan wound an arm around Hayes and pulled him more fully onto his lap. Not caring that he was naked and Hayes was still clothed in his suit pants and white button-down. He'd lost his jacket and his tie somewhere, but Morgan reached up, tucking his other hand in the open neck of his shirt, tracing his collarbone.

"Yeah, I am," Hayes said, dropping his head to Morgan's shoulder. "God, I am." He let out a long, unsteady breath. "Can barely believe it."

"Believe it, angel," Morgan said.

"I listened to what you said," Hayes said after a long pause.

"Hmm?"

"Barty wanted to hold out for more money, and I told him not to. I told him to take it."

"You feel good about it?"

Hayes wiggled closer, nearly giggling, and said, "What do *you* think?"

"Pretty damn good," Morgan said, laughing too now.

He was half-expecting Hayes to crawl down into his lap and do something about his half-hard cock, but instead, Hayes went limp in his arms. Just breathed in and out and in and out again.

"Did you mean it?" Hayes murmured into his neck.

"Did I mean what?" He'd said a lot of shit, so much lovestruck earnestness, over the last two months, and he'd meant every word.

"When you said you'd be around, no matter what. No matter what team I ended up on."

Morgan pulled back, needing Hayes to see his face when he reassured him. "Absolutely," he said. "I'm here for you, always. No matter what."

"When the hockey stuff gets too hard?" Hayes questioned.

It would. They both knew it would. It always did.

Morgan considered how he'd been feeling, right before Hayes showed up. What Hayes himself had told him six years ago.

"Yeah, of course. Of course for the hockey stuff. But also to remind you that hockey isn't all that matters."

Hayes stared at him. Tongue flicked out, licked at his bottom lip.

"I'm never going to stop reminding you, *telling you*, that you can put it down, sometimes. Just like you did for me."

Hayes squeezed his eyes shut. "God, you can't keep saying shit like that."

"I mean it," Morgan said. "I always mean it—"

"I know, *I know*, which is why I just . . .*ugh*. You love me." Hayes didn't say it as a question. Just a statement of fact, which it was.

Morgan Reynolds loved Hayes Montgomery.

"Yeah," he said. "I love you. Always."

EPILOGUE

Eighteen months later

It made a weird, twisted sort of sense that when Hayes won his second Cup and Finn won his first, the only person Morgan got to hug and scream incoherently about it with was Jacob Braun.

He never really regretted retiring when he did. Except this one time. Not because he wanted to be the one lifting the Cup—he'd won his own, and he'd never been prouder that Finn and Hayes had just won their first together—but because he was stuck up in here in this stupid suite instead of down on the ice. Couldn't press his mouth to Hayes' sweaty neck and taste the salt water of the tears that streaked down his cheeks. Had only Jacob to hang on to. Jacob, who was still on the floor, where he'd fallen to his knees, five minutes earlier as Hayes had scored the winning overtime goal.

"Get up," Morgan said, dragging him to his feet, laughing. "Come on, we're gonna have to go down there."

He and Hayes had talked about this—Hayes squirming the whole time, because he hadn't wanted to jinx the Sentinels by assuming they'd win—but he'd needed to know what Hayes wanted. Not just what the general expectations were. Neither he nor Jacob were traditional WAGs. They were both ex-players, and them being down there on the ice, after the trophy presentation, might not be what the team wanted. Might not be what Hayes or Finn wanted.

The last thing Morgan was looking to be was a distraction when the focus should be on the Sentinels.

But Hayes had looked at him like he was crazy for asking. "Of course I want you there," he'd said. "And I can't imagine Finn *not* wanting Jacob there, either."

"What?" Jacob looked at him. His eyes were red, but he was smiling. Maybe even bigger and wider than he had when he'd won his own championships. Morgan understood that because he was pretty sure he was happier now than when he'd last lifted the Cup, seven years ago.

"We gotta go, man," Morgan said, pushing him out of the suite. "Finn's gonna want you down there."

"What?" Jacob repeated.

Morgan laughed. "Are you alright?"

"I think. . .I think my brain is broken," Jacob admitted with a wry laugh, scrubbing a hand across his face. "God, they did it, didn't they?"

"Yeah, they sure fucking did." And Morgan had been there for every moment of it. The good *and* the bad.

Morgan nodded at the security guy at the elevator. "Oh, Mr. Reynolds, I was just about to radio Dom to find you," he said. "You and Mr. Braun both."

"Nicky, you know I told you to call me Morgan, and I don't even know who Mr. Braun is," he teased.

"He really doesn't," Jacob said, apparently snapping out of his fugue state. They stepped into the elevator.

"Monty told me to make sure you were both there," Nicky said as the elevator went down towards the ice level. "He stopped me specially the other day. Told me it was my job to make sure you were both there, even if you protested."

Morgan laughed wetly. Put a hand on his face and realized he was crying now. Of course Hayes had. They'd talked about it, but Hayes had wanted to be *sure*.

"See?" Jacob said, his own laugh not very steady. "I think I aged ten years, watching this playoff run."

Morgan looked over at him. "You look it, with that raggedy-ass beard."

"Like yours is any better," Jacob retorted but he sounded fond.

"Can't wait to shave it off," Morgan admitted.

Jacob patted him on the cheek. "Now you can. God, they did it. I've never been so proud." He glanced at Morgan. "How do you stand it? Finn *and* Hayes?"

The truth was, he didn't. He couldn't. The pride and happiness was too big to be contained inside him, even when he'd learned to carry everything for so long. He'd never imagined he'd face something that would be too big for him.

But this felt like it.

"Not sure I can," Morgan admitted, wiping away another tear. "I'm probably gonna embarrass everyone once we get out there. My son and my boyfriend, for sure."

The elevator dinged. Nicky looked over at them as the doors opened. "You couldn't, Mr. Reynolds. Hayes is so proud of you. Finn, too." Nicky's chin lifted, like he was worried Morgan might argue with him.

Morgan wasn't going to.

He couldn't really.

"This way," Nicky continued, gesturing into the hall. Morgan could already hear the yelling of a celebration going on in the locker room.

But Hayes would probably be the last one out on the ice. And if Morgan knew his son, he'd be with him.

"God, I can't believe we're doing this," Jacob muttered. "We shouldn't—"

Morgan elbowed Jacob in the ribs. "Hayes told me he wanted me there and that Finn wanted *you* there, too. Did you guys not talk about this?"

Jacob winced. "We didn't want to anger the hockey gods!"

"Jesus, logistics are important too," Morgan complained.

They passed by the locker room, doors thrown open, raucous sounds spilling out.

There were still a lot of players out on the ice. Morgan could see them as they walked out of the tunnel.

"There you go," Nicky said, giving them both a nod.

"Thank you, Nicky," Morgan said, nodding his approval. "We'll see you next season?"

"You better count on it." Nicky grinned. "Have a good night."

"Gonna be better than good. It's gonna be great," Jacob muttered.

Morgan elbowed him again. "Don't wanna hear about *that*."

One of the arena staff was by the entrance. "They're waiting for you," she said, gesturing towards the ice. And when Morgan looked up, there Hayes was, holding the Cup, smile on his face wide.

Just waiting for him.

Morgan had never moved faster. They'd put down a carpet to make the presentation easier on anyone not wearing skates, but he would have made it even without that.

They collided. One of them was laughing. One of them was crying. Maybe they were doing both.

"God, angel, you did it," Morgan said, pressing himself firmly into his boyfriend's side. "I'm so fucking proud of you."

Hayes set the Cup down, like *he*, Morgan Reynolds, was the real prize. Gripped him hard, face wet with sweat and tears, and pressed their mouths together.

They hadn't really been bothering with plausible deniability. The first time Morgan had been caught by a fan wearing his Montgomery jersey had pretty much destroyed that entirely. But this was a different level. This was a declaration, and Morgan's heart throbbed with happiness.

He'd never thought he'd have this, and now he had *everything*.

"I love you," he murmured into Hayes' mouth. "No matter what happened. If you'd won. If you lost."

Hayes grinned. "Yeah, but winning is a hell of a lot more fun, isn't it?"

Morgan couldn't deny that. "I'm gonna remind you of this in a year, in two years, in *ten* years."

"Yeah, you'd better. Remind me that I can pick it up and I can put it down again, okay?"

"Always."

Hayes nudged him. "Go congratulate your Stanley Cup-winning son, okay? He deserves it."

"First full year as a starting goalie and he wins the Cup? I'm never gonna stop crowing about *that*," Morgan said, and Hayes laughed. "I will. I just . . .I want one more minute with you, first."

"You can have as long as you want," Hayes said. "I told the boys I wouldn't be coming in, not until we were done out here."

Morgan cleared his throat, emotion clogging it. "How about forever?"

Hayes put a hand on his cheek. "Sounds perfect to me."

-

Don't miss the bonus scene – Finn and Jacob clearly figured out what was going on earlier, but when and how much did they know?

-

If you missed Finn and Jacob or Zach and Gavin's books, you can check out the Portland Evergreens series on Kindle Unlimited and also on audio.

-

My next hockey series is about the three Barnes bros – the Hockey Bros! – and will be out in summer 2026. Preorder *Ethan* here.

INTERESTED IN READING MORE OF
BETH'S BOOKS?

CHECK OUT A FULL LIST OF TILES
BY SCANNING THE QR CODE
OR VISITING HER WEBSITE

WWW.BETHBOLDEN.COM/BOOKLIST

WANT TO FOLLOW BETH?

MAKE SURE YOU NEVER
MISS A RELEASE?

SCAN THE QR CODE BELOW
OR VISIT HER WEBSITE
FOR A SOCIAL MEDIA LIST,
NEWSLETTER SIGNUP,
AND SO MUCH MORE!

WWW.BETHBOLDEN.COM/ABOUT

www.ingramcontent.com/pod-product-compliance
Lightning Source LLC
Chambersburg PA
CBHW060607300726
48975CB00005B/1475